The Deemster

By

Hall Caine

Double9 BOOKS

The Deemster

by Hall Caine

ISBN: 978-93-61152-96-2

Published by

DOUBLE 9 BOOKS
2/13-B, Ansari Road
Daryaganj, New Delhi – 110002
info@double9books.com
www.double9books.com
Tel. 011-40042856

ABOUT THE AUTHOR

Hall Caine CH KBE, better known as Hall Caine, was a British novelist, dramatist, short story writer, poet, and critic in the late nineteenth and early twentieth centuries. Caine enjoyed exceptional fame throughout his lifetime. He published fifteen novels on infidelity, divorce, domestic abuse, illegitimacy, infanticide, religious prejudice, and women's rights, becoming a worldwide literary celebrity and selling 10 million copies. Caine was the highest-paid novelist of his day. The Eternal City is the first novel to sell more than one million copies globally. Caine moved to the Isle of Man in 1895 and served in the Manx House of Keys, the island's lower house of parliament, from 1901 to 1908. Caine was elected President of the Manx National change League in 1903 and chaired the Keys' Committee, which drafted the 1907 constitutional change petition. Caine received the Freedom of the Borough of Douglas on the Isle of Man in 1929. Caine traveled to Russia in 1892 on behalf of the persecuted Jews. Caine traveled to the United States and Canada in 1895, representing the Society of Authors, where he successfully negotiated and obtained significant international copyright concessions from the Dominion Parliament.

CONTENTS

CHAPTER I
THE DEATH OF OLD EWAN

Thorkell Mylrea had waited long for a dead man's shoes, but he was wearing them at length. He was forty years of age; his black hair was thin on the crown and streaked with gray about the temples; the crow's-feet were thick under his small eyes, and the backs of his lean hands were coated with a reddish down. But he had life in every vein, and restless energy in every limb.

His father, Ewan Mylrea, had lived long, and mourned much, and died in sorrow. The good man had been a patriarch among his people, and never a serener saint had trod the ways of men. He was already an old man when his wife died. Over her open grave he tried to say, "The Lord gave, and the Lord hath taken away; blessed—" But his voice faltered and broke. Though he lived ten years longer, he held up his head no more. Little by little he relinquished all active interest in material affairs. The world had lost its light for him, and he was traveling in the dusk.

On his sons, Thorkell, the elder, Gilcrist, the younger, with nearly five years between them, the conduct of his estate devolved. Never were brothers more unlike. Gilcrist, resembling his father, was of a simple and tranquil soul; Thorkell's nature was fiery, impetuous, and crafty. The end was the inevitable one; the heel of Thorkell was too soon on the neck of Gilcrist.

Gilcrist's placid spirit overcame its first vexation, and he seemed content to let his interests slip from his hands. Before he was out Thorkell Mylrea was in effect the master of Ballamona; his younger brother was nightly immersed in astronomy and the Fathers, and the old man was sitting daily, in his slippers, in the high-backed armchair by the ingle, over which these words were cut in the black oak: "God's Providence is mine inheritance."

They were strange effects that followed. People said they had never understood the extraordinary fortunes of Ballamona. Again and again the rents were raised throughout the estate, until the farmers cried in the grip of their poverty that they would neither go nor starve. Then the wagons of Thorkell Mylrea, followed close at their tail-boards by the carts of the clergy, drove into the cornfields when the corn was cut, and picked up the stooks and bore them away amid the deep curses of the bare-armed reapers, who looked on in their impotent rage.

Nevertheless, Thorkell Mylrea said, far and wide, without any show of reserve, and with every accent of sincerity, that never before had his father's affairs worn so grave a look. He told Ewan as much time after time, and then the troubled old face looked puzzled. The end of many earnest consultations between father and son, as the one sat by the open hearth and the other leaned against the lettered ingle, was a speedy recourse to certain moneys that lay at an English bank, as well as the old man's signature to documents of high moment.

Old Ewan's spirits sank yet lower year by year, but he lived on peacefully enough. As time went by, he talked less, and his humid eyes seemed to look within in degree as they grew dim to things without. But the day came at length when the old man died in his chair, before the slumberous peat fire on the hearth, quietly, silently, without a movement, his graspless fingers fumbling a worm-eaten hour-glass, his long waves of thin white hair falling over his drooping shoulders, and his upturned eyes fixed in a strong stare on the text carved on the rannel-tree shelf, "God's Providence is mine inheritance."

That night Thorkell sat alone at the same ingle, in the same chair, glancing at many parchments, and dropping them one by one into the fire. Long afterward, when idle tongues were set to wag, it was said that the elder son of Ewan Mylrea had found a means whereby to sap away his father's personalty. Then it was remembered that through all his strange misfortunes Thorkell had borne an equal countenance.

They buried the old man under the elder-tree by the wall of the churchyard that stands over against the sea. It seemed as if half of the inhabitants of the island came to his funeral, and six sets of bearers claimed their turn to carry him to the grave. The day was a gloomy day of winter; there was not a bird or a breath in the heavy air; the sky was low and empty; the long dead sea was very gray and cold; and over the unplowed land the withered stalks of the last crop lay dank on the mold. When the company returned to Ballamona they sat down to eat and drink and make merry, for "excessive sorrow is exceeding dry." No one asked for the will; there was no will because there was no personalty, and the lands were by law the inheritance of the eldest son. Thorkell was at the head of his table, and he smiled a little, and sometimes reached over the board to touch with his glass the glass that was held out toward him. Gilcrist had stood with these mourners under the empty sky, and his heart was as bare and desolate, but he could endure their company no longer. In an agony of grief and remorse, and rage as well, he got up from his untouched food and walked away to his own room. It was a little, quiet nest of a room that looked out by one small window over the marshy Curraghs that lay between the house and the sea. There Gilcrist sat alone that day in a sort of dull stupor.

The daylight had gone, and the revolving lamps on the headland of Ayre were twinkling red after black over the blank waters, when the door opened and Thorkell entered. Gilcrist stirred the fire, and it broke into a bright blaze. Thorkell's face wore a curious expression.

"I have been thinking a good deal about you, Gilcrist; especially during the last few days. In fact, I have been troubled about you, to say the truth," said Thorkell, and then he paused. "Affairs are in a bad way at Ballamona—very."

Gilcrist made no response whatever, but clasped his hands about his knee and looked steadily into the fire.

"We are neither of us young men now, but if you should think of—of—anything, I should consider it wrong to stand—to put myself in your way—to keep you here, that is—to your disadvantage, you know."

Thorkell was standing with his back to the fire, and his fingers interlaced behind him.

Gilcrist rose to his feet. "Very well," he said, with a strained quietness, and then turned toward the window and looked out at the dark sea. Only the sea's voice from the shore beyond the churchyard broke the silence in that little room.

Thorkell stood a moment, leaning on the mantel-shelf, and the flickering lights of the fire seemed to make sinister smiles on his face. Then he went out without a word.

Next morning, at daybreak, Gilcrist Mylrea was riding toward Derby Haven with a pack in green cloth across his saddle-bow. He took passage by the "King Orry," an old sea-tub plying once a week to Liverpool. From Liverpool he went on to Cambridge to offer himself as a sizar at the University.

It had never occurred to any one that Thorkell Mylrea would marry. But his father was scarcely cold in his grave, the old sea-tub that took his brother across the Channel had hardly grounded at Liverpool, when Thorkell Mylrea offered his heart and wrinkled hand, and the five hundred acres of Ballamona, to a lady twenty years of age, who lived at a distance of some six miles from his estate. It would be more precise to say that the liberal tender was made to the lady's father, for her own will was little more than a cypher in the bargaining. She was a girl of sweet spirit, very tender and submissive, and much under the spell of religious feeling. Her mother had died during her infancy, and she had been brought up in a household that was without other children, in a gaunt rectory that never echoed with children's voices. Her father was Archdeacon of the island, Archdeacon Teare; her own name was Joance.

If half the inhabitants of the island turned out at old Ewan's funeral, the entire population of four parishes made a holiday of his son's wedding. The one followed hard upon the other, and thrift was not absent from either. Thorkell was married in the early spring at the Archdeacon's church, at Andreas.

It would be rash to say that the presence of the great company at the wedding was intended as a tribute to the many virtues of Thorkell Mylrea. Indeed, it was as well that the elderly bridegroom could not overhear the conversation with which some of the homely folk beguiled the way.

"Aw, the murther of it," said one buirdly Manxman, "five-and-forty if he's a day, and a wizened old polecat anyway."

"You'd really think the gel's got no feelin's. Aw, shockin', shockin', extraordinary!"

"And a rael good gel too, they're sayin'. Amazin'! Amazin'!"

The marriage of Thorkell was a curious ceremony. First there walked abreast the fiddler and the piper, playing vigorously the "Black and Gray"; then came the bridegroom's men carrying osiers, as emblems of their superiority over the bridesmaids, who followed them. Three times the company passed round the church before entering it, and then they trooped up toward the communion-rail.

Thorkell went through the ceremony with the air of a whipped terrier. On the outside he was gay in frills and cuffs, and his thin hair was brushed crosswise over the bald patch on his crown. He wore buckled shoes and blue laces to his breeches. But his brave exterior lent him small support as he took the ungloved hand of his girlish bride. He gave his responses in a voice that first faltered, and then sent out a quick, harsh, loud pipe. No such gaunt and grim shadow of a joyful bridegroom ever before knelt beside a beautiful bride, and while the Archdeacon married the spectre of a happy man to his own submissive daughter, the whispered comments of the throng that filled nave and aisles and gallery sometimes reached his own ears.

"You wouldn't think it, now, that the craythur's sold his own gel, and him preaching there about the covenant and Isaac and Rebecca, and all that!"

"Hush, man, it's Laban and Jacob he's meaning."

When the ceremony had come to an end, and the bridegroom's eyes were no longer fixed in a stony stare on the words of the Commandments printed in black and white under the chancel window, the scene underwent a swift change. In one minute Thorkell was like another man. All his abject bearing fell away. When the party was clear of the churchyard four of the groom's men started for the Rectory at a race, and the first to reach it won a flask of brandy, with which he returned at high speed to the wedding company. Then Thorkell, as the custom was, bade his friends to form a circle where they stood in the road, while he drank of the brandy and handed the flask to his wife.

"Custom must be indulged with custom," said he, "or custom will weep."

After that the company moved on until they reached the door of the Archdeacon's house, where the bride cake was broken over the bride's hand, and then thrown to be scrambled for by the noisy throng that blew neat's horns and fired guns and sang ditties by the way.

Thorkell, with the chivalrous bearing of an old courtier, delivered up his wife to the flock of ladies who were ready to pounce upon her at the door of the Rectory. Then he mingled freely with the people, and chattered and bantered, and made quips and quibbles. Finally, he invited all and sundry to partake freely of the oaten cake and ale that he had himself brought from Ballamona in his car for the refreshment of his own tenants there present. The fare was Lenten fare for a wedding day, and some of the straggle-headed troop grumbled, and some sniffled, and some scratched their heads, and some laughed outright. The beer and bread were left almost untouched.

Thorkell was blind to the discontent of his guests, but the Archdeacon perceived it, and forthwith called such of the tumultuous assemblage as came from a distance into his barns. There the creels were turned bottom up, and four close-jointed gates lifted off their hinges were laid on the top for tables. Then from pans and boilers that simmered in the kitchen a great feast was spread. First came the broth, well loaded with barley and cabbage, and not destitute of the flavor of numerous sheep's heads. This was served in wooden piggins, shells being used as spoons. Then suet pudding, as round as a well-fed salmon, and as long as a 30 lb. cod. Last of all a fat hog, roasted whole, and cut with a cleaver, but further dissected only by teeth and fingers, for the unfastidious Manxman cared nothing for knife and fork.

After that there were liquor and lusty song. And all the time there could be heard, over the boisterous harmony of the feasters within the barn, the yet noisier racket of the people without.

By this time, whatever sentiment of doubtful charity had been harbored in the icy breast of the Manxman had been thawed away under the charitable effects of good cheer, and Thorkell Mylrea and Archdeacon Teare began to appear in truly Christian character.

"It's none so ould he is yet, at all at all."

"Ould? He hasn't the hayseed out of his hair, boy."

"And a shocking powerful head-piece at him for all."

There were rough jokes and dubious toasts, and Thorkell enjoyed them all. There was dancing, too, and fiddling, and the pipes at intervals, and all went merry until midnight, when the unharmonious harmonies of fiddle and pipes and unsteady song went off over the Curraghs in various directions.

Next morning Thorkell took his wife home to Ballamona. They drove in the open springless car in which he had brought down the oaten cake and ale. Thorkell had seen that the remains of these good viands were thriftily gathered up. He took them back home with him, carefully packed under the board on which his young wife sat.

CHAPTER II
A MAN CHILD IS BORN

Three years passed and Thorkell's fortunes grew apace. He toiled early and late. Time had no odd days or holiday in his calendar. Every day was working day except Sunday, and then Thorkell, like a devout Christian, went to church. Thorkell believed that he was a devoutly religious man, but rumor whispered that he was better able to make his words fly up than to prevent his thoughts from remaining below.

His wife did not seem to be a happy woman. During the three years of her married life she had not borne her husband children. It began to dawn upon her that Thorkell's sole desire in marriage had been a child, a son, to whom he could leave what no man can carry away.

One Sunday morning, as Thorkell and his wife were on their way to church, a young woman of about twenty passed them, and as she went by she curtsied low to the lady. The girl had a comely, nut-brown face, with dark wavy clusters of hair tumbling over her forehead from beneath a white sun-bonnet, of which the poke had been dexterously rolled back. It was summer, and her light blue bodice was open and showed a white under-bodice and a full neck. Her sleeves were rolled up over the elbows, and her dimpled arms were bare and brown. There was a look of coquetry in her hazel eyes as they shot up their dark lustre under her long lashes, and then dropped as quickly to her feet. She wore buckle shoes with the open clock tops.

Thorkell's quick eyes glanced over her, and when the girl curtsied to his wife he fell back the few paces that he was in front of her.

"Who is she?" he asked.

Thorkell's wife replied that the girl was a net-maker from near Peeltown.

"What's her name?"

Thorkell's wife answered that the girl's name was Mally Kerruish.

"Who are her people? Has she any?"

Thorkell's wife explained that the girl had a mother only, who was poor and worked in the fields, and had come to Ballamona for help during the last hard winter.

"Humph! Doesn't look as if the daughter wanted for much. How does the girl come by her fine feathers if her mother lives on charity?"

Thorkell's wizened face was twisted into grotesque lines. His wife's face saddened, and her voice dropped as she hinted in faltering accents that "scandal did say—say—"

"Well, woman, what does scandal say?" asked Thorkell; and his voice had a curious lilt, and his mouth wore a strange smile.

"It says—I'm afraid, Thorkell, the poor girl is no better than she ought to be."

Thorkell snorted, and then laughed in his throat like a frisky gelding.

"I thought she looked like a lively young puffin," he said, and then trotted on in front, his head rolling between his shoulders, and his eyes down. After going a few yards further he slackened speed again.

"Lives near Peeltown, you say—a net-maker—Mally—is it Mally Kerruish?"

Thorkell's wife answered with a nod of the head, and then her husband faced about, and troubled her with no further conversation until he drew up at the church door, and said, "Quick, woman, quick, and mind you shut the pew door after you."

But "God remembered Rachel and hearkened to her," and then, for the first time, the wife of Thorkell Mylrea began to show a cheerful countenance. Thorkell's own elevation of spirits was yet more noticeable. He had heretofore showed no discontent with the old homestead that had housed his people for six generations, but he now began to build another and much larger house on the rising ground at the foot of Slieu Dhoo. His habits underwent some swift and various changes. He gave away no gray blankets that winter, the itinerant poor who were "on the houses" often went empty from his door, and—most appalling change of all—he promptly stopped his tithe. When the parson's cart drove up to Ballamona, Thorkell turned the horse's head, and gave the flank a sharp cut with his whip. The parson came in white with wrath.

"Let every pig dig for herself," said Thorkell. "I'll daub grease on the rump of your fat pig no more."

Thorkell's new homestead rose rapidly, and when the walls were ready for the roof the masons and carpenters went up to Ballamona for the customary feast of cowree and jough and binjean.

"What! Is it true, then, as the saying is," Thorkell exclaimed at the sight of them, "that when the sport is the merriest it is time to give up?"

They ate no cowree at Ballamona that night and they drank no jough.

"We've been going to the goat's house for wool," grunted one of them as they trudged home.

"Aw, well, man, and what can you get of the cat but his skin?" growled another.

Next day they put on the first timbers of the roof, and the following night a great storm swept over the island, and the roof-timbers were torn away, not a spar or purlin being left in its place. Thorkell fumed at the storm and swore at the men, and when the wind subsided he had the work done afresh. The old homestead of Ballamona was thatched, but the new one must be slated, and slates were quarried at and carted to Slieu Dhoo, and run on to the new roof. A dead calm had prevailed during these operations, but it was the calm that lies in the heart of the storm, and the night after they were completed the other edge of the cyclone passed over the island, tearing up the trees by their roots, and shaking the old Ballamona to its foundations. Thorkell Mylrea slept not a wink, but tramped up and down his bedroom the long night through; and next morning, at daybreak, he drew the blind of his window, and peered through the haze of the dawn to where his new house stood on the breast of Slieu Dhoo. He could just descry its blue walls—it was roofless.

The people began to mutter beneath their breath.

"Aw, man, it's a judgment," said one.

"He has been middlin' hard on the widda and fatherless, and it's like enough that there's Them aloft as knows it."

"What's that they're saying?" said one old crone, "what comes with the wind goes with the water."

"Och, I knew his father—him and me were same as brothers—and a good ould man for all."

"Well, and many a good cow has a bad calf," said the old woman.

Thorkell went about like a cloud of thunder, and when he heard that the accidents to his new homestead were ascribed to supernatural agencies he flashed like forked lightning.

"Where there are geese there's dirt," he said, "and where there are women there's talking. Am I to be frightened if an old woman sneezes?"

But before Thorkell set to work again he paid his tithe. He paid it with a rick of discolored oats that had been cut in the wet and threshed before it was dry. Thorkell had often wondered whether his cows would eat it. The next Sunday morning the parson paused before his sermon to complain that certain of his parishioners, whom he would not name at present, appeared to think that what was too bad for the pigs was good enough for the priests. Let the Church of God have no more of their pig-swill. Thorkell in his pew chuckled audibly, and muttered something about paying for a dead horse.

It was spring when the second roof was blown down, and the new house stood roofless until early summer. Then Thorkell sent four lean pigs across to the Rectory, and got his carpenters together and set them to work. The roofing proceeded without interruption.

The primrose was not yet gone, the swallow had not yet come, and the young grass under the feet of the oxen was still small and sweet, when Thorkell's wife took to her bed. Then all Ballamona was astir. Hommy-beg, the deaf gardener of Ballamona, was sent in the hot haste of his best two miles an hour to the village, commonly known as the Street, to summon the midwife. This good woman was called Kerry Quayle; she was a spinster of forty, and she was all but blind.

"I'm thinking the woman-body is after going on the straw," said Hommy-beg, when he reached the Street, and this was the sum of the message that he delivered.

"Then we'd better be off, as the saying is," remarked Kerry, who never accepted responsibility for any syllable she ever uttered.

When they got to Ballamona, Thorkell Mylrea bustled Hommy-beg into the square springless car, and told him to drive to Andreas, and fetch the Archdeacon without an hour's delay. Hommy-beg set off at fine paces that carried him to the Archdeaconry a matter of four miles an hour.

Thorkell followed Kerry Quayle to the room above. When they stepped into the bedroom Thorkell drew the midwife aside to a table on which a large candle stood in a tall brass candlestick, with gruesome gargoyles carved on the base and upper flange. From this table he picked up a small Testament bound in shiny leather, with silver clasps.

"I'm as great a man as any in the island," said Thorkell, in his shrill whisper, "for laughing at the simpletons that talk about witches and boaganes and the like of that."

"So you are, as the saying is," said Kerry.

"I'd have the law on the lot of them, if I had my way," said Thorkell, still holding the book.

"Aw, and shockin' powerful luck it would be, as the old body said, if all the witches and boaganes in the island could be run into the sea," said Kerry.

"Pshaw! I'm talking of the simpletons that believe in them," said Thorkell, snappishly. "I'd clap them all in Castle Rushen."

"Aw, yes, and clean law and clean justice, too, as the Irishman said."

"So don't think I want the midwife to take her oath in my house," said Thorkell.

"Och, no, of course not. You wouldn't bemean yourself, as they say."

"But, then, you know what the saying is, Kerry. 'Custom must be indulged with custom, or custom will weep;'" and, saying this, Thorkell's voice took a most insinuating tone.

"Aw, now, and I'm as good as here and there one at standing up for custom, as the saying is," said the midwife.

The end of it all was that Kerry Quayle took there and then a solemn oath not to use sorcery or incantation of any kind in the time of travail, not to change the infant at the hour of its birth, not to leave it in the room for a week afterward without spreading the tongs over its crib, and much else of the like solemn purport.

The dusk deepened, and the Archdeacon had not yet arrived. Night came on and the room was dark, but Thorkell would not allow a lamp to be brought in, or a fire to be lighted. Some time later, say six hours after Hommy-beg had set out on his six-mile journey, a lumbrous, jolting sound of heavy wheels came from the road below the Curragh, and soon afterward the Archdeacon entered the room.

"So dark," he said, on stumbling across the threshold.

"Ah, Archdeacon," said Thorkell, with the unaccustomed greeting of an outstretched hand, "the Church shall bring light to the chamber here," and Thorkell handed the tinder-box to the Archdeacon and led him to the side of the table on which the candle stood.

In an instant the Archdeacon, laughing a little, or protesting meekly against his clerical honors, was striking the flint, when Thorkell laid a hand on his arm.

"Wait one moment; of course you know how I despise superstition?"

"Ah! of course, of course," said the Archdeacon.

"But, then, you know the old saying, Archdeacon, 'Custom must be indulged with custom,' you know it?" And Thorkell's face shut up like a nut-cracker.

"So I must bless the candle. Eh, is that it?" said the Archdeacon, with a low gurgle; and the next moment he was gabbling in a quick undertone through certain words that seemed to be all one word: "OLord-Jesus-Christ-bless-Thou-this-creature-of-a-waxen-taper-that-on- what-place-soever-it-be-lighted-or-set-the-devil-may-flee-from-that- habitation-and-no-more-disquiet-them-that-serve—Thee!"

After the penultimate word there was a short pause, and at the last word there was the sharp crack of the flint, and in an instant the candle was lighted.

Then the Archdeacon turned toward the bed and exchanged some words with his daughter. The bed was a mahogany four-post one, with legs like rocks, a hood like a pulpit sounding-board, and tapestry curtains like a muddy avalanche. The Archdeacon—he was a small man, with a face like a russet apple—leaned against one of the bed-posts, and said, in a tone of banter:

"Why, Thorkell, and if you're for indulging custom, how comes it that you have not hung up your hat?"

"My hat—my hat!" said Thorkell, in perplexity.

"Aw, now," said the midwife, "the master's as great a man as any in the island at laughing at the men craythurs that hang up their hats over the straw to fright the boaganes, as the old woman said."

Thorkell's laughter instantly burst forth to justify the midwife's statement.

"Ha, ha! Hang up my hat! Well now, well now! Drives away the black spirits from the birth-bed—isn't that what the dunces say? It's twenty years since I saw the like of it done, and I'd forgotten the old custom. Must look funny, very, the good man's hat perched up on the bed-post? What d'ye say, Archdeacon, shall we have it up? Just for the laugh, you know, ha, ha!"

In another moment Thorkell was gone from the room, and his titter could be heard from the stairs; it ebbed away and presently flowed back again, and Thorkell was once more by the bedside, laughing immoderately, and perching his angular soft hat on the topmost knob of one of the posts at the foot of the bed.

Then Thorkell and the Archdeacon went down to the little room that had once been Gilcrist's room, looking over the Curragh to the sea.

Before daybreak next morning a man child was born to Thorkell Mylrea, and an heir to the five hundred acres of Ballamona.

CHAPTER III
THE CHRISTENING OF YOUNG EWAN

In the dead waste of that night the old wall of Ballamona echoed to the noise of hurrying feet. Thorkell himself ran like a squirrel, hither and thither, breaking out now and again into shrill peals of hysterical laughter; while the women took the kettle to the room above, and employed themselves there in sundry mysterious ordinances on which no male busybody might intrude. Thorkell dived down into the kitchen, and rooted about in the meal casks for the oaten cake, and into the larder for the cheese, and into the cupboard for the bread-basket known as the "peck."

Hommy-beg, who had not been permitted to go home that night, had coiled himself in the settle drawn up before the kitchen fire, and was now snoring lustily. Thorkell roused him, and set him to break the oatcake and cheese into small pieces into the peck, and, when this was done, to scatter it broadcast on the staircase and landing, and on the garden-path immediately in front of the house; while he himself carried a similar peck, piled up like a pyramid with similar pieces of oatcake and cheese, to the room whence there issued at intervals a thin, small voice, that was the sweetest music that had ever yet fallen on Thorkell's ear.

What high commotion did the next day witness! For the first time since that lurid day when old Ewan Mylrea was laid under the elder-tree in the churchyard by the sea, Ballamona kept open house. The itinerant poor, who made the circuit of the houses, came again, and lifted the latch without knocking, and sat at the fire without being asked, and ate of the oatcake and the cheese. And upstairs, where a meek white face looked out with an unfamiliar smile from behind sheets that were hardly more white, the robustious statespeople from twenty miles around sat down in their odorous atmosphere of rude health and high spirits, and noise and laughter, to drink their glass of new brewed jough, and to spread on their oaten bread a thick crust of the rum-butter that stood in the great blue china bowl on the little table near the bed-head. And Thorkell—how nimbly he hopped about, and encouraged his visitors to drink, and rallied them if they ceased to eat!

"Come, man, come," he said a score of times, "shameful leaving is worse than shameful eating—eat, drink!"

And they ate, and they drank, and they laughed, and they sang, till the bedroom reeked with the fumes of a pot-house, and the confusion of tongues therein was worse than at the foot of Babel.

Throughout three long jovial weeks the visitors came and went, and every day the "blithe bread" was piled in the peck for the poor of the earth, and scattered on the paths for the good spirits of the air. And when people jested upon this, and said that not since the old days of their grandfathers had the boaganes and the fairies been so civilly treated, Thorkell laughed noisily, and said what great fun it was that they should think he was superstitious, and that custom must be indulged with custom, or custom would weep!

Then came the christening, and to this ceremony the whole country round was invited. Thorkell was now a man of consequence, and the neighbors high and low trooped in with presents for the young Christian.

Kerry, the midwife, who was nurse as well, carried the child to church, and the tiny red burden lay cooing softly at her breast in a very hillock of white swaddlings. Thorkell walked behind, his little eyes twinkling under his bushy eyebrows; and on his arm his wife leaned heavily after every feeble step, her white waxwork face bright with the smile of first motherhood.

The Archdeacon met the company at the west porch and they gathered for the baptism about the font in the aisle: half-blind Kerry with the infant, Thorkell and his young wife, the two godfathers, the Vicar General and the High Bailiff of Peeltown, and the godmother, the High Bailiff's wife, and behind this circle a mixed throng of many sorts. After the gospel and the prayers, the Archdeacon, in his white surplice, took the infant into his hands and called on the godparents to name the child, and they answered Ewan. Then, as the drops fell over the wee blinking eyes, and all voices were hushed in silence and awe, there came to the open porch and looked into the dusky church a little fleecy lamb, all soft and white and beautiful. It lifted its innocent and dazed face where it stood in the morning sunshine, on the grass of the graves, and bleated, and bleated, as if it had strayed from its mother and was lost.

The Archdeacon paused with his drooping finger half raised over the other innocent face at his breast, Thorkell's features twitched, and the tears ran down the white cheeks of his wife.

In an instant the baby-lamb had hobbled away, and before the Archdeacon had restored the child to the arms of blind Kerry or mumbled the last of the prayers, there came the hum of many voices from the distance. The noise came rapidly nearer, and as it approached it broke into a great tumult of men's deep shouts and women's shrill cries.

The iron hasp of the lych-gate to the churchyard was heard to chink, and at the same moment there was the sound of hurrying footsteps on the paved way. The company that had gathered about the font broke up abruptly, and made for the porch with looks of inquiry and amazement. There, at the head of a mixed throng of the riff-raff of the parish, bareheaded men, women with bold faces, and children with naked feet, a man held a young woman by the arm and pulled her toward the church. He was a stalwart fellow, stern of feature, iron gray, and he gripped the girl's bare brown arm like a vise.

"Make way there! Come, mistress, and no struggling," he shouted, and he tugged the girl after him, and then pushed her before him.

She was young; twenty at most. Her comely face was drawn hard with lines of pain; her hazel eyes flashed with wrath; and where her white sun-bonnet had fallen back from her head on to her shoulders, the knots of her dark hair, draggled and tangled in the scuffle, tumbled in masses over her neck and cheeks.

It was Mally Kerruish, and the man who held her and forced her along was the parish sumner, the church constable.

"Make way, I tell you!" shouted the sumner to the throng that crowded upon him, and into the porch, and through the company that had come for the christening. When the Archdeacon stepped down from the side of the font, the sumner with his prisoner drew up on the instant and the noisy crew stood and was silent.

"I have brought her for her oath, your reverence," said the sumner, dropping his voice and his head together.

"Who accuses her?" the Archdeacon asked.

"Her old mother," said the sumner; "here she is."

From the middle of the throng behind him the sumner drew out an elderly woman with a hard and wizened face. Her head was bare, her eyes were quick and restless, her lips firm and long, her chin was broad and heavy. The woman elbowed her way forward; but when she was brought face to face with the Archdeacon, and he asked her if she charged her daughter, she looked around before answering, and seeing her girl Mally standing there with her white face, under the fire of fifty pairs of eyes, all her resolution seemed to leave her.

"It isn't natheral, I know," she said, "a mother speaking up agen her child," and with that her hard mouth softened, her quick eyes reddened and filled, and her hands went up to her face. "But nature goes down with a flood when you're looking to have another belly to fill, and not a shilling at you this fortnight."

The girl stood without a word, and not one streak of color came to her white cheeks as her mother spoke.

"She denied it, and denied it, and said no, and no; but leave it to a mother to know what way her girl's going."

There was a low murmur among the people at the back and some whispering. The girl's keen ear caught it, and she turned her head over her shoulder with a defiant glance.

"Who is the man?" said the Archdeacon, recalling her with a touch of his finger on her arm.

She did not answer at first, and he repeated the question.

"Who is the guilty man?" he said, in a voice more stern.

"It's not true. Let me go," said the girl, in a quick undertone.

"Who is the partner of your sin?"

"It's not true, I say. Let me go, will you?" and the girl struggled feebly in the sumner's grip.

"Bring her to the altar," said the Archdeacon. He faced about and walked toward the chancel, and entered it. The company followed him and drew up outside the communion rail. He took a Testament from the reading-desk and stepped toward the girl. There was a dead hush.

"The Church provides a remedy for slander," he said, in a cold, clear tone. "If you are not guilty, swear that you are innocent, that he who tampers with your good name may beware." With that the Archdeacon held the Testament toward the girl. She made no show of taking it. He thrust it into her hand. At the touch of the book she gave a faint cry and stepped a pace backward, the Testament falling open on to the penitent-form beneath.

Then the murmur of the bystanders rose again. The girl heard it once more, and dropped on her knees and covered her face, and cried, in a tremulous voice that echoed over the church, "Let me go, let me go."

The company that came for the christening had walked up the aisle. Blinking Kerry stood apart, hushing the infant in her arms; it made a fretful whimper. Thorkell stood behind, pawing the paved path with a restless foot. His wife had made her way to the girl's side, her eyes overflowing with compassion.

"Take her to prison at the Peel," said the Archdeacon, "and keep her there until she confesses the name of her paramour." At that, Thorkell's wife dropped to her knees beside the kneeling girl, and putting one arm about her neck, raised the other against the sumner, and cried, "No, no, no; she will confess."

There was a pause and a long hush. Mally let her hands fall from her face, and turned her eyes full on the eyes of the young mother at her side. In dead silence the two rose to their feet together.

"Confess his name; whoever he is, he does not deserve that you should suffer for him as well," said the wife of Thorkell Mylrea, and as she spoke she touched the girl's white forehead with her pale lips.

"Do *you* ask that?" said Mally, with a strange quietness.

For one swift instant the eyes of these women seemed to see into each other's heart. The face of Thorkell's wife became very pale; she grew faint, and clutched the communion rail as she staggered back.

At the next instant Mally Kerruish was being hurried by the sumner down the aisle; the noisy concourse that had come with them went away with them, and in a moment more the old church was empty, save for the company that had gathered about the font.

There was a great feast at Ballamona that day. The new house was finished, and the young Christian, Ewan Mylrea, of Ballamona, was the first to enter it; for was it not to be his house, and his children's and his children's children's?

Thorkell's wife did not join the revels, but in her new home she went back to her bed. The fatigue and excitement of the day had been too much for her. Thorkell himself sat in his place, and laughed noisily and drank much. Toward sunset the sumner came to say that the girl who had been taken to prison at the Peel had confessed, and was now at large. The Archdeacon got up and went out of the room. Thorkell called lustily on his guests to drink again, and one stupefied old crony clambered to his feet and demanded silence for a toast.

"To the father of the girl's by-blow," he shouted, when the glasses were charged; and then the company laughed till the roof rang, and above all was the shrill laugh of Thorkell Mylrea. Presently the door opened again, and the Archdeacon, with a long, grave face, stood on the threshold and beckoned to Thorkell at the head of his table. Thorkell went out with him, and when they returned together a little later, and the master of Ballamona resumed his seat, he laughed yet more noisily than before, and drank yet more liquor.

On the outside of Ballamona that night an old woman, hooded and caped, knocked at the door. The loud laughter and the ranting songs from within came out to her where she stood in the darkness, under the silent stars. When the door was opened by Hommy-beg the woman asked for Mylrea Ballamona. Hommy-beg repulsed her, and would have shut the door in her face. She called again, and again, and yet again, and at last, by reason of her importunity, Hommy-beg went in and told Thorkell, who got up and followed him out. The Archdeacon heard the message, and left the room at the same moment.

Outside, on the gravel path, the old woman stood with the light of the lamp that burned in the hall on her wizened face. It was Mrs. Kerruish, the mother of Mally.

"It's fine times you're having of it, Master Mylrea," she said, "and you, too, your reverence; but what about me and my poor girl?"

"It was yourself that did it, woman," said Thorkell; and he tried to laugh, but under the stars his laugh fell short.

"Me, you say? Me, was it for all? May the good God judge between us, Master Mylrea. D'ye know what it is that happened? My poor girl's gone."

"Gone!"

"Eh, gone—gone off—gone to hide her shameful face; God help her."

"Better luck," said Thorkell, and a short gurgle rattled in his dry throat.

"Luck, you call it? Luck! Take care, Ballamona."

The Archdeacon interposed. "Come, no threats, my good woman," he said, and waved his hand in protestation. "The Church has done you justice in this matter."

"Threats, your reverence? Justice? Is it justice to punish the woman and let the man go free? What! the woman to stand penance six Sabbaths by the church-door of six parishes, and the man to pay his dirty money, six pounds to you and three to me, and then no mortal to name his name!"

The old woman rummaged in the pocket at her side and pulled out a few coins. "Here, take them back; I'm no Judas to buy my own girl. Here, I say, take them!"

Thorkell had thrust his hands in his pockets, and was making a great show of laughing boisterously.

The old woman stood silent for a moment, and her pale face turned livid. Then by a sudden impulse she lifted her eyes and her two trembling arms. "God in Heaven," she said, in a hoarse whisper, "let Thy wrath rest on this man's head; make this house that he has built for himself and for his children a curse to him and them and theirs; bring it to pass that no birth come to it but death come with it, and so on and on until Thou hast done justice between him and me."

Thorkell's laughter stopped suddenly. As the woman spoke his face quivered, and his knees shook perceptibly under him. Then he took her by the arms and clutched her convulsively. "Woman, woman, what are you saying?" he cried, in his shrill treble. She disengaged herself and went away into the night.

For a moment Thorkell tramped the hall with nervous footsteps. The Archdeacon stood speechless. Then the sound of laughter and of song came from the room they had left, and Thorkell flung in on the merry-makers.

"Go home, go home, every man of you! Away with you!" he shouted, hysterically, and then dropped like a log into a chair.

One by one, with many wise shakes of many sapient heads, the tipsy revelers broke up and went off, leaving the master of Ballamona alone in that chamber, dense with dead smoke, and noisome with the fumes of liquor.

CHAPTER IV
THE DEEMSTER OF MAN

Twenty times that night Thorkell devised expedients to break the web of fate. At first his thoughts were of revengeful defiance. By fair means or foul the woman Kerruish should suffer. She should be turned out of house and home. She should tramp the roads as a mendicant. He would put his foot on her neck. Then they would see what her uncanny threats had come to.

He tried this unction for his affrighted spirit, and put it aside as useless. No, no; he would conciliate the woman. He would settle an annuity of five pounds a year upon her; he would give her the snug gate cottage of old Ballamona to live in; his wife should send her warm blankets in winter, and sometimes a pound of tea, such as old folks love. Then must her imprecation fall impotent, and his own fate be undisturbed.

Thorkell's bedroom in his new house on Slieu Dhoo looked over the Curraghs to the sea. As the day dawned he opened the window, and thrust out his head to drink of the cool morning air. The sun was rising over the land behind, a strong breeze was sweeping over the marshes from the shore, and the white curves of the breakers to the west reflected here and there the glow of the eastern sky. With the salt breath of the sea in his nostrils, it seemed to Thorkell a pitiful thing that a man should be a slave to a mere idea; a thing for shame and humiliation that the sneezing of an old woman should disturb the peace of a strong man. Superstition was the bugbear of the Manxman, but it would die of shame at its sheer absurdity, only that it was pampered by the law. Toleration for superstition! Every man who betrayed faith in omens or portents, or charms or spells, or the power of the evil eye, should be instantly clapped in the Castle. It was but right that a rabid dog should be muzzled.

Thorkell shut the window, closed the shutters, threw off his clothes, and went back to bed. In the silence and the darkness, his thoughts took yet another turn. What madness it was, what pertness and unbelief, to reject that faith in which the best and wisest of all ages had lived and died! Had not omens and portents, and charms and spells, and the evil eye been believed in in all ages? What midget of modern days should now arise with a superior smile and say, "Behold, this is folly: Saul of Israel and Saul of Tarsus, and Samuel and Solomon, rose up and lay down in folly."

Thorkell leaped out of bed, sweating from every pore. The old woman Kerruish should be pensioned; she should live in the cozy cottage at the gates of Ballamona; she should have blankets and tea and many a snug comfort; her daughter should be brought back and married—yes, married—to some honest fellow.

The lark was loud in the sky, the rooks were stirring in the lofty ash, the swallows pecking at the lattice, when sleep came at length to Thorkell's bloodshot eyes, and he stretched himself in a short and fitful slumber. He awoke with a start. The lusty rap of Hommy-beg was at the door of his room. There was no itinerant postman, and it was one of Hommy-beg's daily duties to go to the post-office. He had been there this morning, and was now returned with a letter for his master.

Thorkell took the letter with nervous fingers. He had recognized the seal—it was the seal of the insular Government. The letter came from Castle Rushen. He broke the seal and read:

> "Castle Rushen, June 3d.
>
> "Sir—I am instructed by his Excellency to beg you to come to Castletown without delay, and to report your arrival at the Castle to Madam Churchill, who will see you on behalf of the Duchess.
>
> "I have the honor to be, etc."

The letter was signed by the Secretary to the Governor.

What did it mean? Thorkell could make nothing of it but that in some way it boded ill. In a bewildered state of semi-consciousness he ordered that a horse should be got ready and brought round to the front. Half an hour later he had risen from an untouched breakfast and was seated in the saddle.

He rode past Tynwald Hill and through Foxdale to the south. Twenty times he drew up and half-reined his horse in another direction. But he went on again. He could turn about at any time. He never turned about. At two o'clock that day he stood before the low gate of the Castle and pulled at the great clanging bell.

He seemed to be expected, and was immediately led to a chamber on the north of the courtyard. The room was small and low; it was dimly lighted by two lancet windows set deep into walls that seemed to be three yards thick. The floor was covered with a rush matting; a harp stood near the fireplace. A lady rose as Thorkell entered. She was elderly, but her dress was youthful. Her waist was short; her embroidered skirt was very long; she wore spangled shoes, and her hair was done into a knot on the top of her head.

Thorkell stood before her with the mien of a culprit. She smiled and motioned him to a seat, and sat herself.

"You have heard of the death of one of our two Deemsters?" she asked.

Thorkell's face whitened, and he bowed his head.

"A successor must soon be appointed, and the Deemster is always a Manxman; he must know the language of the common people."

Thorkell's face wore a bewildered expression. The lady's manner was very suave.

"The appointment is the gift of the Lord of the island, and the Duchess is asked to suggest a name."

Thorkell's face lightened. He had regained all his composure.

"The Duchess has heard a good account of you, Mr. Mylrea. She is told that by your great industry and—wisdom—you have raised yourself in life—become rich, in fact."

The lady's voice dropped to a tone of most insinuating suavity. Thorkell stammered some commonplace.

"Hush, Mr. Mylrea, you shall not depreciate yourself. The Duchess has heard that you are a man of enterprise—one who does not begrudge the penny that makes the pound."

Thorkell saw it all. He was to be made Deemster, but he was to buy his appointment. The Duchess had lost money of late, and the swashbuckler court she kept had lately seen some abridgment of its gaieties.

"To be brief, Mr. Mylrea, the Duchess has half an intention of suggesting your name for the post, but before doing so she wished me to see in what way your feelings lie with regard to it."

Thorkell's little eyes twinkled, and his lips took an upward curve. He placed one hand over his breast and bent his head.

"My feelings, madam, lie in one way only—the way of gratitude," he said, meekly.

The lady's face broadened, and there was a pause.

"It is a great distinction, Mr. Mylrea," said the lady, and she drew her breath inward.

"The greater my gratitude," said Thorkell.

"And how far would you go to show this gratitude to the Duchess?"

"Any length, madam," said Thorkell, and he rose and bowed.

"The Duchess is at present at Bath—"

"I would go so far, and—further, madam, further," said Thorkell, and as he spoke he thrust his right hand deep into his pocket, and there—by what accident may not be said—it touched some coins that chinked.

There was another pause, and then the lady rose and held out her hand, and said, in a significant tone:

"I think, sir, I may already venture to hail you as Deemster of Man."

Thorkell cantered home in great elevation of soul. The milestones fell behind him one after one, and he did not feel the burden of the way. His head was in his breast; his body was bent over his saddle-bow; again and again a trill of light laughter came from his lips. Where were his dreams now, his omens, his spells, and the power of the evil eye? He was judge of his island. He was master of his fate.

Passing through St. John's, he covered the bleak top of the hill, and turned down toward the shady copse of Kirk Michael. Where the trees were thickest in the valley he drew rein by a low, long house that stood back to the road. It was the residence of the Bishop of the island, but it was now empty. The bishopric had been vacant these five years, and under the heavy rains from the hills and the strong winds from the sea, the old house had fallen into decay.

Thorkell sat in the saddle under the tall elms in the dim light, and his mind was busy with many thoughts. His memory went back with something akin to tenderness to the last days of old Ewan, his father; to his brother, Gilcrist, and then, by a sudden transition, to the incidents of that morning at Castle Rushen. How far in the past that morning seemed to be!

The last rook had cawed out its low guttural note, and the last gleam of daylight died off between the thick boughs of the dark trees that pattered lightly overhead, as Thorkell set off afresh.

When he arrived at Ballamona the night was dark. The Archdeacon was sitting with his daughter, who had not left her room that day. Thorkell, still booted and spurred, ran like a squirrel up the stairs and into the bedroom. In twenty hot words that were fired off like a cloud of small shot from a blunderbuss, Thorkell told what had occurred. His wife's white face showed no pleasure and betrayed no surprise. Her silence acted on Thorkell as a rebuke, and when her eyes rested on his face he turned his own eyes aside.

The Archdeacon was almost speechless, but his look of astonishment was eloquent, and when Thorkell left the room he followed him out.

At supper the Archdeacon's manner was that of deep amity. "They are prompt to appoint a Deemster," he said. "Has it not struck you as strange that the bishopric has been vacant so long?"

Thorkell laughed a little over his plate, and answered that it was strange.

"Maybe it only needs that a name should be suggested," continued the Archdeacon. "That is to say, suggested by a man of influence—a man of position—by the Deemster, for instance."

"Just that," said Thorkell, with a titter.

Then there was an interchange of further amity. When the two men rose from the table the Archdeacon said, with a conscious smile, "Of course, if you should occur—if you should ever think—if, that is, the Deemster should ever suggest a name for the bishopric—of course, he will remember that—that blood, in short, is thicker than water—*ta fuill my s'chee na ushtey*, as the Manxman says."

"I will remember it," said Thorkell, in a significant tone, and with a faint chuckle.

Satisfied with that day's work, with himself, and with the world, Thorkell then went off to bed, and lay down in peace and content, and slept the sleep of the just.

In due course Thorkell Mylrea became Deemster Ballamona.

He entered upon his duties after the briefest study of the Statute Laws. A Manx judge dispensed justice chiefly by the Breast Laws, the unwritten code locked in his own breast, and supposed to be handed down from Deemster to Deemster. The popular superstition served Thorkell in good stead: there was none to challenge his knowledge of jurisprudence.

As soon as he was settled in his office he began to make inquiries about his brother Gilcrist. He learned that after leaving Cambridge, Gilcrist had taken deacon's orders, and had become tutor to the son of an English nobleman, and afterward chaplain to the nobleman's household. Thorkell addressed him a letter, and received a reply, and this was the first intercourse of the brothers since the death of old Ewan. Gilcrist had lately married; he held a small living on one of the remote moors of Yorkshire; he loved his people and was beloved by them. Thorkell wrote again and again, and yet again, and his letters ran through every tone of remonstrance and entreaty. The end of it was that the Deemster paid yet another visit to the lady deputy at Castle Rushen, and the rumor passed over the island that the same potent influence that had made Thorkell a Deemster was about to make his brother the Bishop of Man.

Then the Archdeacon came down in white wrath to Ballamona, and reminded his son-in-law of his many obligations, touched on benefits forgot, hinted at dark sayings and darker deeds, mentioned, with a significant accent, the girl Mally Kerruish, protested that from causes not to be named he had lost the esteem of his clergy and the reverence of his flock, and wound up with the touching assurance that on that very morning, as he rode from Andreas, he had overheard a burly Manxman say to the tawny-headed fellow who walked with him—both of them the scabbiest sheep on the hills—"There goes the pazon that sold his daughter and bought her husband."

Thorkell listened to the torrent of reproaches, and then said, quietly, as he turned on his heel, "Near is my shirt, but nearer is my skin."

The Deemster's wife held up her head no more. After the christening she rarely left her room. Her cheeks grew thinner, paler they could not grow, and her meek eyes lost their faint lustre. She spoke little, and her interest in life seemed to be all but gone. There was the same abject submission to her husband, but she saw less of him day by day. Only the sight of her babe, when Kerry brought it to be nursed, restored to her face the light of a fleeting joy. If it stayed too long at her breast, if it cried, if its winsome ways made her to laugh outright, the swift recoil of other feelings saddened her to melancholy, and she would put the child from her with a sigh. This went on for several months, and meantime the Deemster was too deeply immersed in secular affairs to make serious note of the shadow that hung over his house. "*Goll sheese ny lhiargagh*—she's going down the steep places," said Kerry.

It was winter when Gilcrist Mylrea was appointed to reach the island, but he wrote that his wife's health was failing her, that it was not unlikely that she was to bear a child, and that he preferred to postpone his journey until the spring. Before the gorse bushes on the mountains had caught their new spears of green, and before the fishermen of Peeltown had gone down to the sea for their first mackerel, Thorkell's wife was lying in her last illness. She sent for her husband and bade him farewell. The Deemster saw no danger, and he laughed at her meek adieu. She was soon to be the mother of another of his children—that was all. But she shook her head when he rallied her, and when he lifted the little creeping, cooing, babbling Ewan from the floor to his mother's bed, and laughed and held up his long, lean, hairy finger before the baby face and asked the little one with a puff how he would like a little sister, the white face on the pillow twitched and fell, and the meek eyes filled, and the shadow was over all.

"Good-by, Thorkell, and for baby's sake—"

But a shrill peal of Thorkell's laughter rang through the chamber, and at the next instant he was gone from the room.

That day the wife of the Deemster passed beyond the sorrows of the life that had no joys. The angels of life and death had come with linked hands to the new homestead of Ballamona, and the young mother had died in giving birth to a girl.

When the Deemster heard what had happened, his loud scream rang through every room of the house. His soul was in ferment; he seemed to be appalled, and to be stricken, not with sorrow, but with fright and horror.

"She's dead; why, she's dead, she's dead," he cried, hysterically; "why did not somebody tell me that she would die?"

The Deemster buried his wife by the side of old Ewan, under the elder-tree that grew by the wall of the churchyard that stands over by the sea. He summoned no mourners, and few stood with him by the open grave. During the short funeral, his horse was tied to the cross-timbers of the lych-gate, and while the earth was still falling in hollow thuds from the sexton's spade, Thorkell got into the saddle and rode away.

Before sunset he waited by the wooden landing jetty at Derby Haven. The old sea-tub, the "King Orry," made the port that day, and disembarked her passengers. Among them was the new Bishop of Man, Gilcrist Mylrea. He looked much older for the six years he had been away. His tall figure stooped heavily; his thick hair fell in wavelets on his shoulders, and was already sprinkled with gray; his long cheeks were deeply lined. As he stepped from the boat on to the jetty he carried something very tenderly in his arms. He seemed to be alone.

The brothers met with looks of constraint and bewilderment.

"Where is your wife?" asked Thorkell.

"She is gone," said Gilcrist. "I have nothing left of her but this," and he looked down at the burden at his breast.

It was a baby boy. Thorkell's face whitened, and terror was in his eyes.

CHAPTER V
THE MANXMAN'S BISHOP

Gilcrist Mylrea had been confirmed Bishop, and consecrated in England; but he had to be installed in his cathedral church at Peeltown with all the honors of the insular decrees. The ceremony was not an imposing one. Few of the native population witnessed it. The Manxman did not love the Church with a love too fervent. "Pazon, pazon," he would say, "what can you expect from the like o' that? Never no duck wasn't hatched by a drake."

It was no merit in the eyes of the people that the new Bishop was himself a Manxman. "Aw, man," they would say, "I knew his father," and knowledge of the father implied a limitation of the respect due to the son. "What's his family?" would be asked again and again across the hearth that scarcely knew its own family more intimately. "Maybe some of the first that's going," would be the answer, and then there would be a laugh.

The Bishop was enthroned by Archdeacon Teare, who filled his function with what grace his chagrin would allow. Thorkell watched his father-in-law keenly during the ceremony, and more than once his little eyes twinkled, and his lips were sucked inward as if he rolled a delectable morsel on his tongue. Archdeacon Teare was conscious of the close fire of his son-in-law's gaze, and after the installation was done, and the clergy that constituted priests and congregation were breaking up, he approached the Deemster with a benevolent smile, and said, "Well, Thorkell, we've had some disagreements, but we'll all meet for peace and harmony in heaven."

The Deemster tittered audibly, and said, "I'm not so sure of that, though."

"No?" said the Archdeacon, with elevated eyebrows. "Why—why?"

"Because we read in the Good Book that there will be no more *tears*, Archdeacon," said Thorkell, with a laugh like the whinny of a colt.

The Bishop and his brother, the Deemster, got on their horses, and turned their heads toward the episcopal palace. It was late when they drove under the tall elms of Bishop's Court. The old house was lighted up for their reception. Half-blind Kerry Quayle had come over from Ballamona to nurse the Bishop's child, and to put him to bed in his new home. "Och, as sweet a baby boy as any on the island, I'll go bail, as the old body said," said Kerry, and the Bishop patted her arm with a gentle familiarity. He went up to the little room where the child lay asleep, and stooped over the cot and touched with his lips the soft lips that breathed gently. The dignity of the Bishop as he stood four hours before under the roof of St. German's had sat less well on this silent man than the tenderness of the father by the side of his motherless child.

Thorkell was in great spirits that night. Twenty times he drank to the health of the new Bishop; twenty times he reminded him of his own gracious offices toward securing the bishopric to one of his own family. Gilcrist smiled, and responded in few words. He did not deceive himself; his eyes were open. He knew that Thorkell had not been so anxious to make him a Bishop as to prevent a place of honor and emolument from going to any one less near to himself than his own brother. "Near is my shirt," as Thorkell had told the Archdeacon, "but nearer is my skin."

Next day the Bishop lost no time in settling to his work. His people watched him closely. He found his palace in a forlorn and dilapidated state, and the episcopal demesne, which was about a square mile of glebe, as fallow as the rough top of the mountains. The money value of this bishopric was rather less than £500 a year, but out of this income he set to work to fence and drain his lands, plant trees, and restore his house to comfort, if not to stateliness. "I find my Patmos in ruins," he said, "and that will oblige me to interrupt my charity to the poor in some measure."

He assumed none of the social dignity of a Bishop. He had no carriage, and no horse for riding. When he made his pastoral visitations he went afoot. The journey to Douglas he called crossing the Pyrenees; and he likened the toilsome tramp across the heavy Curraghs from Bishop's Court to Kirk Andreas to the passing of pilgrims across a desert. "To speak truth," he would say, "I have a title too large for my scant fortune to maintain."

His first acts of episcopal authority did not conciliate either the populace or their superiors in station. He set his face against the contraband trade, and refused communion to those who followed it. "Och, terrible, wonderful hard on the poor man he is, with his laws agen honest trading, and his by-laws and his customs and his canons and the like o' that messing."

It was soon made clear that the Bishop did not court popularity. He started a school in each of the parishes by the help of a lady, who settled a bounty, payable at the Bishop's pleasure, for the support of the teachers. The teachers were appointed by his vicars-general. One day a number of the men of his own parish, with Jabez Gawne, the sleek little tailor, and Matthias Jubman, the buirdly maltster, at their head, came up to Bishop's Court to complain of the schoolmaster appointed to Kirk Michael. According to the malcontents, the schoolmaster was unable to divide his syllables, and his home, which was the schoolhouse also, was too remote for the convenience of the children. "So we beseech your Lordships," said little Jabez, who was spokesman, "to allow us a fit person to discharge the office, *and with submission we will recommend one.*" The Bishop took in the situation at a glance; Jabez's last words had let the cat out of the bag, and it could not be said to be a Manx cat, for it had a most prodigious tail. Next day the Bishop went to the school, examined master and scholars, then called the petitioners together, and said, "I find that James Quirk is qualified to teach an English school, and I can not remove him; but I am of your opinion that his house is in a remote part of the parish, and I shall expect the parishioners to build a new schoolhouse in a convenient place, near the church, within a reasonable time, otherwise the bounty can not be continued to them." The answer staggered the petitioners; but they were men with the saving grace of humor, and through the mouth of little Jabez, which twisted into curious lines, they forthwith signified to his Lordship their earnest desire to meet his wish by building their schoolhouse within the churchyard.

Though a zealous upholder of Church authority, the Bishop was known to temper justice with mercy. He had not been a month in the diocese when his sumner told him a painful story of hard penance. A young girl from near Peeltown had been presented for incontinence, and with the partner of her crime she had been ordered to stand six Sundays at the door of six churches. The man, who was rich, had compounded with the Archdeacon, paying six pounds for exemption, and being thenceforward no more mentioned; but the woman, being penniless and appalled at the disgrace before her, had fled from the island. The Archdeacon had learned her whereabouts in England, and had written to the minister of the place to acquaint him that she was under the Church's censure. The minister, on his part, had laid before her the terror of her position if she died out of communion with God's people. She resisted all appeals until her time came, and then, in her travail, the force of the idea had worked upon her, and she could resist it no more. When she rose from bed she returned voluntarily to the island, with the sign of her shame at her breast, to undergo the penance of her crime. She had stood three Sundays at the doors of three churches, but her health was feeble, and she could scarcely carry her child, so weak was she, and so long the distances from her lodging in Peeltown. "Let her be pardoned the rest of her penance," said the Bishop. "The Church's censure was not passed on her to afflict her with overmuch shame or sorrow."

It was not until years afterward that the Bishop learned the full facts of the woman's case, and comprehended the terrible significance of her punishment. She was Mally Kerruish.

The island was in the province of York, and bound by the English canons, but the Bishop made his own canons, and none were heard to demur. Some of his judgments were strange, but all leaned toward the weaker side. A man named Quayle the Gyke, a blusterous fellow, a thorn in the side of every official within a radius of miles, died after a long illness, leaving nothing to a legitimate son who had nursed him affectionately. This seemed to the Bishop to be contrary to natural piety, and in the exercise of his authority he appointed the son an executor with the others. Quayle the younger lived, as we shall see, to return evil for the Bishop's good. A rich man of bad repute, Thormod Mylechreest, died intestate, leaving an illegitimate son. The Bishop ordered the ordinary to put aside a sum of money out of the estate for the maintenance and education of the child. But Thorkell came down in the name of the civil power, reversed the spiritual judgment, ordered that the whole belongings of the deceased should be confiscated to the Lord of the Isle, and left the base-begotten to charity. We shall also see that the bastard returned good for Thorkell's evil.

The canons and customs of Bishop Mylrea not only leaned—sometimes with too great indulgence—to the weaker side, but they supposed faith in the people by allowing a voluntary oath as evidence, and this made false swearing a terror. Except in the degree of superstition, he encouraged belief in all its forms. He trusted an oath implicitly, but no man ever heard him gainsay his yea or nay.

A hoary old dog known as Billy the Gawk, who had never worked within living memory, who lived, as they said, "on the houses," and frequented the pot-house with more than the regularity of religious observance, was not long in finding out that Bishop's Court had awakened from its protracted sleep. The Bishop had been abroad for his morning's ramble, and sitting on the sunny side of a high turf hedge looking vacantly out to sea, he heard footsteps on the road behind him, and then a dialogue, of which this is a brief summary:

"Going up to the Coort, eh? Ah, well, it's plenty that's there to take the edge off your stomach; plenty, plenty, and a rael welcome too."

"Ah, it's not the stomach that's bothering me. It's the narves, boy—the narves—and a drop of the rael stuff is worth a Jew's eye for studdying a man after a night of it, as the saying is."

"Aw, Billy, Billy—aw well, well, well."

The conversation died off on the Bishop's ear in a loud roystering laugh and a low gurgle as undertone.

Half an hour later Billy the Gawk stood before the Bishop inside the gates of Bishop's Court. The old dog's head hung low, his battered hat was over his eyes, and both his trembling hands leaned heavily on his thick blackthorn stick.

"And how do you live, my man?" asked the Bishop.

"I'm getting a bite here, and a sup there, and I've had terrible little but a bit o' barley bread since yesterday morning," said the Gawk.

"Poor man, that's hard fare," said the Bishop; "but mind you call here every day for the future."

Billy got a measure of corn worth sixpence, and went straightway to the village, where he sold it at the pot-house for as much liquor as could have been bought for three-halfpence. And as Billy the Gawk drank his drop of the real stuff he laughed very loud and boasted that he could outwit the Bishop. But the liquor got into his head, and from laughing he went on to swearing, and thence to fighting, until the innkeeper turned him out into the road, where, under the weight of his measure of corn taken in solution, Billy sank into a dead slumber. The Bishop chanced to take an evening walk that day, and he found his poor penisioner, who fared hard, lodged on a harder bed, and he had him picked up and carried into the house. Next morning, when Billy awoke and found where he was, and remembered what had occurred, an unaccustomed sensation took possession of him, and he stole away unobserved. The hoary old dog was never seen again at Bishop's Court.

But if Billy never came again his kith and kin came frequently. It became a jest that the Bishop kept the beggars from every house but his own, and that no one else could get a beggar.

He had a book, which he called his "Matricula Pauperum," in which he entered the names of his pensioners with notes of their circumstances. He knew all the bits of family history—when Jemmy Corkell's wife was down with lumbago, and when Robbie Quirk was to kill his little pig.

Billy the Gawk was not alone in thinking that he could outwit the Bishop. When the Bishop wanted a new pair of boots or a new coat, the tailor or shoemaker came to Bishop's Court, and was kept there until his job of work was finished. The first winter after his arrival in his Patmos, he wanted a cloak, and sent for Jabez Gawne, the sleek little fox who had been spokesman for the conspirators against James Quirk, the schoolmaster. Jabez had cut out the cloak, and was preparing it for a truly gorgeous adornment, when the Bishop ordered him to put merely a button and a loop on it to keep it together. Jabez thereupon dropped his cloth and held up his hands where he sat cross-legged on the kitchen dresser, and exclaimed, with every accent of aggrieved surprise:

"My Lord, what would become of the poor buttonmakers and their families if every one ordered his tailor in that way?"

"How so, Jabez?"

"Why, they would be starved outright."

"Do you say so, Jabez?"

"Yes, my Lord, I do."

"Then button it all over, Jabez," said the Bishop.

The Deemster was present at that interview, and went away from it tittering audibly.

"Give to the raven and he'll come again," he muttered.

"I forgot that poor Jabez would have his buttons in his breeches-pocket," said the Bishop.

The Manxman had not yet made up his mind concerning the composite character of Bishop Mylrea, his dignity and his humility, his reserve and his simplicity, when a great event settled for the Manxman's heart the problem that had been too much for his head. This was no less a catastrophe than a general famine. It came upon the island in the second year of the Bishop's residence, and was the cause of many changes. One of the changes was that the Bishop came to be regarded by his people with the reverence of Israel for Samuel, and by his brother, the Deemster, with the distrust, envy, and, at length, mingled fear and hatred of Saul for Israel's prophet.

The land of the island had been held under a tenure of straw, known as the three-lives' tenure; the third life was everywhere running out, and the farms were reverting to the Lord of the Isle. This disheartened the farmers, who lost all interest in agriculture, let their lands lie fallow, and turned to the only other industry in which they had an interest, the herring fishing. The herrings failed this season, and without fish, with empty barns, and a scant potato crop, caused by a long summer of drought, the people were reduced to poverty.

Then the Bishop opened wider the gates of Bishop's Court, which since his coming had never been closed. Heaven seemed to have given him a special blessing. The drought had parched up the grass even of the damp Curragh, and left bleached on the whitening mold the poor, thin, dwarfed corn, that could never be reaped. But the glebe of Bishop's Court gave fair crops, and when the people cried in the grip of their necessity the Bishop sent round a pastoral letter to his clergy, saying that he had eight hundred bushels of wheat, barley, and oats more than his household required. Then there came from the north and the south, the east and the west, long, straggling troops of buyers with little or no money to buy, and Bishop's Court was turned into a public market. The Bishop sold to those who had money at the price that corn fetched before the famine, and in his barn behind the house he kept a chest for those who came in at the back with nothing but a sack in their hands. Once a day he inspected the chest, and when it was low, which was frequently, he replenished it, and when it was high, which was rarely, he smiled, and said that God was turning away his displeasure from his people.

The eight hundred bushels were at an end in a month, and still the famine continued. Then the Bishop bought eight hundred other bushels: wheat at ten shillings, barley at six shillings, and oats at four shillings, and sold them at half these prices. He gave orders that the bushel of the poor man was not to be stroked, but left in heaped-up measure.

A second month went by; the second eight hundred bushels were consumed, and the famine showed no abatement. The Bishop waited for vessels from Liverpool, but no vessels came. He was a poor priest, with a great title, and he had little money; but he wrote to England asking for a thousand bushels of grain and five hundred kischen of potatoes, and promised to pay at six days after the next annual revenue. A week of weary waiting ensued, and every day the Bishop cheered the haggard folk that came to Bishop's Court with accounts of the provisions that were coming; and every day they went up on to the head of the hill, and strained their bleared eyes seaward for the sails of an English ship. When patience was worn to despair, the old "King Orry" brought the Bishop a letter saying that the drought had been general, that the famine was felt throughout the kingdom, and that an embargo had been put on all food to forbid traders to send it from English shores. Then the voice of the hungry multitudes went up in one deep cry of pain. "The hunger is on us," they moaned. "Poor once, poor forever," they muttered; and the voice of the Bishop was silent.

Just at that moment a further disaster threatened the people. Their cattle, which they could not sell, they had grazed on the mountains, and the milk of the cows had been the chief food of the children, and the wool of the sheep the only clothing of their old men. With parched meadows and Curraghs, where the turf was so dry that it would take fire from the sun, the broad tops of the furze-covered hills were the sole resource of the poor. At daybreak the shepherd with his six ewe lambs and one goat, and the day laborer with his cow, would troop up to where the grass looked greenest, and at dusk they would come down to shelter, with weary limbs and heavy hearts. "What's it sayin'," they would mutter, "a green hill when far from me; bare, bare, when it is near."

At this crisis it began to be whispered that the Deemster had made an offer to the Lord to rent the whole stretch of mountain land from Ramsey to Peeltown. The rumor created consternation, and was not at first believed. But one day the Deemster, with the Governor of the Grand Enquest, drove to the glen at Sulby and went up the hillside. Not long after, a light cart was seen to follow the highroad to the glen beyond Ballaugh, and then turn up toward the mountains by the cart track. The people who were grazing their cattle on the hills came down and gathered with the people of the valleys at the foot, and there were dark faces and firm-set lips among them, and hot words and deep oaths were heard. "Let's off to the Bishop," said one, and then went to Bishop's Court. Half an hour later the Bishop came from Bishop's Court at the head of a draggled company of men, and his face was white and hard. They overtook the cart half-way up the side of the mountain, and the Bishop called on the driver to stop, and asked what he carried, and where he was going. The man answered that he had provisions for the Governor, the Deemster, and the Grand Enquest, who were surveying the tops of the mountains.

The Bishop looked round, and his lip was set, and his nostrils quivered. "Can any man lend me a knife?" he asked, with a strained quietness.

A huge knife was handed to him, such as shepherds carry in the long legs of their boots. He stepped to the cart and ripped up the harness, which was rope harness, the shafts fell and the horse was free. Then the Bishop turned to the driver and said very quietly:

"Where do you live, my man?"

"At Sulby, my Lord," said the man, trembling with fear.

"You shall have leather harness to-morrow."

Then the Bishop went on, his soiled and draggled company following him, the cart lying helpless in the cart track behind them.

When they got to the top of the mountain they could see the Governor and the Deemster and their associates stretching the chain in the purple distance. The Bishop made in their direction, and when he came up with them, he said:

"Gentlemen, no food will reach you on the mountains to-day; the harness of your cart has been cut, and cart and provisions are lying on the hillside."

At this Thorkell turned white with wrath, and clenched his fists and stamped his foot on the turf, and looked piercingly into the faces of the Bishop's followers.

"As sure as I'm Deemster," he said, with an oath, "the man who has done this shall suffer. Don't let him deceive himself—no one, not even the Bishop himself, shall step in between that man and the punishment of the law."

The Bishop listened with calmness, and then said, "Thorkell, the Bishop will not intercede for him. Punish him if you can."

"And so, by God, I will," cried the Deemster, and his eye traversed the men behind his brother.

The Bishop then took a step forward. "*I* am that man," he said, and then there was a great silence.

Thorkell's face flinched, his head fell between his shoulders, his manner grew dogged, he said not a word, his braggadocio was gone.

The Bishop approached the Governor. "You have no more right to rent these mountains than to rent yonder sea," he said, and he stretched his arm toward the broad blue line to the west. "They belong to God and to the poor. Let me warn you, sir, that as sure as you set up one stone to enclose these true God's acres, I shall be the first to pull that stone down."

The Grand Enquest broke up in confusion, and the mountains were saved to the people.

It blew hard on the hilltop that day, and the next morning the news spread through the island that a ship laden with barley had put in from bad weather at Douglas Harbor. "And a terrible wonderful sight of corn, plenty for all, plenty, plenty," was the word that went round. In three hours' time hundreds of men and women trooped down to the quay with money to buy. To all comers the master shook his head, and refused to sell.

"Sell, man—sell, sell," they cried.

"I can't sell. The cargo is not mine. I'm a poor man myself," said the master.

"Well, and what's that it's sayin', 'When one poor man helps another poor man God laughs.'"

The Bishop came to the ship's side, and tried to treat for the cargo.

"I've given bond to land it all at Whitehaven," said the master.

Then the people's faces grew black, and deep oaths rose to their lips, and they turned and looked into each other's eyes in their impotent rage. "The hunger is on us—we can't starve—let every herring hang by its own gill—let's board her," they muttered among themselves.

And the Bishop heard their threats. "My people," he said, "what will become of this poor island unless God averts his awful judgments, only God himself can know; but this good man has given his bond, and let us not bring on our heads God's further displeasure."

There was a murmur of discontent, and then one long sigh of patient endurance, and then the Bishop lifted his hands, and down on their knees on the quay the people with famished faces fell around the tall, drooping figure of the man of God, and from parched throats, and hearts wellnigh as dry, sent up a great cry to heaven to grant them succor lest they should die.

About a week afterward another ship put in by contrary winds at Castletown. It had a cargo of Welsh oats bound to Dumfries, on the order of the Provost. The contrary winds continued, and the corn began to heat and spoil. The hungry populace, enraged by famine, called on the master to sell. He was powerless. Then the Bishop walked over his "Pyrenees," and saw that the food for which his people hungered was perishing before their eyes. When the master said "No" to him, as to others, he remembered how in old time David, being an hungered, did that which was not lawful in eating of the showbread, and straightway he went up to Castle Rushen, got a company of musketeers, returned with them to the ship's side, boarded the ship, put the master and crew in irons, and took possession of the corn.

What wild joy among the people! What shouts were heard; what tears rolled down the stony cheeks of stern men!

"Patience!" cried the Bishop. "Bring the market weights and scales."

The scales and weights were brought down to the quay and every bushel of the cargo was exactly weighed, and paid for at the prime price according to the master's report. Then the master and crew were liberated, and the Bishop paid the ship's freight out of his own purse. When he passed through the market-place on his way back to the Bishop's Court the people followed with eyes that were almost too dim to see, and they blessed in cheers that were sobs.

And then God remembered his people, and their troubles passed away. With the opening spring the mackerel nets came back to the boats in shining silver masses, and peace and plenty came again to the hearth of the poorest.

The Manxman knew his Bishop now; he knew him for the strongest soul in the dark hour, the serenest saint in the hour of light and peace. That hoary old dog, Billy the Gawk, took his knife and scratched "B.M.," and the year of the Lord on the inside of his cupboard door to record the advent of Bishop Mylrea.

A mason from Ireland, a Catholic named Patrick Looney, was that day at work building the square tower of the church of the market-place, and when he saw the Bishop pass under him he went down on his knees on the scaffold and dropped his head for the good man's blessing.

A little girl of seven, with sunny eyes and yellow hair, stood by at that moment, and for love of the child's happy face the Bishop touched her head and said, "God bless you, my sweet child."

The little one lifted her innocent eyes to his eyes, and answered with a courtesy, "And God bless you, too, sir."

"Thank you, child, thank you," said the Bishop. "I do not doubt that your blessing will be as good as mine."

Such was Gilcrist Mylrea, Bishop of Man. He needed all his strength and all his tenderness for the trials that were to come.

CHAPTER VI
THE COZY NEST AT BISHOP'S COURT

The children of the Deemster and Bishop spent the first five years as one little brood in the cozy nest at Bishop's Court. The arrangement was agreeable to both brothers while it lasted. It left Ballamona a silent place, but the master recked little of that. The Deemster kept no company, or next to none. He dismissed all his domestics except one, and Hommy-beg, who had been gardener hitherto, became groom as well. The new Ballamona began to gather a musty odor, and the old Ballamona took the moss on its wall and the lichen on its roof. The Deemster rose early and went late to bed. Much of the day was spent in the saddle passing from town to town of his northern circuit, for he held a court twice weekly at Ramsey and Peeltown. Toward nightfall he was usually back at his house, sitting alone by the fireplace, whether, as in the long nights of winter, a peat fire burned there, or, as in the summer evenings, the hearth was empty. Hardly a sound broke the dead quiet of the solitary place, save when some litigious farmer who had caught his neighbor in the act of trespass brought him, there and then, for judgment, to the Deemster's house by that most summary kind of summons, the force of superior muscles. On such occasions the plaintiff and defendant, with their noisy witnesses, would troop into the hall with the yaps and snaps of a pack of dogs, and Thorkell would twist in his chair and fine one of them, or perhaps both, and pocket their money, and then drive them all away dissatisfied, to settle their dispute by other means in the darkness of the road outside.

Meantime, Bishop's Court was musical with children's voices, and with the patter of tiny feet that ferreted out every nook and cranny of the old place. There was Ewan, the Deemster's son, a slight, sensitive boy, who listened to you with his head aslant, and with absent looks. There was wee Mona, Ewan's meek sister, with the big eyes and the quiet ways, who liked to be fondled, and would cry sometimes when no one knew why. And then there was Daniel—Danny—Dan, the Bishop's boy, a braw little rogue, with a slice of the man in him, as broad as he was long, with tousled fair head and face usually smudged, laughing a good deal and not crying overmuch, loving a good tug or a delightful bit of a fight, and always feeling high disdain at being kissed. And the Bishop, God bless him! was father and mother both to the motherless brood, though Kerry Quayle was kept as nurse. He would tell a story, or perhaps sing one, while Mona sat on his knee with her pretty head resting on his breast, and Ewan held on to his chair with his shy head hanging on his own shoulder, and his eyes looking out at the window, listening intently in his queer little absent way. And when Dan, in lordly contempt of such doings, would break in on song or story, and tear his way up the back of the chair to the back of the Bishop, Mona would be set on her feet, and the biggest baby of the four there present would slide down on to his hands and knees and creep along the floor with the great little man astride him, and whinny like a horse, or perhaps bark like a dog, and pretend to leap the four-bar gate of the baby's chair tumbled down on its side. And when Dan would slide from his saddle, and the restless horseman would turn coachman and tug the mane of his steed, and all the Bishop's long hair would tumble over his face, what shrieks of laughter, what rolling on the ground and tossing up of bare legs! And then when supper-time came, and the porridge would be brought in, and little Mona would begin to whimper because she had to eat it, and Ewan to fret because it was barley porridge and not oaten cake, and Dan to devour his share with silent industry, and then bellow for more than was good for him, what schemes the good Bishop resorted to, what promises he made, what crafty tricks he learned, what an artful old pate his simple head suddenly became! And then, when Kerry came with the tub and the towels, and three little naked bodies had to be bathed, and the Bishop stole away to his unfinished sermon, and little Mona's wet hands clung to Kerry's dress, and Ewan, standing bolt-upright in the three inches of water, blubbered while he rubbed the sponge over an inch and a half of one cheek, and Dan sat on his haunches in the bottom of the tub splashing the water on every side, and shrieking at every splash; then the fearful commotion would bring the Bishop back from the dusky room upstairs, where the shaded lamp burned on a table that was littered with papers. And at last, when the day's big battle was done, and night's bigger battle began, and three night-dresses were popped over three wary heads that dodged them when they could, the Bishop would carry three sleepless, squealing piggies to bed—Mona at his breast because she was little, Ewan on his back because he was big, and Dan across his shoulders because he could not get to any loftier perch. Presently there would be three little pairs of knees by the crib-side, and then three little flaxen polls on the pillow, tumbling and tossing, and with the great dark head of the Bishop shaking gravely at them from over the counterpane, and then a hush broken by a question lisped drowsily, or a baby-rime that ran a line or two and stopped, and at length the long deep quiet and the silence of sleep, and the Bishop going off on tiptoe to the dusky room with the shaded lamp, and to-morrow's sermon lying half written beneath it.

And so five tearing, romping years went by, and though they were the years of the famine and the pestilence, and of many another dark cloud that hung blackest over Bishop's Court, a world of happiness was crowded into them. Then when Ewan was six years old, and Danny and Mona were five, and the boys were buttoning their own corduroys, the Deemster came over from Ballamona and broke up the little nest of humming-birds.

"Gilcrist," said Thorkell, "you are ruining the children, and I must take my own away from you."

The Bishop's grave face grew suddenly white, and when, after a pause, he said, "No, no, Thorkell, you don't mean that," there was a tremor in his deep voice.

"I do mean it," said the Deemster. "Let a father treat his children as the world will treat them when they have nothing but the world for their father—that's my maxim, and I'll act up to it with my own."

"That's hard treatment, Thorkell," said the Bishop, and his eyes began to fill.

"Spare the rod, spoil the child," said Thorkell.

"Maybe you're right," said the Bishop in a quivering voice, and he could say no more.

But the Deemster was as good as his word. Ewan and Mona were removed to Ballamona. There they had no nurse, and shifted a good deal for themselves. They ate oaten cake and barley porridge three times a day, and that was to build up their bone and brain; they were bathed in cold water summer and winter, and that was to make them hardy; they wore frocks with low necks, and that was to strengthen their lungs; they went to bed without a light and fell asleep while trembling in each other's arms, and that was to make them brave and prevent them from becoming superstitious.

If the spirit and health of the little ones did not sink under their Spartan training it was because Nature was stronger than custom, and because God is very good to the bruised hearts of children. They did not laugh too loud when the Deemster was near, and they were never seen to pull his vest, or to tug him by his hair, or to ride across his back, which was never known to stoop low for their little legs to mount. The house was not much noisier, or dirtier, or less orderly for their presence; they did not fill it with their voices, or tumble it out of its propriety with their busy fingers, as with Cousin Danny's powerful assistance they had filled and tumbled Bishop's Court, until every room in the comfortable old place seemed to say to you with a wink and a nod, "A child lives here; this is his own home, and he is master of the whole house." But when they stole away to their own little room at the back, where no fire burned lest they should grow "nesh," not all the masks that were ever made to make life look like a sorry tragedy could have hidden the joy that was always wanting to break out on their little faces. There they would romp and laugh and crow and sing, and Ewan would play at preaching, with the back of a chair for a pulpit, and his pinafore for surplice, and Mona of the big eyes sitting on the floor below for choir and congregation. And if in the middle of their play it happened that all at once they remembered Danny, then Ewan's head would fall aside, and his look in an instant be far away, and Mona's lower lip would hang suddenly, and the sunshine would straightway die out of her laughing face.

When the Bishop lost the Deemster's children he found a great void in his heart; but little Danny troubled his big head not at all about the change that had taken place. He laughed just as loud, and never cried at all, and when he awoke in the morning and his cousins were not there, their place forthwith knew them no more. In a vague way he missed his playmates, but that only meant that the Bishop had to be his playmate even more than before, and the Bishop was nothing loth. Away they ran through the copse together, these boon companions, and if the Bishop hid behind a tree, of course Danny found him, and if it was Danny that hid, of course the Bishop searched high and low, and never once heard the merry titter that came from behind the gorse bush that was arm's-length away, until, with a burst of laughter, Danny leaped out on him like an avalanche. They talked one jargon, too, for Danny's industrious tongue could not say its *w*, and it made an *s* of its *f*. "How many 'heels has your cart got, carter?" "Sour." "Very srosty to-day, master." "Well, then, come in to the sire."

In a strange and unconscious way the Bishop developed a sort of physical affinity with this sworn ally. When no sound seemed to break the silence he could hear the little man's cry through three stout stone walls and up two flights of stairs. If the child fell and hurt himself half a mile from the house, the Bishop at home felt as if he had himself dropped on a sharp stone and cut his knee. If he clambered to the top of a high wall that was out of sight, the Bishop in his study felt dizzy.

But extraordinary as was this affinity of the Bishop and his boy, the intercourse that subsisted between Danny and his nurse was yet more marvelous. The Bishop had merely a prescience of disaster threatening his darling; but Kerry seemed, by an exercise of some nameless faculty, to know the child's whereabouts at any moment of day or night. Half blind at the time of the birth of little Ewan, Kerry Quayle had grown stone-blind since, and this extraordinary power was in truth her second sight. It was confined to Danny, her nursling, but over his movements it was an absolute gift.

"Och," she cried, leaping up from the spinning-wheel, "the wee craythur's into the chapel, as the sayin' is."

"Impossible!" the Bishop answered; "I've only this moment locked the door."

But Kerry and the Bishop went to the chapel to search for him, and found the fugitive, who had clambered in through an open window, lighting the candle at the reading-desk, after washing his black hands in the font.

"Aw, now," said Kerry, lifting up her hands and her blind face in horror, "what's that it's saying, 'The little hemlock is sister to the big hemlock';" which was as much as to say that the small sin was akin to the great sin, and that little Danny, who had been caught in an act of sacrilege, would one day be guilty of worse.

"Nonsense, woman—nonsense; a child is but a child," said the Bishop, leading the delinquent away.

That day—it was Thursday of Whitsun week—Convocation was to be held at Bishop's Court, and the clergy had already begun to gather in the library that looked west toward the sea. To keep Danny out of further mischief the Bishop led him to his own room, and there he poured water into a bowl and proceeded to bathe his eyes, which had latterly shown signs of weakness. To do this he had need to remove his spectacles, and he set them down on the table by his hand. Danny watched these proceedings with a roguish look, and when the Bishop's face was in the bowl he whipped up the spectacles and pushed them down his neck between his frock and his breast. With a whirr and a puff the Bishop shook the water from his face and dried it, and when the lash comb had tossed back his long hair he stretched his hand out for his spectacles. He could not feel them, and when he looked he could not see them, and then he called on Danny to search for them, and straightway the rogue was on hands and knees hunting in every possible and impossible place. But Danny could not find them—not he. Convocation was waiting for its chief, but the spectacles could not be found, and the Bishop, for all bookish services, was blinder than a bat without them. High and low, up and down, on every table, under every paper, into every pocket, and still no spectacles. At length the Bishop paused and looked steadily into the eyes of the little man sitting on his haunches and tittering audibly.

"Where are the glasses?"

Danny laughed very loud.

"Where are my glasses, Danny veg?"

Danny veg laughed still louder.

There was nothing to be made of an answer like that, so down on his knees went the Bishop again to see if the rogue had hidden the spectacles beneath the hearth-rug, or under the seat of the settle, or inside the shaving pot on the hearth. And all the time Danny, with his hands clasped under his haunches, hopped about the room like a frog with great starry eyes, and crowed and laughed till his face grew scarlet and the tears trickled down his cheeks.

Blind Kerry came to say that the gentlemen wanted to know when the Bishop would be with them, as the saying was; and two minutes afterward the Bishop strode into the library through a line of his clergy, who rose as he entered, and bowed to him in silence when his tall figure bent slightly to each of them in turn.

"Your pardon, gentlemen, for this delay," he said, gravely, and then he settled himself at the head of the table.

Hardly had the clergy taken their seats when the door of the room was dashed open with a lordly bang, and into the muggy room, made darker still by twenty long black coats, there shot a gleam of laughing sunshine—Danny himself, at a hop, skip, and a jump, with a pair of spectacles perched insecurely on the sliding bridge of his diminutive nose.

The Archdeacon was there that day, and when the intruder had been evicted by blind Kerry, who came in hot pursuit of him, he shook his head and looked as solemn and as wise as his little russet face would admit, and said:

"Ah, my Lord, you'll kill that child with kindness. May you never heap up for yourself a bad harvest!"

The Bishop made no answer, but breathed on the restored spectacles, and rubbed them with his red silk handkerchief.

"I hold with the maxim of my son-in-law the Deemster," the Archdeacon continued: "let a child be dealt with in his father's house as the world hereafter will deal with him."

"Nay, nay, but more gently," said the Bishop. "If he is a good man, ten to one the world will whip him—let him remember his father's house as a place of love."

"Ah, my Lord," said the Archdeacon, "but what of the injunction against the neglect of the rod?"

The Bishop bent his head and did not answer.

Once in a way during these early years the Bishop took Danny across to Ballamona, and then the two little exiles in their father's house, banished from the place of love, would rush into the Bishop's arms, Mona at his chin, Ewan with hands clasped about his leg and flaxen head against the great seals that hung from his fob-pocket. But as for Danny and his cousins, and the cousins and Danny, they usually stood a while and inspected one another with that solemnity and aloofness which is one of the phenomena of child manners, and then, when the reserve of the three hard little faces had been softened by a smile, they would forthwith rush at one another with mighty clinched fists and pitch into one another for five minutes together, amid a chorus of squeals. In this form of salutation Danny was never known to fail, and as he was too much of a man to limit his greeting to Ewan, he always pitched into Mona with the same masculine impartiality.

But the time came again when the salutation was unnecessary, for they were sent to school together, and they saw one another daily. There was only one school to which they could be sent, and that was the parish school, the same that was taught by James Quirk, who "could not divide his syllables," according to the account of Jabez Gawne, the tailor.

The parishioners had built their new schoolhouse near the church, and it lay about midway between Bishop's Court and Ballamona. It was also about half-way down the road that led to the sea, and that was a proximity of never-ending delight. After school, in the long summer evenings, the scholars would troop down to the shore in one tumultuous company, the son of the Bishop with the son of the cobbler, the Deemster's little girl with the big girl of Jabez, who sent his child on charity. Ragged and well-clad, clean and dirty, and the biggest lad "rigging" the smallest, and not caring a ha'porth if his name was the name of the Deemster or the name of Billy the Gawk. Hand-in-hand, Danny and Ewan, with Mona between, would skip and caper along the sands down to where the gray rocks of the Head jutted out into the sea and bounded the universe; Mona prattling and singing, shaking out her wavy hair to the wind, dragging Danny aside to look at a seaweed, and pulling Ewan to look at a shell, tripping down to the water's edge, until the big bearded waves touched her boots, and then back once more with a half-frightened, half-affected, laughter-loaded scream. Then the boys would strip and bathe, and Mona, being only a woman, would mind the men's clothes, or they would shout all together at the gulls, and Danny would mock Mother Cary's chicken and catch the doleful cry of the cormorant, and pelt with pebbles the long-necked bird as it sat on the rocks; or he would clamber up over the slippery seaweed, across the sharp slate ribs to where the sea-pinks grew in the corries and the sea-duck laid her eggs, and sing out from some dizzy height to where Ewan held his breath below and Mona stood crying and trembling on the sands.

What times for Danny! How the lad seemed to swell and grow every day of life! Before he was ten he had outgrown Ewan by half an inch, and gone through a stand-up fight with every ruffian under twelve. Then, down among the fishermen on the beach, what sport! Knocking about among the boats, pulling at the oars like mad, or tugging at the sheets, baling out and pushing off, and riding away over the white breakers, and shouting for pure devilment above the plash of the water.

"Aw, man, it's all for the happy the lad feels inside," said Billy Quilleash.

Danny and Billy Quilleash were sworn chums, and the little sand-boy learned all the old salt's racy sayings, and went home to Bishop's Court and fired them off at his father.

"There's a storm coming," the Bishop said one day, looking up at the scudding clouds. "Ay, ay," said Danny, with his small eye askew, "the long cat's tail was going off at a slant a while ago, and now the round thick skate yonder is hanging mortal low." "The wind is rising," the Bishop said on another occasion. "Ay, Davy's putting on the coppers for the parson," said the young heretic.

School, too, was only another playground to Danny, a little less tumultuous but no less delightful than the shore. The schoolmaster had grown very deaf since the days when the Bishop pronounced him qualified to teach an English school. This deafness he did his best to conceal, for he had a lively recollection of the dissatisfaction of the parishioners, and he had a natural unwillingness to lose his bread and butter. But his scholars were not easily hoodwinked, and Danny, the daring young dog, would play on the master's infirmity. "Spell me the word arithmetic," the schoolmaster might ask when the boys were ranged about his desk in class. And Danny would answer with a face of tragic solemnity, "Twice one are two, twice two are four." "Very good," the schoolmaster would reply. "And now, sir, repeat me your multiplication table—twice times." And then, while the master held his head aside, as if in the act of intent listening, and the other boys twisted their faces to hide their grins or sniggered openly, Danny, still with the face of a judge, would repeat a paraphrase of the familiar little hymn, "Jemmy was a Welshman, Jemmy was a thief, Jemmy—" "Don't speak so fast, sir—say your figures more plainly," the schoolmaster would interrupt. And Danny would begin again with a more explicit enunciation, "Jemmy Quirk was a Welshman, Jemmy—" Then the sniggers and the snorts would rise to a tumult. And down would come the master's cane on the desk. "Silence, boys, and let the boy say his table. Some of you big lads might take example by him, and be none the worse. Go on, Daniel—you are quite right so far—twice five are ten, twice six—"

There was one lad in the school who could not see the humor of the situation, a slim, quiet boy, only a little older than Danny, but a long way ahead of him in learning, and one evening this solemn youngster hung behind when school was breaking up, and blurted out the mischief to the schoolmaster. He did not get the reception he expected, for, in dire wrath at the imputation that he was deaf, Mr. Quirk birched the informant soundly. Nor did the reward of his treachery end with birching. It did not take half an hour for the report of both birching and treachery to travel by that swiftest of telephones, the schoolboy tongue, through that widest of kingdoms, the world of school; and the same evening, while Mona, on her way home, was gathering the bluebells that grew on the lea of the yellow-tipped gorse, and Ewan was chasing the humming bee through the hot air that was thick with midges, Danny, with a face as white as a haddock, was striding alone by a long circuit across the moor, to where a cottage stood by the path across the Head. There he bounded in at the porch, caught a boy by the coat, dragged him into the road, pummeled him with silent vigor, while the lad bellowed and struggled to escape.

In another instant, an old woman hobbled out of the cottage on a stick, and with that weapon she made for Danny, and gave him sundry hard raps on the back and head.

"Och, the craythur," she cried, "get off with ye—the damon—extraordinary—would the Lord think it now—it's in the breed of ye—get off, or I'll break every bone in your skin."

Danny paid as little heed to the old woman's blows as to her threats, and was up with his fist for the twentieth time to come down on the craven traitor who bellowed in his grip, when all at once a horse's feet were tramping about their limbs where they struggled in the road, and a stern voice from over their heads shouted, "Stop, stop, or must I bring the whip across your flanks?"

It was the Deemster. Danny fell aside on the right of the horse, and the old woman and the boy on the left.

"What does this mean?" asked the Deemster, turning to his nephew; but Danny stood there panting, his eyes like fire, his fists clinched, his knuckles standing out like ribs of steel, and he made no answer.

"Who is this blubbering coward?" asked the Deemster, pointing with a contemptuous gesture to the boy half hidden by the old woman's dress.

"Coward, is it?" said the woman. "Coward, you say?"

"Who is the brat, Mrs. Kerruish?" said the Deemster, sharply.

At that Mrs. Kerruish, for it was she, pulled the boy from behind her, plucked off his hat, ran her wrinkled hand over his forehead to his hair, and held up his face, and said:

"Look at him, Deemster—look at him. You don't come this way often, but look at him while you're here. Did you ever see his picture before? Never? Never see a face like that? No? Not when you look in the glass, Deemster?"

"Get into the house, woman," said the Deemster, in a low, thick tone, and so saying, he put the spurs to his horse.

"As for this young demon here," said the old woman, pushing the boy back and pointing with her stick at Danny, "he'll have his heel on your neck yet, Deemster—and remember the word I'm saying."

CHAPTER VII
DANNY THE MADCAP

Now, Danny was a great favorite with the Deemster, and nothing that he could do was amiss. The spice of mischief in the lad made him the darling of the Deemster's heart. His own son disappointed the Deemster. He seemed to have no joy in him. Ewan was quiet, and his father thought him a milksop. There was more than one sense in which the Deemster was an indifferent judge of his species, but he found no difficulty in comprehending the idiosyncrasy of his brother's son. Over the pathetic story of Danny's maddest prank, or the last mournful account of his daring devilry, the Deemster would chuckle and shake, and roll his head between his shoulders, then give the boy a slap on his hindmost part, accompanied by a lusty name, and finally rummage for something in his pocket, and smuggle that something into the young rascal's palm.

Danny would be about fifteen years of age—a lump of a lad, and therefore out of the leading-strings of his nurse, Kerry Quayle—when he concocted a most audacious scheme, whereof Kerry was the chief subject and victim. This had nothing less for its aim and object than to get Kerry married to Hommy-beg—the blind woman to the deaf man. Now, Hommy was a gaunt, raw-boned man, dressed in a rough blue jacket and a short gray petticoat. His full and proper name was now quite lost. He was known as Hommy-beg, sometimes as Hommy-beg-Bill, a name which at once embodied a playful allusion to his great physique, and a certain genealogical record in showing that he was little Tom, the son of Bill. Though scarcely short of stone-deaf, he was musical. He played two instruments, the fiddle and the voice. The former squeaked like a rasp, and the latter thundered like a fog-horn. Away to Ballamona Master Danny went, and found Hommy-beg thinning a bed of peonies.

"Aw, man, the terrible fond she is of the like o' that swate flower," said the young rogue, who spoke the homespun to the life. "Aw, dear, the way she smells at them when you bring them up for the Bishop!"

"What, ould Kerry? Smelling, is it? And never a whiff of a smell at the breed o' them!"

"Och, no, it's not the flowers, it's the man—the man, Hommy."

"That'll do, that'll do. And blind, too! Well, well."

"But the swate temper that's at her, Hommy! And the coaxing and coaxing of her! And, man alive, the fond she is of you! *A fine sort of a man anyways*, and *A rael good voice at him*. Aw, extraordinary, extraordinary."

"D'ye raely mane it?"

"Mane it? Aw, well, well, and who but you doesn't know it, Hommy?"

"Astonishing, astonishing!"

"Come up to the Coort and take a cup o' tay with her."

Hommy-beg scratched his head. "Is it rarely true, Danny veg?"

"I'll lave it with you, Hommy," said Danny, and straightway the young rascal went back to Bishop's Court, lighted upon blind Kerry, and entered upon a glowing description of the personal charms of Hommy-beg.

"Aw, the good-looking he is, astonishing! My gough! You should see him in his Sunday hat, or maybe with a frill on his shirt, and smiling, and all to that! Terrible dacent sort is Hommy-beg!"

"What, the loblolly-boy in the petticoat?"

"Aw, but the tender-hearted he is for all, and, bless me, Kerry woman, the swate he is on you!"

"What, the ould red-head that comes singing, as the saying is?"

"Aw, no, woman, but as black as the raven, and the way he looks sorrowful-like when he comes beside of you. You wouldn't believe it! And, bless me, the rael bad he is to come up to the Coort and take a cup of tay with you, and the like o' that."

"Do you raely mane it, Danny, my chree?"

The very next day Hommy-beg arrived at the kitchen door of Bishop's Court in his Sunday hat, in the shirt with the frill to it, and with a peony as big as a March cabbage in his fist. The end of it all was that Kerry and Hommy-beg were forthwith asked in church. Wild as the freak was that made the deaf man and the blind woman man and wife, their marriage was none the less happy for their infirmities.

The Deemster heard of the plot on his way to church on Sunday morning, and he laughed in his throat all through the service, and when the first of the askings was solemnly proclaimed from the reading-desk, he tittered audibly in his pew. "Danny was tired of the woman's second sight—found it inconvenient, very—wanted to be rid of her—good!" he chuckled. But not long afterward he enjoyed a jest that was yet more to his taste, for his own prime butt of ridicule, the Church itself, was then the victim.

It was an old Manx custom that on Christmas Eve the church should be given up to the people for the singing of their native carols or carvals. The curious service was known as Oiel Verree (the Eve of Mary), and at every such service for the last twenty years Hommy-beg, the gardener, and Mr. James Quirk, the schoolmaster, had officiated as singers in the strange Manx ritual. Great had hitherto been the rivalry between these musical celebrities, but word had gone round the town that at length their efforts were to be combined in a carol which they were to sing together. Dan had effected this extraordinary combination of talent by a plot which was expected to add largely to the amusement of the listeners.

Hommy-beg could not read a syllable, yet he never would sing his carol without having the printed copy of it in his hand. Of course, Mr. Quirk, the schoolmaster, could read, but, as we have seen, he resembled Hommy-beg in being almost stone-deaf. Each could hear himself sing, but neither could hear another.

And now for the plot. Master Dan called on the gardener at his cottage on the Brew on the morning of the day before Christmas Day, and "Hommy," said he, "it's morthal strange the way a man of your common-sense can't see that you'd wallop that squeaking ould Jemmy Quirk in a jiffy if you'd only consent to sing a ballad along of him. Bless me, man alive, it's then they'd be seeing what a weak, ould cracked pot of a voice is at him."

Hommy-beg's face began to wear a smile of benevolent condescension. Observing his advantage, the young rascal continued, "Do it at the Oiel Verree to-night, Hommy. He'll sing his treble, and you'll sing seconds to him."

It was an unlucky remark. The gardener frowned austerely. "Me sing seconds to the craythur? No, never!"

Dan explained to Hommy-beg, with a world of abject apologies, that there was a sense in which seconds meant firsts, and at length the gardener was mollified, and consented to the proposal; but one idea was firmly rooted in his mind—namely, that if he was to sing a carol with the schoolmaster, he must take the best of care to sing his loudest, in order to drown at once the voice of his rival, and the bare notion that it was he who was singing seconds to such a poor creature as that.

Then Master Danny trotted off to the schoolhouse, where he was now no longer a scholar, and consequently enjoyed an old boy's privilege of approaching the master on equal terms, and "Jemmy," he said, "it's morthal strange the way a man of your common-sense can't see that you'd wallop that squeaking old Hommy-beg in a jiffy if you'd only consent to sing a ballad along of him. Do it at the Oiel Verree to-night, Jemmy, and, bless me! that's the when they'll be seeing what a weak, ould crack-pot of a voice is at the craythur."

The schoolmaster fell even an easier prey to the plot than the gardener had been. A carol was selected; it was to be the ancient Manx carol on the bad women mentioned in the Bible as having (from Eve downward) brought evil on mankind.

Now, Hommy-beg kept his carols pinned against the walls of his cottage. The "Bad Women" was the carol which was pinned above the mantelpiece, just under the pendulum of the clock with the facetious face. It resembled the other prints in being worn, crumpled, and dirty; but Hommy-beg knew it by its position, and he could distinguish every other carol by its place on the walls.

Danny had somehow got a "skute" into this literary mystery, and after arranging with the schoolmaster the carol that was to be sung, he watched Hommy-beg out of his cottage, and then went into it under pretense of a friendly call upon blind Kerry. Before he left the cottage he had taken down the carol that had been pinned above the mantelpiece, and fixed up another in place of it from the opposite side of the room. The substituted carol happened, oddly enough, to be a second copy of the carol on "Bad Women," with this radical difference: the copy taken from under the clock was the version of the carol in English, and the copy put up was the version in Manx. Toward ten o'clock that night the church bells began to ring, and Hommy-beg looked at the clock, took the carol from under the pendulum, put on his best petticoat, and went off to church.

Now, there were to be seasonable rejoicings at the Court on the morrow, and Kerry had gone over to help at the Christmas preparations. Ewan and Mona had always spent their Christmas at Bishop's Court since the day when they left it as children. That night they had arrived as usual, and after they had spent some hours with Danny in dressing the house in a green-and-red garment of hibbin and hollin, the Bishop had turned them off to bed. Danny's bedroom was the little crib over the library, and Ewan's was the room over that. All three bade the Bishop good-night and went into their rooms. But Danny did not go to bed; he listened until he heard the Bishop in the library twisting his chair and stirring the peats, and then he whipped off his boots and crept upstairs to Ewan's room. There in bated breath he told of the great sport that was to come off at the Oiel Verree, announced his intention of going, and urged Ewan to go with him. They could just jump through the little window of his room, and light on the soft grass by the library wall, and get in again by the same easy means. No one would know that they had been out, and what high jinks they must have! But no, Ewan was not to be persuaded, and Danny set off alone.

Hommy-beg did not reach the church until the parson's sermon was almost over. Prayers had been said in a thin congregation, but no sooner were they done than crowds of young men and maidens tripped down the aisles. The young women went up into the gallery, and from that elevation they shot down at their bachelor friends large handfuls of peas. To what ancient spirit of usage, beyond the ancient spirit of mischief, the strange practise was due, we must be content to leave, as a solemn problem, to the learned and curious antiquaries. Nearly everyboy carried a candle, and the candles of the young women were adorned with a red ribbon or rosette.

In passing out of the church the parson came face to face with Hommy-beg, who was pushing his way up the aisle. The expression on his face was not at the moment one of peculiar grace, and he stopped the gardener and said sharply in his ear, "Mind you see that all is done in decency and order, and that you close my church before midnight."

"Aw, but the church is the people's, I'm thinkin'," said Hommy-beg with a shake of his tousled head.

"The people are as ignorant as goats," said the parson, angrily.

"Aw, well, and you're their shepherd, so just make sheeps of them," said Hommy-beg, and he pushed on.

Danny was there by this time, and, with a face of mighty solemnity, he sat on the right of Hommy-beg, and held a candle in his left hand. When everything was understood to be ready, and Will-as-Thorn, the clerk, had taken his station inside the communion rail, the business of the Oiel Verree began. First one man got up and sung a carol in English; then another sung a Manx carol. But the great event of the night was to be the carol sung by the sworn enemies and rivals, Hommy-beg and Mr. James Quirk.

At last the time came for these worthies. They rose from opposite sides of the church, eyed each other with severe looks, stepped out of their pews, and walked down the aisle to the door of the porch. Then they turned about in silence, and, standing side by side, faced the communion.

The tittering in the gallery and whispering in the body were audible to all except the persons who were the cause of both. "Hush, hush, man alive, that's him, that's him." "Bless me, look at Hommy-beg and the petticut, and the handkercher pinnin' round his throat." "Aw, dear, it's what he's used of." "A regular Punch and Judy."

Danny was exerting himself at that moment to keep order and silence. "Hush, man, let them make a start for all."

The carol the rivals were about to sing contained some thirty verses. It was an ancient usage that after each verse the carol singers should take a long stride toward the communion. By the time the carol of "Bad Women" came to an end the carol singers must, therefore, be at the opposite end of the church.

There was now a sublime scorn printed on the features of Mr. Quirk. As for Hommy-beg, he looked, at this last instant, like a man who was rather sorry than otherwise for his rash adversary.

"The rermantic they're looking," whispered a girl in the gallery to the giggling companion beside her.

Expectation was at its highest when Hommy-beg thrust his hand into his pocket and brought out the printed copy of the carol. Hommy unfolded it, glanced at it with the air of a conductor taking a final look at his score, nodded his head at it as if in approval, and then, with a magnanimous gesture, held it between himself and Mr. Quirk. The schoolmaster in turn glanced at it, glanced again, glanced a third time at the paper, and up into the face of Hommy-beg.

Anxiety was now on tiptoe. "Hush, d'ye hear, hush," whispered Danny from his pew; "hush, man, or it's spoiling it all you'll be, for sure."

At the moment when Mr. Quirk glanced into the face of Hommy-beg there was a smile on that countenance. Mr. Quirk mistook that smile. He imagined he saw a trick. The schoolmaster could read, and he perceived that the carol which the gardener held out to him was not the carol for which he had been told by Master Danny to prepare. They were, by arrangement, to have sung the English version of "Bad Women." This was the Manx version, and though the metre was the same, it was always sung to a different tune. Ah! Mr. Quirk understood it all! The monster wanted to show that he, James Quirk, schoolmaster, could only sing one carol; but, as sure as his name was Jemmy, he would be equal with him! He could sing this Manx version, and he would. It was now Mr. Quirk's turn to smile.

"Aw, look at them—the two of them—grinnin' together like a pair of old gurgoils on the steeple!"

At a motion of the gardener's hand, intended to beat the time, the singers began. Hommy-beg sang the carol agreed upon—the English version of "Bad Women." Mr. Quirk sang the carol they held in their hands—the Manx version of "Bad Women." Neither heard the other, and to dispel the bare notion that either was singing seconds, each bawled at the utmost reach of his lung-power. To one tune Hommy-beg sang:

> "Thus from the days of Adam
> Her mischief you may trace."

And to another Mr. Quirk sang:

> "She ish va'n voir ain ooilley
> Son v'ee da Adam ben."

Such laughter! How the young women in the gallery lay back in their seats with hysterical shrieks! How the young fellows in the body made the sacred edifice ring with guffaws! But the singers, with eyes steadfastly fixed on the paper, heard nothing but each his own voice.

Three verses had been sung, and three strides made toward the communion, when suddenly the laughter and shouting of the people ceased. All eyes had turned toward the porch. There the Bishop stood, with blank amazement printed on his face, his head bare, and one hand on the half-opened door.

If a spectre had appeared the consternation had scarcely been greater. Danny had been rolling in his pew with unconstrained laughter, but at sight of the Bishop his candle fell from his hand and sputtered on the book-rail. The Bishop turned about, and before the people had recovered from their surprise he was gone. At the next moment everybody got up without a word and left the church. In two minutes more not a soul remained except Hommy-beg and Mr. Jemmy Quirk, who, with eyes riveted on the printed carol in their hands, still sang lustily, oblivious of the fact that they had no audience.

When Danny left the church that night it was through the lancet-window of the vestry. Dropping on the turf at the northeast of the church, he leaped the wall that divided the churchyard from a meadow on the north, and struck upon a path that went round to Bishop's Court by way of the cliff-head. The path was a long one, but it was lonesome, and its lonesomeness was no small merit in Danny's view that night. The Bishop must return to the Court by the highway through the village, and the Bishop must be in front of him.

The night was dark and dumb, and, laden with salt scent, the dank vapor floated up from the sea. Danny walked quickly. The deep boom of the waters rolling on the sand below came up to him through the dense air. Late as was the hour, he could hear the little sandpiper screaming at Orris Head. The sea-swallow shot over him too, with its low, mournful cry. Save for these sounds, and the quick beat of his own feet, all was still around him.

Beneath his stubborn bit of skepticism Danny was superstitious. He was full to the throat of fairy-lore and stories of witchcraft. He had learned both from old Billy Quilleash and his mates as they sat barking their nets on the shore. And that night the ghostly memories would arise, do what he might to keep them down. To banish them Danny began to whistle, and, failing to enliven himself much by that exercise, he began to sing. His selection of a song was not the happiest under the circumstances. It was the doleful ballad of "Myle Charaine." Danny sang it in Manx, but here is a stave of it in English:

> "Oh, Myle Charaine, where got you your gold?
> Lone, lone, you have left me here;
> Oh, not in the Curragh, deep under the mold—
> Lone, lone, and void of cheer."

He had come up to Bishop's Court on the sea-front, and there the Bishop's library stood out from the body of the old house, between the chapel porch and the kitchen offices. A light was in the library, and passing over the soft grass with the soft flight of a lapwing, Danny peered in at the curtainless window. The familiar room was empty. On the hearth a turf fire burned without flame, and bathed the book-encased walls in a rosy red. The Bishop's easy-chair, in its white covering, stood at one side of the ingle, his slippers in front of it; and beside it, on the little three-legged mahogany table, were the inkhorn and the long quill, and the Bishop's four-cornered library cap. The door stood ajar, and the two candles in the two brass brackets at each side of the fireplace were tipped by their extinguishers.

The Bishop had not returned; but the faint smile of triumph which at that thought rested like a ray of pale sunshine on Danny's face suddenly vanished. In a lad's vague way Danny now realized that it had not been merely because the night was dark and the road lonely that he had whistled and sung. He hung his head where he stood in the night, and as if by an involuntary movement, he lifted his cap and fumbled it.

At the next instant Danny was clambering up the angle of the wall to the lead flat that covered the projecting part of the library. From this lead flat there opened the window of his own bedroom, and in a moment he was striding through it. All was darkness within, but he needed no light to see his way in that room. He knew every crib and corner; the place where he kept his fishing lines, the nail from which his moth-net hung, the bottle on the drawers in which he had his minnows, and the can with the lid well down that contained the newts that were the terror of all the women in the house. If Danny had been as blind as old Kerry he could have found everything his room had in it, except, perhaps, his breeches, or his shirt, or his other coat, or that cap that was always getting itself lost, and of course no sight and no light would help a lad to find things like these.

Hardly had Danny taken a step into his room before he realized that some one had been there since he left it. Derry, his white-eyed collie, who had been lying on the bed, dropped on the floor, and frisked about him. "Down, Derry, down!" he whispered, and for a moment he thought it might have been Derry that had pushed open the door. But the dog's snout could not have turned down the counterpane of the bed, or opened the top drawer that held the fishing flies, or rummaged among the long rods in the corner. The counterpane lay double, the drawer stood open, the rods were scattered—some one had been there to look for him, and, not finding him, had tried to find a reason for his absence, and that some one had either come into the room in the dark, or—been blind.

"Aw, it's always Kerry that's in it," Danny told himself, and with an unpleasant remembrance of Kerry's strange faculty, whereof he was the peculiar victim, he reflected that his race home had been vain. Then on the instant Danny found himself concocting a trick to defeat appearances. He had a foot on the stairs to carry out his design, when he heard the door at the front of the house open and close, and a familiar step pass through the hall. The Bishop had returned. Danny waited and listened. Now there was talking in the library. Danny's quick ear could scarcely distinguish the words, but the voices he could not mistake—they were the voices of the Bishop and blind Kerry. With a stealthy stride Danny went up to Ewan's room. Ewan was sleeping. Feeling hot and cold together, Danny undressed and turned into bed. Before he had time to bury his head under the clothes he heard the Bishop on the stairs. The footsteps passed into the room below, and then after an interval they were again on the stairs. In another moment Danny knew, though of course his eyes were fast shut, and he was sleeping most profoundly, that the Bishop with a lighted candle in his hand was leaning over him.

It would wrong the truth to say that Master Danny's slumber was disturbed that night; but next morning when the boys awoke together, and Ewan rose on his elbow with a puzzled gaze at his unexpected bed-fellow, Danny sidled out of the bed on to the floor, and, without looking too much into Ewan's face, he began his toilet, as was his wont, by putting on his cap. He had got this length, and was standing in cap and shirt, when he blurted out the mischief of last night's adventure, the singing, the sudden appearance of the Bishop, the race home along the cliff, and the coming up to bed. "But you won't let on, Ewan, will you?" he said. Ewan looked at that moment as if the fate of the universe hung on his answer, but he gave the promise that was required of him. Then the boys went downstairs and found Mona, and imparted the dread secret to her. Presently the Bishop came in to breakfast with a face that was paler than usual, and more than ordinarily solemn.

"Danny," he said, "why did you not sleep in your own bed last night, my boy?"

"I slept with Ewan, father," Danny answered, promptly.

The Bishop said no more then, and they all sat down at the table.

"And so you two boys went to bed together—*together*?" he said, and, with a dig of emphasis on his last word, repeated, he looked at Ewan.

Ewan's face crimsoned, and his tongue faltered, "Yes, uncle."

The Bishop's eyes fell. "Boys," he said, in another tone, "would you think it? I have done you a great wrong."

The boys were just then most intent on the tablecloth.

"You must know," the Bishop went on, "that there was a most unseemly riot at the Oiel Verree, and all night long I have been sore troubled by the bad thought that Danny was in the midst of it."

The boys held their heads very low over their plates, and Mona's big eyes filled visibly. Danny's impulse was to blurt out the whole mischief there and then, but he reflected that to do so would be to charge Ewan with falsehood. Ewan, on his part, would have confessed to the deception, but he knew that this would mean that Danny must be punished. The boy's wise head could see no way out of a tangle like that. The breakfast was the quietest ever eaten on a Christmas morning at Bishop's Court, and, little as the talking was, the Bishop, strangely enough, did it all. But when they rose from the table, and the boys slunk out of the room with most portentous gravity, Mona went up to the Bishop with a face full of liquid grief, and, turning the whole depths of her great troubled eyes upon him, the little maiden said: "Ewan didn't mean to tell you what wasn't true—and cousin Danny didn't intend to deceive—but he was—that is, Danny—I mean—dear uncle, you won't—"

"You mean that Danny was at the Oiel Verree last night—I know it, child, I know it," said the Bishop, and he patted her head and smiled.

But the Bishop knew also that Danny had that day made one more step down the steep of life, and left a little ghost of his child-self behind him, and in his secret heart the Bishop saw that shadowy form, and wept over it.

CHAPTER VIII
PASSING THE LOVE OF WOMEN

Now the facts of this history must stride on some six years, and in that time the Deemster had lost nearly all the little interest he ever felt in his children. Mona had budded into womanhood, tender, gracious, quiet—a tall fair-haired maiden of twenty, with a drooping head like a flower, with a voice soft and low, and the full blue eyes with their depths of love and sympathy shaded by long fluttering lashes as the trembling sedge shades the deep mountain pool. It was as ripe and beautiful a womanhood as the heart of a father might dream of, but the Deemster could take little pleasure in it. If Mona had been his son, her quiet ways and tractable nature might have counted for something; but a woman was only a woman in the Deemster's eyes, and the Deemster, like the Bedouin chief, would have numbered his children without counting his daughter. As for Ewan, he had falsified every hope of the Deemster. His Spartan training had gone for nothing. He was physically a weakling; a tall spare youth of two-and-twenty, fair-haired, like his sister, with a face as spiritual and beautiful, and hardly less feminine. He was of a self-torturing spirit, constantly troubled with vague questionings, and though in this regard he was very much his father's son, the Deemster held his temperament in contempt.

The end of all was that Ewan showed a strong desire to enter the Church. The Deemster had intended that his son should study the law and follow him in his place when his time came. But Ewan's womanly temperament coexisted with a manly temper. Into the law he would not go, and the Church he was resolved to follow. The Bishop had then newly opened at Bishop's Court a training college for his clergy, and Ewan sought and obtained admission. The Deemster fumed, but his son was not to be moved even by his wrath. This was when Ewan was nineteen years of age, and after two more years the spirituality of his character overcame the obstacle of his youth, and the Bishop ordained him at twenty-one. Then Ewan was made chaplain to the household at Bishop's Court.

Hardly had this been done when Ewan took another step in life. With the knowledge of the Bishop, but without consulting the Deemster, he married, being now of age, a pretty child of sixteen, the daughter of his father's old foe, the vicar of the parish. When knowledge of this act of unwisdom reached the Deemster his last remaining spark of interest in his son expired, and he sent Mona across to Bishop's Court with a curt message saying that Ewan and his wife were at liberty, if they liked, to take possession of the old Ballamona. Thus he turned his back upon his son, and did his best to wipe him out of his mind.

Ewan took his young wife to the homestead that had been the place of his people for six generations, the place where he himself had been born, the place where that other Ewan, his good grandfather, had lived and died.

More than ever for these events the Deemster became a solitary man. He kept no company; he took no pleasures. Alone he sat night after night in his study at Ballamona, and Ballamona was asleep before he slept, and before it awoke he was stirring. His daughter's presence in the house was no society for the Deemster. She grew beside him like her mother's youth, a yet fairer vision of the old days coming back to him hour by hour, but he saw nothing of all that. Disappointed in his sole hope, his son, whom truly he had never loved for love's sake, but only for his own sorry ambitions, he sat down under his disappointment a doubly soured and thrice-hardened man. He had grown noticeably older, but his restless energy suffered no abatement. Biweekly he kept his court, but few sought the law whom the law did not first find, for word went round that the Deemster was a hard judge, and deemed the laws in rigor. If men differed about money, they would say, "Och, why go to the Deemster? It's throwing a bone into the bad dog's mouth," and then they would divide their difference.

The one remaining joy of the Deemster's lonely life was centred in his brother's son, Dan. That lusty youth had not disappointed his expectations. At twenty he was a braw, brown-haired, brown-eyed lad of six feet two inches in stature, straight and upright, and with the thews and sinews of an ox. He was the athlete of the island, and where there was a tough job of wrestling to be had, or a delightful bit of fighting to be done, there was Dan in the heart of it. "Aw, and middling few could come anigh him," the people used to say. But more than in Dan's great stature and great strength, the little Deemster took a bitter pleasure in his daring irreverence for things held sacred. In this regard Dan had not improved with improving years. Scores of tricks his sad pugnacity devised to help the farmers to cheat the parson of his tithe, and it added not a little to the Deemster's keen relish of freaks like these that it was none other than the son of the Bishop who perpetrated them. As for the Bishop himself, he tried to shut his eyes to such follies. He meant his son to go into the Church, and, in spite of all outbursts of spirit, notwithstanding wrestling matches and fights, and even some tipsy broils of which rumor was in the air, he entered Dan as a student at the college he kept at Bishop's Court.

In due course the time of Dan's examination came, and then all further clinging to a forlorn hope was at an end. The Archdeacon acted as the Bishop's examining chaplain, and more than once the little man had declared in advance his conscientious intention of dealing with the Bishop's son as he would deal with any other. The examination took place in the library of Bishop's Court, and besides the students and the examiner there were some six or seven of the clergy present, and Ewan Mylrea, then newly ordained, was among them. It was a purely oral examination, and when Dan's turn came the Archdeacon assumed his loftiest look, and first tackled the candidate where he was known to be weakest.

"I suppose, sir, you think you can read your Greek Testament?"

Dan answered that he had never thought anything about it.

"I dare say for all your modesty that you have an idea that you know it well enough to teach it," said the Archdeacon.

Dan hadn't an idea on the subject.

"Take down the Greek Testament, and imagine that I'm your pupil, and proceed to expound it," said the Archdeacon.

Dan took the book from the bookcase and fumbled it in his fingers.

"Well, sir, open at the parable of the tares."

Dan scratched his big head leisurely, and he did his best to find the place. "So I'm to be tutor—is that it?" he said, with a puzzled look.

"That is so."

"And you are to be the pupil?"

"Precisely—suppose yourself my tutor—and now begin."

At this Ewan stepped out with a look of anxiety. "Is not that a rather difficult supposition, Archdeacon?" he said, timidly.

The Archdeacon glanced over his grandson loftily and made no reply.

"Begin, sir, begin," he said, with a sweep of his hand toward Dan, and at that he sat down in the high-backed oak chair at the head of the table.

Then on the instant there came into Dan's quick eyes a most mischievous twinkle. He was standing before the table with the Greek Testament open at the parable of the tares, and he knew too well he could not read the parable.

"When do we change places, Archdeacon?" he asked.

"We have changed places—you are now the tutor—I am your pupil—begin, sir."

"Oh! we have changed places, have we?" said Dan, and at that he lifted up the Archdeacon's silver-tipped walking-cane which lay on the table and brought it down again with a bang. "Then just you get up off your chair, sir," he said, with a tone of command.

The Archdeacon's russet face showed several tints of blue at that moment, but he rose to his feet. Thereupon Dan handed him the open book.

"Now, sir," he said, "first read me the parable of the tares."

The clergy began to shuffle about and look into each other's faces. The Archdeacon's expression was not amiable, but he took the book and read the parable.

"Very fair, very fair indeed," said Dan, in a tone of mild condescension—"a few false quantities, but very fair on the whole."

"Gentlemen, gentlemen, this is going too far," said one of the clergy.

"Silence, sir," said Dan, with a look of outraged authority.

Then there was dire confusion. Some of the clergy laughed outright, and some giggled under their breath, and some protested in white wrath, and the end of it all was that the examination came to a sudden termination, and, rightly or wrongly, wisely or foolishly, Dan was adjudged to be unfit for the ministry of the Church.

When the Bishop heard the verdict his pale face whitened visibly, and he seemed to see the beginning of the end. At that moment he thought of the Deemster with bitterness. This blow to his hopes did not cement the severed lives of the brothers. The forces that had been dividing them year by year since the days of their father appeared to be drawing them yet wider apart in the lives and fortunes of their children. Each felt that the other was frustrating his dearest expectations in his son, and that was an offense that neither could forgive. To the Deemster it seemed that the Bishop was bearing down every ambition of his life, tearing him up as a naked trunk, leaving him a childless man. To the Bishop it seemed that the Deemster was wrecking the one life that was more to him than his own soul, and standing between him and the heart that with all its follies was dearer than the world beside. From the time of Ewan's marriage and Dan's disgrace the Bishop and the Deemster rarely met, and when they passed on the road they exchanged only the coldest salutation.

But if the fates were now more than ever fostering an unnatural enmity between the sons of old Ewan they were cherishing at the same time the loves of their children. Never were cousins more unlike or more fondly attached. Between Dan, the reckless scapegrace, and Mona, with the big soft eyes and the quiet ways, the affection was such as neither understood. They had grown up side by side, they had seen each other daily, they had scampered along the shore with clasped hands, they had screamed at the sea-gulls with one voice, and still they were boy and girl together. But once they were stooking the barley in the glebe, and, the day being hot, Mona tipped back her white sun-bonnet, and it fell on to her shoulders. Seeing this, Dan came stealthily behind and thought very craftily to whisk it away unobserved; but the strings by which it was tied caught in her hair and tugged at its knot, and the beautiful wavy shower fell rip-rip-rippling down her back. The wind caught the loosened hair and tossed it about her, and she stood up erect among the corn with the first blush on her cheeks that Dan had ever brought there, and turned full upon him all the glorious light of her deep blue eyes. Then, then, oh then, Dan seemed to see her for the first time a girl no longer, but a woman, a woman, a woman! And the mountains behind her were in one instant blotted out of Dan's eyes, and everything seemed to spin about him.

When next he knew where he was, and what he was doing, behold, there were Mona's rosy lips under his, and she was panting and gasping for breath.

But if the love of Dan and Mona was more than cousinly, though they knew it not as yet, the love of Ewan for Dan was wonderful and passing the love of women. That pure soul, with its vague spiritual yearnings, seemed to have nothing in common with the jovial roysterer, always fighting, always laughing, taking disgrace as a duck takes water, and losing the trace of it as easily. Twenty times he stood between the scapegrace and the Bishop, twenty times he hid from the good father the follies of the son. He thought for that thoughtless head that never had an ache or a care under its abundant curls; he hoped for that light heart that hoped for nothing; he trembled for the soul that felt no fear. Never was such loyalty between man and man since David wept for Jonathan. And Ewan's marriage disturbed this affection not at all, for the love he bore to Dan was a brotherly passion for which language has yet no name.

Let us tell one story that shall show this friendship in its double bearings—Ewan's love and temper and Dan's heedless harshness and the great nature beneath it, and then we will pass on with fuller knowledge to weightier matters.

Derry, the white-eyed collie that had nestled on the top of his master's bed the night Dan sneaked home in disgrace from Oiel Verree, was a crafty little fox, with cunning and duplicity bred in his very bones. If you were a tramp of the profession of Billy the Gawk, he would look up at you with his big innocent eyes, and lick your hand, and thrust his nose into your palm, and the next moment he would seize you by the hindmost parts and hold on like a leech. His unamiable qualities grew as he grew in years, and one day Dan went on a long journey, leaving Derry behind, and when he returned he had another dog with him, a great shaggy Scotch collie, with bright eyes, a happy phiz, and a huge bush of a tail. Derry was at the gate when his master came home, and he eyed the new-comer with looks askance. From that day Derry turned his back on his master, he would never answer his call, and he did not know his whistle from the croak of a corn-crake. In fact, Derry took his own courses, and forthwith fell into all manner of dissolute habits. He went out at night alone, incognito, and kept most unchristian hours. The farmers around complained that their sheep were found dead in the field, torn and worried by a dog's teeth. Derry was known to be a dog that did not live a reputable life, and suspicion fell on him. Dan took the old fox in hand, and thenceforward Derry looked out on the world through a rope muzzle.

One day there was to be a sheep-dog match, and Dan entered his Scotch collie, Laddie. The race was to be in the meadow at the foot of Slieu Dhoo, and great crowds of people came to witness it. Hurdles were set up to make all crooks and cranks of difficulty, and then a drift of sheep were turned loose in the field. The prize was to the dog that would, at the word of its master, gather the sheep together and take them out at the gate in the shortest time. Ewan, then newly married, was there, and beside him was his child-wife. Time was called, and Dan's turn came to try the mettle of his Laddie. The dog started well, and in two or three minutes he had driven the whole flock save two into an alcove of hurdles close to where Ewan and his wife stood together. Then at the word of his master Laddie set off over the field for the stragglers, and Dan shouted to Ewan not to stir a hand or foot, or the sheep would be scattered again. Now, just at that instant who should pop over the hedge but Derry in his muzzle, and quick as thought he shot down his head, put up his paws, threw off his muzzle, dashed at the sheep, snapped at their legs, and away they went in twenty directions.

Before Ewan had time to cry out Derry was gone, with his muzzle between his teeth. When Dan, who was a perch or two up the meadow, turned round and saw what had happened, and that his dog's chances were gone, his anger overcame him, and he turned on Ewan with a torrent of reproaches.

"There—you've done it with your lumbering—curse it."

With complete self-possession Ewan explained how Derry had done the mischief.

Then Dan's face was darker with wrath than it had ever been before.

"A pretty tale," he said, and his lip curled in a sneer. He turned to the people around. "Anybody see the dog slip his muzzle?"

None had seen what Ewan had affirmed. The eyes of every one had been on the two stragglers in the distance pursued by Dan and Laddie.

Now, when Ewan saw that Dan distrusted him, and appealed to strangers as witness to his word, his face flushed deep, and his delicate nostrils quivered.

"A pretty tale," Dan repeated, and he was twisting on his heel, when up came Derry again, his muzzle on his snout, whisking his tail, and frisking about Dan's feet with an expression of quite lamb-like simplicity.

At that sight Ewan's livid face turned to a great pallor, and Dan broke into a hard laugh.

"We've heard of a dog slipping his muzzle," he said, "but who ever heard of a dog putting a muzzle on again?"

Then Ewan stepped from beside his girl-wife, who stood there with heaving breast. His eyes were aflame, but for an instant he conquered his emotions and said, with a constrained quietness, but with a deep pathos in his tone, "Dan, do you think I've told you the truth?"

Dan wheeled about. "I think you've told me a lie," he said, and his voice came thick from his throat.

All heard the word, and all held their breath. Ewan stood a moment as if rooted to the spot, and his pallid face whitened every instant. Then he fell back, and took the girl-wife by the hand and turned away with her, his head down, his very heart surging itself out of his choking breast. And, as he passed through the throng, to carry away from that scene the madness that was working in his brain, he overheard the mocking comments of the people. "Aw, well, well, did ye hear that now?—called him a liar, and not a word to say agen it." "A liar! Och, a liar? and him a parzon, too!" "Middling chicken-hearted, anyways—a liar! Aw, well, well, well!"

At that Ewan flung away the hand of his wife, and, quivering from head to foot, he strode toward Dan.

"You've called me a liar," he said, in a shrill voice that was like a cry. "Now, you shall prove your word—you shall fight me—you shall, by God."

He was completely carried away by passion.

"The parzon, the parzon!" "Man alive, the young parzon!" the people muttered, and they closed around.

Dan stood a moment. He looked down from his great height at Ewan's quivering form and distorted face. Then he turned about and glanced into the faces of the people. In another instant his eyes were swimming in tears; he took a step toward Ewan, flung his arms about him, and buried his head in his neck, and the great stalwart lad wept like a little child. In another moment Ewan's passion was melted away, and he kissed Dan on the cheek.

"Blubbering cowards!" "Aw, blatherskites!" "Och, man alive, a pair of turtle-doves!"

Dan lifted his head and looked around, raised himself to his full height, clinched his fists, and said:

"Now, my lads, you did your best to make a fight, and you couldn't manage it. I won't fight my cousin, and he shan't fight me; but if there's a man among you would like to know for himself how much of a coward I am, let him step out—I'm ready."

Not a man budged an inch.

CHAPTER IX
THE SERVICE ON THE SHORE

It was the spring of the year when the examining chaplain gave the verdict which for good or ill put Dan out of the odor of sanctity. Then in disgrace with fortune and men's eyes, he haunted the shore where old Billy and his mates were spreading their nets and barking them in preparation for the herring season that was soon to begin. There it was, while stretched on the warm shingle, with old Billy Quilleash sitting near, smoking his black cutty and mending the meshes broken by the dogfish of last year, that Dan hit on the idea of a new course in life. This was nothing better or worse than that of turning fisherman. He would buy a smack and make old Billy his skipper; he would follow the herrings himself, and take up his own share and the share of the boat. It would be delightful, and, of course, it would be vastly profitable. Everything looked plain and straight and simple, and though old Billy more than half shook his gray head at the project, and let fall by several inches his tawny face, and took his pipe out of his mouth and cleared his throat noisily, and looked vacantly out to sea, and gave other ominous symptoms of grave internal dubitation, Dan leaped to his feet at the sudden access of new purpose, and bowled off in hot haste to tell the Bishop.

The Bishop listened in silence at first, and with a sidelong look out at the window up to the heights of Slieu Dhoo, and when Dan, in a hang-dog manner, hinted at certain new-born intentions of reform, there was a perceptible trembling of the Bishop's eyelids; and when he gathered voice and pictured the vast scheme of profit without loss, the Bishop turned his grave eyes slowly upon him, and then Dan's own eyes suddenly fell, and the big world began to shrivel up to the pitiful dimensions of an orange with the juice squeezed out of it. But the end of it all was that the Bishop undertook to become responsible for the first costs of the boat, and, having made this promise with the air of a man who knows too well that he is pampering the whim of a spoiled boy, he turned away rather suddenly, with his chin a thought deeper than ever in his breast.

What hurry and bustle ensued. What driving away to north, south, east, and west, to every fishing port in the island where boats were built or sold! At length a boat was bought on the chocks at Port le Mary, a thirty-ton boat of lugger build, and old Billy Quilleash was sent south to bring it up through the Calf Sound to the harbor at Peeltown.

Then there was the getting together of a crew. Of course old Billy was made skipper. He had sailed twenty years in a boat of Kinvig's with three nets to his share, and half that time he had been admiral of the Peeltown fleet of herring boats, with five pounds a year for his post of honor. In Dan's boat he was to have four nets by his own right, and one for his nephew, Davy Fayle. Davy was an orphan, brought up by Billy Quilleash. He was a lad of eighteen, and was to sail as boy. There were four other hands—Crennel, the cook; Teare, the mate; Corkell, and Corlett.

Early and late Dan was down at the harbor, stripped to the woolen shirt, and tackling any odd job of painting or carpentry, for the opening of the herring season was hard upon them. But he found time to run up to the new Ballamona to tell Mona that she was to christen his new boat, for it had not been named when it left the chocks; and then to the old Ballamona, to persuade Ewan to go with him on his first trip to the herrings.

The day appointed by custom for the first takings of the herring came quickly round. It was a brilliant day in early June. Ewan had been across to Slieu Dhoo to visit his father, for the first time since his marriage, more than half a year ago, in order to say that he meant to go out for the night's fishing in Dan's new boat, and to beg that his young wife, who was just then in delicate health, might be invited to spend the night of his absence with Mona at the new Ballamona. The Deemster complied with a grim face; Ewan's young wife went across in the early morning, and in the afternoon all four, the Deemster and Mona, Ewan and his wife, set off in a lumbering, springless coach—the first that the island had yet seen—to witness the departure of the herring fleet from Peeltown, and to engage in that day's ceremony.

The salt breath of the sea was in the air, and the light ripples of the bay glistened through a drowsy haze of warm sunshine. It was to be high water at six o'clock. When the Deemster's company reached Peeltown, the sun was still high over Contrary Head, and the fishing boats in the harbor, to the number of two hundred, were rolling gently, with their brown sails half set, to the motion of the rising tide.

There was Dan in his guernsey on the deck of his boat, and, as the coach drew up near the bottom of the wooden pier, he lifted his red cap from his curly head, and then went on to tie a bottle by a long blue ribbon to the tiller. There was old Billy Quilleash in his sea-boots, and there was Davy Fayle, a shambling sort of lad, long rather than tall, with fair hair tangled over his forehead, and a face which had a simple, vacant look that came of a lagging lower lip. Men on every boat in the harbor were washing the decks, or bailing out the dingey, or laying down the nets below. The harbor-master was on the quay, shouting to this boat to pull up or to that one to lie back. And down on the broad sands of the shore were men, women, and children in many hundreds, sitting and lying and lounging about an empty boat with a hole in the bottom that lay high and dry on the beach. The old fishing town itself had lost its chill and cheerless aspect, and no longer looked hungrily out over miles of bleak sea. Its blind alleys and dark lanes, its narrow, crabbed, crooked streets were bright with little flags hung out of the little stuffed-up windows, and yet brighter with bright faces that hurried to and fro.

About five o'clock, as the sun was dipping seaward across the back of Contrary, leaving the brown sails in the harbor in shade, and glistening red on the sides of the cathedral church on the island-rock that stood twenty yards out from the mainland, there was a movement of the people on the shore toward the town behind them, and of fisher-fellows from their boats toward the beach. Some of the neighboring clergy had come down to Peeltown, and the little Deemster sat in his coach, thrown open, blinking in the sun under his shaggy gray eyebrows. But some one was still looked for, and expectation was plainly evident in every face until a cheer came over the tops of the houses from the market-place. Then there was a general rush toward the mouth of the quay, and presently there came, laboring over the rough cobbles of the tortuous Castle Street, flanked by a tumultuous company of boys and men, bareheaded women, and children, who halloed and waved their arms and tossed up their caps, a rough-coated Manx pony, on which the tall figure of the Bishop sat.

The people moved on with the Bishop at their head until they came to the beach, and there, at the disused boat lying dry on the sand, the Bishop alighted. In two minutes more every fisherman in the harbor had left his boat and gathered with his fellows on the shore. Then there began a ceremony of infinite pathos and grandeur.

In the open boat the pale-faced Bishop stood, his long hair, sprinkled with gray, lifted gently over his drooping shoulders by the gentle breeze that came with its odor of brine from the sea. Around him, on their knees on the sand, were the tawny-faced, weather-beaten fishermen in their sea-boots and guernseys, bareheaded, and fumbling their soft caps in their hands. There, on the outside, stood the multitude of men, women, and young children, and on the skirts of the crowd stood the coach of the Deemster, and it was half encircled by the pawing horses of some of the black-coated clergy.

The Bishop began the service. It asked for the blessing of God on the fishing expedition which was about to set out. First came the lesson, "And God said, let the waters bring forth abundantly"; and then the story of Jesus in the ship, when there arose a great tempest while He slept, and His disciples awoke Him, and He arose and rebuked the waves; and then that other story of how the disciples toiled all night and took nothing, but let down their nets again at Christ's word, and there came a great multitude of fishes, and their nets brake. "Restore and continue to us the harvest of the sea," prayed the Bishop, with his face uplifted; and the men on their knees on the sand, with uncovered heads and faces in their caps, murmured their responses in their own tongue, "Yn Meailley."

And while they prayed, the soft boom of the unruffled waters on the shore, and the sea's deep murmur from away beyond the headland, and the wild jabbering cries of a flight of sea-gulls disporting on a rock in the bay, were the only sounds that mingled with the Bishop's deep tones and the men's hoarse voices.

Last of all, the Bishop gave out a hymn. It was a simple old hymn, such as every man had known since his mother had crooned it over his cot. The men rose to their feet, and their lusty voices took up the strain; the crowd behind, and the clergy on their horses, joined it; and from the Deemster's coach two women's voices took it up, and higher, higher, higher, like a lark, it floated up, until the soft boom and deep murmur of the sea and the wild cry of the sea-birds were drowned in the broad swell of the simple old sacred song.

The sun was sinking fast through a red haze toward the sea's verge, and the tide was near the flood, when the service on the shore ended, and the fishermen returned to their boats.

Billy Quilleash leaped aboard the new lugger, and his four men followed him. "See all clear," he shouted to Davy Fayle; and Davy stood on the quay with the duty of clearing the ropes from the blocks, and then following in the dingey that lay moored to the wooden steps.

Dan had gone up to the Deemster's coach and helped Mona and the young wife of Ewan to alight. He led them to the quay steps, and when the company had gathered about, and all was made ready, he shouted to old Billy to throw him the bottle that lay tied by the blue ribbon to the tiller. Then he handed the bottle to Mona, who stood on the step, a few feet above the water's edge.

Mona was looking very fresh and beautiful that day, with a delicious joy and pride in her deep eyes. Dan was talking to her with an awkward sort of consciousness, looking askance at his big brown hands when they came in contact with her dainty white fingers, then glancing down at his great clattering boots, and up into her soft, smooth face.

"What am I to christen her?" said Mona, with the bottle held up in her hand.

"Mona," answered Dan, with a shamefaced look and one hand in his brown hair.

"No, no," said she, "not that."

"Then what you like," said Dan.

"Well, the 'Ben-my-Chree,'" said Mona, and with that the bottle broke on the boat's side.

In another instant Ewan was kissing his meek little wife, and bidding her good-by, and Dan, in a fumbling way, was, for the first time in his life, demurely shaking Mona's hand, and trying hard to look her in the face.

"Tail on there," shouted Quilleash from the lugger. Then the two men jumped aboard, Davy Fayle ran the ropes from the blocks, the admiral's boat cleared away from the quay, and the admiral's flag was shot up to the masthead. The other boats in the harbor followed one by one, and soon the bay was full of the fleet.

As the "Ben-my-Chree" stood out to sea beyond the island-rock, Dan and Ewan stood aft, Dan in his brown guernsey, Ewan in his black coat; Ewan waving his handkerchief, and Dan his cap; old Billy was at the tiller, Crennel, the cook, had his head just above the hatchways, and Davy was clambering hand-over-hand up the rope by which the dingey was hauled to the stern.

Then the herring fleet sailed away under the glow of the setting sun.

CHAPTER X
THE FIRST NIGHT WITH THE HERRINGS

The sun went down, and a smart breeze rose off the land as the "Ben-my-Chree," with the fleet behind her, rounded Contrary Head, and crossed the two streams that flow there. For an hour afterward there was still light enough to see the coast-line curved into covelets and promontories, and to look for miles over the hills with their moles of gorse, and tussocks of lush grass. The twilight deepened as the fleet rounded Niarbyl Point, and left the islet on their lee, with Cronk-ny-Irey-Lhaa towering into the gloomy sky. When they sailed across Fleshwick Bay the night gradually darkened, and nothing was seen of Ennyn Mooar. But after an hour of darkness the heavens lightened again, and glistened with stars, and when old Billy Quilleash brought his boat head to the wind in six fathoms of water outside Port Erin, the moon had risen behind Bradda, and the rugged headland showed clear against the sky. One after another the boats and the fleet brought to about the "Ben-my-Chree."

Dan asked old Billy if he had found the herrings on this ground at the same time in former seasons.

"Not for seven years," said the old man.

"Then why try now?"

Billy stretched out his hand to where a flight of sea-gulls were dipping and sailing in the moonlight. "See the gull there?" he said. "She's skipper to-night; she's showing us the fish."

Davy Fayle had been leaning over the bow, rapping with a stick at the timbers near the water's edge.

"Any signs?" shouted Billy Quilleash.

"Ay," said Davy, "the mar-fire's risin'."

The wind had dropped, and luminous patches of phosphorescent light in the water were showing that the herrings were stirring.

"Let's make a shot; up with the gear," said Quilleash, and preparations were made for shooting the nets over the quarter.

"Ned Teare, you see to the line. Crennel, look after the corks. Davy—where's that lad?—look to the seizings, d'ye hear?"

Then the nets were hauled from below, and passed over a bank-board placed between the hatchway and the top of the bulwark. Teare and Crennel shot the gear, and as the seizings came up, Davy ran aft with them, and made them fast to the warp near the taffrail.

When the nets were all paid out, every net in the drift being tied to the next, and a solid wall of meshes nine feet deep had been swept away along the sea for half a mile behind them, Quilleash shouted, "Down with the sheets."

The ropes were hauled, the sails were taken in, the mainmast—which was so made as to lower backward—was dropped, and only the drift-mizzen was left, and that was to keep the boat head on to the wind.

"Up with the light there," said Quilleash.

At this word Davy Fayle popped his head out of the hatchways.

"Aw, to be sure, that lad's never ready. Get out of that, quick."

Davy jumped on deck, took a lantern, and fixed it to the top of the mitch board. Then vessel and nets drifted together, and Dan and Ewan, who had kept the deck until now, went below together.

It was now a calm, clear night, with just light enough to show two or three of the buoys on the back of the net nearest to the boat, as they floated under water. Old Billy had not mistaken his ground. Large white patches came moving out of the surrounding pavement of deep black, lightened only by the image of a star where the vanishing ripples left the dark sea smooth. Once or twice countless faint popping sounds were to be heard, and minute points of shooting silver were to be seen on the water around. The herrings were at play, and shoals on shoals soon broke the black sea into a glistening foam.

But no "strike" was made, and after an hour's time Dan popped his head over the hatchways and asked the skipper to try the "look-on" net. The warp was hauled in until the first net was reached. It came up as black as coal, save for a single dogfish or two that had broken a mesh here and there.

"Too much moon to-night," said Quilleash; "they see the nets, and 'cute they are extraordinary."

But half an hour later the moon went out behind a thick ridge of cloud that floated over the land; the sky became gray and leaden, and a rising breeze ruffled the sea. Then hour after hour wore on, and not a fish came to the look-on net. Toward one o'clock in the morning, the moon broke out again. "There'll be a heavy strike now," said Quilleash, and in another instant a luminous patch floated across the line of the nets, sank, disappeared, and finally pulled three of the buoys down with them.

"Pull up now," shouted Quilleash, in another tone.

Then the nets were hauled. Davy, the boy, led the warp through a snatch-block fixed to the mast-hole on to the capstan. Ned Teare disconnected the nets from the warps, and Crennel and Corlett pulled the nets over the gunwale. They came up silver-white in the moonlight, a solid block of fish. Billy Quilleash and Dan passed them over the scudding-pole and shook the herrings into the hold.

"Five maze at least," said Quilleash, with a chuckle of satisfaction. "Try again." And once more the nets were shot. The other boats of the fleet were signaled, by a blue light run up the drift-mizzen, that the "Ben-my-Chree" had struck a scale of fish. In a few minutes more the blue light was answered by other blue lights on every side, and these reported that the fishery was everywhere faring well.

One, two, three o'clock came and went. The night was wearing on; the moon went out once more, and in the darkness which preceded the dawn the lanterns burning on the fleet of drifting boats gave out an eerie glow across the waters that lay black and flat around. The gray light came at length in the east, and the sun rose over the land. Then the nets were hauled in for the last time and that night's fishing was done.

The mast was lifted, but before the boat was brought about the skipper shouted, "Men, let us do as we're used of," and instantly the admiral's flag was run up to the masthead, and at this sign the men dropped on one knee, with their faces in their caps, and old Billy offered up a short and simple prayer of thanks for the blessings of the sea.

When this was done every man leaped to his feet, and all was work, bustle, shouting, singing out, and some lusty curses.

"Tumble up the sheets—bear a hand there—d—— the lad," bawled Quilleash; "get out of the way, or I'll make you walk handsome over the bricks."

In five minutes more the "Ben-my-Chree," with the herring fleet behind her, was running home before a stiff breeze.

"Nine maze—not bad for the first night," said Dan to Ewan.

"Souse them well," said Quilleash, and Ned Teare sprinkled salt on the herrings as they lay in the hold.

Crennel, the cook, better known as the "slushy," came up the hatchways with a huge saucepan, which he filled with the fish. As he did so there was a faint "cheep, cheep" from below—the herrings were still alive.

All hands went down for a smoke except Corlett, who stood at the tiller, Davy, who counted for nobody and stretched himself out at the bow, and Ewan. The young parson, who had been taking note of the lad during the night, now seated himself on a coil of rope near where Davy lay. The "cheep, cheep" was the only sound in the air except the plash of the waters at the boat's bow, and with an inclination of the head in the direction of the fish in the hold, Ewan said, "It seems cruel, Davy, doesn't it?"

"Cruel? Well, pozzible, pozzible. Och, 'deed now, they've got their feelings same as anybody else."

The parson had taken the lad's measure at a glance.

"You should see the shoals of them lying round the nets, watching the others—their mothers and sisters, as you might say—who've got their gills 'tangled. And when you haul the net up, away they go at a slant in millions and millions, just the same as lightning going through the water. Och, yes, yes, leave them alone for having their feelings."

"It does seem cruel, Davy, eh?"

Davy looked puzzled; he was reasoning out a grave problem.

"Well, sir, that's the mortal strange part of it. It does look cruel to catch them, sarten sure; but then the herrings themselves catch the sand-eels, and the cod catch the herring, and the porpoises and grampuses catch the cod."

Ewan did his best to look astonished.

"Aw, that's the truth, sir. It's terrible, wonderful strange, but I suppose it's all nathur. You see, sir, we do the same ourselves."

"How do you mean, Davy? We don't eat each other, I hope," said the young parson.

"Och, don't we, though? Lave us alone for that."

Ewan tried to look appalled.

"Well, of coorse, not to say *ate*, not 'xactly *ate;* but the biggest chap allis rigs the rest; and the next biggest chap allis rigs a littler one, you know, and the littlest chap, he gets rigged by everybody all round, doesn't he, sir?"

Davy had got a grip of the knotty problem, but the lad's poor, simple face looked sadly burdened, and he came back to his old word.

"Seems to me it must be all nathur, sir."

Ewan began to feel some touch of shame at playing with this simple, earnest, big little heart. "So you think it all nature, Davy?" he said, with a lump gathering in his throat.

"Well, well, I do, you know, sir; it does make a fellow fit to cry a bit, somehow; but it must be nathur, sir."

And Davy took off his blue worsted cap and fumbled it and gave his troubled young head a grave shake.

Then there was some general talk about Davy's early history. Davy's father had been pressed into the army before Davy was born, and had afterward been no more heard of; then his mother had died, and Billy Quilleash, being his mother's elder brother, had brought him up. Davy had always sailed as boy with Uncle Billy, he was sailing as boy then, and that was to the end that Uncle Billy might draw his share, but the young master (Mastha Dan) had spoken up for him, so he had, and he knew middlin' well what that would come to. "'He's a tidy lump of a lad now,' says Mastha Dan, 'and he's well used of the boats, too,' says he, 'and if he does well this time,' he says, 'he must sail man for himself next season.' Aw, yes, sir, that was what Mastha Dan said."

It was clear that Dan was the boy's hero. When Dan was mentioned that lagging lip gave a yearning look to Davy's simple face. Dan's doubtful exploits and his dubious triumphs all looked glorious in Davy's eyes. Davy had watched Dan, and listened to him, and though Dan might know nothing of his silent worship, every word that Dan had spoken to him had been hoarded up in the lad's heart like treasure. Davy had the dog's soul, and Dan was his master.

"Uncle Billy and him's same as brothers," said Davy; "and Uncle Billy's uncommon proud of the young master, and middlin' jealous, too. Aw, well! who's wondering at it?"

Just then Crennel, the cook, came up to say that breakfast was ready, and Ewan and Davy went below, the young parson's hand resting on the boy's shoulder. In the cabin Dan was sitting by the stove, laughing immoderately. Ewan saw at a glance that Dan had been drinking, and he forthwith elbowed his way to Dan's side and lifted a brandy bottle from the stove-top into the locker, under pretense of finding a place for his hat. Then all hands sat down to the table. There was a huge dish of potatoes boiled in their jackets, and a similar dish of herrings. Every man dipped into the dishes with his hands, lifted his herring on to his plate, ran his fingers from tail to head, swept all the flesh off the fresh fish, and threw the bare backbone into the crock that stood behind.

"Keep a corner for the Meailley at the 'Three Legs,'" said Dan.

There was to be a herring breakfast that morning at the "Three Legs of Man," to celebrate the opening of the fishing season.

"You'll come, Ewan, eh?"

The young parson shook his head.

Dan was in great spirits, to which the spirits he had imbibed contributed a more than common share. Ewan saw the too familiar light of dangerous mischief dancing in Dan's eyes, and made twenty attempts to keep the conversation within ordinary bounds of seriousness. But Dan was not to be restrained, and breaking away into the homespun—a sure indication that the old Adam was having the upper hand—he forthwith plunged into some chaff that was started by the mate, Ned Teare, at Davy Fayle's expense.

"Aw, ye wouldn't think it's true, would ye, now?" said Ned, with a wink at Dan and a "glime" at Davy.

"And what's that?" said Dan, with another "glime" at the lad.

"Why, that the like o' yander is tackin' round the gels."

"D'ye raely mane it?" said Dan, dropping his herring and lifting his eyes.

Ewan coughed with some volume, and said, "There, there, Dan—there, there."

"Yes, though, and sniffin' and snuffin' abaft of them astonishin'," Ned Teare put it again.

"Aw, well, well, well," said Dan, turning up afresh the whites of his eyes.

There was not a sign from Davy; he broke his potato more carefully, and took both hands and both eyes to strip away its jacket.

"Yes, yes, the craythur's doing somethin' in the spooney line," said Billy Quilleash; "him as hasn't the hayseed out of his hair yet."

"Aw, well," said Dan, pretending to come to Davy's relief, "it isn't raisonable but the lad should be coortin' some gel now."

"What's that?" shouted Quilleash, dropping the banter rather suddenly. "What, and not a farthing at him? And owin' me fortune for the bringin' up."

"No matter, Billy," said Dan, "and don't ride a man down like a main-tack. One of these fine mornings Davy will be payin' his debt to you with the foretopsail."

Davy's eyes were held very low, but it was not hard to see that they were beginning to fill.

"That will do, Dan, that will do," said Ewan. The young parson's face had grown suddenly pale, but Dan saw nothing of that.

"And look at him there," said Dan, reaching round Ewan to prod Davy in the ribs—"look at him there, pretendin' he never knows nothin'."

The big tears were near to toppling out of Davy's eyes. He could have borne the chaff from any one but Dan.

"Dan," said Ewan, with a constrained quietness, "stop it; I can't stand it much longer."

At that Davy got up from the table, leaving his unfinished breakfast, and began to climb the hatchways.

"Aw, now, look at that," said Dan, with affected solemnity, and so saying, and not heeding the change in Ewan's manner, Dan got up too and followed Davy out, put an arm round the lad's waist, and tried to draw him back. "Don't mind the loblolly-boys, Davy veg," he said, coaxingly. Davy pushed him away with an angry word.

"What's that he's after saying?" asked Quilleash.

"Nothin'; he only cussed a bit," said Dan.

"Cussed, did he? He'd better show a leg if he don't want the rat's tail."

Then Ewan rose from the table, and his eyes flashed and his pale face quivered.

"I'll tell you what it is," he said in a tense, tremulous voice, "there's not a man among you. You're a lot of skulking cowards."

At that he was making for the deck; but Dan, whose face, full of the fire of the liquor he had taken, grew in one moment old and ugly, leaped to his feet in a tempest of wrath, overturned his stool, and rushed at Ewan with eyes aflame and uplifted hand, and suddenly, instantly, like a flash, his fist fell, and Ewan rolled on the floor.

Then the men jumped up and crowded round in confusion. "The parzon! the parzon! God preserve me, the parzon!"

There stood Dan, with a ghastly countenance, white and convulsed, and there at his feet lay Ewan.

"God A'mighty! Mastha Dan, Mastha Dan," cried Davy. Before the men had found time to breathe, Davy had leaped back from the deck to the cockpit, and had lifted Ewan's head on to his knee.

Ewan drew a long breath and opened his eyes. He was bleeding from a gash above the temple, having fallen among some refuse of iron chain. Davy, still moaning piteously, "Oh, Mastha Dan, God A'mighty, Mastha Dan," took a white handkerchief from Ewan's breast, and bound it about his head over the wound. The blood oozed through and stained the handkerchief.

Ewan rose to his feet pale and trembling, and without looking at any one, steadied himself by Davy's shoulder, and clambered weakly to the deck. There he stumbled forward, sat down on the coil of rope that had been his seat before, and buried his uncovered head in his breast.

The sun had now risen above Contrary, and the fair young morning light danced over the rippling waters far and near. A fresh breeze blew from the land, and the boats of the fleet around and about scudded on before the wind like a flight of happy birds, with outspread wings.

The "Ben-my-Chree" was then rounding the head, and the smoke was beginning to coil up in many a slender shaft above the chimneys of the little town of Peel. But Ewan saw nothing of this; with head on his breast, and his heart cold within him, he sat at the bow.

Down below, Dan was then doing his best to make himself believe that he was unconcerned. He whistled a little, and sang a little, and laughed a good deal; but the whistle lost its tune, and the song stopped short, and the laugh was loud and empty. When he first saw Ewan lie where he fell, all the fire of his evil passion seemed to die away, and for the instant his heart seemed to choke him, and he was prompted to drop down and lift Ewan to his feet; but at that moment his stubborn knees would not bend, and at the next moment the angel of God troubled the waters of his heart no more. Then the fisher-fellows overcame their amazement, and began to crow, and to side with him, and to talk of his pluck, and what not.

"The parzons—och, the parzons—they think they may ride a man down for half a word inside his gills."

"'Cowards'—och, 'skulking cowards,' if you plaize—right sarved, say I!"

Dan tramped about the cabin restlessly, and sometimes chuckled aloud and asked himself what did he care, and then laughed noisily, and sat down to smoke, and presently jumped up, threw the pipe into the open stove, and took the brandy bottle out of the locker. Where was Ewan? What was he doing? What was he looking like? Dan would rather have died than humbled himself to ask; but would none of these grinning boobies tell him? When Teare, the mate, came down from the deck and said that sarten sure the young parzon was afther sayin' his prayers up forrard Dan's eyes flashed again, and he had almost lifted his hand to fell the sniggering waistrel. He drank half a tumbler of brandy, and protested afresh, though none had yet disputed it, that he cared nothing, not he, let them say what they liked to the contrary.

In fifteen minutes from the time of the quarrel the fleet was running into harbor. Dan had leaped on deck just as the "Ben-my-Chree" touched the two streams outside Contrary. He first looked forward, and saw Ewan sitting on the cable in the bow with his eyes shut and his pallid face sunk deep in his breast. Then a strange, wild light shot into Dan's eyes, and he reeled aft and plucked the tiller from the hand of Corlett, and set it hard aport, and drove the boat head on for the narrow neck of water that flowed between the mainland and the island-rock on which the old castle stood.

"Hould hard," shouted old Billy Quilleash, "there's not water enough for the like o' that—you'll run her on the rocks."

Then Dan laughed wildly, and his voice rang among the coves and caves of the coast.

"Here's for the harbor or—hell," he screamed, and then another wild peal of his mad laughter rang in the air and echoed from the land.

"What's agate of the young mastha?" the men muttered one to another; and with eyes of fear they stood stock-still on the deck and saw themselves driven on toward the shoals of the little sound.

In two minutes more they breathed freely. The "Ben-my-Chree" had shot like an arrow through the belt of water and was putting about in the harbor.

Dan dropped the tiller, reeled along the deck, scarcely able to bear himself erect, and stumbled under the hatchways. Old Billy brought up the boat to its moorings.

"Come, lay down, d'ye hear? Where's that lad?"

Davy was standing by the young parson.

"You idiot waistrel, why d'ye stand prating there? I'll pay you, you beachcomber."

The skipper was making for Davy, when Ewan got up, stepped toward him, looked him hard in the face, seemed about to speak, checked himself, and turned away.

Old Billy broke into a bitter little laugh, and said, "I'm right up and down like a yard o' pump-water, that's what I am."

The boat was now at the quay-side, and Ewan leaped ashore. Without a word or a look more, he walked away, the white handkerchief, clotted with blood, still about his forehead, and his hat carried in his hand.

On the quay there were numbers of women with baskets waiting to buy the fish. Teare, the mate, and Crennel, the cook, counted the herrings and sold them. The rest of the crew stepped ashore.

Dan went away with the rest. His face was livid in the soft morning sunlight. He was still keeping up his brave outside, while the madness was growing every moment fiercer within. As he stumbled along the paved way with an unsteady step his hollow laugh grated on the quiet air.

CHAPTER XI
THE HERRING BREAKFAST

It was between four o'clock and five when the fleet ran into Peeltown harbor after the first night of the herring season, and toward eight the fisher-fellows, to the number of fifty at least, had gathered for their customary first breakfast in the kitchen of the "Three Legs of Man." What sport! What noisy laughter! What singing and rollicking cheers! The men stood neither on the order of their coming nor their going, their sitting nor their standing. In they trooped in their woolen caps or their broad sou'westers, their oilskins or their long sea-boots swung across their arms. They wore their caps or not as pleased them, they sang or talked as suited them, they laughed or sneezed, they sulked or snarled, they were noisy or silent, precisely as the whim of the individual prescribed the individual rule of manners. Rather later than the rest Dan Mylrea came swinging in, with a loud laugh and a shout, and something like an oath, too, and the broad homespun on his lips.

"Billy Quilleash—I say, Billy, there—why don't you put up the young mastha for the chair?"

"Aw, lave me alone," answered Billy Quilleash, with a contemptuous toss of the head.

"Uncle Billy's proud uncommon of the mastha," whispered Davy Fayle, who sat meekly on a form near the door, to the man who sat cross-legged on the form beside him.

"It's a bit free them chaps is making," said old Billy, in a confidential undertone to Dan, who was stretching himself out on the settle. Then rising to his feet with gravity, "Gen'l'men," said Quilleash, "what d'ye say now to Mistha Dan'l Mylrea for the elber-cheer yander?"

At that there was the response of loud raps on the table with the heels of the long boots swung over various arms, and with several clay pipes that lost their heads in the encounter. Old Billy resumed his seat with a lofty glance of patronage at the men about him, which said as plainly as words themselves, "I tould ye to lave it all to me."

"Proud, d'ye say? Look at him," muttered the fisherman sitting by Davy Fayle.

Dan staggered up and shouldered his way to the elbow-chair at the head of the table. He had no sooner taken his seat than he shouted for the breakfast, and without more ado the breakfast was lifted direct on to the table from the pans and boilers that simmered on the hearth.

First came the broth, well loaded with barley and cabbage; then suet puddings; and last of all the frying-pan was taken down from the wall, and four or five dozen of fresh herrings were made to grizzle and crackle and sputter over the fire.

Dan ate ravenously, and laughed noisily, and talked incessantly as he ate. The men at first caught the contagion of his boisterous manners, but after a time they shook their tousled heads and laid them together in gravity, and began to repeat in whispers, "What's agate of the young mastha, at all, at all?"

Away went the dishes, away went the cloth, an oil-lamp with its open mouth—a relic of some monkish sanctuary of the Middle Ages—was lifted from the mantel-shelf and put on the table for the receipt of custom; a brass censer, choked with spills, was placed beside it; pipes emerged from waistcoat-pockets, and pots of liquor with glasses and bottles came in from the outer bar.

"Is it heavy on the liquor you're going to be, Billy?" said Ned, the mate; and old Billy replied with a superior smile and the lifting up of a whisky bottle, from which he had just drawn the cork.

Then came the toasts. The chairman arose amid hip, hip, hooraa! and gave "Life to man and death to fish!" and Quilleash gave "Death to the head that never wore hair!"

Then came more noise and more liquor, and a good deal of both in the vicinity of the chair. Dan struck up a song. He sang "Drink to Me Only," and the noisy company were at first hushed to silence and then melted to audible sobs.

"Aw, man, the voice he has, anyway!"

"And the loud it is, and the tender, too, and the way he slidders up and down, and no squeaks and jumps."

"No, no; nothin' like squeezin' a tune out of an ould sow by pulling the tail at her."

Old Billy listened to this dialogue among the fisher-fellows about him, and smiled loftily. "It's nothin'," he said, condescendingly—"that's nothin'. You should hear him out in the boat, when we're lying at anchor, and me and him together, and the stars just makin' a peep, and the moon, and the mar-fire, and all to that, and me and him lying aft and smookin', and having a glass maybe, but nothin' to do no harm—that's the when you should hear him. Aw, man alive, him and me's same as brothers."

"More liquor there," shouted Dan, climbing with difficulty to his feet.

"Ay, look here. D'ye hear, down yander? Give us a swipe o' them speerits. Right. More liquor for the chair!" said Billy Quilleash. "And for some one besides?—is that what they're saying, the loblolly-boys? Well, look here, bad cess to it, of coorse, some for me, too. It's terrible good for the narves, and they're telling me it's morthal good for steddyin' the vi'ce. Going to sing? Coorse, coorse. What's that from the elber-cheer? Enemy, eh? Confound it, and that's true, though. What's that it's sayin'? 'Who's fool enough to put the enemy into his mouth to stale away his brains?' Aw, now, it's the good ould Book that's fine at summin' it all up."

Then there was more liquor and yet more, till the mouth of the monastic lamp ran over with chinking coin. Old Billy struck up his song. It was a doleful ditty on the loss of the herring fleet on one St. Matthew's Day not long before.

> An hour before day,
> Tom Grimshaw, they say,
> To run for the port had resolved;
> Himself and John More
> Were lost in that hour,
> And also unfortunate Kinved.

The last three lines of each verse were repeated by the whole company in chorus. Doleful as the ditty might be, the men gave it voice with a heartiness that suggested no special sense of sorrow, and loud as were the voices of the fisher-fellows, Dan's voice was yet louder.

"Aw, Dan, man, Dan, man alive, Dan," the men whispered among themselves. "What's agate of Mastha Dan? it's more than's good, man, aw, yes, yes, yes."

Still more liquor and yet more noise, and then, through the dense fumes of tobacco-smoke, old Billy Quilleash could be seen struggling to his feet. "Silence!" he shouted; "aisy there!" and he lifted up his glass. "Here's to Mistha Dan'l Mylrea, and if he's not going among the parzons, bad cess to them, he's going among the Kays, and when he gets to the big house at Castletown, I'm calkerlatin' it'll be all up with the lot o' them parzons, with their tithes and their censures, and their customs and their canons, and their regalashuns agen the countin' of the herrin', and all the rest of their messin'. What d'ye say, men? 'Skulking cowards?' Coorse, and right sarved, too, as I say. And what's that you're grinning and winkin' at, Ned Teare? It's middlin' free you're gettin' with the mastha anyhow, and if it wasn't for me he wouldn't bemane himself by comin' among the like of you, singin' and makin' aisy. Chaps, fill up your glasses every man of you, d'ye hear? Here's to the best gen'l'man in the island, bar none—Mistha Dan'l Mylrea, hip, hip, hooraa!"

The toast was responded to with alacrity, and loud shouts of "Dan'l Mylrea—best gen'l'man—bar none."

But what was going on at the head of the table? Dan had risen from the elbow-chair; it was the moment for him to respond, but he stared wildly around, and stood there in silence, and his tongue seemed to cleave to his mouth. Every eye was now fixed on his face, and that face quivered and turned white. The glass he had held in his hand fell from his nerveless fingers and broke on the table. Laughter died on every lip, and the voices were hushed. At last Dan spoke; his words came slowly, and fell heavily on the ear.

"Men," he said, "you have been drinking my health. You call me a good fellow. That's wrong. I'm the worst man among you. Old Billy says I'm going to the House of Keys. That's wrong, too. Shall I tell you where I am going? Shall I tell you? I'm going to the devil," and then, amid breathless silence, he dropped back in his seat and buried his head in his hands.

No one spoke. The fair head lay on the table among broken pipes and the refuse of spilled liquor. There could be no more drinking that morning. Every man rose to his feet, and picking up his waterproofs or his long sea-boots, one after one went shambling out. The room was dense with smoke; but outside the air was light and free, and the morning sun shone brightly.

"Strange now, wasn't it?" muttered one of the fellows.

"Strange uncommon!"

"He's been middlin' heavy on the liquor lately."

"And he'd never no right to strike the young parzon, and him his cousin, too, and terrible fond of him, as they're saying."

"Well, well, it's middlin' wicked anyway."

And so the croakers went their way. In two minutes more the room was empty, except for the stricken man, who lay there with hidden face, and Davy Fayle, who, with big tears glistening in his eyes, was stroking the tangled curls.

CHAPTER XII
DAN'S PENANCE

Dan rose to his feet a sobered man, and went out of the smoky pot-house without a word to any one, and without lifting his bleared and bloodshot eyes unto any face. He took the lane to the shore, and behind him, with downcast eyes, like a dog at the heels of his master, Davy Fayle slouched along. When they reached the shore Dan turned toward Orris Head, walking within a yard or two of the water's edge. Striding over the sands, the past of his childhood came back to him with a sense of pain. He saw himself flying along the beach with Ewan and Mona, shouting at the gull, mocking the cormorant, clambering up the rocks to where the long-necked bird laid her spotted eggs, and the sea-pink grew under the fresh grass of the corries. Under the head Dan sat on a rock and lifted away his hat from his burning forehead; but not a breath of wind stirred his soft hair.

Dan rose again with a new resolve. He knew now what course he must take. He would go to the Deemster, confess to the outrage of which he had been guilty, and submit to the just punishment of the law. With quick steps he strode back over the beach, and Davy followed him until he turned up to the gates of the new Ballamona, and then the lad rambled away under the foot of Slieu Dhoo. Dan found the Deemster's house in a tumult. Hommy-beg was rushing here and there, and Dan called to him, but he waved his arm and shouted something in reply, whereof the purport was lost, and then disappeared. Blind Kerry was there, and when Dan spoke to her as she went up the stairs, he could gather nothing from her hurried answer except that some one was morthal bad, as the saying was, and in another moment she, too, had gone. Dan stood in the hall with a sense of impending disaster. What had happened? A dread idea struck him at that moment like a blow on the brain. The sweat started from his forehead. He could bear the uncertainty no longer, and had set foot on the stairs to follow the blind woman, when there was the sound of a light step descending. In another moment he stood face to face with Mona. She colored deeply, and his head fell before her.

"Is it Ewan?" he said, and his voice came like a hoarse whisper.

"No, his wife," said Mona.

It turned out that not long after daybreak that morning the young wife of Ewan, who had slept with Mona, had awakened with a start, and the sensation of having received a heavy blow on the forehead. She had roused Mona, and told her what seemed to have occurred. They had looked about and seen nothing that could have fallen. They had risen from bed and examined the room, and had found everything as it had been when they lay down. The door was shut and there was no hood above the bed. But Mona had drawn up the window blind, and then she had seen, clearly marked on the white forehead of Ewan's young wife, a little above the temple, on the spot where she had seemed to feel the blow, a streak of pale color such as might have been made by the scratch of a thorn that had not torn the skin. It had been a perplexing difficulty, and the girls had gone back to bed, and talked of it in whispers until they had fallen asleep in each other's arms. When they had awakened again, the Deemster was rapping at their door to say that he had taken an early breakfast, that he was going off to hold his court at Ramsey, and expected to be back at midday. Then half-timidly, Mona had told her father of their strange experience, but he had bantered them on their folly, and they had still heard his laughter when he had leaped to the saddle in front of the house, and was cantering away over the gravel. Reassured by the Deemster's unbelief, the girls had thrown off their vague misgivings, and given way to good spirits. Ewan's young wife had said that all morning she had dreamed of her husband, and that her dreams had been bright and happy. They had gone down to breakfast, but scarcely had they been seated at the table before they had heard the click of the gate from the road.

Then they had risen together, and Ewan had come up the path with a white bandage about his head, and with a streak of blood above the temple. With a sharp cry, Ewan's young wife had fallen to the ground insensible, and when Ewan himself had come into the house they had carried her back to bed. There she was at that moment, and from a peculiar delicacy of her health at the time, there was but too much reason to fear that the shock might have serious results.

All this Mona told to Dan from where she stood, three steps up the stairs, and he listened with his head held low, one hand gripping the stair-rail, and his foot pawing the mat at the bottom. When she finished, there was a pause, and then there came from overhead a long, deep moan of pain.

Dan lifted his face; its sudden pallor was startling. "Mona," he said, in a voice that was husky in his throat, "do you know who struck Ewan that blow?"

There was silence for a moment and then, half in a whisper, half with a sob, Mona answered that she knew. It had not been from Ewan himself, but by one of the many tongues of scandal, that the news had come to Ballamona.

Dan railed at himself in bitter words, and called God to witness that he had been a curse to himself and every one about him. Mona let the torrent of his self-reproach spend itself, and then she said:

"Dan, you must be reconciled to Ewan."

"Not yet," he answered.

"Yes, yes, I'm sure he would forgive you," said Mona, and she turned about as if in the act of going back to seek for Ewan.

Dan grasped her hand firmly. "No," he said, "don't heap coals of fire on my head, Mona; don't, don't." And after a moment, with a calmer manner, "I must see the Deemster first."

Hardly had this been spoken when they heard a horse's hoofs on the gravel path, and the Deemster's voice calling to Hommy-beg as he threw the reins over the post near the door and entered the house. The Deemster was in unusual spirits, and slapped Dan on the back and laughed as he went into his room. Dan followed him, and Mona crept nervously to the open door. With head held down, Dan told what had occurred. The Deemster listened and laughed, asked further particulars and laughed again, threw off his riding boots and leggings, looked knowingly from under his shaggy brows, and then laughed once more.

"And what d'ye say you want me to do for you, Danny veg?" he asked, with one side of his wrinkled face twisted awry.

"To punish me, sir," said Dan.

At that the Deemster, who was buckling his slippers, threw himself back in his chair, and sent a shrill peal of mocking laughter through the house.

Dan was unmoved. His countenance did not bend as he said slowly, and in a low tone, "If you don't do it, sir, I shall never look into Ewan's face again."

The Deemster fixed his buckles, rose to his feet, slapped Dan on the back, and said: "Go home, man veen, go home," and then hurried away to the kitchen, where in another moment his testy voice could be heard directing Hommy-beg to put up the saddle on the "lath."

Mona looked into Dan's face. "Will you be reconciled to Ewan now?" she said, and took both his hands and held them.

"No," he answered firmly, "I will see the Bishop." His eyes were dilated; his face, that had hitherto been very mournful to see, was alive with a strange fire. Mona held his hands with a passionate grasp.

"Dan," she said, with a great tenderness, "this is very, very noble of you; this is like our Dan, this—"

She stopped; she trembled and glowed; her eyes were close to his.

"Don't look at me like that," he said.

She dropped his hands, and at the next instant he was gone from the house.

Dan found the Bishop at Bishop's Court, and told him all. The Bishop had heard the story already, but he said nothing of that. He knew when Dan hid his provocation and painted his offense at its blackest. With a grave face he listened while Dan accused himself, and his heart heaved within him.

"It is a serious offense," he said; "to strike a minister is a grievous offense, and the Church provides a censure."

Dan held his face very low, and clasped his hands in front of him.

"The censure is that on the next Sabbath morning following, in the presence of the congregation, you shall walk up the aisle of the parish church from the porch to the communion behind the minister, who shall read the 51st Psalm meantime."

The Bishop's deep tones and quiet manner concealed his strong emotion, and Dan went out without another word.

This was Friday, and on the evening of the same day Ewan heard what had passed between Dan and the Deemster and between Dan and the Bishop, and with a great lump in his throat he went across to Bishop's Court to pray that the censure might be taken off.

"The provocation was mine, and he is penitent," said Ewan; and with heaving breast the Bishop heard him out, and then shook his head.

"The censures of the Church were never meant to pass by the house of the Bishop," he said.

"But he is too deeply abased already," said Ewan.

"The offense was committed in public, and before the eyes of all men the expiation must be made."

"But I, too, am ashamed—think of it, and remove the censure," said Ewan, and his voice trembled and broke.

The Bishop gazed out at the window with blurred eyes that saw nothing. "Ewan," he said, "it is God's hand on the lad. Let it be; let it be."

Next day the Bishop sent his sumner round the parish, asking that every house might send one at least to the parish church next morning.

On Sunday Ewan's young wife kept her bed; but when Ewan left her for the church the shock of her nerves seemed in a measure to have passed away. There was still, however, one great disaster to fear, and Mona remained at the bedside.

The meaning of the sumner's summons had eked out, and long before the hour of service the parish church was crowded. The riff-raff that never came to church from year's end to year's end, except to celebrate the Oiel Verree, were there with eager eyes. While Willas-Thorn tolled the bell from the rope suspended in the porch, there was a low buzz of gossip, but when the bell ceased its hoarse clangor, and Will-as-Thorn appeared with his pitch-pipe in the front of the gallery, there could be heard, in the silence that followed over the crowded church, the loud tick of the wooden clock in front of him.

Presently from the porch there came a low, tremulous voice reading the Psalm that begins, "Have mercy upon me, O God, after Thy great goodness: according to the multitude of Thy mercies do away mine offenses."

Then the people who sat in front turned about, and those who sat at the side strained across, and those who sat above craned forward.

Ewan was walking slowly up the aisle in his surplice, with his pale face and scarred forehead bent low over the book in his hand, and close behind him, towering above him in his great stature, with head held down, but with a steadfast gaze, his hat in his hands, his step firm and resolute, Dan Mylrea strode along.

There was a dead hush over the congregation.

"Wash me thoroughly from my wickedness, and cleanse me from my sin. For I acknowledge my faults; and my sin is ever before me."

The tremulous voice rose and fell, and nothing else broke the silence except the uncertain step of the reader, and the strong tread of the penitent behind him.

"Against Thee only have I sinned, and done this evil in Thy sight—"

At this the tremulous voice deepened, and stopped, and went on and stopped again, and when the words came once more they came in a deep, low sob, and the reader's head fell into his breast.

Not until the Psalm came to an end, and Ewan and Dan had reached the communion, and the vicar had begun the morning prayer, and Will-as-Thorn had sent out a blast from his pitch-pipe, was the hard tension of that moment broken.

When the morning service ended, the Deemster rose from his pew and hurried down the aisle. As usual, he was the first to leave the church. The ghostly smile with which he had witnessed the penance that had brought tears to the eyes of others was still on the Deemster's lip, and a chuckle was in his throat when at the gate of the churchyard he met Hommy-beg, whose face was livid from a long run, and who stood for an instant panting for breath.

"Well, well, well?" said the Deemster, sending the words like small shot into Hommy-beg's deaf ear.

"Terrible, terrible, terrible," said Hommy-beg, and he lifted his hands.

"What is it? What? What?"

"The young woman-body is dead in child-bed."

Then the ghostly smile fled from the Deemster's face.

CHAPTER XIII
HOW EWAN MOURNED FOR HIS WIFE

What passed at the new Ballamona on that morning of Dan's penance was very pitiful. There, in the death-chamber already darkened, lay Ewan's young wife, her eyes lightly closed, her girlish features composed, and a faint tinge of color in her cheeks. Her breast was half open, and her beautiful head lay in a pillow of her soft brown hair. One round arm was stretched over the counterpane, and the delicate fingers were curved inward until the thumb-nail, like an acorn, rested on the inner rim of a ring. Quiet, peaceful, very sweet and tender, she lay there like one who slept. After a short, sharp pang she had died gently, without a struggle, almost without a sigh, merely closing her eyes as one who was weary, and drawing a long, deep breath. In dying she had given premature birth to a child, a girl, and the infant was alive, and was taken from the mother at the moment of death.

When the Deemster entered the room, with a face of great pallor and eyes of fear, Mona was standing by the bed-head gazing down, but seeing nothing. The Deemster felt the pulse of the arm over the counterpane with fingers that trembled visibly. Then he shot away from the room, and was no more seen that day. The vicar, the child-wife's father, came with panting breath and stood by the bedside for a moment, and then turned aside in silence. Ewan came, too, and behind him Dan walked to the door and there stopped, and let Ewan enter the chamber of his great sorrow alone. Not a word was said until Ewan went down on his knees by the side of his wife, and put his arms about her, and kissed her lips, still warm, with his own far colder lips, and called to her softly by her name, as though she slept gently, and must not be awakened too harshly, and drew her to his breast, and called again, in a tenderer tone that brushed the upturned face like a caress:

"Aileen! Aileen! Aileen!"

Mona covered her eyes in her hands, and Dan, where he stood at the door, turned his head away.

"Aileen! Ailee! Ailee! My Ailee!"

The voice went like a whisper and a kiss into the deaf ear, and only one other sound was heard, and that was the faint cry of an infant from the room below.

Ewan raised his head and seemed to listen; he paused and looked at the faint color in the quiet cheeks; he put his hand lightly on the heart, and looked long at the breast that did not heave. Then he drew his arms very slowly away, and rose to his feet.

For a moment he stood as one dazed, like a man whose brain is benumbed, and, with the vacant light still in his eyes, he touched Mona on the arm and drew her hand from her eyes, and he said, as one who tells you something that you could not think, "She is dead!"

Mona looked up into his face, and at sight of it the tears rained down her own. Dan had stepped into the room noiselessly, and came behind Ewan, and when Ewan felt his presence, he turned to Dan with the same vacant look, and repeated in the same empty tone, "She is dead!"

And never a tear came into Ewan's eyes to soften their look of dull torpor; never again did he stretch out his arms to the silent form beneath him; only with dazed, dry eyes, he looked down, and said once more, "She is dead!"

Dan could bear up no longer; his heart was choking, and he went out without a word.

It was the dread silence of feeling that was frozen, but the thaw came in its time. They laid out the body of the young wife in the darkened room, and Ewan went away and rambled over the house all day long, and when night fell in, and the lighted candles were set in the death-chamber, and all in Ballamona were going off to bed, Ewan was still rambling aimlessly from room to room. He was very quiet, and he spoke little and did not weep at all. In the middle of that night the Deemster opened his bedroom door and listened, and Ewan's step was still passing from room to room, and Mona heard the same restless footfall in every break of her fitful sleep. But later on, in the dark hour that comes before day, the Deemster opened his door and listened again, and then all was quiet in the house. "He has gone to bed at last," thought the Deemster; but in the early morning, as he passed by Ewan's room, he found the door open, and saw that the bed had not been slept in.

The second day went by like the first, and the next night like the former one, and again in the dead of night the Deemster opened his door and heard Ewan's step. Once more, in the dark hour that goes before the day, he opened his door and listened again, and all was quiet as before. "Surely he is in bed now," thought the Deemster. He was turning back into his own room, when he felt a sudden impulse to go to Ewan's room first and see if it was as he supposed. He went, and the door was open and Ewan was not there, and again the bed had not been slept in.

The Deemster crept back on tiptoe, and a gruesome feeling took hold of him. He could not lie, and no sleep had come near his wakeful eyes, so he waited and listened for that unquiet beat of restless feet, but the sound did not come. Then, as the day was breaking over the top of Slieu Dhoo, and all the Curraghs around lay veiled in mist, and far away to the west a deep line stretched across where the dark sea lay with the lightening sky above it, the Deemster opened his door yet again, and went along the corridor steadily until he came to the door of the room where the body was. "Perhaps he is sitting with her," he thought, with awe, and he turned the handle. But when the door swung open the Deemster paused; a faint sound broke the silence; it was a soft and measured breathing from within. Quivering with dread, the Deemster stepped into the death-chamber, and his head turned rigidly toward the bed. There, in the gloom of the dawn that came over the light of the last candle that flickered in its socket, Ewan lay outstretched by the side of the white, upturned face of his dead wife, and his hand lay on her hand, and he was in a deep sleep.

To the Deemster it was as if a spirit had passed before his face, and the hair of his flesh stood up.

They buried Ewan's young wife side by side with his mother, under the elder-tree (now thick with clusters of the green berry) by the wall of the churchyard that stood over by the sea. The morning was fine, but the sun shone dimly through a crust of hot air that gathered and slumbered and caked above. Ewan passed through all without a word, or a sigh, or a tear. But when the company returned to the Deemster's house, and Mona spoke to Ewan and he answered her without any show of feeling, and Dan told him of his own remorse and accused himself of every disaster, and still Ewan gave no sign, but went in and out among them all with the vacant light in his eyes, then the Bishop whispered to Mona, and she went out and presently came again, and in her arms was the infant in its white linen clothes.

The sun was now hidden by the heavy cloud overhead, and against the window-panes at that moment there was a light pattering of rain-drops. Ewan had watched with his vacant gaze when Mona went out, but when she came again a new light seemed to come into his eyes, and he stepped up to her and looked down at the little face that was sleeping softly against her breast. Then he put out his arms to take the child, and Mona passed it to him, and he held it, and sat down with it, and all at once the tears came into his dry eyes and he wept aloud.

CHAPTER XIV
WRESTLING WITH FATE

So far as concerned the Deemster, the death of Ewan's wife was the beginning of the end. Had she not died under the roof of the new Ballamona? Was it not by the strangest of accidents that she had died there, and not in her own home? Had she not died in child-bed? Did not everything attending her death suggest the force of an irresistible fate? More than twenty years ago the woman Kerruish, the mother of Mally Kerruish, had cursed this house, and said that no life would come to it but death would come with it.

And for more than twenty years the Deemster had done his best to laugh at the prediction and to forget it. Who was he that he should be the victim of fear at the sneezing of an old woman? What was he that he should not be master of his fate? But what had occurred? For more than twenty years one disturbing and distinct idea had engrossed him. In all his waking hours it exasperated him, and even in his hours of sleep it lay heavy at the back of his brain as a dull feeling of dread. On the bench, in the saddle, at table, alone by the winter's fire, alone in summer walks, the obstinate idea was always there. And nothing but death seemed likely to shake it off.

Often he laughed at it in his long, lingering, nervous laugh; but it was a chain that was slowly tightening about him. Everything was being fulfilled. First came the death of his wife at the birth of Mona, and now, after an interval of twenty years, the death of his son's wife at the birth of her child. In that stretch of time he had become in his own view a childless man; his hopes had been thwarted in the son on whom alone his hopes had been built; the house he had founded was but an echoing vault; the fortune he had reared an empty bubble. He was accursed; God had heard the woman's voice; he looked too steadily at the facts to mistake them, and let the incredulous fools laugh if they liked.

When, twenty years before, the Deemster realized that he was the slave of one tyrannical idea, he tried to break the fate that hung over him. He bought up the cottage on the Brew, and turned the woman Kerruish into the roads. Then he put his foot on every sign of superstitious belief that came in his way as judge.

But not with such brave shows of unbelief could he conquer his one disturbing idea. His nature had never been kindly, but now there grew upon him an obstinate hatred of everybody. This was in the days when his children, Ewan and Mona, lived in the cozy nest at Bishop's Court. If in these days any man mentioned the Kerruishes in the Deemster's presence, he showed irritation, but he kept his ears open for every syllable said about them. He knew all their history; he knew when the girl Mally fled away from the island on the day of Ewan's christening; he knew by what boat she sailed; he knew where she settled herself in England; he knew when her child was born, and when, in terror at the unfulfilled censure of the Church that hung over her (separating her from all communion with God's people in life or hope of redemption in death), she came back to the island, drawn by an irresistible idea, her child at her breast, to work out her penance on the scene of her shame.

Thereafter he watched her daily, and knew her life. She had been taken back to work at the net-looms of Kinvig, the Peeltown net-maker, and she lived with her mother at the cottage over the Head, and there in poverty she brought up her child, her boy, Jarvis Kerruish, as she had called him. If any pointed at her and laughed with cruelty; if any pretended to sympathize with her and said, with a snigger, "The first error is always forgiven, Mally woman"; if any mentioned the Deemster himself, and said, with a wink, "I'm thinking it terrible strange, Mally, that you don't take a slue round and put a sight on him"; if any said to her when she bought a new garment out of her scant earnings, a gown, or even a scarf or bit of bright ribbon such as she loved in the old days, "Dearee dear! I thought you wouldn't take rest, but be up and put a sight on the ould crooky"—the Deemster knew it all. He saw the ruddy, audacious girl of twenty sink into the pallid slattern of thirty, without hope, without joy in life, and with only a single tie.

And the Deemster found that there grew upon him daily his old malicious feeling; but so far as concerned his outer bearing, matters took a turn on the day he came upon the boys, Dan Mylrea and Jarvis Kerruish, fighting in the road. It was the first time he had seen the boy Jarvis. "Who is he?" he had asked, and the old woman Kerruish had made answer, "Don't you know him, Deemster? Do you never see a face like that? Not when you look in the glass?"

There was no need to look twice into a mirror like the face of that lad to know whose son he was.

The Deemster went home to Ballamona, and thought over the fierce encounter. He could tolerate no longer the living reproach of this boy's presence within a few miles of his own house, and, by an impulse no better than humbled pride, he went back to the cottage of the Kerruishes at night, alone, and afoot. The cottage was a lone place on the top of a bare heath, with the bleak sea in front, and the purple hills behind, and with a fenceless cart-track leading up to it. A lead mine, known as the Cross Vein, had been worked there forty years before. The shaft was still open, and now full of dark, foul water almost to the surface. One roofless wall showed where the gear had stood, and under the shelter of this wall there crouched a low thatched tool-shed, having a door and a small window. This was the cottage; and until old Mrs. Kerruish had brought there her few rickety sticks when, by the Deemster's orders, they had been thrown into the road, none had ever occupied the tool-shed as a house.

The door was open, and the Deemster stepped in. One of the women, old Mrs. Kerruish, was sitting on a stool by the fire—it was a fire of sputtering hazel sticks—shredding some scraps of green vegetables into a pot of broth that swung from the iron hook of the chimney. The other woman, Mally, was doing something in the dark crib of a sleeping-room, shut off from the living-room by a wooden partition like the stanchion-board of a stable. The boy was asleep; his soft breathing came from the dark crib.

"Mrs. Kerruish," said the Deemster, "I am willing to take the lad, and rear him, and when the time comes, to set him to business, and give him a start in life."

Mrs. Kerruish had risen stiffly from her stool, and her face was set hard.

"Think of it, woman, think of it, and don't answer in haste," said the Deemster.

"We'd have to be despard hard put to for a bite and a sup before we'd take anything from you, Deemster," said the old woman.

The Deemster's quick eyes, under the shaggy gray brows, glanced about the room. It was a place of poverty, descending to squalor. The floor was of the bare earth trodden hard, the roof was of the bare thatch, with here and there a lath pushed between the uphewn spars to keep it up, and here and there a broken patch dropping hayseed.

"You are desperate hard put to, woman," said the Deemster, and at that Mally herself came out of the sleeping-crib. Her face was thin and pale, and her bleared eyes had lost their sharp light; it was a countenance without one ray of hope.

"Stop, mother," she said; "let us hear what the Deemster has to offer."

"Offer? Offer?" the old woman rapped out; "you've had enough of the Deemster's offers, I'm thinking."

"Be quiet, mother," said Mally, and then she turned to the Deemster and said, "Well, sir, and what is it?"

"Aw, very nate and amazing civil to dirks like that—go on, girl, go on," said the old woman, tossing her head and hand in anger toward Mally.

"Mother, this is my concern, I'm thinking—what is it, sir?"

But the old woman's wrath at her daughter's patience was not to be kept down. "Behold ye!" she said, "it's my own girl that's after telling me before strangers that I've not a farthing at me, and me good for nothing at working, and only fit to hobble about on a stick, and fix the house tidy maybe, and to have no say in nothing—go on, och, go on, girl."

The Deemster explained his proposal. It was that the boy Jarvis should be given entirely into his control, and be no more known by his mother and his mother's mother, and perhaps no more seen or claimed or acknowledged by them, and that the Deemster should provide for him and see him started in life.

Mrs. Kerruish's impatience knew no bounds. "My gough!" she cried—"my gough, my gough!" But Mally listened and reflected. Her spirit was broken, and she was thinking of her poverty. Her mother was now laid aside by rheumatism, and could earn nothing, and she herself worked piecework at the net-making—so much for a piece of net, a hundred yards long by two hundred meshes deep, toiling without heart from eight to eight, and earning four, five, and six shillings a week. And if there was a want, her boy felt it. She did not answer at once, and after a moment the Deemster turned to the door. "Think of it," he said; "think of it."

"Hurroo! hurroo!" cried the old woman, derisively, from her stool, her untamable soul aflame with indignation.

"Be quiet, mother," said Mally, and the hopelessness that had spoken from her eyes seemed then to find a way into her voice.

The end of it was that Jarvis Kerruish was sent to a school at Liverpool, and remained there three years, and then became a clerk in the counting-house of Benas Brothers, of the Goree Piazza, ostensibly African merchants, really English money-lenders. Jarvis did not fret at the loss of his mother, and of course he never wrote to her; but he addressed a careful letter to the Deemster twice a year, beginning "Honored Sir," and ending "Yours, with much respect, most obediently."

Mally had miscalculated her self-command. If she had thought of her poverty, it had been because she had thought of her boy as well. He would be lifted above it all if she could but bring herself to part with him. She wrought up her feelings to the sacrifice, and gave away her son, and sat down as a broken-spirited and childless woman. Then she realized the price she had to pay. The boy had been the cause of her shame; but he had been the centre of her pride as well. If she had been a hopeless woman before, she was now a heartless one. Little by little she fell into habits of idleness and intemperance. Before young Jarvis sat in his frilled shirt on the stool in the Goree Piazza, and before the down had begun to show on his lean cheeks, his mother was a lost and abandoned woman.

But not yet had the Deemster broken his fate. When Ewan disappointed his hopes and went into the Church, and married without his sanction or knowledge, it seemed to him that the chain was gradually tightening about him. Then the Deemster went over once more to the cottage at the Cross Vein, alone, and in the night.

"Mrs. Kerruish," he said, "I am willing to allow you six pounds a year pension, and I will pay it in three pound notes on Lady Day and Martinmas," and putting his first payment on the table he turned about and was gone before the rheumatic old body could twist in her chair.

The Deemster had just made his third visit to the cottage at the Cross Vein, and left his second payment, when the death of Ewan's young wife came as a thunderbolt and startled him to the soul. For days and nights thereafter he went about like a beaten horse, trembling to the very bone. He had resisted the truth for twenty years; he had laughed at it in his long lingering laugh at going to bed at night and at rising in the morning; he had ridiculed superstition in others, and punished it when he could; he was the judge of the island, and she through whose mouth his fate fell upon him was a miserable ruin cast aside on life's highway; but the truth would be resisted no longer: the house over his head was accursed—accursed to him, and to his children, and to his children's children.

The Deemster's engrossing idea became a dominating terror. Was there no way left to him to break the fate that hung over him? None? The Deemster revolved the problem night and day, and meantime lived the life of the damned. At length he hit on a plan, and then peace seemed to come to him, a poor paltering show of peace, and he went about no longer like a beaten and broken horse. His project was a strange one; it was the last that prudence would have suggested, but the first that the evil spirit of his destiny could have hoped for—it was to send to Liverpool for Jarvis Kerruish, and establish him in Ballamona as his son.

In that project the hand of his fate was strongly upon him; he could not resist it; he seemed to yield himself to its power; he made himself its willing victim; he was even as Saul when the Spirit of the Lord had gone from him and an evil spirit troubled him, sending for the anointed son of Jesse to play on the harp to him and to supplant him on the throne.

CHAPTER XV
THE LIE THAT EWAN TOLD

It was not for long that Dan bore the signs of contrition. As soon as Ewan's pale face had lost the weight of its gloom, Dan's curly poll knew no more trouble. He followed the herrings all through that season, grew brown with the sun and the briny air, and caught the sea's laughter in his rollicking voice. He drifted into some bad habits from which he had hitherto held himself in check. Every morning when the boats ran into harbor, and Teare, the mate, and Crennel, the cook, stayed behind to sell the fish, Dan and old Billy Quilleash trooped up to the "Three Legs of Man" together. There Dan was made much of, and the lad's spirit was not proof against the poor flattery. It was Mastha Dan here, and Mastha Dan there, and Where is Mastha Dan? and What does Mastha Dan say? and great shoutings, and tearings, and sprees; and all the time the old cat with the whiskers who kept the pot-house was scoring up against Dan at the back of the cupboard door.

Did the Bishop know? Know? Did ever a young fellow go to the dogs but some old woman of either sex found her way to the very ear that ought not to be tormented with Job's comfort, and whisper, "Aw, dear! aw, dear!" and "Lawk-a-day!" and "I'm the last to bring bad newses, as the saying is," and "Och, and it's a pity, and him a fine, brave young fellow too!" and "I wouldn't have told it on no account to another living soul!"

The Bishop said little, and tried not to hear; but when Dan would have hoodwinked him, he saw through the device as the sun sees through glass. Dan never left his father's presence without a sense of shame that was harder to bear than any reproach would have been. Something patient and trustful, and strong in hope, and stronger in love, seemed to go out from the Bishop's silence to Dan's reticence. Dan would slink off with the bearing of a whipped hound, or perhaps, with a muttered curse under his teeth, and always with a stern resolve to pitch himself or his cronies straightway into the sea. The tragical purpose usually lasted him over the short mile and a half that divided Bishop's Court from the "Three Legs of Man," and then it went down with some other troubles and a long pint of Manx jough.

Of all men, the most prompt to keep the Bishop informed of Dan's sad pranks was no other than the Deemster. Since the death of Ewan's wife the

Deemster's feelings toward Dan had undergone a complete change. From that time forward he looked on Dan with eyes of distrust, amounting in its intensity to hatred. He forbade him his house, though Dan laughed at the prohibition and ignored it. He also went across to Bishop's Court for the first time for ten years, and poured into the Bishop's ears the story of every bad bit of business in which Dan got involved. Dan kept him fully employed in this regard, and Bishop's Court saw the Deemster at frequent intervals.

If it was degrading to the Bishop's place as father of the Church that his son should consort with all the "ragabash" of the island, the scum of the land, and the dirtiest froth of the sea, the Bishop was made to know the full bitterness of that degradation. He would listen with head held down, and when the Deemster, passing from remonstrance to reproach, would call upon him to set his own house in order before he ever ascended the pulpit again, the Bishop would lift his great heavy eyes with an agonizing look of appeal, and answer in a voice like a sob, "Have patience, Thorkell—have patience with the lad; he is my son, my only son."

It chanced that toward the end of the herring season an old man of eighty, one William Callow, died, and he was the captain of the parish of Michael. The captaincy was a semi-civil, semi-military office, and it included the functions of parish head-constable. Callow had been a a man of extreme probity, and his walk in life had been without a slip.

"The ould man's left no living craythur to fill his shoes," the people said when they buried him, but when the name of the old man's successor came down from Castletown, who should be the new captain but Daniel Mylrea? The people were amazed, the Deemster laughed in his throat, and Dan himself looked appalled.

Hardly a month after this event, the relations of Dan and the Deemster, and Dan and the Bishop, reached a climax.

For months past the Bishop had been hatching a scheme for the subdivision of his episcopal glebe, the large extent of which had long been a burden on the dwindling energies of his advancing age; and he had determined that, since his son was not to be a minister of the Church, he should be its tenant, and farm its lands. So he cut off from the demesne a farm of eighty acres of fine Curragh land, well drained and tilled. This would be a stay and a solid source of livelihood to Dan when the herring fishing had ceased to be a pastime. There was no farmhouse on the eighty acres, but barns and stables were to be erected, and Dan was to share with Ewan the old Ballamona as a home.

Dan witnessed these preparations, but entered into them with only a moderate enthusiasm. The reason of his lukewarmness was that he found himself deeply involved in debts whereof his father knew nothing. When the fishing season finished and the calculations were made, it was found that the boat had earned no more than £240. Of this, old Billy Quilleash took four shares, every man took two shares, there was a share set aside for Davy, the boy, and the owner was entitled to eight shares for himself, his nets, and his boat. So far, all was reasonably satisfactory. The difficulty and dissatisfaction arose when Dan began to count the treasury. Then it was discovered that there was not enough in hand to pay old Billy and his men and the boy, leaving Dan's eight shares out of the count Dan scratched his head and pondered. He was not brilliant at figures, but he totted up his numbers again with the same result. Then he computed the provisioning—tea, at four shillings a pound, besides fresh meat four times a week, and fine flour biscuits. It was heavy, but not ruinous, and the season had been poor, but not bad, and whatever the net results, there ought not to have been a deficit where the principle of cooperation between master and man was that of share and share.

Dan began to see his way through the mystery—it was most painfully transparent in the light of the score that had been chalked up from time to time on the inside of the cupboard of the "Three Legs of Man." But it was easier to see where the money had gone than to make it up, and old Billy and his chums began to mutter and to grumble.

"It's raely wuss till ever," said one.

"The tack we've been on hasn't been worth workin'," said another.

Dan heard their murmurs, and went up to Bishop's Court. After all, the deficit was only forty pounds, and his father would lend him that much. But hardly had Dan sat down to breakfast than the Bishop, who was clearly in lower spirits than usual, began to lament that his charities to the poor had been interrupted by the cost of building the barns and stables on the farm intended for his son.

"I hope your fishing will turn out well, Dan," he said, "for I've scarce a pound in hand to start you."

So Dan said nothing about the debt, and went back to the fisher-fellows with a face as long as a haddock's. "I'll tell you, men, the storm is coming," he said.

Old Billy looked as black as thunder, and answered with an impatient gesture, "Then keep your weather eye liftin', that's all."

Dan measured the old salt from head to foot, and hitched his hand into his guernsey. "You wouldn't talk to me like that, Billy Quilleash, if I hadn't been a fool with you. It's a true saying, that when you tell your servant your secret you make him your master."

Old Billy sniggered, and his men snorted. Billy wanted to know why he had left Kinvig's boat, where he had a sure thirty pounds for his season; and Ned Teare wished to be told what his missus would say when he took her five pound ten; and Crennel, the slushy, asked what sort of a season the mastha was aftha callin' it, at all, at all.

Not a man of them remembered his share of the long scores chalked up on the inside of the cupboard door.

"Poor old dad," thought Dan, "he must find the money after all—no way but that," and once again he turned toward Bishop's Court.

Billy Quilleash saw him going off, and followed him. "I've somethin' terrible fine up here," said Billy, tapping his forehead mysteriously.

"What is it?" Dan asked.

"Och, a shockin' powerful schame. It'll get you out of the shoal water anyways," said Billy.

It turned out that the "shockin' powerful schame" was the ancient device of borrowing the money from a money-lender. Old Billy knew the very man to serve the turn. His name was Kisseck, and he kept the "Jolly Herrings" in Peeltown, near the bottom of the crabbed little thoroughfare that wound and twisted and descended to that part of the quay which overlooked the castle rock.

"No, no; that'll not do," said Dan.

"Aw, and why not at all?"

"Why not? Why not? Because it's blank robbery to borrow what you can't pay back."

"Robbery? Now, what's the use of sayin' the like o' that? Aw, the shockin' notions! Well, well, and do you raely think a person's got no feelin's? Robbery? Aw, well now, well now."

And old Billy tramped along with the air of an injured man.

But the end of it was that Dan said nothing to the Bishop that day, and the same night found him at the "Jolly Herrings." The landlord had nothing to lend, not he, but he knew people who would not mind parting with money on good security, or on anybody's bail, as the sayin' was. Couldn't Mastha Dan get a good man's name to a bit o' paper, like? Coorse he could, and nothing easier, for a gen'l'man same as him. Who was the people? They belonged to Liverpool, the Goree Peaizy—Benas they were callin' them.

Three days afterward the forty pounds, made up to fifty for round numbers, came to Kisseck, the landlord, and the bit o' paper came with it. Dan took the paper and went off with it to the old Ballamona. Ewan would go bail for him, and so the Bishop need know nothing of the muddle. But when Dan reached his new home Ewan was away—a poor old Quaker named Christian, who had brought himself to beggary by neglecting Solomon's injunction against suretyship, was dying, and had sent for the parson.

Dan was in a hurry; the fisher-fellows were grumbling, and their wives were hanging close about their coat-tails; the money must be got without delay, and of course Ewan would sign for it straight-away if he were there. An idea struck Dan, and made the sweat to start from his forehead. He had put the paper on the table and taken up a pen, when he heard Ewan's voice outside, and then he threw the pen down and his heart leaped with a sense of relief.

Ewan came in, and rattled on about old Christian, the Quaker. He hadn't a week to live, poor old soul, and he hadn't a shilling left in the world. Once he farmed his hundred acres, but he had stood surety for this man and surety for that man, and paid up the defalcations of both, and now, while they were eating the bread of luxury, he was dying as a homeless pauper.

"Well, he has been practising a bad virtue," said Ewan. "I wouldn't stand surety for my own brother—not for my own brother if I had one. It would be helping him to eat to-day the bread he earns to-morrow."

Dan went out without saying anything of the bit of paper from Liverpool. The fisher-fellows met him, and when they heard what he had to say their grumblings broke out again.

"Well, I'm off for the Bishop—and no disrespec'," said old Billy.

He did not go; the bit o' paper was signed, but not by Ewan; the money was paid; the grateful sea-dogs were sent home with their wages in their pockets and a smart cuff on either ear.

A month or two went by, and Dan grew quiet and thoughtful, and sometimes gloomy, and people began to say, "It's none so wild the young mastha is at all, at all," or perhaps, "Wonderful studdy he's growing," or even, "I wouldn't trust but he'll turn out a parson after all." One day in

November Dan went over to new Ballamona and asked for Mona, and sat with her in earnest talk. He told her of some impending disaster, and she listened with a whitening face.

From that day forward Mona was a changed woman. She seemed to share some great burden of fear with Dan, and it lay heavy upon her, and made the way of life very long and cheerless to the sweet and silent girl.

Toward the beginning of December, sundry letters came out of their season from the young clerk of Benas Brothers, Jarvis Kerruish. Then the Deemster went over more than once to Bishop's Court, and had grave interviews with the Bishop.

"If you can prove this that you say, Thorkell, I shall turn my back on him forever—yes, forever," said the Bishop, and his voice was husky and his sad face was seamed with lines of pain.

A few days passed and a stranger appeared at Ballamona, and when the stranger had gone the Deemster said to Mona, "Be ready to go to Bishop's Court with me in the morning."

Mona's breath seemed to be suddenly arrested. "Will Ewan be there?" she asked.

"Yes—isn't it the day of his week-day service at the chapel—Wednesday—isn't it?"

"And Dan?" she said.

"Dan? Why Dan? Well, woman, perhaps Dan too—who knows?"

The Bishop had sent across to the old Ballamona to say that he wished to see his son in the library after service on the following morning.

At twelve next day, Dan, who had been plowing, turned in at Bishop's Court in his long boots and rough red shirt, and there in the library he found Mona and the Deemster seated. Mona did not speak when Dan spoke to her. Her voice seemed to fail; but the Deemster answered in a jaunty word or two; and then the Bishop, looking very thoughtful, came in with Ewan, whose eyes were brighter than they had been for many a day, and behind them walked the stranger whom Mona had seen at Ballamona the day before.

"Why, and how's this?" said Ewan, on perceiving that so many of them were gathered there.

The Bishop closed the door, and then answered, with averted face, "We have a painful interview before us, Ewan—be seated."

It was a dark day; the clouds hung low, and the dull rumble of the sea came through the dead air. A fire of logs and peat burned on the hearth, and the Deemster rose and stood with his back to it, his hands interlaced behind him. The Bishop sat on his brass-clamped chair at the table, and rested his pale cheek on his hand. There was a pause, and then without lifting his eyes the Bishop said, "Ewan, do you know that it is contrary to the customs of the Church for a minister to stand security for a debtor?"

Ewan was standing by the table, fumbling the covers of a book that he had lifted. "I know it," he said, quietly.

"Do you know that the minister who disregards that custom stands liable to suspension at the hands of his Bishop?"

Ewan looked about with a stare of bewilderment, but he answered again, and as quietly, "I know it."

There was silence for a moment, and then the Deemster, clearing his throat noisily, turned to where Dan was pawing up a rug that lay under a column and bust of Bunyan.

"And do you know, sir," said the Deemster, in his shrill tones, "what the punishment of forgery may be?"

Dan's face had undergone some changes during the last few minutes, but when he lifted it to the Deemster's, it was as firm as a rock.

"Hanging, perhaps," he answered, sullenly; "transportation, perhaps. What of it? Out with it—be quick."

Dan's eyes flashed; the Deemster tittered audibly; the Bishop looked up at his son from under the rims of his spectacles and drew a long breath. Mona had covered her face in her hands where she sat in silence by the ingle, and Ewan, still fumbling the book in his nervous fingers, was glancing from Dan to the Deemster, and from the Bishop to Dan, with a look of blank amazement.

The Deemster motioned to the stranger, who thereupon advanced from where he had stood by the door, and stepped up to Ewan.

"May I ask if this document was drawn by your authority?" and saying this the stranger held out a paper, and Ewan took it in his listless fingers.

There was a moment's silence. Ewan glanced down at the document. It showed that fifty pounds had been lent to Daniel Mylrea, by Benas Brothers, of the Goree Piazza, Liverpool, and it was signed by Ewan's own name as that of surety.

"Is that your signature?" asked the stranger.

Ewan glanced at Dan, and Dan's head was on his breast and his lips quivered. The Bishop was trembling visibly, and sat with head bent low by the sorrow of a wrecked and shattered hope.

The stranger looked from Ewan to Dan, and from Dan to the Bishop. The Deemster gazed steadily before him, and his face wore a ghostly smile.

"Is it your signature?" repeated the stranger, and his words fell on the silence like the clank of a chain.

Ewan saw it all now. He glanced again at the document, but his eyes were dim, and he could read nothing. Then he lifted his face, and its lines of agony told of a terrible struggle.

"Yes," he answered, "the signature *is* mine—what of it?"

At that the Bishop and Mona raised their eyes together. The stranger looked incredulous.

"It is quite right if you say so," the stranger replied, with a cold smile.

Ewan trembled in every limb. "I do say so," he said.

His fingers crumpled the document as he spoke, but his head was erect, and the truth seemed to sit on his lips. Dan dropped heavily into a chair and buried his face in his hands.

The stranger smiled again the same cold smile. "The lenders wish to withdraw the loan," he said.

"They may do so—in a month," said Ewan.

"That will suffice."

The Deemster's face twitched; Mona's cheeks were wet with tears; the Bishop had risen and gone to the window, and was gazing out through blurred eyes into the blinding rain that was now pelting against the glass.

"It would be cruel to prolong a painful interview," said the stranger; and then, with a glance toward Dan where he sat convulsed with distress that he made no effort to conceal, he added, in a hard tone:

"Only the lenders came to have reasons to fear that perhaps the document had been drawn without your knowledge."

Ewan handed the paper back with a nerveless hand. He looked at the stranger through swimming eyes and said gently, but with an awful inward effort, "You have my answer, sir—I knew of it."

The stranger bowed and went out. Dan leaped to his feet and threw his arms about Ewan's neck, but dared not to look into his troubled face. Mona covered her eyes and sobbed.

The Deemster picked up his hat to go, and in passing out he paused in front of Ewan and said, in a bitter whisper:

"Fool! fool! You have taken this man's part to your own confusion."

When the door closed behind the Deemster the Bishop turned from the window. "Ewan," he said, in a voice like a cry, "the Recording Angel has set down the lie you have told to-day in the Book of Life to your credit in heaven."

Then the Bishop paused, and Dan lifted his head from Ewan's neck.

"As for you, sir," the Bishop added, turning to his son, "I am done with you forever—go from me—let me see your face no more."

Dan went out of the room with bended head.

CHAPTER XVI
THE PLOWING MATCH

When Ewan got back home there was Dan sitting before the fire in the old hall, his legs stretched out before him, his hands thrust deep in his pockets, his head low in his breast, and his whole mien indicative of a crushed and broken spirit. He glanced up furtively as Ewan entered, and then back with a stony stare to the fire. If Ewan had then given him one word of cheer, God knows what tragic consequences would have been spared to them both. But Ewan had saved Dan from the penalty of his crime at the cost of truth and his self-esteem.

"Dan," he said, "you and I must part—we can be friends no longer."

He spoke with a strong effort, and the words seemed to choke him. Dan shambled to his feet; he appeared to collect his thoughts for a moment, like one who had fainted and returns to consciousness.

"Mind—I don't turn you out of the house," said Ewan, "only if we are to share this place together we must be strangers."

A hard smile broke out on Dan's face. He seemed to be trying to speak, but not a word would come. He twisted slowly on his heel, and lifted the latch of the door that led to the inner part of the house.

"One thing more," said Ewan, speaking quickly, and in a tremulous voice, "I will ask you to look upon yourself as a stranger to my sister also."

Dan stopped and turned about. Over the forced smile his hard face told of a great struggle for self-command. He said nothing, and after a moment he went out, drawing his breath audibly.

Then straightway Ewan flung himself into the chair from which Dan had risen, and his slight frame shook with suppressed sobs. After some minutes the sense of his own degradation diminished, and left room for a just idea of Dan's abject humiliation. "I have gone too far," he thought; "I will make amends." He had risen to follow Dan, when another thought trod heavily on the heels of the first. "Leave him alone, it will be best for himself—leave him alone, for his own sake." And so, with the madness of wrath fermenting in his own brain, he left it to ferment in Dan's brain as well.

Now, when Dan found himself left alone he tried to carry off his humiliation by a brave show of unconcern. He stayed on at the old Ballamona, but he never bothered himself—not he, forsooth—to talk to folks who passed him on the stairs without a word of greeting, or met in the hall without a glance of recognition.

It chanced just then that, in view of a threatened invasion, the authorities were getting up a corps of volunteers, known as the Manx Fencibles, and that they called on the captains of the parishes to establish companies. Dan threw himself into this enterprise with uncommon vigor, took drills himself, acquired a competent knowledge of the rudiments in a twinkling, and forthwith set himself to band together the young fellows of his parish. It was just the sort of activity that Dan wanted at the moment, and in following it up the "Three Legs" saw him something oftener than before, and there the fellows of the baser sort drank and laughed with him, addressing him sometimes as captain, but oftener as Dan, never troubling themselves a ha'p'orth to put a handle to his name.

This was a turn of events which Ewan could not understand. "I have been mistaken in the man," he thought; "there's no heart left in him."

Toward the middle of December Jarvis Kerruish arrived at Ballamona, and forthwith established himself there in a position that would have been proper to the Deemster's heir. He was a young man of medium height and size, closely resembling the Deemster in face and figure. His dress was English: he wore a close-fitting undercoat with tails, and over it a loose cloak mounted with a brass buckle at the throat; he had a beaver hat of the shape of a sugar-loaf; and boots that fitted to his legs like gloves. His manner was expansive, and he betrayed a complete unconsciousness of the sinister bar of his birth, and of the false position he had taken up in the Deemster's house. He showed no desire to visit the cottage at the Cross Vein; and he spoke of the poor with condescension. When he met with Ewan he displayed no uneasiness, and Ewan on his part gave no sign of resentment. Mona, on the other hand, betrayed an instinctive repulsion, and in less than a week from his coming their relations had reached an extraordinary crisis, which involved Ewan and Dan and herself in terrible consequences. This is what occurred:

On the day before Christmas Day there was to be a plowing match in a meadow over the Head, and Ewan stood pledged by an old promise to act as judge. The day came, and it was a heavy day, with snow-clouds hanging overhead, and misty vapors floating down from the hills and up from the Curraghs, and hiding them. At ten in the morning Mona muffled herself in a great cloak, and went over to the meadow with Ewan. There a crowd had already gathered, strong men in blue pilots, old men in sheepskin coats, women with their short blue camblet gowns tucked over their linen caps, boys and girls on every side, all coming and going like shadows in the mist. At one end of the meadow several pairs of horses stood yoked to plows, and a few lads were in charge of them. On Ewan's arrival there was a general movement among a group of men standing together, and a respectful salutation to the parson. The names were called over of the plowmen who had entered for the prize—a pound note and a cup—and last of all, there was a show of hands for the election of six men to form a jury.

Then the stretch was staked out. The prize was to the plowman who would make the stretch up and down the meadow in the shortest time, cutting the furrows straightest, cleanest, and of the most regular depth.

When all was ready, Ewan took up his station where the first furrow would be cut into the field, with Mona at his side, and the six jurors about him. The first plowman to bring up his plow was a brawny young fellow with a tanned face. The plowman had brought up his horses in front of the stake, and had laid hands on his plow-handles, and was measuring the stretch with his eye for a landmark to sight by, when Jarvis Kerruish came into the meadow, and walked through the crowd, and took up a place by Mona's side. There were audible comments, and some racy exclamations as he pushed through the crowd, not lifting an eye to any face; but he showed complete indifference, and began to talk to Mona in a loud, measured tone.

"Ah! this is very gratifying," he was saying, "to see the peasantry engaged in manly sports—useful sports—is, I confess, very gratifying to me."

"My gough!" said a voice from one side.

"Hurroo!" said a voice from the other side.

"Lawk-a-day!" came from behind, in a shrill female treble. "Did ye ever see a grub turn butterfly?"

Jarvis seemed not to hear. "Now there *are* sports—" he began; but the plowman was shouting to his horses, "Steady, steady," the plow was dipping into the succulent grass, the first swish of the upturned soil was in the air, and Jarvis's wise words were lost.

All eyes were on the bent back of the plowman plodding on in the mist. "He cuts like a razor," said one of the spectators. "He bears his hand too much on," said another. "Do better yourself next spell," said a third.

When the horses reached the far end of the stretch the plowman whipped them round like the turn of a wheel, and in another moment he was toiling back, steadily, firmly, his hand rigid, and his face set hard. When he got back to where Ewan, with his watch in his hand, stood surrounded by the jurors, he was covered with sweat. "Good, very good—six minutes ten seconds," said Ewan, and there were some plaudits from the people looking on, and some banter of the competitors who came up to follow.

Jarvis Kerruish, at Mona's elbow, was beginning again, "I confess that it has always been my personal opinion—" but in the bustle of another pair of horses whipped up to the stake no one seemed to be aware that he was speaking.

Five plowmen came in succession, but all were behind the first in time and cut a less regular furrow. So Ewan and the jurors announced that the prize was to the stranger. Then as Ewan twisted about, his adjudication finished, to where Mona stood with Jarvis by her side, there was a general rush of competitors and spectators to a corner of the meadow, where, from a little square cart, the buirdly stranger who was victor proceeded to serve out glasses of ale from a small barrel.

While this was going on, and there was some laughter and shouting and singing, there came a loud "Hello," as of many voices from a little distance, and then the beat of many irregular feet, and one of the lads in the crowd, who had jumped to the top of the broad turf hedge, shouted, "It's the capt'n—it's Mastha Dan."

In another half-minute, Dan and some fifty or sixty of the scum of the parish came tumbling into the meadow on all sides—over the hedge, over the gate, and tearing through the gaps in the gorse. They were the corps that Dan had banded together toward the Manx Fencibles, but the only regimentals they yet wore were a leather belt, and the only implement of war they yet carried was the small dagger that was fitted into the belt. That morning they had been drilling, and after drill they had set off to see the plowing match, and on the way they had passed the "Three Legs," and being exceeding dry, they had drawn up in front thereof, and every man had been served with a glass, which had been duly scored off to the captain's account.

Dan saw Mona with Ewan as he vaulted the gate, but he gave no sign of recognition, and in a moment he was in the thick of the throng at the side of the cart, hearing all about the match, and making loud comments upon it in his broadest homespun.

"What!" he said, "and you've let yourselves be bate by a craythur like that. Hurroo!"

He strode up to the stranger's furrow, cocked his eye along it, and then glanced at the stranger's horses.

"Och, I'll go bail I'll bate it with a yoke of oxen."

At that there was a movement of the crowd around him, and some cheering, just to egg on the rupture that was imminent.

The big stranger heard all, and strode through the people with a face like a thunder-cloud.

"Who says he'll bate it with a yoke of oxen?" he asked.

"That's just what I'm afther saying, my fine fellow. Have you anything agen it?"

In half a minute a wager had been laid of a pound a side that Dan, with a pair of oxen, would beat the stranger with a pair of horses in two stretches out of three.

"Davy! Davy!" shouted Dan, and in a twinkling there was Davy Fayle, looking queer enough in his guernsey, and his long boots, and his sea-cap, and withal his belt and his dagger. Davy was sent for a pair of oxen to where they were leading manure, not far away. He went off like a shot, and in ten minutes he was back in the meadow, driving the oxen before him.

Now, these oxen had been a gift of the Bishop to Dan. They were old, and had grown wise with their years. For fifteen years they had worked on the glebe at Bishop's Court, and they knew the dinner hour as well as if they could have taken the altitude of the sun. When the dinner bell rang at the Court at twelve o'clock, the oxen would stop short, no matter where they were or what they were doing, and not another budge would they make until they had been unyoked and led off for their midday mash.

It was now only a few minutes short of twelve, but no one took note of that circumstance, and the oxen were yoked to a plow.

"Same judge and jury," said the stranger, but Ewan excused himself.

"Aw, what matter about a judge," said Dan, from his plow-handles; "let the jury be judge as well."

Ewan and Mona looked on in silence for some moments. Ewan could scarce contain himself. There was Dan, stripped to his red flannel shirt, his face tanned and glowing, his whole body radiant with fresh life and health, and he was shouting and laughing as if there had never been a shadow to darken his days.

"Look at him," whispered Ewan, with emotion, in Mona's ear. "Look! this good-nature that seems so good to others is almost enough to make me hate him."

Mona was startled, and turned to glance into Ewan's face.

"Come, let us go," said Ewan, with head aside.

"Not yet," said Mona.

Then Jarvis Kerruish, who had stepped aside for a moment, returned and said:

"Will you take a wager with me, Mona—a pair of gloves?"

"Very well," she answered.

"Who do you bet on?"

"Oh, on the stranger," said Mona, coloring slightly, and laughing a little.

"How lucky," said Jarvis, "I bet on the captain."

"I can stand it no longer," whispered Ewan, "will you come?" But Mona's eyes were riveted on the group about the oxen. She did not hear, and Ewan turned away, and walked out of the meadow.

Then there was a shout, and the oxen started with Dan behind them. On they went through the hard, tough ground, tranquilly, steadily, with measured pace, tearing through roots of trees that lay in their way as if nothing could stop them in their great strength.

When the oxen got back after the first stretch the time was called—five minutes thirty seconds—and there was a great cheer, and Mona's pale face was triumphant.

The stranger brought up his horses, and set off again, straining every muscle. He did his stretch in six minutes four seconds, and another cheer—but it was a cheer for Dan—went up after the figures were called.

Then Dan whipped round his oxen once more, and brought them up to the stake. The excitement among the people was now very great. Mona clutched her cloak convulsively, and held her breath. Jarvis was watching her closely, and she knew that his cold eyes were on her face.

"One would almost imagine that you were anxious to lose your bet," he said. She made no answer. When the oxen started again her lips closed tightly, as if she was in pain.

On the oxen went, and made the first half of the stretch without a hitch, and, with the blade of the plow lifted, they were wheeling over the furrow end, when a bell rang across the Curragh—it was the bell for the midday meal at Bishop's Court—and instantly they came to a dead stand. Dan called to them, but they did not budge; then his whip fell heavily across their snouts, and they snorted, but stirred not an inch. The people were in a tumult, and shouted with fifty voices at once. Dan's passion mastered him. He brought his whip down over the flanks and across the eyes and noses of the oxen; they winced under the blows that rained down on them, and then shot away across the meadow, tearing up the furrows they had made.

Then there was a cry of vexation and anger from the people, and Dan, who had let go his reins, strode back to the stake. "I've lost," said Dan, with a muttered oath at the oxen.

All this time Jarvis Kerruish had kept his eye steadily fixed on Mona's twitching face. "You've won, Mona," he said, in a cold voice and with an icy smile.

"I must go. Where is Ewan?" she said, tremulously, and before Jarvis was aware she had gone over the grass.

Dan had heard when Ewan declined to act as judge, he had seen when Ewan left the meadow, and, though he did not look, he knew when Mona was no longer there. His face was set hard, and it glowed red under his sunburned skin.

"Davy, bring them up," he said; and Davy Fayle led back the oxen to the front of the stake.

Then Dan unyoked them, took out the long swinging tree that divided them—a heavy wooden bar clamped with iron—and they stood free and began to nibble the grass under their feet.

"Look out!" he shouted, and he swung the bar over his shoulder.

The crowd receded and left an open space in which Dan stood alone with the oxen, his great limbs holding the ground like their own hoofs, his muscles standing out like bulbs on his bare arms.

"What is he going to do—kill them?" said one.

"Look out!" Dan shouted again, and in another moment there was the swish of the bar through the air. Then down the bar came on the forehead of one of the oxen, and it reeled, and its legs gave way, and it fell dead.

The bar was raised again, and again it fell, and the second of the oxen reeled like the first and fell dead beside its old yoke-fellow.

A cry of horror ran through the crowd, but heeding it not at all, Dan threw on his coat and buckled his belt about him, and strode through the people and out at the gate.

CHAPTER XVII
THE WRONG WAY WITH DAN

What happened next was one of those tragedies of bewildering motive, so common and so fatal, in which it is impossible to decide whether evil passion or evil circumstances plays the chief malicious part.

Dan walked straight to the new Ballamona, and pushed through the house without ceremony, as it had been his habit to do in other days, to the room where Mona was to be found. She was there, and she looked startled at his coming.

"Is it you, Dan?" she said, in a tremulous whisper.

He answered sullenly:

"It is I. I have come to speak with you. I have something to say—but no matter—"

He stopped and threw himself into a chair. His head ached, his eyes were hot, and his mind seemed to him to be in darkness and confusion.

"Mona, I think I must be going mad," he stammered after a moment.

"Why talk like that?" she said. Her bosom heaved and her face was troubled.

He did not answer, but after a pause turned toward her, and said in a quick, harsh tone, "You did not expect to see me here, and you have been forbidden to receive me. Is it not so?"

She colored deeply, and did not answer at once, and then she began, with hesitation:

"My father—it is true, my father—"

"It *is* so," he said sharply. He got on to his feet and tramped about the room. After a moment he sat down again, and leaned his elbows on his knees and his head in his hands.

"But what of Ewan?" he asked.

"Ewan loves you, Dan, and you have been at fault," said Mona, in broken accents.

"At fault?"

There was a sudden change in his manner. He spoke bruskly, even mockingly, and laughed a short, grating laugh.

"They are taking the wrong way with me, Mona—that's the fact," he said, and now his breast heaved and the words came with difficulty.

Mona was gazing absently out at the window, her head aslant, her fingers interlaced before her. "Oh, Dan, Dan," she murmured in a low tone, "there is your dear, dear father, and Ewan, and—and myself—"

Dan had leapt to his feet again. "Don't turn my eyes into my head, Mona," he said.

He tramped to and fro in the room for a moment and then broke out nervously, "All last night I dreamt such an ugly dream. I dreamt it three times, and, O God! what an ugly dream it was! It was a bad night, and I was walking in the dark, and stumbling first into bogs and then in cart ruts, when all of a sudden a man's hand seized me unawares. I could not see the man, and we struggled long in the darkness, and it seemed as if he would master me. He gripped me by the waist, and I held him by the shoulders. We reeled and fell together, and when I would have risen his knee was on my chest. But a great flood of strength seemed to come to me and I threw him off, and rose to my feet and closed with him again, and at last I was over him, covering him, with his back across my thigh and my hand set hard in his throat. And all this time I heard his loud breathing in the darkness, but never once the sound of his voice. Then instantly, as if by a flash of lightning, I saw the face that was close to mine, and—God Almighty! it was my own face—my own—and it was black already from the pressure of my stiff fingers at the throat."

He trembled as he spoke, and sat again and shivered, and a cold chill ran down his back.

"Mona," he said, half in a sob, "do you believe in omens?"

She did not reply. Her breast heaved visibly, and she could not speak.

"Tush!" he said, in another voice, "omens!" and he laughed bitterly, and rose again and picked up his hat, and then said, in a quieter way, "Only, as I say, they're taking the wrong way with me, Mona."

He had opened the door, and she had turned her swimming eyes toward him.

"It was bad enough to make himself a stranger to me, but why did he want to make you a stranger, too? Stranger, stranger!" He echoed the word in a mocking accent, and threw back his head.

"Dan," said Mona, in a low, passionate tone, and the blinding tears rained down her cheeks, "nothing and nobody can make us strangers, you and me—not my father, or your dear father, or Ewan, or"—she dropped her voice to a deep whisper—"or any misfortune or any disgrace."

"Mona!" he cried, and took a step toward her, and stretched out one arm with a yearning gesture.

But at the next moment he had swung about, and was going out at the door. At sight of all that tenderness and loyalty in Mona's face his conscience smote him as it had never smitten him before.

"Ewan was right, Mona. He is the noblest man on God's earth, and I am the foulest beast on it."

He was pulling the door behind him when he encountered Jarvis Kerruish in the hall. That gentleman had just come into the house, and was passing through the hall in hat and cloak. He looked appalled at seeing Dan there, and stepped aside to let him go by; but Dan did not so much as recognize his presence by lifting his head as he strode out at the porch.

With head still bent, Dan had reached the gate to the road and pushed through it, and sent it back with a swing and a click, when the Deemster walked up to it, and half halted, and would have stopped. But Dan went moodily on, and the frown on the Deemster's wizened face was lost on him. He did not take the lane toward the old Ballamona, but followed the turnpike that led past Bishop's Court, and as he went by the large house behind the trees Ewan came through the smaller gate, and turned toward the new Ballamona. They did not speak, or even glance at each other's faces.

Dan went on until he came to the parish church. There was singing within, and he stopped. He remembered that this was Christmas Eve. The choir was practising the psalms for the morrow's services.

"Before I was troubled, I went wrong; but now have I kept Thy word."

Dan went up to the church porch, and stood there and listened.

"It is good for me that I have been in trouble, that I may learn Thy statutes."

The wooden door, clamped and barred and worm-eaten and cut by knives, was ajar, and from where he stood Dan could see into the church. There were the empty pews, the gaunt, square, green-clad boxes on which he had sat on many a Christmas Eve at Oiel Verree. He could picture the old place as it used to be in those days of his boyhood, the sea of faces, some solemn and some bubbling over with mischief, the candles with their ribbons, the old clerk, Will-as-Thorn, standing up behind the communion rail with his pitch-pipe in his hand, and Hommy-beg in his linsey-woolsey petticoat, singing lustily from a paper held upside down. The singing stopped. Behind were the hills Slieu Dhoo and Slieu Volley, hidden now under a thick veil of mist, and from across the flat Curragh there came in the silence the low moan of the sea. "Once more," said a voice within the church, and then the psalm was sung again. Dan began to breathe easier, he scarce knew why, and a great weight seemed to be lifted off his breast.

As he turned away from the porch a heavy web of cloud was sweeping on and sweeping on from over the sea. He looked up and saw that a snow-storm was coming, and that the snow-cloud would break when it reached the mountains.

The clock in the gray tower was striking—one—two—three—so it was now three o'clock. Dan went down toward the creek known as the Lockjaw, under Orris Head. There he expected to see old Billy Quilleash and his mates, who had liberty to use the "Ben-my-Chree" during the winter months for fishing with the lines. When he got to the creek it was an hour after high water, and the lugger, with Quilleash and Teare, had gone out for cod. Davy Fayle, who, like Dan himself, was still wearing his militia belt and dagger, had been doing something among scraps of net and bits of old rope, which lay in a shed that the men had thrown together for the storing of their odds-and-ends.

Davy was looking out to sea. Down there a stiff breeze was blowing, and the white curves of the breakers outside could just be seen through the thick atmosphere.

"The storm is coming, Mastha Dan," said Davy. "See the diver on the top of the white wave out there! D'ye hear her wild note?"

Davy shaded his eyes from the wind, which was blowing from the sea, and looked up at the stormy petrel that was careering over the head of the cliff above them and uttering its dismal cry: "Ay, and d'ye see Mother Carey's chickens up yonder?" said Davy again. "The storm's coming, and wonderful quick too."

Truly, a storm was coming, and it was a storm more terrible than wind and snow.

CHAPTER XVIII
THE BLIND WOMAN'S SECOND SIGHT

Now, when Jarvis Kerruish encountered Dan in the act of coming out of Mona's room, his surprise was due to something more than the knowledge that Dan had been forbidden the house. On leaving the meadow after the plowing match, and the slaughter of the oxen that followed it, Jarvis had made a long circuit of the Curragh, and returned to Ballamona by the road. He had been pondering on Mona's deportment during the exciting part of the contest between Dan and the stranger, and had just arrived at obvious conclusions of his own by way of explaining the emotion that she could not conceal, when he recognized that he was approaching the cottage occupied by Hommy-beg and his wife Kerry. A droning voice came from within, accompanied by some of the most doleful wails that ever arrested mortal ears.

Jarvis was prompted to stop and enter. He did so, and found both the deaf husband and the blind wife at home. Hommy was squatting on a low three-legged stool, with his fiddle at his shoulder, playing vigorously and singing as he played. It was Christmas Eve to Hommy-beg also, and he was practising the carol that he meant to sing at the Oiel Verree that night. Blind Kerry was sitting by the fire knitting with gray yarn. The deaf man's eyes and the blind woman's ears simultaneously announced the visit of Jarvis, and as Hommy-beg dropped his fiddle from his shoulder, Kerry let fall the needles on her lap, and held up her hand with an expression of concern.

"Och, and didn't I say that something was happening at Ballamona?" said Kerry.

"And so she did," said Hommy-Beg.

"I knew it," said Kerry. "I knew it, as the sayin' is."

All this in return for Jarvis's casual visit and mere salutation surprised him.

"The sight! The sight! It's as true as the ould Book itself. Aw, yes, aw, yes," continued Kerry, and she began to wring her hands.

Jarvis felt uneasy. "Do you know, my good people," he said, largely, "I'm at a loss to understand what you mean. What is it that has happened at Ballamona?"

At that the face of the blind wife looked puzzled.

"Have ye not come from Ballamona straight?" she asked.

"No—it's four hours since I left there," said Jarvis.

"Aw, dear, aw dearee dear!" said Kerry. "The sight! the sight!"

Jarvis's uneasiness developed into curiosity, and in answer to many questions he learned that blind Kerry had that day been visited by another of those visions of Dan which never came to her except when her nursling was in some disgrace or danger, and never failed to come to her then. On this occasion the vision had been one of great sorrow, and Kerry trembled as she recounted it.

"I saw him as plain as plain, and he was standing in Misthress Mona's room, atween the bed and the wee craythur's cot, and he went down on his knees aside of it, and cried, and cried, and cried morthal, and Misthress Mona herself was there sobbing her heart out, as the sayin' is, and the wee craythur was sleeping soft and quiet, and it was dark night outside, and the candle was in the misthress's hand. Aw, yes, I saw it, sir, I saw it, and I tould my man here, and, behould ye, he said, 'Drop it, woman, drop it,' says he, 'it's only drames, it's only drames.'"

Jarvis did not find the story a tragic one, but he listened with an interest that was all his own.

"You saw Mr. Dan in Miss Mona's room—do you mean her chamber?"

"Sure, and he climbed in at the window, and white as a haddock, and all amuck with sweat."

"Climbed in at the window—the window of her chamber—her bedroom—you're sure it was her bedroom?"

"Sarten sure. Don't I know it same as my own bit of a place? The bed, with the curtains all white and dimity, as they're sayin', and the wee thing's cot carved over with the lions, and the tigers, and the beasties, and the goat's rug, and the sheepskin—aw, yes, aw, yes."

The reality of the vision had taken such a hold of Kerry that she had looked upon it as a certain presage of disaster, and when Jarvis had opened the door she had leapt to the conclusion that he came to announce the catastrophe that she foresaw, and to summon her to Ballamona.

Jarvis smiled grimly. He had heard in the old days of Kerry's second sight, and now he laughed at it. But the blind woman's stupid dreams had given him an idea, and he rose suddenly and hurried away.

Jarvis knew the Deemster's weakness, for he knew why he found himself where he was. Stern man as the Deemster might be, keen of wit and strong of soul, Jarvis knew that there was one side of his mind on which he was feebler than a child. On that side of the Deemster Jarvis now meant to play to his own end and profit.

He was full to the throat of the story which he had to pour into credulous ears, that never listened to a superstitious tale without laughing at it, and mocking at it, and believing it, when he stepped into the hall at Ballamona, and came suddenly face to face with Dan, and saw the door of Mona's sitting-room open before and close behind him.

Jarvis was bewildered. Could it be possible that there was something in the blind woman's second sight? He had scarcely recovered from his surprise when the Deemster walked into the porch, looking as black as a thunder-cloud.

"That man has been here again," he said. "Why didn't you turn him out of the house?"

"I have something to tell you," said Jarvis.

They went into the Deemster's study. It was a little place to the left of the hall, half under the stairs, and with the fireplace built across one corner. Over the mantel-shelf a number of curious things were hung from hooks and nails—a huge silver watch with a small face and great seals, a mask, a blunderbuss, a monastic lamp and a crucifix, a piece of silvered glass, and a pistol.

"What now?" asked the Deemster.

Jarvis told the blind woman's story with variations, and the Deemster listened intently, and with a look of deadly rage.

"And you saw him come out of her room—you yourself saw him?" said the Deemster.

"With my own eyes, dear sir," said Jarvis.

The Deemster's lip quivered. "My God! it must be true," he said.

At that moment they heard a foot in the hall, and going to the door in his restless tramping to and fro, the Deemster saw that Ewan had come into the house. He called to him, and Ewan went into the study, and on Ewan going in Jarvis went out.

There was a look of such affright on the Deemster's face that before a word was spoken Ewan had caught the contagion of his father's terror. Then, grasping his son by the wrist in the intensity of his passion, the

Deemster poured his tale into Ewan's ear. But it was not the tale that blind Kerry had told to Jarvis, it was not the tale that Jarvis had told to him; it was a tale compounded of superstition and of hate. Blind Kerry had said of her certain knowledge that Dan was accustomed to visit Mona in her chamber at night alone, entering in at the window. Jarvis Kerruish himself had seen him there—and that very day, not at night, but in the broad daylight, Jarvis had seen Dan come from Mona's room. What? Had Ewan no bowels that he could submit to the dishonor of his own sister?

Ewan listened to the hot words that came from his father in a rapid and ceaseless whirl. The story was all so fatally circumstantial as the Deemster told it; no visions; no sights; no sneezings of an old woman; all was clear, hard, deadly, damning circumstance, or seemed to be so to Ewan's heated brain and poisoned heart.

"Father," he said, very quietly, but with visible emotion, "you are my father, but there are only two persons alive from whose lips I would take a story like this, and you are not one of them."

At that word the Deemster's passion overcame him. "My God," he cried, "what have I done that I should not be believed by my own son? Would I slander my own daughter?"

But Ewan did not hear him. He had turned away, and was going toward the door of Mona's room. He moved slowly; there was an awful silence. Full half a minute his hand rested on the door handle, and only then did his nervous fingers turn it.

He stepped into the room. The room was empty. It was Mona's sitting-room, her work-room, her parlor, her nursery. Out of it there opened another room by a door at the further end of the hall on the left.

The door of that other room was ajar, and Ewan could hear, from where he now stood quivering in every limb, the soft cooing of the child—his child, his dead wife's child—and the inarticulate nothings that Mona, the foster-mother, babbled over it.

"Boo-loo-la-la-pa-pa," "Dearee-dearee-dear," and then the tender cooing died off into a murmur, and an almost noiseless, long kiss on the full round baby-neck.

Ewan stood irresolute for a moment, and the sweat started from his forehead. He felt like one who has been kneeling at a shrine when a foul hand besmudges it. He had half swung about to go back, when his ear caught the sound of the Deemster's restless foot outside. He could not go back: the poison had gone to his heart.

He stepped into the bedroom that led out of the sitting-room. Mona raised her eyes as her brother entered. She was leaning over the cot, her beautiful face alive with the light of a tender love—a very vision of pure and delicious womanhood. Almost she had lifted the child from the cot to Ewan's arms when at a second glance she recognized the solemn expression of his face, and then she let the little one slide back to its pillow.

"What has happened?"

"Is it true," he began very slowly, "that Dan has been here?"

Then Mona blushed deeply, and there was a pause.

"Is it true?" he said again, and now with a hurried and startled look; "is it true that Dan has been here—here?"

Mona misunderstood his emphasis. Ewan was standing in her chamber, and when he asked if Dan had been there, he was inquiring if Dan had been with her in that very room. She did not comprehend the evil thought that had been put in his heart. But she remembered the prohibition placed upon her both by Ewan and her father, never to receive Dan again, and her confusion at the moment of Ewan's question came of the knowledge that, contrary to that prohibition, she had received him.

"Is it true?" he asked yet again, and he trembled with the passion he suppressed.

After a pause he answered himself, with an awful composure, "It *is* true."

The child lifted itself and babbled at Mona with its innocent face all smiles, and Mona turned to hide her confusion by leaning over the cot.

"Boo—loo—la-la."

Then a great wave of passion seemed to come to Ewan, and he stepped to his sister, and took her by both hands. He was like a strong man in a dream, who feels sure that he can only be dreaming—struggling in vain to awake from a terrible nightmare, and knowing that a nightmare it must be that sits on him and crushes him.

"No, no, there must be a mistake; there must, there must," he said, and his hot breathing beat on her face. "He has never been here —here—never."

Mona raised herself. She loosed her hands from his grasp. Her woman's pride had been stung. It seemed to her that her brother was taking more than a brother's part.

"There is no mistake," she said, with some anger; "Dan has been here."

"You confess it?"

She looked him straight in the eyes and answered, "Yes, if you call it so—I confess it. It is of no use to deceive you."

Then there was an ominous silence. Ewan's features became death-like in their rigidity. A sickening sense came over him. He was struggling to ask a question that his tongue would not utter.

"Mona—do you mean—do you mean that Dan has—has—outrage—Great God! what am I to say? How am I to say it?"

Mona drew herself up.

"I mean that I can hide my feelings no longer," she said. "Do with me as you may; I am not a child, and no brother shall govern me. Dan has been here—outrage or none—call it what you will—yes, and—" she dropped her head over the cot, "I love him."

Ewan was not himself: his heart was poisoned, or then and there he would have unraveled the devilish tangle of circumstance. He tried again with another and yet another question. But every question he asked, and every answer Mona gave, made the tangle thicker. His strained jaw seemed to start from his skin.

"I passed him on the road," he said to himself, in a hushed whisper. "Oh, that I had but known!"

Then with a look of reproach at Mona he turned aside and went out of the room.

He stepped back to the study, and there the Deemster was still tramping to and fro.

"Simpleton, simpleton, to expect a woman to acknowledge her own dishonor," the Deemster cried.

Ewan did not answer at once; but in silence he reached up to where the pistol hung over the mantel-shelf and took it down.

"What are you doing?" cried the Deemster.

"She *has* acknowledged it," said Ewan, still in a suppressed whisper.

For a moment the Deemster was made speechless and powerless by that answer. Then he laid hold of his son's hand and wrenched the pistol away.

"No violence," he cried.

He was now terrified at the wrath that his own evil passions had aroused; he locked the pistol in a cabinet.

"It is better so," said Ewan, and in another moment he was going out at the porch.

The Deemster followed him, and laid a hand on his arm.

"Remember—no violence," he said; "for the love of God, see there is no violence."

But Ewan, without a word more, without relaxing a muscle of his hard, white face, without a glance or a sign, but with bloodshot eyes and quivering nostrils, with teeth compressed and the great veins on his forehead large and dark over the scar that Dan had left there, drew himself away, and went out of the house.

CHAPTER XIX
HOW EWAN FOUND DAN

Ewan went along like a man whose reason is clogged. All his faculties were deadened. He could not see properly. He could not hear. He could not think. Try as he might to keep his faculties from wandering, his mind would not be kept steady.

Time after time he went back to the passage of Scripture which he had fixed on that morning for his next lesson and sermon. It was the story how Esau, when robbed of his birthright blessing, said in his heart, "I will slay my brother Jacob"; how Jacob fled from his brother's anger to the home of Laban; how after many years Esau married the daughter of Ishmael, and Jacob came to the country of Edom; how, in exceeding fear of Esau's wrath, Jacob sent before him a present for Esau out of the plenty with which God had blessed him; and how Jacob lifted up his eyes and beheld Esau, and ran to meet him and embraced him, and fell on his neck and kissed him, and they wept.

Ewan would see the goats and the ewes, and the rams, and the milch camels toiling along through the hot lush grass by the waters of the Jordan; then all at once these would vanish and he would find himself standing alone in the drear winter day, with the rumble of the bleak sea far in front, and close overhead the dark snow-clouds sweeping on and on.

His strong emotion paralyzed all his faculties. He could neither fix his mind on the mission on which he had set out, nor banish the thought of it. Mission! What was it? At one moment he thought he knew, and then his eyes seemed to jump from their sockets. "Am I going mad?" he asked himself, and his head turned giddy.

He went on; a blind force impelled him. At length he reached the old Ballamona. His own especial room in the house was the little book-encased closet, looking over the Curraghs toward the sea—the same that had been the study of Gilcrist Mylrea, before he went away and came back as bishop.

But Ewan turned mechanically toward another part of the house and entered a room hung about with muskets and the horns of deer, fishing rods and baskets, a watchman's truncheon lettered in red, loose pieces of net, and even some horse harness. A dog, a brown collie, lay asleep before the fire, and over the rannel-tree shelf a huge watch was ticking.

But Dan was not in his room. Then Ewan remembered in a dazed way—how had the memory escaped him so long?—that when Dan passed him on the road he was not going homeward, but toward the village. No doubt the man was on his way to the low pot-house he frequented.

Ewan left Ballamona and went on toward the "Three Legs of Man." He crossed the fields which the Bishop had cut off from the episcopal demesne for his son's occupation as a farm. As he walked, his wandering, aimless thoughts were arrested by the neglected state of the land and the stock upon it. In one croft the withered stalks of the last crop of cabbage lay rotten on the ground; in a meadow a sheep was lying dead of the rot, and six or seven of the rest of the flock were dragging their falling wool along the thin grass.

Ewan came out of the fields to the turnpike by the footpath that goes by Bishop's Court, and as he passed through the stile he heard the Bishop in conversation with some one on the road within.

"What is the balance that I owe you, Mr. Looney, for building those barns on my son's farm?" the Bishop was saying.

"Seven pounds five shillings, my lord," the man answered, "and rael bad I'm wanting the money, too, my lord, and three months I'm afther waiting for it."

"So you are, Mr. Looney. You would have been paid before this if I'd had wherewith to pay you."

Then there was silence between the two, and Ewan was going on, when the Bishop added:

"Here—here—take this;" there was a sound as of the rattle of keys, and seals, and a watch chain—"it was my old father's last gift to me, all he had to give to me—God bless his memory!—and I little thought to part with it—but there, take it and sell it, and pay yourself, Mr. Looney."

The man seemed to draw back.

"Your watch!" he said. "Aw, no, no, no! Och, if I'm never paid, never, it's not Patrick Looney that is the man to take the watch out of your pocket."

"Take it—take it! Why, my good man"—the Bishop's voice was all but breaking—"you should not refuse to take the time of day from your Bishop." Then there was a jaunty laugh, with a great sob at the back of it. "Besides, I've found the old thing a sore tax on my failing memory this many day, to wind it and wear it. Come, it will wipe out my debt to you."

Ewan went on; his teeth were set hard. Why had he overheard that conversation? Was it to whet his purpose? It seemed as if there might be some supernatural influence over him. But this was not the only conversation he overheard that day. When he got to the "Three Legs of Man" a carrier's cart stood outside. Ewan stepped into the lobby of the house. The old cat was counting up the chalk marks, vertical and horizontal, at the back of the cupboard door, and the carrier was sitting on a round table, recounting certain mad doings at Castletown.

"'Let's down with the watch and take their lanterns,' says the captain, says he, laughing morthal and a bit sprung, maybe; and down they went, one a top o' the other, Jemmy the Red, and Johnny-by-Nite, and all the rest of them, bellowing strong, and the capt'n and his pals whipping up their lanterns and their truncheons, and away at a slant Aw, it was right fine."

The carrier laughed loud at his story.

"Was that when Mastha Dan was down at Castletown, fixing the business for the Fencibles?"

"Aw, yes, woman, and middlin' stiff it cost him. Next morning Jemmy the Red and Johnny-by-Nite were off for the Castle, but the captain met them, and 'I'm not for denying it,' says he, and 'a bit of a spree,' he says, and Take this, Jemmy,' says he, 'and say no more.'"

"And what did he give the watch to sweeten them?"

"Three pound, they're saying. Aw, yes, woman, woman—liberal, very. None o' yer close-fisted about the captain."

The blood rushed to Ewan's heart. In a moment he found himself asking for Dan and hearing from the old woman with the whiskers, who spoke with a curtsey after every syllable, that Master Dan had been seen to go down toward the creek, the Lockjaw, under Orris Head.

Ewan went out of the pot-house and turned the lane toward the creek. What was the mysterious influence on his destiny, that he of all men must needs overhear two such conversations, and hear them now of all times? The neglected lands, the impoverished old Bishop, the reckless spendthrift, all rose before Ewan's mind in a bewildering haze.

The lane to the Lockjaw led past the shambles, that stood a little out of the village. Ewan had often noticed the butcher's low wagon on the road, with sheep penned in by a rope across the sternboard, or with a calf in a net. All at once he now realized that he was walking behind this wagon, and that a dead ox lay in it, and that the driver at the horse's head was talking to a man who plodded along beside him. Ewan's faculties were now more clouded than before, but he could hear, with gaps in which his sense of hearing seemed to leave him, the conversation between the two men.

"Well, well, just to think—killing the poor beast for stopping when the dinner bell rang at the Coort! And them used of it for fifteen years! Aw, well, well."

"He's no Christian, anyway, and no disrespec'."

"Christian? Christian, is it? Brute beast, as I'm sayin'. The ould Bishop's son? Well, well."

Bit by bit, scarcely listening, losing the words sometimes, as one loses at intervals the tick of a clock when lying awake at night with a brain distraught, Ewan gathered up the story of the bad business at the plowing match after he had left the meadow.

"Christian? Och, Christian?" one of the men repeated with a bitter laugh of mockery. "I'm thinking it would be a middlin' little crime to treat a Christian like that same as he treated the poor dumb craythurs."

Ewan's temples beat furiously, and a fearful tumult was rife in his brain. One wild thought expelled all other thoughts. Why had he overheard three such conversations? There could be but one answer—he was designed by supernatural powers to be the instrument of a fixed purpose. It was irrevocably decided—he was impelled to the terrible business that was in his mind by an irresistible force to which he was blind and powerless. It was so, it was so.

Ewan pushed on past the wagon, and heard the men's voices die off to an indistinct mumble behind him. How hideous were the meditations of the next few minutes! The beating of his temple drew the skin hard about the scar above it. He thought of his young wife in her grave, and of the shock that sent her there. He felt afresh the abject degradation of that bitter moment in the library at Bishop's Court, when, to save the honor of a forger, he had lied before God and man. Then he thought of the gray head of that august old man, serenest of saints, fondest of fathers, the Bishop, bowed down to the dust with shame and a ruined hope. And after his mind had oscillated among these agonizing thoughts, there came to him over all else and more hideous than all else, the memory of what his own father, the Deemster, had told him an hour ago.

Ewan began to run, and as he ran all his blood seemed to rush to his head, and a thousand confused and vague forms danced before his eyes. All at once he recognized that he was at the mouth of the creek, going down the steep gate to the sea that ended in the Lockjaw. Before he was aware, he was talking with Davy Fayle, and asking for Dan. He noticed that his voice would scarcely obey him.

"He's in the crib on the shore, sir," said Davy, and the lad turned back to his work. He was hammering an old bent nail out of a pitch-pine plank that had washed ashore with the last tide. After a moment Davy stopped and looked after the young parson, and shook his head and muttered something to himself. Then he threw down his hammer, and followed slowly.

Ewan went on. His impatience was now feverish. He was picturing Dan as he would find him—drinking, smoking, laughing, one leg thrown over the end of a table, his cap awry, his face red, his eyes bleared, and his lips hot.

It was growing dark, the snow-cloud was very low overhead, the sea-birds were screaming down at the water's edge, and the sea's deep rumble came up from the shingle below and the rocks beyond.

Ewan saw the tent and made for it. As he came near to it he slipped and fell. Regaining his feet, he perceived that in the dusk he had tripped over some chips that lay about a block. Davy had been chopping firewood of the driftwood that the sea had sent up. Ewan saw the hatchet lying among the loose chips. In an instant he had caught it up. Recognizing in every event of that awful hour the mysterious influence of supernatural powers, he read this incident as he had read all the others. Until then he had thought of nothing but the deed he was to do; never for one instant of how he was to do it. But now the hatchet was thrust into his hand. Thus was everything irrevocably decided.

And now Ewan was in front of the tent, panting audibly, the hatchet in his hand, his eyes starting from their sockets, the great veins on his forehead hard and black. Now, O God! for a moment's strength, one little moment's strength, now, now!

The smoke was rising from the gorse-covered roof; the little black door was shut. Inside was Dan, Dan, Dan; and while Ewan's young wife lay in her grave, and Ewan's sister was worse than in her grave, and the good Bishop was brought low, Dan was there, there, and he was drinking and laughing, and his heart was cold and dead.

Ewan lifted the latch and pushed the door open, and stepped into the tent.

Lord of grace and mercy, what was there? On the floor of earth, in one corner of the small place, a fire of gorse, turf, and logs burned slowly; and near the fire Dan lay outstretched on a bed of straw, his head pillowed on a coil of old rope, one hand twisted under his head, the other resting lightly on his breast, and he slept peacefully like a child.

Ewan stood for a moment shuddering and dismayed. The sight of Dan, helpless and at his mercy, unnerved his arm and drove the fever from his blood. There was an awful power in that sleeping man, and sleep had wrapped him in its own divinity.

The hatchet dropped from Ewan's graspless fingers, and he covered his face. As a drowning man is said to see all his life pass before him at the moment of death, so Ewan saw all the past, the happy past—the past of love and of innocence, whereof Dan was a part—rise up before him.

"It is true, I am going mad," he thought, and he fell back on to a bench that stood by the wall. Then there came an instant of unconsciousness, and in that instant he was again by the waters of the Jordan, and the ewes and the rams and the milch camels were toiling through the long grass, and Esau was falling on the neck of Jacob, and they were weeping together.

CHAPTER XX
BLIND PASSION AND PAIN

Dan moved uneasily, and presently awoke, opened his eyes, and saw Ewan, and betrayed no surprise at his presence there.

"Ah! Is it you, Ewan?" he said, speaking quietly, partly in a shamefaced way, and with some confusion. "Do you know, I've been dreaming of you—you and Mona?"

Ewan gave no answer. Because sleep is a holy thing, and the brother of death, whose shadow also it is, therefore Ewan's hideous purpose had left him while Dan lay asleep at his feet; but now that Dan was awake, the evil passion came again.

"I was dreaming of that Mother Carey's chicken—you remember it? when we were lumps of lads, you know—why, you can't have forgotten it—the old thing I caught in its nest just under the Head?"

Still Ewan gave no sign, but looked down at Dan resting on his elbows. Dan's eyes fell upon Ewan's face, but he went on in a confused way:

"Mona couldn't bear to see it caged, and would have me put it back. Don't you remember I clambered up to the nest, and put the bird in again? You were down on the shore, thinking sure I would tumble over the Head, and Mona—Mona—"

Dan glanced afresh into Ewan's face, and its look of terror seemed to stupefy him; still he made shift to go on with his dream in an abashed sort of way:

"My gough! If I didn't dream it all as fresh, as fresh, and the fight in the air, and the screams when I put the old bird in the nest—the young ones had forgotten it clean, and they tumbled it out, and set on it terrible, and drove it away—and then the poor old thing on the rocks sitting by itself as lonesome as lonesome—and little Mona crying and crying down below, and her long hair rip-rip-rippling in the wind, and—and—"

Dan had got to his feet, and then seated himself on a stool as he rambled on with the story of his dream. But once again his shifty eyes came back to Ewan's face, and he stopped short.

"My God, what is it?" he cried.

Now Ewan, standing there with a thousand vague forms floating in his brain, had heard little of what Dan had said, but he had noted his confused manner, and had taken this story of the dream as a feeble device to hide the momentary discomfiture.

"What does it mean?" he said. "It means that this island is not large enough to hold both you and me."

"What?"

"It means that you must go away."

"Away!"

"Yes—and at once."

In the pause that followed after his first cry of amazement, Dan thought only of the bad business of the killing of the oxen at the plowing match that morning, and so, in a tone of utter abasement, with his face to the ground, he went on, in a blundering, humble way, to allow that Ewan had reason for his anger.

"I'm a blind headstrong fool, I know that—and my temper is—well, it's damnable, that's the fact—but no one suffers from it more than I do, and if I could have felled myself after I had felled the oxen, why down ... Ewan, for the sake of the dear old times when we were good chums, you and I and little Mona, with her quiet eyes, God bless her—!"

"Go away, and never come back to either of us," cried Ewan, stamping his foot.

Dan paused, and there was a painful silence.

"Why should I go away?" he said, with an effort at quietness.

"Because you are a scoundrel—the basest scoundrel on God's earth—the foulest traitor—the blackest-hearted monster—"

Dan's sunburnt face whitened under his tawny skin.

"Easy, easy, man veen, easy," he said, struggling visibly for self-command, while he interrupted Ewan's torrent of reproaches.

"You are a disgrace and a by-word. Only the riff-raff of the island are your friends and associates."

"That's true enough, Ewan," said Dan, and his head fell between his hands, his elbows resting on his knees.

"What are you doing? Drinking, gambling, roistering, cheating—yes—"

Dan got on his feet uneasily and took a step to and fro about the little place; then sat again, and buried his head in his hands as before.

"I've been a reckless, self-willed, mad fool, Ewan, but no worse than that. And if you could see me as God sees me, and know how I suffer for my follies and curse them, for all I seem to make so light of them, and how I am driven to them one on the head of another, perhaps—perhaps—perhaps—you would have pity—ay, pity."

"Pity? Pity for you? You who have brought your father to shame? He is the ruin of the man he was. You have impoverished him; you have spent his substance and wasted it. Ay, and you have made his gray head a mark for reproach. 'Set your own house in order'—that's what the world says to the man of God whose son is a child of the—"

"Stop!" cried Dan.

He had leapt to his feet, his fist clenched, his knuckles showing like nuts of steel.

But Ewan went on, standing there with a face that was ashy white above his black coat. "Your heart is as dead as your honor. And that is not all, but you must outrage the honor of another."

Now, when Ewan said this, Dan thought of his forged signature, and of the censure and suspension to which Ewan was thereby made liable.

"Go away," Ewan cried again, motioning Dan off with his trembling hand.

Dan lifted his eyes. "And what if I refuse?" he said in a resolute way.

"Then take the consequences."

"You mean the consequences of that—that—that forgery?"

At this Ewan realized the thought in Dan's mind, and perceived that Dan conceived him capable of playing upon his fears by holding over his head the penalty of an offense which he had already taken upon himself. "God in heaven!" he thought, "and this is the pitiful creature whom I have all these years taken to my heart."

"Is that what your loyalty comes to?" said Dan, and his lip curled.

"Loyalty!" cried Ewan, in white wrath. "Loyalty, and you talk to me of loyalty—you who have outraged the honor of my sister—"

"Mona!"

"I have said it at last, though the word blisters my tongue. Go away from the island forever, and let me never see your face again."

Dan rose to his feet with rigid limbs. He looked about him for a moment in a dazed silence, and put his hand to his forehead as if he had lost himself.

"Do you believe *that*?" he said, in a slow whisper.

"Don't deny it—don't let me know you for a liar as well," Ewan said, eagerly; and then added in another tone, "I have had her own confession."

"Her confession?"

"Yes, and the witness of another."

"The witness of another!"

Dan echoed Ewan's words in a vague, half-conscious way.

Then, in a torrent of hot words that seemed to blister and sting the man who spoke them no less than the man who heard them, Ewan told all, and Dan listened like one in a stupor.

There was silence, and then Ewan spoke again in a tone of agony. "Dan, there was a time when in spite of yourself I loved you—yes, though I'm ashamed to say it, for it was against God's own leading; still I loved you, Dan. But let us part forever now, and each go his own way, and perhaps, though we can never forget the wrong that you have done us, we may yet think more kindly of you, and time may help us to forgive—"

But Dan had awakened from his stupor, and he flung aside.

"Damn your forgiveness!" he said, hotly, and then, with teeth set and lips drawn hard and eyes aflame, he turned upon Ewan and strode up to him, and they stood together face to face.

"You said just now that there was not room enough in the island for you and me," he said, in a hushed whisper. "You were right, but I shall mend your words: if you believe what you have said—by Heaven, I'll not deny it for you!—there is not room enough for both of us in the world."

"It was my own thought," said Ewan, and then for an instant each looked into the other's eyes and read the other's purpose.

The horror of that moment of silence was broken by the lifting of the latch. Davy Fayle came shambling into the tent on some pretended errand. He took off his militia belt with the dagger in the sheath attached to it, and hung it on a long rusty nail driven into an upright timber at one corner. Then he picked up from among some ling on the floor a waterproof coat and put it on. He was going out, with furtive glances at Dan and Ewan, who said not a word in his presence, and were bearing themselves toward each other with a painful constraint, when his glance fell on the hatchet which lay a few feet from the door. Davy picked it up and carried it out, muttering to himself, "Strange, strange, uncommon!"

Hardly had the boy dropped the latch of the door from without than Ewan took the militia belt from the nail and buckled it about his waist. Dan understood his thought; he was still wearing his own militia belt and dagger. There was now not an instant's paltering between them—not a word of explanation.

"We must get rid of the lad," said Dan.

Ewan bowed his head. It had come to him to reflect that when all was over Mona might hear of what had been done. What they had to do was to be done for her honor, or for what seemed to be her honor in that blind tangle of passion and circumstance. But none the less, though she loved both of them now, would she loathe that one who returned to her with the blood of the other upon him.

"She must never know," he said. "Send the boy away. Then we must go to where this work can be done between you and me alone."

Dan had followed his thought in silence, and was stepping toward the door to call to Davy, when the lad came back, carrying a log of driftwood for the fire. There were some small flakes of snow on his waterproof coat.

"Go up to the shambles, Davy," said Dan, speaking with an effort at composure, "and tell Jemmy Curghey to keep me the ox-horns."

Davy looked up in a vacant way, and his lip lagged low. "Aw, and didn't you tell Jemmy yourself, and terrible partic'lar, too?"

"Do you say so, Davy?"

"Sarten sure."

"Then just slip away and fetch them."

Davy fixed the log on the fire, tapped it into the flame, glanced anxiously at Dan and Ewan, and then in a lingering way went out. His simple face looked sad under its vacant expression.

The men listened while the lad's footsteps could be heard on the shingle, above the deep murmur of the sea. Then Dan stepped to the door and threw it open.

"Now," he said.

It was rapidly growing dark. The wind blew strongly into the shed. Dan stepped out, and Ewan followed him.

They walked in silence through the gully that led from the creek to the cliff head. The snow that had begun to fall was swirled about in the wind that came from over the sea, and spinning in the air, it sometimes beat against their faces.

Ewan went along like a man condemned to death. He had begun to doubt, though he did not know it, and would have shut his mind to the idea if it had occurred to him. But once, when Dan seemed to stop as if only half resolved, and partly turn his face toward him, Ewan mistook his intention. "He is going to tell me that there is some hideous error," he thought. He was burning for that word. But no, Dan went plodding on again, and never after shifted his steadfast gaze, never spoke, and gave no sign. At length he stopped, and Ewan stopped with him. They were standing on the summit of Orris Head.

It was a sad, a lonesome, and a desolate place, in sight of a wide waste of common land, without a house, and with never a tree rising above the purple gorse and tussocks of long grass. The sky hung very low over it; the steep red cliffs, with their patches of green in ledges, swept down from it to the shingle and the sharp shelves of slate covered with seaweed. The ground swell came up from below with a very mournful noise, but the air seemed to be empty, and every beat of the foot on the soft turf sounded near and large. Above their heads the sea-fowl kept up a wild clamor, and far out, where sea and sky seemed to meet in the gathering darkness, the sea's steady blow on the bare rocks of the naze sent up a deep, hoarse boom.

Dan unbuckled his belt, and threw off his coat and vest. Ewan did the same, and they stood there face to face in the thin flakes of snow, Dan in his red shirt, Ewan in his white shirt open at the neck, these two men whose souls had been knit together as the soul of Jonathan was knit to the soul of David, and each ready to lift his hand against his heart's best brother. Then all at once a startled cry came from near at hand.

It was Davy Fayle's voice. The lad had not gone to the shambles. Realizing in some vague way that the errand was a subterfuge and that mischief was about, he had hidden himself at a little distance, and had seen when Dan and Ewan came out of the tent together. Creeping through the ling, and partly hidden by the dusk, he had followed the men until they had stopped on the Head. Then Davy had dropped to his knees. His ideas were obscure, he scarcely knew what was going on before his eyes, but he held his breath and watched and listened. At length, when the men threw off their clothes, the truth dawned on Davy; and though he tried to smother an exclamation, a cry of terror burst from his husky throat.

Dan and Ewan exchanged glances, and each seemed in one moment to read the other's thoughts. In another instant, at three quick strides, Dan had taken Davy by the shoulders.

"Promise," he said, "that you will never tell what you have seen."

Davy struggled to free himself, but his frantic efforts were useless. In Dan's grip he was held as in a vice.

"Let me go, Mastha Dan," the lad cried.

"Promise to hold your tongue," said Dan; "promise it, promise it."

"Let me go, will you? let me go," the lad shouted sullenly.

"Be quiet," said Dan.

"I won't be quiet," was the stubborn answer. "Help! help! help!" and the lad screamed lustily.

"Hold your tongue, or by G—"

Dan held Davy by one of his great hands hitched into the lad's guernsey, and he lifted the other hand threateningly.

"Help! help! help!" Davy screamed still louder, and struggled yet more fiercely, until his strength was spent, and his breath was gone, and then there was a moment's silence.

The desolate place was still as desolate as before. Not a sign of life around; not an answering cry.

"There's nobody to help you," said Dan. "You have got to promise never to tell what you have seen to man, woman, or child."

"I won't promise, and I won't hould my tongue," said the lad, stoutly. "You are goin' to fight, you and Mastha Ewan, and—"

Dan stopped him. "Hearken here. If you are to live another hour, you will promise—"

But Davy had regained both strength and voice.

"I don't care—help! help! help!" he shouted.

Dan put his hand over the lad's mouth, and dragged him to the cliff head. Below was the brant steep, dark and jagged, and quivering in the deepening gloom, and the sea-birds were darting through the mid-air like bats in the dark.

"Look," said Dan, "you've got to swear never to tell what you have seen to-night, so help you God!"

The lad, held tightly by the breast and throat, and gripping the arms that held him with fingers that clung like claws, took one horrified glance down into the darkness. He struggled no longer. His face was very pitiful to see.

"I can not promise," he said, in a voice like a cry.

At that answer Dan drew Davy back from the cliff edge, and loosed his hold of him. He was abashed and ashamed. He felt himself a little man by the side of this half-daft fisher-lad.

All this time Ewan had stood aside looking on while Dan demanded the promise, and saying nothing. Now he went up to Davy, and said, in a quiet voice:

"Davy, if you should ever tell any one what you have seen, Dan will be a lost man all his life hereafter."

"Then let him pitch me over the cliff," said Davy, in a smothered cry.

"Listen to me, Davy," Ewan went on; "you're a brave lad, and I know what's in your head, but—"

"Then what for do you want to fight him?" Davy broke out. The lad's throat was dry and husky, and his eyes were growing dim.

Ewan paused. Half his passion was spent. Davy's poor dense head had found him a question that he could not answer.

"Davy, if you don't promise, you will ruin Dan—yes, it will be you who will ruin him, you, remember that. He will be a lost man, and my sister, my good sister Mona, she will be a broken-hearted woman."

Then Davy broke down utterly, and big tears filled his eyes, and ran down his cheeks.

"I promise," he sobbed.

"Good lad—now go."

Davy turned about and went away, at first running, and then dragging slowly, then running again, and then again lingering.

What followed was a very pitiful conflict of emotion. Nature, who looks down pitilessly on man and his big, little passions, that clamor so loud but never touch her at all—even Nature played her part in this tragedy.

When Davy Fayle was gone, Dan and Ewan stood face to face as before, Dan with his back to the cliff, Ewan with his face to the sea. Then, without a word, each turned aside and picked up his militia belt.

The snowflakes had thickened during the last few moments, but now they seemed to cease and the sky to lighten. Suddenly in the west the sky was cloven as though by the sweep of a sword, and under a black bar of cloud and above a silvered water-line the sun came through very red and hazy in its setting, and with its ragged streamers around it.

Ewan was buckling the belt about his waist when the setting sun rose upon them, and all at once there came to him the Scripture that says, "Let not the sun go down on your wrath." If God's hand had appeared in the heavens, the effect on Ewan could not have been greater. Already his passion was more than half gone, and now it melted entirely away.

"Dan," he cried, and his voice was a sob, "Dan, I can not fight—right or wrong I can not," and he flung himself down, and the tears filled his eyes.

Then Dan, whose face was afire, laughed loud and bitterly. "Coward," he said, "coward and poltroon!"

At that word all the evil passion came back to Ewan and he leapt to his feet.

"That is enough," he said; "the belts—buckle them together."

Dan understood Ewan's purpose. At the next breath the belt about Dan's waist was buckled to the belt about the waist of Ewan, and the two men stood strapped together. Then they drew the daggers, and an awful struggle followed.

With breast to breast until their flesh all but touched, and with thighs entwined, they reeled and swayed, the right hand of each held up for thrust, the left for guard and parry. What Dan gained in strength Ewan made up in rage, and the fight was fierce and terrible, Dan still with his back to the cliff, Ewan still with his face to the sea.

At one instant Dan, by his great stature, had reached over Ewan's shoulder to thrust from behind, and at the next instant Ewan had wrenched his lithe body backward and had taken the blow in his lifted arm, which forthwith spouted blood above the wrist. In that encounter they reeled about, changing places, and Ewan's back was henceforward toward the cliff, and Dan fought with his face toward the sea.

It was a hideous and savage fight. The sun had gone down, the cleft in the heavens had closed again, once more the thin flakes of snow were falling, and the world had dropped back to its dark mood. A stormy petrel came up from the cliff and swirled above the men as they fought, and made its direful scream over them.

Up and down, to and fro, embracing closely, clutching, guarding, and meantime panting hoarsely, and drawing hard breath, the two men fought in their deadly hate. At last they had backed and swayed to within three yards of the cliff, and then Ewan, with the gasp of a drowning man, flung his weapon into the air, and Dan ripped his dagger's edge across the belts that bound them together, and at the next breath the belts were cut, and the two were divided, and Ewan, separated from Dan, and leaning heavily backward, was reeling, by force of his own weight, toward the cliff.

Then Dan stood as one transfixed with uplifted hand, and a deep groan came from his throat. Passion and pain were gone from him in that awful moment, and the world itself seemed to be blotted out. When he came to himself, he was standing on the cliff head alone.

The clock in the old church was striking. How the bell echoed on that lonely height! One—two—three—four—five. Five o'clock! Everything else was silent as death. The day was gone. The snow began to fall in thick, large flakes. It fell heavily on Dan's hot cheeks and bare neck. His heart seemed to stand still, and the very silence itself was awful. His terror stupefied him. "What have I done?" he asked himself. He could not think. He covered his eyes with his hands, and strode up and down the cliff head, up and down, up and down. Then in a bewildered state of semi-consciousness he looked out to sea, and there far off, a league away, he saw a black thing looming large against the darkening sky. He recognized that it was a sail, and then perceived that it was a lugger, and quite mechanically he tried to divide the mainmast and mizzen, the mainsail and yawlsail, and to note if the boat were fetching to leeward or beating down the Channel.

All at once sea and sky were blotted out, and he could not stand on his legs, but dropped to his knees, and great beads of perspiration rolled down his face and neck. He tried to call "Ewan! Ewan!" but he could not utter the least cry. His throat was parched; his tongue swelled and filled his mouth. His lips moved, but no words came from him. Then he rose to his feet, and the world flowed back upon him; the sea-fowl crying over his head, the shrillness of the wind in the snow-capped gorse, and the sea's hoarse voice swelling upward through the air, while its heavy, monotonous blow on the beach shook the earth beneath him. If anything else had appeared to Dan at that moment, he must have screamed with terror.

Quaking in every limb, he picked up his clothes and turned back toward the shore. He was so feeble that he could scarcely walk through the snow that now lay thick on the short grass. When he reached the mouth of the gully he did not turn into the shed, but went on over the pebbles of the creek. His bloodshot eyes, which almost started from their sockets, glanced eagerly from side to side. At last he saw the thing he sought, and now that it was under him, within reach of his hand, he dare hardly look upon it.

At the foot of a jagged crag that hung heavily over from the cliff the body of Ewan Mylrea lay dead and cold. There was no mark of violence upon it save a gash on the wrist of the left hand, and over the wound there was a clot of blood. The white face lay deep in the breast, as if the neck had been dislocated. There were no other outward marks of injury from the fall. The body was outstretched on its back, with one arm—the left arm—lying half over the forehead, and the other, the right arm, with the hand open and the listless fingers apart, thrown loosely aside.

Dan knelt beside the body, and his heart was benumbed like ice. He tried to pray, but no prayer would come, and he could not weep.

"Ewan! Ewan!" he cried at length, and his voice of agony rolled round the corpse like the soughing of the wind.

"Ewan! Ewan!" he cried again; but only the sea's voice broke the silence that followed. Then his head fell on the cold breast, and his arms covered the lifeless body, and he cried upon God to have mercy on him, and to lift up His hand against him and cut him off.

Presently he got on his feet, and scarcely knowing what he was doing, he lifted the body in his arms, with the head lying backward on his shoulder, and the white face looking up in its stony stare to the darkening heavens. As he did so his eyes were raised to the cliff, and there, clearly outlined over the black crags and against the somewhat lighter sky, he saw the figure of a man.

He toiled along toward the shed. He was so weak that he could scarce keep on his legs, and when he reached the little place at the mouth of the creek he was more dead than alive. He put the body to lie on the bed of straw on which he had himself slept and dreamed an hour before. Then all at once he felt a low sort of cunning coming over him, and he went back to the door and shut it, and drew the long wooden bolt into its iron hoop on the jamb.

He had hardly done so when he heard an impatient footstep on the shingle outside. In another instant the latch was lifted and the door pushed heavily. Then there was a knock. Dan made no answer, but stood very still and held his breath. There was another knock, and another. Then, in a low tremulous murmur there came the words:

"Where is he? God A'mighty! where is he?" It was Davy Fayle. Another knock, louder, and still no reply.

"Mastha Dan, Mastha Dan, they're coming; Mastha Dan, God A'mighty!—"

Davy was now tramping restlessly to and fro. Dan was trying to consider what it was best to do, whether to open to Davy and hear what he had to say, or to carry it off as if he were not within, when another foot sounded on the shingle and cut short his meditations.

"Have you seen Mr. Ewan—Parson Ewan?"

Dan recognized the voice. It was the voice of Jarvis Kerruish.

Davy did not answer immediately.

"Have you seen him, eh?"

"No, sir," Davy faltered.

"Then why didn't you say so at once? It is very strange. The people said he was walking toward the creek. There's no way out in this direction, is there?"

"Way out—this direction? Yes, sir," Davy stammered.

"How? show me the way."

"By the sea, sir."

"The sea! Simpleton, what are you doing here?"

"Waiting for the boat, sir."

"What shed is this?"

Dan could hear that at this question Davy was in a fever of excitement.

"Only a place for bits of net and cable, and all to that," said Davy, eagerly.

Dan could feel that Jarvis had stepped up to the shed, and that he was trying to look in through the little window.

"Do you keep a fire to warm your nets and cables?" he asked in a suspicious tone.

At the next moment he was trying to force the door. Dan stood behind. The bolt creaked in the hasp. If the hasp should give way, he and Jarvis would stand face to face.

"Strange—there's something strange about all this," said the man outside. "I heard a scream as I came over the Head. Did you hear anything?"

"I tell you I heard nothing," said Davy, sullenly.

Dan grew dizzy, and groping for something to cling to, his hand scraped across the door.

"Wait! I could have sworn I heard something move inside. Who keeps the key of this shed?"

"Kay? There's never a kay at the like of it."

"Then how is it fastened? From within? Wait—let me see."

There was a sound like the brushing of a hand over the outside face of the door.

"Has the snow stopped up the keyhole, or is there no such thing? Or is the door fastened by a padlock?"

Dan had regained his self-possession by this time. He felt an impulse to throw the door open. He groped at his waist for the dagger, but belt and dagger were both gone.

"All this is very strange," said Jarvis, and then he seemed to turn from the door and move away.

"Stop. Where is the man Dan—the captain?" he asked, from a little distance.

"I dunno," said Davy, stoutly.

"That's a lie, my lad."

Then the man's footsteps went off in dull beats on the snow-clotted pebbles.

After a moment's silence there was a soft knocking; Davy had crept up to the door.

"Mastha Dan," he whispered, amid panting breath.

Dan did not stir. The latch was lifted in vain.

"Mastha Dan, Mastha Dan." The soft knocking continued.

Dan found his voice at last.

"Go away, Davy—go away," he said, hoarsely.

There was a short pause, and then there came from without an answer like a sob.

"I'm going, Mastha Dan."

After that all was silent as death. Half an hour later, Dan Mylrea was walking through the darkness toward Ballamona. In his blind misery he was going to Mona. The snow was not falling now, and in the lift of the storm the sky was lighter than it had been. As Dan passed the old church, he could just descry the clock. The snow lay thick on the face, and clogged the hands. The clock had stopped. It stood at five exactly.

The blind leading that is here of passion by accident is everywhere that great tragedies are done. It is not the evil in man's heart more than the deep perfidy of circumstance that brings him to crime.

CHAPTER XXI
THE VOICE IN THE NIGHT

However bleak the night, however dark the mood of the world might be, there was a room in Ballamona that was bright with one beautiful human flower in bloom. Mona was there—Mona of the quiet eyes and the silent ways and the little elfish head. It was Christmas Eve with her as with other people, and she was dressing the house in hibbin and hollin from a great mountain of both that Hommy-beg had piled up in the hall. She was looking very smart and happy that night in her short body of homespun turned in from neck to waist, showing a white habit-shirt and a white handkercheif crossed upon it; a quilted overskirt and linen apron that did not fall so low as to hide the open-work stockings and the sandal-shoes. Her room, too, was bright and sweet, with its glowing fire of peat and logs on the wide hearth, its lamp on the square oak table, and the oak settle drawn up between them.

In one corner of the settle, bubbling and babbling and spluttering and cooing amid a very crater of red baize cushions, was Mona's foster-child, Ewan's motherless daughter, lying on her back and fighting the air with clinched fists.

While Mona picked out the hibbin from the hollin, dissected both, made arches and crosses and crowns and rosettes, and then sprinkled flour to resemble snow on the red berries and the green leaves, she sung an old Manx ballad in snatches, or prattled to the little one in that half-articulate tongue that comes with the instinct of motherhood to every good woman that God ever makes.

> I rede ye beware of the Carrasdoo men
> As ye come up the wold;
> I rede ye beware of the haunted glen—

But a fretful whimper would interrupt the singer.

"Hush, hush, Ailee darling—hush."

The whimper would be hushed, and again there would be a snatch of the ballad:

> In Jorby curragh they dwell alone
> By dark peat bogs, where the willows moan,
> Down in a gloomy and lonely glen—

Once again the whimper would stop the song.

"Hush, darling; papa is coming to Ailee, yes; and Ailee will see papa, yes, and papa will see Ailee, yes, and Ailee—"

Then a long, low gurgle, a lovely head leaning over the back of the settle and dropping to the middle of the pillow like a lark to its nest in the grass, a long liquid kiss on the soft round baby legs, and then a perfect fit of baby laughter.

It was as pretty a picture as the world had in it on that bleak Christmas Eve. Whatever tumult might reign without, there within was a nest of peace.

Mona was expecting Ewan at Ballamona that night, and now she was waiting for his coming. It was true that when he was there three hours ago it was in something like anger that they had parted, but Mona recked nothing of that. She knew Ewan's impetuous temper no better than his conciliatory spirit. He would come to-night, as he had promised yesterday, and if there had been anger between them it would then be gone.

Twenty times she glanced at the little clock with the lion face and the pendulum like a dog's head that swung above the ingle. Many a time, with head aslant, with parted lips, and eyes alight, she cried "Hark!" to the little one when a footstep would sound in the hall But Ewan did not come, and meantime the child grew more and more fretful as her bedtime approached. At length Mona undressed her and carried her off to her crib in the room adjoining, and sang softly to her while she struggled hard with sleep under the oak hood with the ugly beasts carved on it, until sleep had conquered and all was silence and peace. Then, leaving a tallow dip burning on the table between the crib and the bed, lest perchance the little one should awake and cry from fear of the darkness, Mona went back to her sitting-room to finish off the last bunch of the hibbin and hollin.

The last bunch was a bit of prickly green, with a cluster of the reddest berries, and Mona hung it over a portrait of her brother, which was painted by a great artist from England when Ewan was a child. The Deemster had turned the portrait out of the dining-room after the painful interview at Bishop's Court about the loan and surety, and Mona had found it, face to the wall, in a lumber-room. She looked at it now with a new interest. When she hung the hollin over it she recognized for the first time a resemblance to the little Aileen whom she had just put to bed. How strange it seemed that Ewan had once been a child like Aileen!

Then she began to feel that Ewan was late in coming, and to make conjectures as to the cause of his delay. Her father's house was fast becoming a cheerless place to her. More than ever the Deemster was lost to her. Jarvis

Kerruish, her stranger-brother, was her father's companion; and this seemed to draw her closer to Ewan for solace and cheer.

Then she sat on the settle to thread some loose berries that had fallen, and to think of Dan—the high-spirited, reckless, rollicking, headstrong, tender-hearted, thoughtless, brave, stubborn, daring, dear, dear Dan—Dan, who was very, very much to her in her great loneliness. Let other people rail at Dan if they would; he was wrapped up with too many of her fondest memories to allow of disloyalty like that. Dan would yet justify her belief in him. Oh, yes, he would yet be a great man, all the world would say it was so, and she would be very proud that he was her cousin—yes, her cousin, or perhaps, perhaps—. And then, without quite daring to follow up that delicious train of thought, even in her secret heart, though none might look there and say if it was unmaidenly, Mona came back to the old Manx ballad, and sang to herself another verse of it:

"Who has not heard of Adair, the youth?
Who does not know that his soul was truth?
Woe is me! how smoothly they speak,
And Adair was brave, and a man, but weak."

All at once her hand went up to her forehead, and the words of the old song seemed to have a new significance. Hardly had her voice stopped and her last soft note ceased to ring in the quiet room, when she thought she heard her own name called twice—"Mona! Mona!"

The voice was Ewan's voice, and it seemed to come from her bedroom. She rose from the settle, and went into her room. There was no one there save the child. The little one was disturbed in her sleep at the moment, and was twisting restlessly, making a faint cry. It was very strange. The voice had been Ewan's voice, and it had been deep and tremulous, as the voice of one in trouble.

Presently the child settled itself to sleep, all was silent as before, and Mona went back to the sitting-room. Scarcely was she seated afresh when she heard the voice again, and it again called her twice by name, "Mona! Mona!" in the same tremulous tone, but very clear and distinct.

Then tremblingly Mona rose once more and went into her room, for thence the voice seemed to come. No one was there. The candle burned fitfully, and suddenly the child cried in its sleep—that strange night-cry that freezes the blood of one who is awake to hear it. It was very, very strange.

Feeling faint, hardly able to keep on her feet, Mona went back to the sitting-room and opened the door that led into the hall. No one seemed to be stirring. The door of her father's study opposite was closed, and there was talking—the animated talking of two persons—within.

Mona turned back, closed her door quietly, and then, summoning all her courage, she walked to the window and drew the heavy curtains aside. The hoops from which they hung rattled noisily over the pole. Putting her face close to the glass, and shading her eyes from the light of the lamp behind her, she looked out. She saw that the snow had fallen since the lamp had been lit at dusk. There was snow on the ground, and thin snow on the leafless boughs of the trees. She could see nothing else. She even pushed up the sash, and called:

"Who is there?"

But there came no answer. The wind moaned about the house, and the sea rumbled in the distance. She pulled the sash down again.

Then, leaving the curtain back, she turned again into the room, and partly to divert her mind from the mysterious apprehensions that had seized it, she sat down at the little harpsichord that stood on the farther side of the ingle against the wall that ran at right angles from the window.

At first her fingers ran nervously over the keys, but they gained force as she went on, and the volume of sound seemed to dissipate her fears.

"It is nothing," she thought. "I have been troubled about what Ewan said to-day, and I'm nervous—that is all."

And as she played her eyes looked not at the finger-board, but across her shoulder toward the bare window. Then suddenly there came to her a sensation that made her flesh creep. It was as if from the darkness outside there were eyes which she could not see looking steadily in upon her where she sat.

Her blood rushed to her head, she felt dizzy, the playing ceased, and she clung by one hand to the candle-rest of the harpsichord. Then once more she distinctly heard the same deep, tremulous voice call her by her name—"Mona! Mona!"

Faint and all but reeling, she rose again, and again made her way to the bedroom. As before, the child was restless in her sleep. It seemed as if all the air were charged. Mona had almost fallen from fright, when all at once she heard a sound that she could not mistake, and instantly she recovered some self-possession.

It was the sound of the window of her sitting-room being thrown open from without. She ran back, and saw Dan Mylrea climbing into the room.

"Dan!" she cried.

"Mona."

"Did you call?"

"When?"

"Now—a little while ago?"

"No."

A great trembling shook Dan's whole frame. Mona perceived it, and a sensation of disaster not yet attained to the clearness of an idea took hold of her.

"Where is Ewan?" she said.

He tried to avoid her gaze. "Why do you ask for him?" said Dan, in a faltering voice.

"Where is he?" she asked again.

He grew dizzy, and laid hold of the settle for support. The question she asked was that which he had come to answer, but his tongue clave to his mouth.

Very pale and almost rigid from the heaviness of a great fear which she felt but could not understand, she watched him when he reeled like a drunken man.

"He has called me three times. Where is he? He was to be here to-night," she said.

"Ewan will not come to-night," he answered, scarcely audibly; "not to-night, Mona, or to-morrow—or ever—no, he will never come again."

The horrible apprehension that had taken hold of her leaped to the significance of his words, and, almost before he had spoken, a cry burst from her.

"Ewan is dead—he is dead; Mona, our Ewan, he is dead," he faltered.

She dropped to the settle, and cried, in the excess of her first despair, "Ewan, Ewan! to think that I shall see him no more!" and then she wept. All the time Dan stood over her, leaning heavily to bear himself up, trembling visibly, and with a look of great agony fixed upon her, as if he had not the strength to turn his eyes away.

"Yes, yes, our Ewan is dead," he repeated in a murmur that came up from his heart. "The truest friend, the fondest brother, the whitest soul, the dearest, bravest, purest, noblest—O God! O God! dead, dead! Worse, a hundredfold worse—Mona, he is murdered."

At that she raised herself up, and a bewildered look was in her eyes.

"Murdered? No, that is not possible. He was beloved by all. There is no one who would kill him—there is no one alive with a heart so black."

"Yes, Mona, but there is," he said; "there is one man with a heart so black."

"Who is he?"

"Who! He is the foulest creature on God's earth. Oh, God in heaven! why was he born?"

"Who is he?"

He bowed his head where he stood before her and beads of sweat started from his brow.

"Cursed be the hour when that man was born!" he said in an awful whisper.

Then Mona's despair came upon her like a torrent, and she wept long. In the bitterness of her heart she cried:

"Cursed indeed, cursed forever! Dan, Dan, you must kill him—you must kill that man!"

But at the sound of that word from her own lips the spirit of revenge left her on the instant, and she cried, "No, no, not that." Then she went down on her knees and made a short and piteous prayer for forgiveness for her thought. "O Father," she prayed, "forgive me. I did not know what I said. But Ewan is dead! O Father, our dear Ewan is murdered. Some black-hearted man has killed him. Vengeance is Thine. Yes, I know that. O Father, forgive me. But to think that Ewan is gone forever, and that base soul lives on. Vengeance is Thine; but, O Father, let thy vengeance fall upon him. If it is Thy will, let Thy hand be on him. Follow him, Father; follow him with Thy vengeance—"

She had flung herself on her knees by the settle, her upturned eyes wide open, and her two trembling hands held above her head. Dan stood beside her, and as she prayed a deep groan came up from his heart, his breast swelled, and his throat seemed to choke. At last he clutched her by the shoulders and interrupted her prayer, and cried, "Mona, Mona, what are you saying—what are you saying? Stop, stop!"

She rose to her feet. "I have done wrong," she said, more quietly. "He is in God's hands. Yes, it is for God to punish him."

Then Dan said, in a heart-rending voice:

"Mona, he did not mean to kill Ewan—they fought—it was all in the heat of blood."

Once more he tried to avoid her gaze, and once more, pale and immovable, she watched his face.

"Who is he?" she asked, with an awful calmness.

"Mona, turn your face away from me, and I will tell you," he said.

Then everything swam about her, and her pale lips grew ashy.

"Don't you know?" he asked in a whisper.

She did not turn her face, and he was compelled to look at her now. His glaring eyes were fixed upon her.

"Don't you know?" he whispered again, and then, in a scarcely audible voice, he said, "It was I, Mona."

At that she grew cold with horror. Her features became changed beyond recognition. She recoiled from him, stretched her trembling hands before her as if to keep him off.

"Oh, horror! Do not touch me!" she cried, faintly, through the breath that came so hard.

"Do not spare me, Mona," he said in a great sob. "Do not spare me. You do right not to spare me. I have stained my hands with your blood."

Then she sank to the settle, and held her head, while he stood by her and told her all—all the bitter, blundering truth—and bit by bit she grasped the tangled tale, and realized the blind passion and pain that had brought them to such a pass, and saw her own unwitting share in it.

And he on his part saw the product of his headstrong wrath, and the pitiful grounds for it, so small and so absurd as such grounds oftenest are. And together these shipwrecked voyagers on the waters of life sat and wept, and wondered what evil could be in hell itself if man in his blindness could find the world so full of it.

And Dan cursed himself and said:

"Oh, the madness of thinking that if either were gone the other could ever again know one hour's happiness with you, Mona. Ay, though the crime lay hidden, yet would it wither and blast every hour. And now, behold, at the first moment, I am bringing my burden of sin, too heavy for myself, to you. I am a coward—yes, I am a coward. You will turn your back upon me, Mona, and then I shall be alone."

She looked at him with infinite compassion, and her heart surged within her as she listened to his voice of great agony.

"Ah me! and I asked God to curse you," she said. "Oh, how wicked that prayer was! Will God hear it? Merciful Father, do not hear it. I did not know what I said. I am a blind, ignorant creature, but Thou seest and knowest best. Pity him, and forgive him. Oh, no, God will not hear my wicked prayer."

Thus in fitful outbursts she talked and prayed. It was as if a tempest had torn up every tie of her soul. Dan listened, and he looked at her with swimming eyes.

"And do you pray for me, Mona?" he said.

"Who will pray for you if I do not? In all the world there will not be one left to speak kindly of you if I speak ill. Oh, Dan, it will become known, and every one will be against you."

"And can you think well of him who killed your brother?"

"But you are in such sorrow; you are so miserable."

Then Dan's great frame shook wofully, and he cried in his pain—"Mercy, mercy, have mercy! What have I lost? What love have I lost?"

At that Mona's weeping ceased; she looked at Dan through her lashes, still wet, and said in another tone:

"Dan, do not think me unmaidenly. If you had done well, if you had realized my hopes of you, if you had grown to be the good and great man I longed to see you, then, though I might have yearned for you, I would rather have died with my secret than speak of it. But now, now that all this is not so, now that it is a lost faith, now that by God's will you are to be abased before the whole world—oh, do not think me unmaidenly, now I tell you, Dan, that I love you, and have always loved you."

"Mona!" he cried, in a low, passionate tone, and took one step toward her and held out his hands. There was an unspeakable language in her face.

"Yes; and that where you go I must go also, though it were to disgrace and shame—"

She had turned toward him lovingly, yearningly, with heaving breast. With a great cry he flung his arms about her, and the world of pain and sorrow was for that instant blotted out.

But all the bitter flood came rushing back upon them. He put her from him with a strong shudder.

"We are clasping hands over a tomb, Mona. Our love is known too late. We are mariners cast on a rock within a cable's length of harbor, but cut off from it by a cruel sea that may never be passed. We are hopeless within sight of hope. Our love is known in vain. It is a vision of what might have been in the days that are lost forever. We can never clasp hands, for, O God! a cold hand is between us, and lies in the hand of both."

Then again she fell to weeping, but suddenly she arose as if struck by a sudden idea.

"You will be taken," she said; "how can I have forgotten it so long? You must fly from the island. You must get away to-night. To-morrow all will be discovered."

"I will not leave the island," said Dan, firmly. "Can you drive me from you?" he said, with a suppliant look. "Yes, you do well to drive me away."

"My love, I do not drive you from me. I would have you here forever. But you will be taken. Quick, the world is wide."

"There is no world for me save here, Mona. To go from you now is to go forever, and I would rather die by my own hand than face such banishment."

"No, no, not that; never, never that. That would imperil your soul, and then we should be divided forever."

"It is so already, Mona," said Dan, with solemnity. "We are divided forever—as the blessed are divided from the damned."

"Don't say that, don't say that."

"Yes, Mona," he said, with a fearful calmness, "we have thought of my crime as against Ewan, as against you, myself, the world, and its law. But it is a crime against God also, and surely it is the unpardonable sin."

"Don't say that, Dan. There is one great anchor of hope."

"What is that, Mona?"

"Ewan is with God. At this moment, while we stand here together, Ewan sees God."

"Ah!"

Dan dropped to his knees with awe at that thought, and drew off the cap which he had worn until then, and bent his head.

"Yes, he died in anger and in strife," said Mona; "but God is merciful. He knows the feebleness of His creatures, and has pity. Yes, our dear Ewan is with God; now he knows what you suffer, my poor Dan; and he is taking blame to himself and pleading for you."

"No, no; I did it all, Mona. He would not have fought. He would have made peace at the last, but I drove him on. 'I can not fight, Dan,' he said. I can see him saying it, and the sun was setting. No, it was not fight, it was murder. And God will punish me, my poor girl. Death is my just punishment—everlasting death."

"Wait. I know what is to be done."

"What, Mona?"

"You must make atonement."

"How?"

"You must give yourself up to justice and take the punishment of the law. And so you will be redeemed, and God will forgive you."

He listened, and then said:

"And such is to be the end of our love, Mona, born in the hour of its death. You, even you, give me up to justice."

"Don't say that. You will be redeemed by atonement. When Ewan was killed it was woe enough, but that you are under God's wrath is worse than if we were all, all slain."

"Then we must bid farewell. The penalty of my crime is death."

"No, no; not that."

"I must die, Mona. This, then, is to be our last parting."

"And even if so, it is best. You must make your peace with God."

"And you, my last refuge, even you send me to my death. Well, it is right, it is just, it is well. Farewell, my poor girl; this is a sad parting."

"Farewell."

"You will remember me, Mona?"

"Remember you? When the tears I shed for Ewan are dry, I shall still weep for you."

There was a faint cry at that moment.

"Hush!" said Mona, and she lifted one hand.

"It is the child," she added. "Come, look at it."

She turned, and walked toward the bedroom. Dan followed her with drooping head. The little one had again been restless in her sleep, but now, with a long breath, she settled herself in sweet repose.

At sight of the child the great trembling shook Dan's frame again. "Mona, Mona, why did you bring me here?" he said.

The sense of his crime came with a yet keener agony when he looked down at the child's unconscious face. The thought flashed upon him that he had made this innocent babe fatherless, and that all the unprotected years were before her wherein she must realize her loss.

He fell to his knees beside the cot, and his tears rained down upon it.

Mona had lifted the candle from the table, and she held it above the kneeling man and the sleeping child.

It was the blind woman's vision realized.

When Dan rose to his feet he was a stronger man.

"Mona," he said, resolutely, "you are right. This sin must be wiped out."

She had put down the candle and was now trying to take his hand.

"Don't touch me," he said, "don't touch me."

He returned to the other room, and threw open the window. His face was turned toward the distant sea, whose low moan came up through the dark night.

"Dan," she murmured, "do you think we shall meet again?"

"Perhaps we are speaking for the last time, Mona," he answered.

"Oh, my heart will break!" she said. "Dan," she murmured again, and tried to grasp his hand.

"Don't touch me. Not until later—not until—until *then*."

Their eyes met. The longing, yearning look in hers answered to the wild light in his. She felt as if this were the last she was ever to see of Dan in this weary world. He loved her with all his great, broken, bleeding heart. He had sinned for her sake. She caught both his hands with a passionate grasp. Her lips quivered, and the brave, fearless, stainless girl put her quivering lips to his.

To Dan that touch was as fire. With a passionate cry he flung his arms about her. For an instant her head lay on his breast.

"Now go," she whispered, and broke from his embrace. Dan tore himself away, with heart and brain aflame. Were they ever to meet again? Yes. At one great moment they were yet to stand face to face.

The night was dark, but Dan felt the darkness not at all, for the night was heavier within him. He went down toward the creek. To-morrow he would give himself up to the Deemster; but to-night was for himself—himself and *it*.

He went by the church. A noisy company were just then trooping out of the porch into the churchyard. There they gathered in little knots, lit lanterns, laughed, and drank healths from bottles that were brought out of their pockets.

It was the breaking up of the Oiel Verree.

CHAPTER XXII
ALONE, ALONE—ALL, ALL ALONE!

When Dan got down to the creek the little shed was full of the fisher-fellows. There were Quilleash, Teare, Crennell, and the lad Davy. The men wore their oilskins, as if they had just stepped out of the dingey on the beach, and on the floor were three baskets of cod and ray, as if they had just set them down. The fire of gorse was crackling on the hearth, and Davy sat beside it, looking pale and ill. He had watched Dan away from the shed, and then, trembling with fear, but girding up his young heart to conquer it, he had crept back and kept guard by the body.

"I couldn't give myself liberty to lave it," he said, half fearfully, lifting his eyes to Dan's as Dan entered. Then the men, who in the first moment of horror had asked Davy fifty questions, and got never an answer to any of them, seemed to understand everything at once. They made way for Dan, and he strode through them, and looked down at the body, for it was still lying where he had left it. He said not a word.

When the men had time to comprehend in its awful fulness what had occurred, they stood together and whispered, cast side looks at Dan, and then long, searching looks at the body. The certainty that Ewan was dead did not at first take hold of them. There was no mark of violence on the body except the wound above the wrist, and suddenly, while the men stood and looked down, the wound bled afresh. Then old Quilleash, who was reputed to possess a charm to stop blood, knelt beside Ewan, and while all looked on and none spoke, he whispered his spell in the deaf ear.

"A few good words can do no harm," said Crennell, the cook, who was a Quaker.

Old Quilleash whispered again in the dead ear, and then he made a wild command to the blood to cease flowing, in the name of the three godly men who came to Rome—Christ, Peter, and Paul.

There was a minute of silence, and the blood seemed to stop. The men trembled; Davy, the lad, grew more pale than before, and Dan stood as if in a stupor, looking down and seeing all, yet seeing nothing.

Then the old man lifted his tawny face. "Cha marroo as clagh," he said, in another hoarse whisper. "He is dead as a stone."

There was a deep groan from the throats of the men; they dropped aside, and awe fell upon them. None of them spoke to Dan, and none questioned the lad again; but all seemed to understand everything in some vague way. Billy Quilleash sat on a block of a tree-trunk that stood at one side, and there was silence for a space. Then the old man turned his face to his mates and said, "I'm for a man sticking up for a frien', I am."

At that there was an uneasy movement among the others.

"Aw, yes, though, a man should stick to his frien', he should, alow or aloft, up or down," continued Billy; and after some twisting and muttering among the other fisher-fellows he went on: "You have to summer and winter a man before you know him, and lave it to us to know Mastha Dan. We've shared meat, shared work with him, and d—— me sowl! nothing will hould me, but I'll stand up for him now, sink or swim."

Then one of the fellows said "Ay," and another said "Ay," and a third—it was Crennell—said, "A friend in need was more preciouser nor goold;" and then old Billy half twisted his head toward Dan, but never once lifted his eyes to Dan's face, and speaking at him but not to him, said they were rough chaps maybe, and couldn't put out no talk at all, never being used of it, but if there was somethin' wrong, as was plain to see, and keepin' a quiet tongue in your head was the way it was goin', and buckin' up for them as was afther buckin' up for his chums, why, a frien' was a frien', and they meant to stand by it.

At that, these rough sea-dogs, with the big hearts in their broad breasts, took hold of each other's hard hands in a circle about the body of Ewan, whose white face looked up at them in its stony stare, and there in the little lonely shed by the sea they made their mutual pledge.

All that time Dan had stood and looked on in silence, and Davy, sitting by the spluttering fire, sobbed audibly while Uncle Billy spoke.

"We must put it away," said old Billy, in a low tone, with his eyes on the body.

"Ay," said Ned Teare.

"What's o'clock?"

"A piece past twelve."

"Half-flood. It will be near the turn of the ebb at three," said Quilleash.

Not another word of explanation was needed, all understanding that they must take the body of Ewan out to sea, and bury it there after three o'clock next morning, so that, if it stirred after it was sent down to its long home, it must be swept away over the Channel.

"Heise," said one, as he put his hand down to lift the body.

"Shoo!"

Dan himself stepped aside to let them pass out. He had watched their movements with wide eyes. They went by him without a word. When they were gone, he followed them mechanically, scarcely knowing what he did. Davy went after him.

The fishermen stepped out into the night. In silence they carried the body of Ewan to the dingey that lay on the beach. All got into the boat and pushed off. It was very dark now, but soon they came athwart the hawse of the "Ben-my-Chree," which was lying at anchor below low-water. They pulled up, lifted the body over the gunwale, and followed it into the fishing-boat.

"There's a good taste of a breeze," said old Quilleash.

In five minutes more they were standing out to sea, with their dread freight of horror and crime. They had put the body to lie by the hatchways, and again and again they turned their heads toward it in the darkness. It was as though it might even yet stand up in their midst, and any man at any moment might find it face to face with him, eye to eye.

The wind was fresh outside. It was on their larboard quarter as they made in long tacks for the north. When they were well away the men gathered about the cockpit and began to mourn over Ewan, and to recount their memories concerning him.

"Well, the young pazon's cruise is up, and a rael good man anyway."

"Aw, yes, there's odds of pazons, but the like of him isn't in."

"Poor Pazon Ewan," said Quilleash, "I remember him since he was a wee skute in his mother's arms—and a fine lady too. And him that quiet, but thinking a dale maybe, with his head a piece to starboard and his eyes fixed like a figure-head, but more natheral, and tender uncommon. And game too. Aw, dear, you should 'a seen him buck up to young Dan at whiles."

"Game? A hot temper at him for all, and I wouldn't trust but it's been the death of him."

"Well, man, lave it at that; lave it, man. Which of us doesn't lie ever in a bit of a breeze aither to port or starboard? God won't be hard on him for the temper. No, no, God'll never be hard on a warm heart because it keeps company with a hot head."

"Aw, but the tender he was!" said Crennell, the Quaker. "And the voice like an urgan when it's like a flute, soft and low, and all a-tremblin'! D'ye mind the day ould Betty Kelly lost her little gel by the faver, the one with the slander little stalk of a body, and the head like a flower, and the eyes like a pair of bumbees playing in it? You mind her, the millish? Well, young Pazon Ewan up and went to Ballig-beg immadietly, and ould Betty scraming and crying morthal, and 'she'd die!' so she would, and 'what for should you live?' but och, boy, the way the pazon put out the talk at him, and the bit of a spell at the prayin'—aw, man alive, he calked the seams of the ould body wonderful."

"The man was free, as free as free," said old Quilleash. "When he grew up it was, 'How are you, Billy Quilleash?' And when he came straight from the college at Bishop's Court, and all the larning at him, and the fine English tongue, and all to that, it was 'And how are you to-day, Billy?' 'I'm middlin' to-day, Mastha Ewan.' Aw, yes, yes, though, a tender heart at him anyway, and no pride at all, at all."

The old man's memories were not thrilling to relate, but they brought the tears to his eyes, and he wiped them away with his sleeve.

"Still a quick temper for all, and when his blood was up it was batten down your hatches, my boys—a storm's coming," said Ned Teare.

All at once they turned their faces in the darkness to where Dan sat on the battened hatches, his elbows on his knees, his head on his hands, and a sort of shame took hold of them at all this praise of Ewan. It was as if every word must enter into Dan's soul like iron. Then, hardly knowing what they did, they began to beat about to undo the mischief. They talked of the Deemster in his relation to his son.

"Deed on Ewan—there was not much truck atween them—the Deemster and him. It wasn't natheral. It's like as if a sarpent crawled in his ould sowl, the craythur, and spat out at the young pazon."

Then they talked of Jarvis Kerruish.

"Och, schemin' and plannin' reg'lar, and stirrin' and stirrin' and stirrin' at the devil's own gruel."

"Aw, the Deemster's made many a man toe the mark, but I'm thinking he'll have to stand to it when the big day comes. I'll go bail the ould polecat's got summat to answer for in this consarn."

Dan said nothing. Alone, and giving no sign, he still sat on the hatches near where the body lay, and, a little to aft of him, Davy Fayle was stretched out on the deck. The lad's head rested on one hand, and his eyes were fixed with a dog's yearning look on the dark outlines of Dan's figure.

They were doubling the Point of Ayre, when suddenly the wind fell to a dead calm. The darkness seemed to grow almost palpable.

"More snow comin'—let the boat driff," said old Billy Quilleash, and the men turned into the cabin, only Dan and the body, with Davy, the lad, remaining on deck.

Then, through the silence and the blank darkness, there was the sound of large drops of rain falling on the deck. Presently there came a torrent which lasted about ten minutes. When the rain ceased the darkness lifted away, and the stars came out. This was toward two o'clock, and soon afterward the moon rose, but before long it was concealed again by a dense black turret-cloud that reared itself upward from the horizon.

When Dan stepped aboard a dull, dense aching at his heart was all the consciousness he had. The world was dead to him. He had then no clear purpose of concealing his crime, and none of carrying out the atonement that Mona had urged him to attempt. He was stunned. His spirit seemed to be dead. It was as though it could awake to life again only in another world. He had watched old Billy when he whispered into Ewan's deaf ear the words of the mystic charm. Without will or intention he had followed the men when they came to the boat. Later on a fluttering within him preceded the return of the agonizing sense. Had he not damned his own soul forever? That he had taken a warm human life; that Ewan, who had been alive, lay dead a few feet away from him—this was nothing to the horrible thought that he himself was going, hot and unprepared, to an everlasting hell. "Oh, can this thing have happened?" his bewildered mind asked itself a thousand times as it awoke as often from the half-dream of a paralyzed consciousness. Yes, it was true that such a thing had occurred. No, it was not a nightmare. He would never awake in the morning sunlight and smile to know that it was not true. No, no, true, true, true it was, even until the Day of Judgment, and he and Ewan stood once more face to face, and the awful voice would cry aloud, "Go, get thee hence."

Then Dan thought of Mona, and his heart was nigh to breaking. With a dumb longing his eyes turned through the darkness toward the land, and while the boat was sailing before the wind it seemed to be carrying him away from Mona forever. The water that lay between them was as the river that for all eternity would divide the blessed and the damned.

And while behind him the men talked, and their voices fell on his ear like a dull buzz, the last ray of his hope was flying away. When Mona had prompted him to the idea of atonement, it had come to him like a gleam of sunlight that, though he might never, never clasp her hands on earth, in heaven she would yet be his, to love for ever and ever. But no, no, no; between them now the great gulf was fixed.

Much of this time Dan lay on the deck with only the dead and the lad Davy for company, and the fishing-boat lay motionless with only the lap of the waters about her. The stars died off, the darkness came again, and then, deep in the night, the first gray streaks stretching along the east foretold the dawn. Over the confines of another night the soft daylight was about to break, but more utterly lonely, more void, to Dan, was the great waste of waters now that the striding light was chasing the curling mists than when the darkness lay dead upon it. On one side no object was visible on the waters until sky and ocean met in that great half-circle far away. On the other side was the land that was once called home.

When the gray light came, and the darkness ebbed away, Dan still sat on the hatches, haggard and pale. Davy lay on the deck a pace or two aside. A gentle breeze was rising in the southwest. The boat had drifted many miles, and was now almost due west off Peeltown, and some five miles out to sea. The men came up from below. The cold white face by the hatchway looked up at them, and at heaven.

"We must put it away now," said Billy Quilleash.

"Ay, it's past the turn of the ebb," said Crennell.

Not another word was spoken. A man went below and brought up an old sail, and two heavy iron weights, used for holding down the nets, were also fetched from the hold. There was no singing out, no talking. Silently they took up what lay there cold and stiff, and wrapped it in canvas, putting one of the weights at the head and another at the feet. Then one of the men—it was old Billy himself, because he had been a rigger in his young days—sat down with a sail-maker's needle and string, and began to stitch up the body in the sail.

"Will the string hold?" asked one.

"It will last him this voyage out—it's a short one," said old Billy.

Awe and silence sat on the crew. When all was made ready, the men brought from below a bank-board used for shooting the nets. They lifted the body on to it, and then with the scudding-pole they raised one end of the board on to the gunwale. It was a solemn and awful sight. Overhead the heavy clouds of night were still rolling before the dawn.

Dan sat on the hatches with his head in his hands and his haggard face toward the deck. None spoke to him. A kind of awe had fallen on the men in their dealings with him. They left him alone. Davy Fayle had got up and was leaning against the mitch-board. All hands else gathered round the bank-board and lifted their caps. Then old Quilleash went down on one knee and laid his right hand on the body, while two men raised the other end of the board. "*Dy bishee jeeah shin*—God prosper you," murmured the old fisherman.

"God prosper you," echoed the others, and the body of Ewan slid down into the wide waste of waters.

And then there occurred one of those awful incidents which mariners say have been known only thrice in all the strange history of the sea. Scarcely had the water covered up the body, when there was a low rumble under the wave-circles in which it had disappeared. It was the noise of the iron weights slipping from their places at the foot and at the head. The stitching was giving away, and the weights were tearing open the canvas in which the body was wrapped. In another minute these weights had rolled out of the canvas and sunk into the sea. Then a terrible thing happened. The body, free of the weights that were to sink it, rose to the surface. The torn canvas, not yet thoroughly saturated, opened out, and spread like a sail in the breeze that had risen again. The tide was not yet strong, for the ebb had only just begun, and the body, floating on the top of the water like a boat began to drive athwart the hawse of the fishing-boat straight for the land. Nor was the marvel ended yet. Almost instantly a great luminous line arose and stretched from the boat's quarter toward the island, white as a moon's waterway, but with no moon to make it. Flashing along the sea's surface for several seconds, it seemed to be the finger of God marking the body's path on the waters. Old mariners, who can interpret aright the signs of sea and sky, will understand this phenomenon if they have marked closely what has been said of the varying weather of this fearful night.

To the crew of the "Ben-my-Chree" all that had happened bore but one awful explanation. The men stood and stared into each other's faces in speechless dismay. They strained their eyes to watch the body until—the strange light being gone—it became a speck in the twilight of the dawn and could be seen no more. It was as though an avenging angel had torn the murdered man from their grasp. But the worst thought was behind, and it was this: the body of Ewan Mylrea would wash ashore, the murder would become known, and they themselves, who had thought only to hide the crime of Dan Mylrea, would now, in the eyes of the law, become participators in that crime or accessories to it.

Dan saw it all, and in a moment he was another man. He read that incident by another light. It was God's sign to the guilty man, saying, "Blood will have blood." The body would not be buried; the crime would not be hidden. The penalty must be paid. Then in an instant Dan thrust behind him all his vague fears, and all his paralyzing terrors. Atonement! atonement! atonement! God himself demanded it. Dan leaped to his feet and cried: "Come, my lads, we must go back—heave hearty and away."

It was the first time Dan had spoken that night, and his voice was awful in the men's ears.

CHAPTER XXIII
ALONE ON A WIDE, WIDE SEA

The wind strengthened, and the men hoisted sail and began to beat into the island. The breeze filled the canvas, and for half an hour the jib lay over the side, while the fishing-boat scudded along like a startled bird. The sun rose over the land, a thin gauze obscuring it. The red light flashed and died away, and fanned the air as if the wind itself were the sunshine. The men's haggard faces caught at moments a lurid glow from it. In the west a mass of bluish cloud rested a little while on the horizon, and then passed into a nimbus of gray rain-cloud that floated above it. Such was the dawn and sunrise of a fateful day.

Dan stood at the helm. When the speck that had glided along the waters like a spectre boat could be no more seen, he gazed in silence toward the eastern light and the green shores of morning. Then he had a sweet half-hour's blessed respite from terrible thoughts. He saw calmly what he had done, and in what a temper of blind passion he had done it. "Surely God is merciful," he thought, and his mind turned to Mona. It relieved him to think of her. She intertwined herself with his yearning hope of pardon and peace. She became part of his scheme of penitence. His love for her was to redeem him in the Father's eye. He was to take it to the foot of God's white throne, and when his guilt came up for judgment, he was to lay it meekly there, and look up into the good Father's face.

The crew had now recovered from their first consternation, and were no longer obeying Dan's orders mechanically. They had come aboard with no clear purpose before them, except that of saving their friend; but nature is nature, and a pitiful thing at the best, and now every man began to be mainly concerned about saving himself. One after one they slunk away forward and sat on the thwart, and there they took counsel together. The wind was full on their starboard beam, the mainsail and yawl were bellied out, and the boat was driving straight for home. But through the men's half-bewildered heads there ran like a cold blast of wind the thought that home could be home no longer. The voices of girls, the prattle of children, the welcome of wife, the glowing hearth—these could be theirs no more. Davy Fayle stayed aft with Dan, but the men fetched him forward and began to question him.

"'Tarprit all this mysterious trouble to us," they said.

Davy held down his head and made no answer.

"You were with him—what's it he's afther doin'?"

Still no answer from the lad.

"Out with it, you cursed young imp," said old Billy.

"Damn his fool's face, why doesn't he spake?"

"It's the mastha's saycret, and I wunnit tell it," said Davy.

"You wunnit, you idiot waistrel?"

"No, I wunnit," said Davy, stoutly.

"Look here, ye beachcomber, snappin' yer fingers at yer old uncle that's after bringin' you up, you pauper—what was it goin' doin' in the shed yander?"

"It's his saycret," repeated Davy.

Old Billy took Davy by the neck as if he had been a sack with an open mouth, and brought down his other hand with a heavy slap on the lad's shoulder.

"Gerr out, you young devil," he said.

Davy took the blow quietly, but he stirred not an inch, and he turned on his uncle with great wide eyes.

"Gerr out, scollop eyes;" and old Billy lifted his hand again.

"Aisy, aisy," said Crennell, interposing; and then, while Davy went back aft, the men compared notes again.

"It's plain to see," said Ned Teare, "it's been a quarrel and maybe a fight, and he's had a piece more than the better, as is only natheral, and him a big strapping chap as strong as a black ox and as straight as the backbone of a herring, and he's been in hidlins, and now he's afther takin' a second thought, and goin' back and chance it."

This reading of the mystery commended itself to all.

"It's aisy for him to lay high like that," said Ned again. "If I was the old Bishop's son I'd hould my luff too, and no hidlins neither. But we've got ourselves in for it, so we have, and we're the common sort, so we are, and there's never no sailin' close to the wind for the like of us."

And to this view of the situation there were many gruff assents. They had come out to sea innocently enough and by a kindly impulse, but they had thereby cast in their lot with the guilty man; and the guilty man had favor in high places, but they had none. Then their tousled heads went together again.

"What for shouldn't we lay high, too?" whispered one, which, with other whispers, was as much as to say, why should they not take the high hand and mutiny, and put Dan into irons, and turn the boat's head and stand out to sea? Then it would be anywhere, anywhere, away from the crime of one, and the guilt of all.

"Hould hard," said old Billy Quilleash, "I'll spake to himself."

Dan, at the tiller, had seen when the men went forward, and he had also seen when some of them cast sidelong looks over their shoulders in his direction. He knew—he thought he knew—the thought wherewith their brave hearts were busy. They were thinking—so thought Dan—that if he meant to throw himself away they must prevent him. But they should see that he could make atonement. Atonement? Empty solace, pitiful unction for a soul in its abasement, but all that remained to him—all, all.

Old Quilleash went aft, sidled up to the helm, and began to speak in a stammering way, splicing a bit of rope while he spoke, and never lifting his eyes to Dan's face.

"What for shouldn't we gerr away to Shetlands?" he said.

"Why to Shetlands?" asked Dan.

"Aw, it's safe and well we'll be when we're there. Aw, yes, I've been there afore to-day. They're all poor men there, but right kind; and what's it sayin', 'When one poor man helps another poor man, God laughs.'"

Dan thought he saw into the heart of the old fellow. His throat grew hard and his eyes dim, and he twisted his face away, keeping one hand on the tiller. They should yet be justified of their loyalty, these stout sea-dogs—yes, God helping him.

"No, no, Billy," he said, "there's to be no running away. We're going back to see it out."

At that old Quilleash threw off some of his reserve.

"Mastha Dan," he said, "we came out to sea just to help you out of this jeel, and because we've shared work, shared meat with you, and a frien' should stand to a frien'; but now we're in for it too, so we are, and what you'll have to stand to we'll have to stand to, and it'll be unknownst to the law as we are innocent as kittens; and so it's every man for himself and God for us all."

Then Dan understood them—how had he been blind so long to their position?

"You want me to put about; is that it?" he asked.

Old Quilleash nodded his head, still keeping his eyes down.

"You think you'll be taken with me?"

Old Quilleash made an abashed mutter of assent. "Aw, yes, as 'cessories before the fac's," he added.

At that Dan's great purpose began to waver.

"Don't fear, Billy," he said, "I'll speak up for you."

"And what'll that go for? Nothin'. Haven't we been tryin' to put 'it' away?"

"That's true."

It was a fearful situation. The cold sweat rose in big beads on Dan's forehead. What had he done? He had allowed these brave fellows to cast in their lot with him. They were with him now for good or ill. He might say they were innocent, but what would his word avail? And he had no proof. They had tried to cover up his crime; they could not cover it; God had willed that the crime should not be hidden. And now, if he wished to lose his life to save his soul, what right had he to take the lives of these men also? The brave fellows had wives that waited for them, and children that claimed their knees. Atonement? Empty heroics to be bought at the price of the blood of five loyal fellows whose only crime was that they had followed him. He had dressed himself in a proud armor of self-sacrifice, but a righteous God, that sees into the heart of man and hates pride and brings it to the dust, had stripped him naked.

Dan's soul was in a turmoil. What should he do? On the one hand were love, honor, Mona, even everlasting life; and on the other were five innocent men. The agony of that moment was terrible. Atonement? God must have set his face against it.

Dan's hand rested on the tiller, but there was no strength in his arm, because there was now no resolve in his heart. The fishing-boat was about three miles west of Jurby Point, going well before the wind. In half an hour more it would run into the creek. It was now to act or never. What was he to do? What? What?

It was, then, in that moment of awful doubt, when the will of a strong man might have shriveled up, that nature herself seemed to give the answer.

All at once the wind fell again to a dead calm. Then Dan knew, or seemed to know, that God was with the men, and against him. There was to be no atonement. No, there was to be no proud self-sacrifice.

Dan's listless hand dropped from the tiller, and he flung himself down in his old seat by the hatches. The men looked into each other's faces and smiled a grisly smile. The sails flapped idly; the men furled them, and the boat drifted south.

The set of the tide was still to ebb, and every boat's length south took the boat a fathom farther out to sea. This was what the men wanted, and they gathered in the cockpit, and gave way to more cheerful spirits.

Dan lay by the hatches, helpless and hopeless, and more haggard and pale than before. An unearthly light now fired his eyes, and that was the first word of a fearful tale. A witch's Sabbath, a devil's revelry, had begun in his distracted brain. It was as though he were already a being of another world. In a state of wild hallucination he saw his own spectre, and he was dead. He lay on the deck; he was cold; his face was white, and it stared straight up at the sky. The crew were busy about him; they were bringing up the canvas and the weights. He knew what they were going to do; they were going to bury him in the sea.

Then a film overspread his sight, and when he awoke he knew that he had slept. He had seen his father and Mona in a dream. His father was very old, the white head was bent, and the calm, saintly gaze was fixed upon him. There was a happy thought in Mona's face. Everything around her spoke of peace. The dream was fresh and sweet and peaceful to Dan when he woke where he lay on the deck. It was like the sunshine and the caroling of birds and the smell of new-cut grass. Was there no dew in Heaven for parched lips, no balm for the soul of a man accursed?

Hours went by. The day wore on. A passing breath sometimes stirred the waters, and again all was dumb, dead, pulseless peace. Hearing only the faint flap of the rippling tide, they drifted, drifted, drifted.

Curious and very touching were the changes that came over the feelings of the men. They had rejoiced when they were first becalmed, but now another sense was uppermost. The day was cold to starvation. Death was before them—slow, sure, relentless death. There could be no jugglery. Then let it be death at home rather than death on this desert sea! Anything, anything but this blind end, this dumb end, this dying bit by bit on still waters. To see the darkness come again, and the sun rise afresh, and once more the sun sink and the darkness deepen, and still to lie there with nothing around but the changeless sea, and nothing above but the empty sky, and only the eye of God upon them, while the winds and the waters lay in His avenging hands—let it rather be death, swift death, just or unjust.

Thus despair took hold of them, and drove away all fear, and where there is no fear there is no grace.

"Share yn olk shione dooin na yn olk nagh nhione dooin," said old Billy, and that was the old Manx proverb that says that better is the evil we know than the evil we do not know.

And with such shifts they deceived themselves, and changed their poor purposes, and comforted their torn hearts.

The cold, thick, winter day was worn far toward sunset, and still not a breath of wind was stirring. Gilded by the sun's hazy rays, the waters to the west made a floor of bleared red. The fishing-boat had drifted nearly ten miles to the south. If she should drift two miles more she must float into the south-eastern current that flows under Contrary Head. At the thought of that, and the bare chance of drifting into Peeltown Harbor, a little of the vague sense of hopelessness seemed to lift away. The men glanced across at Dan, and one murmured: "Let every herring hang by its own gill;" and another muttered: "Every man to the mill with his own sack."

Davy Fayle lay on the deck a few paces from Dan. The simple lad tried to recall the good words that he had heard in the course of his poor, neglected, battered life. One after one they came back to him, most of them from some far-away dreamland, strangely bright with the vision of a face that looked fondly upon him, and even kissed him tenderly. "Gentle Jesus," and "Now I lay me down to sleep"—he could remember them both pretty well, and their simple words went up with the supplicatory ardor of his great-grown heart to the sky on which his eyes were bent.

The men lounged about, and were half frozen. No one cared to go below. None thought of a fire. Silence and death were in their midst. Once again their hearts turned to home, and now with other feelings. They could see the island through the haze, and a sprinkling of snow dotted its purple hills. This brought to mind the bright days of summer, and out of their hopelessness they talked of the woods, and the birds, and the flowers. "D'ye mind my ould mother's bit of a place up the glen," said Crennell, "an' the wee croft afore it swaying and a-flowing same as the sea in the softest taste of a south breeze, and the red ling like a rod of goold running up the hedge, and the fuchsia stretchin' up the wall of the loft, and drooping its red wrack like blood, and the green trammon atop of the porch—d'ye mind it?" And the men said "Ay," and brushed their eyes with their sleeves. Each hard man, with despair seated on his rugged face, longed, like a sick child, to lay his head in the lap of home.

It was Christmas Day. Old Quilleash remembered this, and they talked of Christmas Days gone by, and what happy times they had been. Billy began to tell a humorous story of the two deaf men, Hommy-beg, the gardener, and Jemmy Quirk, the schoolmaster, singing against each other at Oiel Verree; and the old fellow's discolored teeth, with their many gaps between, grinned horribly like an ape's between his frozen jaws when he laughed so hard. But this was too tender a chord, and soon the men were silent once more. Then, while the waters lay cold and clear and still, and the sun was sinking in the west, there came floating to them from the land, through the breathless air, the sound of the church bells ringing at home.

It was the last drop in their cup. The poor fellows could bear up no longer. More than one dropped his head to his knees and sobbed aloud. Then old Quilleash, in a husky voice, and coarsely, almost swearing as he spoke, just to hide his shame in a way, said, spitting from his quid, "Some chap pray a spell." "Ay, ay," said another. "Aw, yes," said a third. But no one prayed. "You, Billy," said Ned Teare. Billy shook his head. The old man had never known a prayer. "It was Pazon Ewan that was powerful at prayer," said Crennell. "You, Crennell." Crennell could not pray.

All lay quiet as death around them, and only the faint sound of the bells was borne to them as a mellow whisper. Then, from near where Dan sat by the hatches, Davy Fayle rose silently to his feet. None had thought of him. With the sad longing in his big, simple eyes, he began to sing. This was what he sang:

"Lo! He comes with clouds descending,
Once for favored sinners slain."

The lad's voice, laden with tears, floated away over the great waters. The men hung their heads, and were mute. The dried-up well of Dan's eyes moistened at last, and down his hard face ran the glistening tears in gracious drops like dew.

CHAPTER XXIV
"THERE'S GOLD ON THE CUSHAGS YET"

Then there came a breath of wind. At first it was soft as an angel's whisper. It grew stronger, and ruffled the sea. Every man lifted his eyes and looked at his mates. Each was struggling with a painful idea that perhaps he was the victim of a delusion of the sense. But the chill breath of the wind was indeed among them.

"Isn't it beginning to puff up from the sou'west?" asked Crennell, in an uncertain whisper. At that old Quilleash jumped to his feet. The idea of the supernatural had gone from him. "Now for the sheets and to make sail," he cried, and spat the quid.

One after one the men got up and bustled about. Their limbs were wellnigh frozen stiff. All was stir and animation in an instant. Pulling at the ropes, the men had begun to laugh, yes, with their husky, grating, tear-drowned voices, even to laugh through their grisly beards. A gruesome sense of the ludicrous had taken hold of them. It was the swift reaction from solemn thoughts. When the boat felt her canvas she shook herself like a sea-bird trying her wings, then shot off at full flight.

"Bear a hand there. Lay on, man alive. Why, you're going about like a brewing-pan, old fellow. Pull, boy, pull. What are your arms for, eh?" Old Quilleash's eyes, which had been dim with tears a moment ago, glistened with grisly mischief. "Who hasn't heard that a Manxman's arms are three legs?" he said with a hungry grin. How the men laughed! What humor there was now in the haggard old saw!

"Where are you for, Billy?" cried Corkell.

"Peel, boy, Peel, d—— it, Peel," shouted Quilleash.

"Hurroo! Bould fellow! Ha, ha, he, he."

"Hurroo! There's gold on the cushags yet."

How they worked! In two minutes the mast was stepped, the mainsail and mizzen were up, and they filled away and stood out. From the shores of death they had sailed somehow into the waters of life, and hope was theirs once more.

They began to talk of what had caused the wind. "It was the blessed St. Patrick," said Corkell. St. Patrick was the patron saint of that sea, and Corkell was more than half a Catholic, his mother being a fish-wife from Kinsale.

"Saint Patrick be ——," cried Ned Teare, with a scornful laugh, and they got to words and at length almost to blows.

Old Quilleash was at the tiller. "Drop it," he shouted, "we're in the down stream for Contrary, and we'll be in harbor in ten minutes."

"God A'mighty! it's running a ten-knots tide," said Teare.

In less than ten minutes they were sailing under the castle islet up to the wooden pier, having been eighteen hours on the water.

Not a man of the four had given a thought to Dan, whether he wished to go back to the island, or to make a foreign port where his name and his crime would be unknown. Only the lad Davy had hung about him where he sat by the hatches. Dan's pale face was firm and resolute, and the dream of a smile was on his hard-drawn lips. But his despair had grown into courage, and he knew no fear at all.

The sun was down, the darkness was gathering, and through the day-mist the dew fog was rising as the fishing-boat put to under the lee of a lantern newly lighted, that was stuck out from the end of the pier on a pole. The quay was almost deserted. Only the old harbor-master was there, singing out, as by duty bound, his lusty oaths at their lumberings. Never before did the old grumbler's strident voice sound so musical as now, and even his manifest ill-temper was sweet to-night, for it seemed to tell the men that thus far they were not suspected.

The men went their way together, and Dan went off alone. He took the straightest course home. Seven long miles over a desolate road he tramped in the darkness and never a star came out, and the moon, which was in its last quarter, struggling behind a rack of cloud, lightened the sky sometimes, but did not appear. As he passed through Michael he noticed, though his mind was preoccupied and his perception obscure, that the street was more that usually silent, and that few lights burned behind the window-blinds. Even the low porch of the "Three Legs," when Dan came to it, was deserted, and hardly the sound of a voice came from within the little pot-house. Only in a vague way did these impressions communicate themselves to Dan's stunned intelligence as he plodded along, but hardly had he passed out of the street when he realized the cause of the desolation. A great glow came from a spot in front of him, as of many lanterns and torches burning together, and though in his bewilderment he had not noticed it before, the lights lit all the air about them. In the midst of these lights there came and went out of the darkness the figures of a great company of people, sometimes bright with the glare on their faces, sometimes black with the deep shadow of the torchlight.

Obscure as his ideas were, Dan comprehended everything in an instant, and, chilled as he was to the heart's core by the terrors of the last night and day, his very bones seemed now to grow cold within him.

It was a funeral by torchlight, and these maimed rites were, by an ancient usage, long disused, but here revived, the only burial of one whose death had been doubtful, or whose body had washed ashore on the same day.

The people were gathered on the side of the churchyard near to the high road, between the road and the church. Dan crept up to the opposite side, leaped the low cobble wall, and placed himself under the shadow of the vestry by the chancel. He was then standing beneath the window he had leaped out of in his effort to escape the Bishop on that Christmas Eve long ago of his boyish freak at Oiel Verree.

About an open vault three of four mourners were standing, and, a little apart from them a smoking and flickering torch cast its light on their faces. There was the Bishop, with his snowy head bare and deeply bowed, and there by his elbow was Jarvis Kerruish in his cloak and beaver, with arms folded under his chin. And walking to and fro, from side to side, with a quick nervous step, breaking out into alternate shrill cries and harsh commands to four men who had descended into the vault, was the little, restless figure of the Deemster. Behind these, and about them was the close company of the people, with the light coming and going on their faces, a deep low murmur, as of many whispers together, rising out of their midst.

Dan shook from head to foot. His heart seemed to stand still. He knew on what business the mourners were met; they were there to bury Ewan. He felt an impulse to scream, and then another impulse to turn and fly. But he could not utter the least cry, and quivering in every limb he could not stir. Standing there in silence he clung to the stone wall with trembling fingers.

The body had been lowered to its last home, and the short obsequies began. The service for the dead was not read, but the Bishop stretched out his hands above the open vault and prayed. Dan heard the words, but it was as if he heard the voice only. They beat on his dazed, closed mind as a sea-gull, blown by the wind, beats against a window on a stormy night. While the Bishop prayed in broken accents, the deep thick boom of the sea came up from the distant shore between the low-breathed murmurs of the people.

Dan dropped to his knees, breathless and trembling. He tried to pray, too, but no prayer would come. His mind was beaten, and his soul was barren. His father's faltering voice ceased, and then a half-stifled moan burst from his own lips. In the silence the moan seemed to fall on every ear, and the quick ear of the Deemster was instantly arrested. "Who's that?" he cried, and twisted about.

But all was still once more, and then the people began to sing. It was a strange sight, and a strange sound: the torches, the hard furrowed faces in the flickering light, the white-headed Bishop, the restless Deemster, and the voices ringing out in the night over the open grave. And from where he knelt Dan lifted his eyes, and by the light of the torches he saw the clock in the church tower; the hands still stood at five.

He rose to his feet and turned away. His step fell softly on the grass of the churchyard. At one instant he thought that there were footsteps behind him. He stopped and stretched his arms half-fearfully toward the sound. There was nothing. After he had leaped the cobble wall, he was conscious that he had stopped again, and was listening as though to learn if he had been observed.

CHAPTER XXV
A RESURRECTION INDEED

And now a strange accident befell him—strange enough in itself, mysterious in its significance, and marvelous as one of God's own miracles in its results. He was going to give himself up to the Deemster at Ballamona, but he did not any longer take the high road through the village, for he shrank from every human face. Almost without consciousness he followed the fenceless cart-track that went by the old lead mine known as the Cross Vein. The disused shaft had never been filled up and never even enclosed by a rail. It had been for years a cause of anxiety, which nothing but its remoteness on the lone waste of the headland had served to modify. And now Dan, who knew every foot of the waste, and was the last man to whom danger from such an occasion might have been feared, plodding along with absent mind in the darkness, fell down the open shaft.

The shaft was forty-five fathoms deep, yet Dan was not so much as hurt. At the bottom were nearly twenty-five fathoms of water, the constant drainage of the old workings, which rose almost to the surface, or dropped to a great depth, according to weather. This had broken his fall. On coming to the surface, one stroke in the first instance of dazed consciousness had landed him on a narrow ledge of rock that raked downward from the seam. But what was his position when he realized it? It seemed to be worse than death itself; it was a living death; it was burial in an open grave.

Hardly had he recovered his senses when he heard something stirring overhead. Were they footsteps, those thuds on the ear, like the first rumble of a distant thunder-cloud? In the agony of fear he tried to call, but his tongue clave to his mouth. Then there was some talking near the mouth of the shaft. It came down to him like words shouted through a black, hollow, upright pillar.

"No use, men," said one speaker, "not a foot farther after the best man alive. It's every man for himself now, and I'll go bail it's after ourselves they'll be going next."

And then another voice, laden with the note of pain, cried, "But they'll take him, Uncle Billy, they'll take him, and him knowin' nothing'."

"Drove it, drove it! Come along, man alive. Lave the lad to this d—d blather—you'd better. Let's make a slant for it. The fac's is agen us."

Dan shuddered at the sound of human voices. Buried, as he was, twenty-five fathoms beneath the surface, the voices came to him like the voice that the wind might make on a tempestuous night, if, as it reaches your ear, it whispered words and fled away.

The men had gone. Who were they? What had happened? Dan asked himself if he had not remembered one of the voices, or both. His mind was stunned and he could not think. He could hardly be sure that in very truth he was conscious of what occurred.

Time passed—he knew not how long or short—and again he heard voices overhead, but they were not the voices that he had heard before.

"I apprehend that they have escaped us. But they were our men nevertheless. I have had advices from Peel that the boat put into the harbor two hours ago."

"Mind the old lead shaft, sir."

Dan was conscious that a footstep approached the mouth of the shaft.

"What a gulf! Lucky we didn't tumble down."

There was a short laugh—as of one who was panting after a sharp run—at the mouth of Dan's open grave.

"This was the way they took, sir; over the head toward the Curraghs. They were not half wise, or they would have taken the mountains for it."

"They do not know that we are in pursuit of *them*. Depend upon it they are following *him* up to warn him. After all, it may have been his voice that the Deemster heard in the churchyard. He is somewhere within arm's reach. Let us push on."

The voices ceased, the footsteps died off. Forty feet of dull, dead rock and earth had carried the sounds away in an instant. "Stop!" cried Dan, in the hurry of fear. Despair made him brave; fear made him fearless. There was no response. He was alone once more, but Death was with him. Then in the first moment of recovered consciousness he knew whose voice it was that he had heard last, and he thanked God that his call had not been answered. It was the voice of Jarvis Kerruish. In agony of despair Dan perceived that the first company of men had been Quilleash and the fisher-fellows. What fatality had prevented him from crying aloud to the only persons on earth who could have rescued and saved him? Dan realized that his crime was known, and that he was now a hunted man.

It was then that he knew how hopeless was his plight. He must not cry for help; he must stand still as death in his deep tomb. To be lifted out of this pit by the men who were in search of him would be, as it would seem, to be dragged from his hiding-place, and captured in a feeble effort to escape. What then of his brave atonement? Who would believe that he meant to make it? It would be a mockery at which the veriest poltroon might laugh.

Dan saw now that death encircled him on every side. To remain in the pit was death; to be lifted out of it was death no less surely; to escape was hopeless. But not so soon is hope conquered when it is hope of life. Cry for help he must; be dragged out of this grave he should, let the issue be what it could or would. To lie there and die was not human. To live was the first duty, the first necessity, be the price of life no less than future death.

Dan looked up at the sky; it was a small square patch of leaden gray against the impenetrable blackness of his prison-walls. Standing on the ledge of the rock, and steadying himself with one hand, he lifted the other cautiously upward to feel the sides of the shaft. They were of rock, and were quite precipitous, but had rugged projecting pieces on which it was possible to lay hold. As he grasped one of these, a sickening pang of hope shot through him, and wounded him worse than despair. But it was gone in an instant. The piece of rock gave way in his hand, and tumbled into the water below him with a hollow splash. The sides of the shaft were of crumbling stone!

It was then, in that blind laboring of despair, that he asked himself why he should struggle with this last of the misfortunes that had befallen him. Was life so dear to him? Not so, or, being dear, he was willing to lay it down. Was he not about to deliver himself to the death that must be the first punishment of his crime? And what, after all, was there to choose between two forms of death? Nay, if he must die, who was no longer worthy of life, better to die there, none knowing his way of death, than to die on the gallows.

At that thought his hair rose from its roots. He had never rightly put it to himself until now that if he had to die for the death of Ewan he must die the death of hanging. That horror of hanging which all men have was stronger in Dan than in most. With the grim vision before him of a shameful and damning death it came to him to tell himself that better, a thousand times better, was death in that living tomb than the death that awaited him outside it. Then he thought of his father, and of the abasement of that good man if so great a shame overtook his son, and thereupon, at the same breath with a prayer to God that he might die where he was, a horrible blasphemy bolted from his lips. He was in higher hands than his own. God had saved him from himself. At least he was not to die on the gallows. He had but one prayer now, and it cried in its barrenness of hope, "Let me never leave this place!" His soul was crushed as the moth that will never lift wing again.

But at that his agony took another turn. He reflected that, if God's hand was keeping him from the just punishment of his crime, God was holding him back from the atonement that was to wash his crime away. At this thought he was struck with a great trembling. He wrestled with it, but it would not be overcome. Had he not parted with Mona with the firm purpose of giving himself up to the law? Yet at every hour since that parting some impediment had arisen. First, there were the men in the shed at the creek, their resolve to bury the body, and his own weak acquiescence; then came the dead calm out at sea when he stood at the tiller, and the long weary drifting on the wide waters; and now there was this last strange accident. It was as if a higher will had willed it that he should die before his atonement could be made. His spirit sank yet lower, and he was for giving up all as lost. In the anguish of despair he thought that in very deed it must be that he had committed the unpardonable sin. This terrible idea clung to him like a leech at a vein. And then it came to him to think what a mockery his dream of atonement had been. What atonement could a bad man make for spilling the blood of a good one? He could but send his own wasted life after a life well spent. Would a righteous God take that for a just balance? Mockeries of mockeries! No, no; let him die where he now was, and let his memory be blotted out, and his sin be remembered no more.

He tried to compose himself, and pressed one hand hard at his breast to quiet the laboring of his heart. He began to reckon the moments. In this he had no object, or none save only that mysterious longing of a dying man to know how the hour drags on. With the one hand that was free he took out his watch, intending to listen for the beat of its seconds; but his watch had stopped; no doubt it was full of water. His heart beat loud enough. Then he went on to count—one, two, three. But his mind was in a whirl, and he lost his reckoning. He found that he had stopped counting, and forgotten the number. Whether five minutes or fifty had passed, he could not be sure.

But time was passing. The wind began to rise. At first Dan felt nothing of it as he stood in his deep tomb. He could hear its thin hiss over the mouth of the shaft, and that was all. But presently the hiss deepened to a sough. Dan had often heard of the wind's sob. It was a reality, and no metaphor, as he listened to the wind now. The wind began to descend. With a great swoop it came down the shaft, licked the walls, gathered voice from the echoing water at the bottom, struggled for escape, roared like a caged lion, and was once more sucked up to the surface, with a noise like the breaking of a huge wave over a reef. The tumult of the wind in the shaft was hard to bear, but when it was gone it was the silence that seemed to be deafening. Then the rain began to fall. Dan knew this by the quick, monotonous patter overhead. But no rain touched him. It was driven aslant by the wind, and fell only against the uppermost part of the walls of the shaft. Sometimes a soft thin shower fell over him. It was like a spray from a cataract, except that the volume of water from which it came was above and not beneath him.

It was then in the deadly sickness of fear that there came to Dan the dread of miscarrying forever if he should die now. He seemed to see what it was to die unredeemed. Not to be forgiven, but to be forever accursed, to be cut off from the living that live in God's peace?—the dead darkness of that doom stood up before him. Life had looked very dear to him before, but what now of everlasting death? He was as one who was dead before his death came. Live he could not, die he dared not. His past life rose up in front of him, and he drank of memory's very dregs. It was all so fearsome and strange that as he recalled its lost hours one by one it was as if he were a stranger to himself. He saw himself, like Esau, who for a morsel of meat had sold his birthright, and could thereafter find no acceptance, though he sought it with tears. The Scripture leaped to his mind which says, "It is a fearful thing to fall into the hands of the living God."

And then from the past to the future his mind went on in a rapid and ceaseless whirl. He saw himself fleeing as from the face of a dreadful judge. Tossed with the terror of a dreadful doom, he saw his place in the world, cold, empty, forsaken. He saw his old father, too, the saintly Bishop, living under the burden of a thousand sorrows, while he who was the life of the good man's life, but his no longer, was a restless, wandering soul, coming as a cold blast of wind between him and his heaven. That thought was the worst terror of all, and Dan heard a cry burst from his throat that roused echoes of horror in the dark pit.

Then, as if his instinct acted without help from his mind, Dan began to contemplate measures for escape. That unexpected softness of the rock which had at first appalled him began now to give him some painful glimmerings of hope. If the sides of the shaft had been of the slate rock of the island the ledge he had laid hold of would not have crumbled in his hand. That it was soft showed that there must be a vein of sandstone running across the shaft. Dan's bewildered mind recalled the fact that Orris Head was a rift of red sand and soft sandstone. If this vein were but deep enough his safety was assured. He could cut niches into it with a knife, and so, perhaps, after infinite pain and labor, reach the surface.

Steadying himself with one hand, Dan felt in his pockets for his knife. It was not there! Now indeed his death seemed certain. He was icy cold and feverishly hot at intervals. His clothes were wet; the water still dripped from them, and fell into the hidden tarn beneath in hollow drops. But not to hope now would have been not to fear. Dan remembered that he had a pair of small scissors which he had used three days ago in scratching his name on the silver buckle of his militia belt. When searching for his knife he had felt it in his pocket, and spurned it for resembling the knife to the touch of his nervous fingers. Now, it was to be his sole instrument. He found it again, and with this paltry help he set himself to his work of escape from the dark, deep tunnel that stood upright.

The night was wearing on; hour after hour went by. The wind dropped; the rain ceased to patter overhead. Dan toiled on step over step. Resting sometimes on the largest and firmest of the projecting ledges, he looked up at the sky. The leaden gray had changed to a dark blue, studded with stars. The moon arose very late, being in its last quarter, and much beset by rain-clouds. It shone a little way down the shaft, lighting all the rest. Dan knew it must be early morning. One star, a large, full globe of light, twinkled directly above him. He sat long and watched it, and turned again and again in his toilsome journey to look at it. At one moment it crept into his heart that the star was a symbol of hope to him. Then he twisted back to his work, and when he looked again the star was gone—it had moved beyond his ken, it had passed out of the range of his narrow spot of heaven. Somehow, it had been a mute companion.

Dan's spirit sank in his cheerless solitude, but he toiled on. His strength was far spent. The moon died off, and the stars went out one after one. Then a deep cloud of darkness overspread the little sky above. Dan knew it must be the darkness that precedes the dawn. He had reached a ledge of rock that was wider than any of the ledges that were beneath it. Clearly enough a wooden rafter had lain along it. Dan rested and looked up. At that moment he heard the light patter of little feet overhead. It was a stray sheep, a lamb of last year's flock, wandering and lost. Though he could not see it, he knew it was there, and it bleated down the shaft. The melancholy cry of the lost creature in that dismal place touched a seared place on Dan's heart, and made the tears which he had not shed until now to start from his eyes. What old memory did it awaken? He could not recall it at first, but then he remembered the beautiful story which he had heard many times of the lost lamb that came to the church porch at the christening of Ewan. Was it strange that there and then his thoughts turned to Ewan's child, the babe that was innocent of its great sorrows to come? He began to wish himself a little child again, walking by his father's hand, with all the years rolled back, and all the transgressions of the years blotted out as a cloud, and with a new spirit sweet and fresh, where now was a spirit seared and old, and one great aching wound. In a moment the outcast lamb went off, sending up, as it went, its pitiful cry into the night. Dan was alone once more, but that visitation had sweetly refreshed his spirit.

Then it came back to him to think that of a surety it was not all one whether he died where he was, never coming alive from his open tomb, or died for his crime before the faces of all men. He must live, he must live, though not for life's sake, but to rob death of its worst terrors. And as for the impediments that had arisen to prevent the atonement on which his mind was set, they were not from God to lay his soul outside the reach of mercy, but from the devil to beset him and keep him back from the washing away of his sin. This thought revived him, and he turned to his task with a new resolve.

His fingers were chilled to the bone, and his clothes clung like damp cerements to his body. The meagre blades of the scissors were worn short; they could not last long. He rose to his feet on the ledge of rock, and plunged the scissors into the blank wall above him, and at that a fresh disaster seemed to overwhelm him. His hand went into soft earth; the vein of rock had finished, and above it must be loose, uncertain mold!

He gasped at the discovery. A minute since life had looked very dear. Must he abandon his hopes after all? He might have been longer vexed with this new fear, but that he recalled at that moment the words spoken by Jarvis Kerruish as he went by on the road that ran near the mouth of the shaft. Was it not clear that Quilleash and the fisher-fellows were being pursued as his associates? Without his evidence to clear them, would they not surely suffer, innocent though they might be, and even though he himself lay dead in this place? Now, indeed, he saw that he must of a certainty escape from this death in life, no difficulties conquering him.

Dan paused and reflected. As nearly as he could remember, he had made twenty niches in the rock. Hence, he must be fully thirty-five feet from the water and ten from the surface. Only ten feet, and then freedom! Yet these ten seemed to represent an impossibility. To ascend by holes dug deep in the soft earth was a perilous enterprise. A great clod of soil might at any moment give away above or beneath him, and then he would be plunged once more into the pit. If he fell from the side of the shaft he would be more likely than at first, when he fell from the top, to strike on one of the projecting ledges and be killed before reaching the water.

There was nothing left but to wait for the dawn. Perhaps the daylight would reveal some less hazardous method of escape. Slowly the dull, dead, impenetrable blackness was lifted off. It was as though a spirit had breathed on the night, and it fled away. When the woolly hue of morning dappled his larger sky, Dan could hear the slow beat of the waves on the shore. The coast rose up before his vision then, silent, solemn, alone with the dawn. The light crept into his prison-house, and he looked down at the deep black tarn beneath him.

And now hope rose in his hearth again. Overhead he saw timbers running around and across the shaft. These had been used to bank up the earth, and to make two grooves in which the ascending and descending cages had once worked. Dan lifted up his soul in thankfulness. The world was once more full of grace even for him. He could climb from stay to stay, and so reach the surface. Catching one of the stays in his uplifted hands, he swung his knee on to another. One stage he accomplished, and then how stiff were his joints, and how sinewless his fingers! Another and another stage he reached, and then four feet and no more were between him and the gorse that waved in the light of the risen sun across the mouth of his night-long tomb.

But the rain of years had eaten into these timbers. In some places they crumbled, and were rotten. God! how the one on which he rested creaked under him at that instant! Another minute, and then his toilsome journey would be over. Another minute, and his dead self would be left behind him, buried forever in this grave. Then there would be a resurrection in very truth. Yes, truly, God helping him.

Half an hour later Dan Mylrea, with swimming eyes and a big heart, was walking toward the Deemster at Ballamona. The flush of the sun newly risen, and the brighter glory of a great hope newly born, was on his worn and pallid cheek. What terrors had life for him now? It had none. And very soon death also would lose its sting. Atonement! atonement! It was even as he had thought: a wasted life for a life well spent, the life of a bad man for the life of a good one, but all he had to give—all, all!

And when he came to lay his offering at the merciful Father's feet it would not be spurned.

CHAPTER XXVI
HOW EWAN CAME TO CHURCH

It is essential to the progress of this history that we should leave Dan where he now is, in the peace of a great soul newly awakened, and go back to the beginning of this Christmas Day on shore.

The parish of Michael began that day with all its old observances. While the dawn of Christmas morning was struggling but feebly with the night of Christmas-eve a gang of the baser sort went out with lanterns and long sticks into the lanes, there to whoop and beat the bushes. It was their annual hunting of the wren. Before the parish had sat down to its Christmas breakfast two of these lusty enemies of the tiny bird were standing in the street of the village with a long pole from shoulder to shoulder and a wee wren suspended from the middle of it. Their brave companions gathered round and plucked a feather from the wren's breast now and again. At one side of the company, surrounded by a throng of children, was Hommy-beg, singing a carol, and playing his own accompaniment on his fiddle. The carol told a tragic story of an evil spirit in the shape of a woman who pestered the island in the old days, of how the people rose up against her to drive her into the sea, and of how she turned herself into a wren, and all on the holy day of the blessed Saint Stephen. A boy whose black eyes danced with a mischievous twinkle held a crumpled paper upside down before the gardener, and from this inverted text and score the unlettered cox-comb pretended to play and sing. The women came to their doors to listen, and the men with their two hands in their breeches-pockets leaned against the ends of their houses and smoked and looked on sleepily.

When the noisy crowd had passed, the street sank back to its customary repose, broken only by the voice of a child—a little auburn-haired lassie, in a white apron tucked up in fish-wife fashion—crying, "Shrimps, fine shrimps, fresh shrimps!" and then by a lustier voice that drowned the little lassie's tones, and cried, "Conger—conger eel—fine, ladies—fresh, ladies—and bellies as big as bishops! Conger eel—conger!"

It was not a brilliant morning, but the sun was shining drowsily through a white haze like a dew-fog that hid the mountains. The snow of the night before was not quite washed away by the sharp rain of the morning; it still lay at the eaves of the thatched houses, and among the cobbles of the paved pathway. The blue smoke was coiling up through the thick air from every chimney when the bells at Bishop's Court began to ring for Christmas service. An old woman here and there came out of her cabin in her long blue cape and her mutch, and hobbled along on a stick to church. Two or three men in sea-boots, with shrimping nets over their shoulders and pipes in their mouths, sauntered down the lane that led by the shambles to the shore.

Half an hour later, while the bells were still ringing, and the people were trooping into the chapel, the Bishop came out of his house and walked down the path toward the vestry. He had a worn and jaded look that morning, as if the night had gone heavily with him, but he smiled when the women courtesied as they passed, and waved his hand when the men fumbled their caps.

"Good-morning, and a merry Christmas to you," he said, as he went by the open porch, to Will-as-Thorn, the parish clerk, who was tugging at the bell-rope there, bareheaded, stripped to his sheepskin waistcoat with its gray flannel sleeves, and sweating.

He hailed Billy the Gawk, too, the hoary old dog turned penitent in his latter days. "A merry Christmas, Billy, and may you live to see many of them yet, please God!"

Billy was leaning against the porch buttress and taking alms if any offered them.

"Then it's not living it will be, my lord; it's lingering," said this old Bartimeus.

And Jabez Gawne, the sleek little tailor, had the Bishop's salutation as he passed on in the ancient cloak with many buttons.

"A merry Christmas to you, Jabez, and a good New Year."

"Aw, 'deed, my lord," said Jabez, with a face as long as a fiddle, "if the New Year's no better than the ould one, what with quiet times and high rents and the children's schooling, it's going on the houses I'll be, middlin' safe."

"Nay, nay, remember our old saying, Jabez: The greater the calm the nearer the south wind."

As the Bishop was turning in at the vestry door, blind Kerry and her husband Hommy passed him, and he hailed them as he had hailed the others.

"I'm taking joy to see you so hearty, my lord," said the blind woman.

"Yes, I'm well, on the whole, thank God!" said the Bishop; "and how are you, Kerry?"

"I'm in, my lord—I'm in; but distracted mortal with the sights. Och, sir, it's allis the sights, and the sights, and the sights; and it's Mastha Dan that's in them still. This morning, bless ye, when I woke, what should it be, behould ye, but a company of great ones from the big house itself, going down to the churchyard with lanterns. Aw, 'deed it was, sir, my lord, begging your pardon, though it's like enough you'll think it's wake and a kind of silly, as the sayin' is."

The Bishop listened to the blind woman's garrulous tongue with a downcast head and a look of pain, and said, in a subdued voice, as he put his hand on the wooden latch of the vestry door:

"It is not for me to laugh at you, Kerry, woman. All night long I have myself been tortured by an uneasy feeling, which would not be explained or yet be put away. But let us say no more of such mysteries. There are dark places that we may never hope to penetrate. Let it content us if, in God's mercy and His wisdom, we can see the step that is at our feet."

So saying, the Bishop turned about and passed in at the door. Kerry and her husband went into the chapel at the west porch.

"It's just an ould angel he is," whispered Kerry, reaching up to Hommy's ear, as they went by Will-as-Thorn.

"Aw, yes, yes," said Hommy-beg, "a rael ould archangel, so he is."

And still the bells rang for service of Christmas morning.

Inside the chapel the congregation was larger than common. There was so much hand-shaking and "taking of joy" to be gone through in the aisles and the pews that Christmas morning that it was not at first observed—except by malcontents like Billy the Gawk and Jabez Gawne, to whom the wine of life was mostly vinegar—when the hour for beginning the service had come and gone. The choir in the west gallery had taken their places on either side of Will-as-Thorn's empty seat over the clock, with the pitch-pipe resting on the rail above it, and opening their books, they faced about for gossip. Then the bell stopped, having rung some minutes longer than was its wont; the whispering was hushed from pew to choir, and only the sound of the turning of the leaves of many books disturbed the silence a moment afterward.

The Bishop entered the chancel, and while he knelt to pray, down like corn before a south wind went a hundred heads on to the book-rail before the wind of custom. When the Bishop rose there was the sound of shuffling and settling in the pews, followed by some craning of necks in his direction and some subdued whispering.

"Where is Pazon Ewan?"

"What's come of the young pazon?"

The Bishop sat alone in the chancel, and gave no sign of any intention to commence the service. In the gallery, the choir, books in hand, waited for Will-as-Thorn to take his seat over the clock; but his place remained empty. Then, to the universal surprise, the bell began to ring again. Steadily at first and timidly, and after that with lusty voice the bell rang out over the heads of the astonished people. Forth-with the people laid those same heads together and whispered.

What was agate of Pazon Ewan? Had he forgotten that he had to preach that morning? Blind Kerry wanted to know if some of the men craythurs shouldn't just take a slieu round to the ould Ballamona and wake him up, as the saying is; but Mr. Quirk, in more "gintale" phraseology, as became his scholastic calling, gave it out as probable that the young pazon had only been making a "little deetower" after breakfast, and gone a little too far.

Still the bell rang, and the uneasy shuffling in the pews grew more noticeable. Presently, in the middle of an abridged movement of the iron tongue in the loft, the head and shoulders of Will-as-Thorn appeared in the opening of the green curtain that divided the porch from the body of the chapel, and the parish clerk beckoned to Hommy-beg. Shambling to his feet and down the aisle, Hommy obeyed the summons, and then, amid yet more vigorous bobbing together of many heads in the pews, the schoolmaster, not to be eclipsed at a moment of public excitement, got up also and followed the gardener into the porch. The whispering had risen to a sibilant hiss that deadened even the bell's loud clangor when little Jabez Gawne himself felt a call to rise and go out after the others.

All this time the Bishop sat motionless in the chancel, his head down, his face rather paler than usual, his whole figure somewhat weak and languid, as if continued suffering in silence and in secret had at length taken the power of life out of him. Presently the bell stopped suddenly, and almost instantly little Jabez, with a face as sharp as a pen, came back to his pew, and Mr. Quirk also returned to his place, shaking his head meantime with portentous gravity. A moment later Will-as-Thorn appeared inside the communion-rail, having put on his coat and whipped the lash comb through his hair, which now hung like a dozen of wet dip-candles down his forehead straight for his eyes.

The dull buzz of gossip ceased, all was dead silence in the chapel, and many necks were craned forward as Will-as-Thorn was seen to go up to the Bishop and speak to him. Listening without much apparent concern, the Bishop nodded his head once or twice, then rose immediately and walked to the reading-desk. Almost at the same moment Will-as-Thorn took his seat over the clock in the little west gallery, and straightway the service began.

The choir sang the psalm which they had practised at the parish church the evening before—"It is good for me that I have been in trouble, that I may learn thy statutes." For the first of his lessons the Bishop read the story of Eli and of Samuel, and of the taking by the Philistines of the ark of the covenant of God. His voice was deep and measured, and when he came to read of the death of Eli's sons, and of how the bad news was brought to Eli, his voice softened and all but broke.

"And there ran a man of Benjamin out of the army, and came to Shiloh the same day with his clothes rent, and with earth upon his head.

"And when he came, lo, Eli sat upon a seat by the wayside watching: for his heart trembled for the ark of God. And when the man came into the city, and told it, all the city cried out.

"And when Eli heard the noise of the crying, he said, What meaneth the noise of this tumult? And the man came in hastily, and told Eli.

"Now Eli was ninety and eight years old; and his eyes were dim, that he could not see.

"And the man said unto Eli, I am he that came out of the army, and I fled to-day out of the army. And he said, What is there done, my son?"

The Bishop preached but rarely now, and partly for the reverence they always owed the good man, and partly for the reason that they did not often hear him, the people composed themselves to a mood of sympathy as he ascended the pulpit that Christmas morning. It was a beautiful sermon that he gave them, and it was spoken without premeditation, and was loose enough in its structure. But it was full of thought that seemed to be too simple to be deep, and of emotion that was too deep to be anything but simple. It touched on the life of Christ, from his birth in Bethlehem to his coming as a boy to the Temple where the doctors sat, and so on to the agony in the garden. And then it glanced aside, as touchingly as irrelevantly, at the story of Eli and his sons, and the judgment of God on Israel's prophet. In that beautiful digression the Bishop warned all parents that it was their duty before God to bring up their children in God's fear, or theirs would be the sorrow, and their children's the suffering and the shame everlasting.

And then in a voice that could barely support itself he made an allusion that none could mistake.

"Strange it is, and very pitiful," he said, "that what we think in our weakness to be the holiest of our human affections may be a snare and a stumbling-block. Strange enough, surely, and very sad, that even as the hardest of soul among us all may be free from blame where his children stand for judgment, so the tenderest of heart may, like Eli of old, be swept from the face of the living God for the iniquity of his children, which he has not restrained. But the best of our earthly passions, or what seem to be the best, the love of the mother for the babe at her breast, the pride of the father in the son that is flesh of his flesh, must be indulged with sin if it is not accepted with grace. True, too true, that there are those of us who may cast no stone, who should offer no counsel. Like Eli, we know that the word of God has gone out against us, and we can but bend our foreheads and say, 'It is the Lord, let him do what seemeth him good.'"

When the sermon ended there was much needless industry in searching for books under the book-rail, much furtive wiping of the eyes, much demonstrative blowing of the nose, and in the midst of the benediction a good deal of subdued whispering.

"Aw, 'deed, the ould Bishop bates the young pazon himself at putting out the talk—studdier-like, and not so fiery maybe; but, man alive, the tender he is!"

"And d'ye mind that taste about Eli and them two idiot waistrels Hoffnee and Fin-e-ass?"

"And did ye observe the ould man thrembling mortal?"

"Och, yes, and I'll go bail it wasn't them two blackyards he was thinking of, at all, at all."

When the service came to an end, and the congregation was breaking up, and Billy the Gawk was hobbling down the aisle on a pair of sticks, that hoary old sinner, turned saint because fallen sick, was muttering something about "a rael good ould father," and "dirts like than Dan," and "a thund'rin rascal with all."

A strange scene came next. The last of the congregation had not yet reached the porch, when all at once there was an uneasy move among them like the ground-swell among the shoalings before the storm comes to shore. Those who were in front fell back or turned about and nodded as if they wished to say something; and those who were behind seemed to think and wonder. Then sudden as the sharp crack of the first breaker on a reef, the faces of the people fell to a great heaviness of horror, and the air was full of mournful exclamations, surprise, and terror.

"Lord ha' massy!"

"Dead, you say?"

"Aw, dead enough."

"Washed ashore by the Mooragh?"

"So they're sayin', so they're sayin'."

"*Hiain Jean myghin orrin*—Lord have mercy upon us!"

Half a minute later the whole congregation were gathered outside the west porch. There, in the recess between the chapel and the house, two men, fisher-fellows of Michael, stood surrounded by a throng of people. Something lay at their feet, and the crowd made a circle about it, looked down at it, and drew long breaths. And when one after another came up, reached over the heads of others, and saw what lay within, he turned away with uplifted hands and a face that was white with fear.

"Lord ha' massy! Lord ha' massy!" cried the people on every side, and their senses were confused and overpowered.

What the dread thing was that lay at the feet of the two fishermen does not need to be said.

"At the Mooragh, d'ye say—came ashore at the Mooragh?"

"Ay, at the top of the flood."

"God bless me!"

"I saw it an hour before it drifted in," said one of the two grave fellows. "I was down 'longshore shrimping, and it was a good piece out to sea, and a heavy tide running. 'Lord ha' massy, what's that?' I says. 'It's a gig with a sail,' I was thinking, but no, it was looking too small. 'It's a diver, or maybe a solan goose with its wings stretched out'; but no, it was looking too big."

"Bless me! Lord bless me!"

"And when it came a piece nearer it was into the sea I was going, breast-high and a more, and I came anigh it, and saw what it was—and frightened mortal, you go bail—and away to the street for Jemmy here, and back middlin' sharp, and it driffin' and driffin' on the beach by that time, and the water flopping on it, and the two of us up with it on to our shoulders, and straight away for the Coort."

And sure enough the fisherman's clothes were drenched above his middle, and the shoulders of both men were wet.

"Bless me! bless me! Lord ha' massy!" echoed one, and then another, and once again they craned their necks forward and looked down.

The loose canvas that had been ripped open by the weights was lying where the seams were stretched, and none uncovered the face, for the sense of human death was strong on all. But word had gone about whose body it was, and blind Kerry, wringing her hands and muttering something about the sights, pushed her way to the side of the two men, and asked why they had brought their burden to Bishop's Court instead of taking it to Ballamona.

"Aw, well," they answered, "we were thinking the Bishop was his true father, and Bishop's Coort his true home for all."

"And that's true, too," said Kerry, "for his own father has been worse than a haythen naygro to him, and lave it to me to know, for didn't I bring the millish into the world?"

Then there came a rush of people down the road from the village. A rumor that something horrible had washed ashore had passed quickly from mouth to mouth, after the fisherman had run up to the village for help. And now, in low, eager tones, questions and answers came and went among the crowd. "Who is it?" "Is it the captain?" "What, Mastha Dan?" "That's what they're saying up the street anyway." "Wrapped in a hammock—good Lord preserve us!" "Came up in the tideway at the Mooragh—gracious me! and I saw him myself on'y yesterday."

The Bishop was seen to come out of the vestry door, and at the sight of him the crowd seemed to awake out of its first stupor. "God help the Bishop!" "Here he's coming." "Bless me, he'll have to pass it by, going into the house." "The shock will kill the ould man." "Poor thing, poor thing!" "Some one must up and break the bad newses to him." "Aw, yes, for sure."

And then came the question of who was to tell the Bishop. First the people asked one Corlett Ballafayle. Corlett farmed a hundred acres, and was a churchwarden, and a member of the Keys. But the big man said no, and edged away. Then they asked one of the Tubmans, but the brewer shook his head. He could not look into the Bishop's face and tell him a tale like that. At length they thought of blind Kerry. She at least would not see the face of the stricken man when she took him the fearful news.

"Aw, yes, Kerry, woman, it's yourself for it, and a rael stout heart at you, and blind for all, thank the Lord."

"I'll try, please God," said Kerry, and with that she moved slowly toward the vestry door, where the Bishop had stopped to stroke the yellow curls of a little shy boy, and to ask him his age next birthday, and to wish him a merry Christmas and eighty more of them, and all merry ones. It was observed that the good man's face was brighter now than it had been when he went into the chapel.

The people watched Kerry as she moved up to the Bishop. Could she be telling him? He was smiling! Was it not his laugh that they heard? Kerry was standing before him in an irresolute way, and now with a wave of the hand he was leaving her. He was coming forward. No, he had stopped again to speak to old Auntie Nan from the Curragh, and Kerry had passed him in returning to the crowd.

"I couldn't do it; he spoke so cheerful, poor thing," said Kerry; "and when I was goin' to speak he looked the spitten picture of my ould father."

The Bishop parted from the old woman of the Curragh, and then on raising his eyes he became conscious of the throng by the porch.

"Lave it to me," said a rough voice, and Billy the Gawk stepped out. The crowd fell aside, and the fishermen placed themselves in front of the dread thing on the ground. Smiling and bowing on the right and left, the Bishop was passing on toward the door that led to the house, when the old beggar of the highways hobbled in front of him.

"We're right sorry, sir, my lord, to bring ye bad newses," the old man stammered, lifting the torn cap from his head.

The Bishop's face fell to a sudden gravity. "What is it?" he said, and his voice sank.

"We're rael sorry, and we know your heart was gript to him with grapplin's."

"Ay, ay," said some in the crowd.

"What is it, man? Speak," said the Bishop, and all around was silence and awe.

The old man stood irresolute for a moment. Then, just as he was lifting his head to speak, and every eye was on the two who stood in the midst, the Bishop and the old beggar, there came a loud noise from near at hand, and voices that sounded hoarse and jarring were in the air.

"Where is it? When did they bring it up? Why is it not taken into the house?"

It was the Deemster, and he came on with great flashing eyes, and behind him was Jarvis Kerruish. In an instant the crowd had fallen aside for him, and he had pushed through and come to a stand in front of the Bishop.

"We know what has happened. We have heard it in the village," he said. "I knew what it must come to sooner or later. I told you a hundred times, and you have only yourself to thank for it."

The Bishop said not a word. He saw what lay behind the feet of the fishermen, and stepped up to it.

"It's of your own doing," shouted the Deemster in a voice of no ruth or pity. "You would not heed my warning. It was easy to see that the devil's own dues were in him. He hadn't an ounce of grace in his carcass. He put his foot on your neck, and threatened to do as much for me some day. And see where he is now! Look at him! This is how your son comes home to you!"

As he spoke, the Deemster pointed contemptuously with the handle of his walking-cane to the thing that lay between them.

Then the hard tension of the people's silence was broken; they began to mutter among themselves and to propose and demur to something. They saw the Deemster's awful error, and that he thought the dead man was Dan.

The Bishop still stood immovable, with not the sign of a tear on his white face, but over it the skin was drawn hard.

"And let me tell you one thing more," said the Deemster. "Whoever he may be that brought matters to this pass, he shall not suffer. I will not lift a finger against him. The man who brings about his own death shall have the burden of it on his own head. The law will uphold me."

Then a hoarse murmur ran from lip to lip among the people who stood around, and one man, a burly fellow, nerved by the Deemster's error, pushed forward and said:

"Deemster, be merciful, as you hope for mercy; you don't know what you're saying."

At that the Deemster turned about hotly and brought down his walking-cane with a heavy blow on the man's breast.

The stalwart fellow took the blow without lifting a hand. "God help you! Deemster," he said, in a thick voice. "God help you! you don't know what you're doing. Go and look at it, Deemster. Go and look, if you've the heart for it. Look at it, man, and may the Lord have mercy on you, and on us all in our day of trouble, and may God forgive you the cruel words you've spoken to your own brother this day!"

There was then a great silence for a moment. The Deemster gazed in a sort of stupor into the man's face, and his stick dropped out of his hand. With a look of majesty and of suffering the Bishop stood at one side of the body, quiet, silent, giving no sign, seeing nothing but the thing at his feet, and hardly hearing the reproaches that were being hurled at him in the face of his people. The beating of his heart fell low.

There was a moment of suspense, and then, breathing rapid, audible breath, the Deemster stooped beside the body, stretched out a half-palsied hand, and drew aside the loose canvas, and saw the face of his own son Ewan.

One long exclamation of surprise and consternation broke from the Deemster, and after that there came another fearful pause, wherein the Bishop went down on his knees beside the body.

In an instant the Deemster fell back to his savage mood. He rose to his full height; his face became suddenly and awfully discolored and stern, and, tottering almost to falling, he lifted his clenched fist to the sky in silent imprecation of heaven.

The people dropped aside in horror, and their flesh crawled over them. "Lord ha' massy!" they cried again, and Kerry, who was blind and could not see the Deemster, covered her ears that she might not hear him.

And from where he knelt the Bishop, who had not spoken until now, said, with an awful emphasis, "Brother, the Lord of heaven looks down on us."

But the Deemster, recovering himself, laughed in scorn of his own weakness no less than of the Bishop's reproof. He picked up the walking-cane that he had dropped, slapped his leg with it, ordered the two fishermen to shoulder their burden again and take it to Ballamona, and sent straightway for the coroner and the joiner, "For," said he, "my son having come out of the sea, must be buried this same day."

CHAPTER XXVII
HOW THE NEWS CAME TO THE BISHOP

The Deemster swung aside and went off, followed by Jarvis Kerruish. Then the two fishermen took up their dread burden and set their faces toward Ballamona. In a blind agony of uncertainty the Bishop went into his house. His mind was confused; he sat and did his best to compose himself. The thing that had happened perplexed him cruelly. He tried to think it out, but found it impossible to analyze his unlinked ideas. His faculties were benumbed, and not even pain, the pain of Ewan's loss, could yet penetrate the dead blank that lay between him and a full consciousness of the awful event. He shed no tears, and not a sigh broke from him. Silent he sat, with an expression of suffering that might have been frozen in his stony eyes and on his whitening lips, so rigid was it, and as if the power of life had ebbed away like the last ebb of an exhausted tide.

Then the people from without began to crowd in upon him where he sat in his library. They were in a state of great excitement, and all reserve and ceremony were broken down. Each had his tale to tell, each his conjecture to offer. One told what the longshore shrimper had said of finding the body near the fishing-ground known as the Mooragh. Another had his opinion as to how the body had sailed ashore instead of sinking. A third fumbled his cap, and said, "I take sorrow to see you in such trouble, my lord, and wouldn't bring bad newses if I could give myself lave to bring good newses instead, but I'll go bail there's been bad work goin', and foul play, as they're sayin', and I wouldn't trust but Mastha Dan—I'm saying I wouldn't trust but Mastha Dan could tell us something—"

The Bishop cut short the man's garrulity with a slight gesture, and one by one the people went out. He had listened to them in silence and with a face of saintly suffering, scarcely hearing what they had said. "I will await events," he thought, "and trust in God." But a great fear was laying hold of him, and he had to gird up his heart to conquer it. "I will trust in God," he told himself a score of times, and in his faith in the goodness of his God he tried to be calm and brave. But one after another his people came back and back and back with new and still newer facts. At every fresh blow from damning circumstances his thin lips trembled, his nervous fingers ran through his flowing white hair, and his deep eyes filled without moving.

And after the first tempest of his own sorrow for the loss of Ewan, he thought of Dan, and of Dan's sure grief. He remembered the love of Ewan for Dan, and the love of Dan for Ewan. He recalled many instances of that beautiful affection, and in the quickening flow of the light of that love half the follies of his wayward son sank out of sight. Dan must be told what had occurred, and if none had told him already, it was best that it should be broken to him from lips that loved him.

Thus it was that this brave and long-harassed man, trying to think ill of his own harshness, that looked so impotent and so childish now, remembering no longer his vow never to set eyes on the face of his son, or hold speech with him again, sent a messenger to the old Ballamona to ask for Dan, and to bring him to Bishop's Court without delay.

Half an hour later, at the sound of a knock at his door, the Bishop, thinking it was Dan himself, stood up to his stately height, and tried to hide his agitation, and answered in an unsteady voice, that not all the resolution of his brave heart could subdue to calmness. But it was the messenger, and not Dan, and he had returned to say that Mastha Dan had not been home since yesterday, and that when Mastha Ewan was last seen at home, he had asked for Mastha Dan, and, not finding him, had gone down to the Lockjaw Creek to seek him.

"When was that?" the Bishop asked.

"The ould body at the house said it might be a piece after three o'clock yesterday evening," said the man.

Beneath the cold quietness of the regard with which the Bishop dismissed his messenger, a keener eye than his might have noted a fearful tumult. The Bishop's hand grew cold and trembled. At the next instant he had become conscious of his agitation, and had begun to reproach himself for his want of faith. "I will trust in God and await events," he told himself again. "No, I will not speak; I will maintain silence. Yes, I will await the turn of events, and trust in the good Father of all."

Then there came another knock at his door. "Surely it is Dan at length; his old housekeeper has sent him on," he thought. "Come in," he called, in a voice that shook.

It was Hommy-beg. The Deemster had sent him across with a message.

"And what is it?" the Bishop asked, speaking at the deaf man's ear.

Hommy-beg scratched his tousled head and made no answer at first, and the Bishop repeated the question.

"We're all taking sorrow for you, my lord," said Hommy, and then he stopped.

"What is it?" the Bishop repeated.

"And right sorry I am to bring his message."

The Bishop's pale face took an ashy gray, but his manner was still calm.

"What did the Deemster send you to say, Hommy?"

"The Dempster—bad cess to him, and no disrespec'—he sent me to tell you that they're after stripping the canvas off, and, behould ye, it's an ould sail, and they're knowing it by its number, and what fishing-boat it came out of, and all to that."

"Where did the sailcloth come from?" asked the Bishop, and his deep eyes were fixed on Hommy.

"It's an ould—well, the fact is—to tell you not a word of a lie—aw, my lord, what matter—what if it is—"

"Where?" said the Bishop calmly, though his lips whitened and quivered.

"It's an old drift yawlsail of the 'Ben-my-Chree.' Aw, yes, yes, sarten sure, and sorry I am to bring bad newses."

Hommy-beg went out, and the Bishop stood for some minutes in the thrall of fear. He had been smitten hard by other facts, but this latest fact seemed for the moment to overthrow his great calm faith in God's power to bring out all things for the best. He wrestled with it long and hard. He tried to persuade himself that it meant nothing. That Ewan was dead was certain. That he came by his death through foul play seemed no less sure and terrible. But that his body had been wrapped in sailcloth once belonging to Dan's fishing-boat was no sufficient ground for the terrible accusation that was taking shape in other minds. Could he accept the idea? Ah, no, no, no. To do so would be to fly in the face of all sound reason, all fatherly love, and all trust in the good Father above. Though the sailcloth came from the "Ben-my-Chree," the fact said nothing of where the body came from. And even though it were certain that the body must have been dropped into the sea from the fishing-boat that belonged to Dan, it would still require proof that Dan himself was aboard of her.

With such poor shifts the Bishop bore down the cruel facts as one after one they beat upon his brain. He tried to feel shame of his own shame, and to think hard of his own hard thoughts. "Yes, I will trust in God," he told himself afresh, "I will await events, and trust in the good Father of all mercies." But where was Dan? The Bishop had made up his mind to send messengers to skirr the island round in search of his son, when suddenly there came a great noise as of many persons talking eagerly, and drawing hurriedly near and nearer.

A minute afterward his library door was opened again without reserve or ceremony, and there came trooping into the room a mixed throng of the village folk. Little Jabez Gawne was at their head with a coat and a hat held in his hands before him.

Cold as the day was the people looked hot and full of puzzled eagerness, and their smoking breath came in long jets into the quiet room.

"My lord, look what we've found on the top of Orrisdel," said Jabez, and he stretched out the coat, while one of the men behind him relieved him of the beaver.

The coat was a long black-cloth coat, with lappets and tails and wristbands turned over.

The Bishop saw at a glance that it was the coat of a clergyman.

"Leave it to me to know this coat, my lord, for it was myself that made it," said Jabez.

The Bishop's brain turned giddy, and the perspiration started from his temples, but his dignity and his largeness did not desert him.

"Is it my poor Ewan's coat?" he asked, as he held out his hand to take it; but his tone was one of almost hopeless misery and not of inquiry.

"That's true, my lord," said Jabez, and thereupon the little tailor started an elaborate series of identifications, based chiefly on points of superior cut and workmanship. But the Bishop cut the tailor short with a wave of the hand.

"You found it on Orrisdale Head?" asked the Bishop.

And one of the men behind pushed his head between the shoulders of those who were before him, and said:

"Aw, yes, my lord, not twenty yards from the cliff, and I found something else beside of it."

Just then there was a further noise in the passage outside the library, and a voice saying:

"Gerr out of the way, you old loblolly-boys, bringing bad newses still, and glad of them, too."

It was Hommy-beg returned to Bishop's Court with yet another message, but it was a message of his own and not of the Deemster's. He pushed his way through the throng until he came face to face with the Bishop, and then he said:

"The Dempster is afther having the doctor down from Ramsey, and the big man is sayin' the neck was broken, and it was a fall that killed the young pazon, and nothing worse, at all at all."

The large sad eyes of the Bishop seemed to shine without moving as Hommy spoke, but in an instant the man who had spoken before thrust his word in again, and then the Bishop's face grew darker than ever with settled gloom.

"It was myself that found the coat and hat, my lord; and a piece nearer the cliff I found this, and this; and then, down the brew itself—maybe a matter of ten feet down—I saw this other one sticking in a green corry of grass and ling, and over I went, hand-under-hand, and brought it up."

While he spoke the man struggled to the front, and held out in one hand a belt, or what seemed to be two belts buckled together and cut across as with a knife, and in the other hand two daggers.

A great awe fell upon every one at sight of the weapons. The Bishop's face still showed a quiet grandeur, but his breathing was labored and harassed.

"Give them to me," he said, with an impressive calmness, and the man put the belts and daggers into the Bishop's hands. He looked at them attentively, and saw that one of the buckles was of silver, while the other was of steel.

"Has any one recognized them?" he asked.

A dozen voice answered at once that they were the belts of the newly-banded militia.

At the same instant the Bishop's eye was arrested by some scratches on the back of the silver buckle. He fixed his spectacles to examine the marks more closely. When he had done so he breathed with gasps of agony, and all the cheer of life seemed in one instant to die out of his face. His nerveless fingers dropped the belts and daggers on to the table, and the silver and the steel clinked as they fell.

There had been a dead silence in the room for some moments, and then, with a labored tranquillity, the Bishop said, "That will do," and stood mute and motionless while the people shambled out, leaving their dread treasures behind them.

To his heart's core the Bishop was struck with an icy chill. He tried to link together the terrible ideas that had smitten his brain, but his mind wandered and slipped away. Ewan was last seen going toward the creek; he was dead; he had been killed by a fall; his body had come ashore in an old sail of the "Ben-my-Chree"; his coat and hat had been picked up on the top of Orrisdale Head, and beside them lay two weapons and two belts, whereof one had belonged to Dan, whose name was scratched upon it.

In the crushing coil of circumstance that was every moment tightening about him the Bishop's great calm faith in the goodness of his Maker seemed to be benumbed. "Oh, my son, my son!" he cried, when he was left alone. "Would to God I had died before I saw this day! Oh, my son, my son!" But after a time he regained his self-control, and said to himself again, "I will trust in God; He will make the dark places plain," Then he broke into short, fitful prayers, as if to drive away, by the warmth of the spirit, the chill that was waiting in readiness to freeze his faith—"Make haste unto me, O God! Hide not Thy face from Thy servant, for I am in trouble."

The short winter's day had dragged on heavily, but the arms of darkness were now closing round it. The Bishop put on his cloak and hat and set off for Ballamona. In length of days he was but little past his prime, but the dark sorrow of many years had drained his best strength, and he tottered on the way. Only his strong faith that God would remember His servant in the hour of trouble gave power to his trembling limbs.

And as he walked he began to reproach himself for the mistrust whereby he had been so sorely shaken. This comforted him somewhat, and he stepped out more boldly. He was telling himself that, perplexing though the facts might be, they were yet so inconclusive as to prove nothing except that Ewan was dead, when all at once he became conscious that in the road ahead of him, grouped about the gate of Ballamona, were a company of women and children, all agitated and some weeping, with the coroner in their midst, questioning them.

The coroner was Quayle the Gyke, the same who would have been left penniless by his father but for the Bishop's intervention.

"And when did your husband go out to sea?" the coroner asked.

"At floodtide yesterday," answered one of the women; "and my man, he said to me, 'Liza,' he said, 'get me a bite of priddhas and salt herrin's for supper,' he said; 'we'll be back for twelve,' he said; but never a sight of him yet, and me up all night till daylight."

"But they've been in and gone out to sea again," said another of the women.

"How d'ye know that, Mother Quilleash?" asked the coroner.

"Because I've been taking a slieu round to the creek, and there's a basket of ray and cod in the shed," the woman answered.

At that the Bishop drew up at the gate, and the coroner explained to him the trouble of the women and children.

"Is it you, Mrs. Corkell?" the Bishop asked of a woman near him.

"Aw, yes, my lord."

"And you, too, Mrs. Teare?"

The woman courtesied; the Bishop named them one by one, and stroked the bare head of the little girl who was clinging to her mother's cloak and weeping.

"Then it's the 'Ben-my-Chree' that has been missing since yesterday at high-water?" the Bishop said, in a sort of hushed whisper.

"Yes, sure, my lord."

At that the Bishop turned suddenly aside, without a word more, opened the gate, and walked up the path. "Oh, my son, my son," he cried, in his bleeding heart, "how have you shortened my days! How have you clothed me with shame! Oh, my son, my son!"

Before Ballamona an open cart was standing, with the tail-board down, and the horse was pawing the gravel which had once—on a far different occasion—been strewn with the "blithe-bread." The door of the house stood ajar, and a jet of light from within fell on the restless horse without. The Bishop entered the house, and found all in readiness for the hurried night burial. On chairs that were ranged back to back a rough oak coffin, like an oblong box, was resting, and from the rafter of the ceiling immediately over it a small oil-lamp was suspended. On either side of the hall were three or four men holding brands and leathern lanterns, ready for lighting. The Deemster was coming and going from his own room beyond, attended in bustling eagerness by Jarvis Kerruish. Near the coffin stood the vicar of the parish, father of the dead man's dead wife, and in the opening of a door that went out from the hall Mona stood weeping, with the dead man's child in her arms.

And even as it is only in the night that the brightest stars may truly be seen, so in the night of all this calamity the star of the Bishop's faith shone out clearly again, and his vague misgivings fell away. He stepped up to Mona, whose dim eyes were now fixed on his face in sadness of sympathy, and with his dry lips he touched her forehead.

Then, in the depth of his own sorrow and the breadth of shadow that lay upon him, he looked down at the little one in Mona's arms, where it leaped and cooed and beat its arms on the air in a strange wild joy at this gay spectacle of its father's funeral, and his eyes filled for what the course of its life would be.

Almost as soon as the Deemster was conscious of the Bishop's presence in the house, he called on the mourners to make ready, and then six men stepped to the side of the coffin.

"Thorkell," said the Bishop, calmly, and the bearers paused while he spoke, "this haste to put away the body of our dear Ewan is unseemly, because it is unnecessary."

The Deemster made no other answer than a spluttered expression of contempt, and the Bishop spoke again:

"You are aware that there is no canon of the Church requiring it, and no law of State demanding it. That a body from the sea shall be buried within the day it has washed ashore is no more than a custom."

"Then custom shall be indulged with custom," said Thorkell, decisively.

"Not for fifty years has it been observed," continued the Bishop; "and here is an outrage on reason and on the respect we owe to our dead."

At this the Deemster said: "The body is mine, and I will do as I please with it."

Even the six carriers, with their hands on the coffin, caught their breath at these words; but the Bishop answered without anger: "And the graveyard is mine, in charge for the Church and God's people, and if I do not forbid the burial, it is because I would have no wrangling over the grave of my dear boy."

The Deemster spat on the floor, and called on the carriers to take up their burden. Then the six men lifted the coffin from the chairs, and put it into the cart at the door. The other mourners went out on to the gravel, and such of them as carried torches and lanterns lighted them there. The Old Hundred was then sung, and when its last notes had died on the night air the springless cart went jolting down the path. Behind it the mourners ranged themselves two abreast, with the Deemster walking alone after the cart, and the Bishop last of all.

Mona stood a moment at the open door, in the hall that was now empty and desolate and silent, save for the babblings of the child in her arms. She saw the procession through the gate into the road. After that she went into the house, drew aside the curtain of her window, and watched the moving lights until they stopped, and then she knew that they were gathered about an open grave, and that half of all that had been very dear to her in this weary world was gone from it forever.

CHAPTER XXVIII
THE CHILD GHOST IN THE HOUSE

After the coroner, Quayle the Gyke, had gone through one part of his dual functions at Ballamona, and thereby discovered that the body of Ewan had been wrapped in a sailcloth of the "Ben-my-Chree," he set out on the other part of his duty, to find the berth of the fishing-boat, and, if need be, to arrest the crew. He was in the act of leaving Ballamona when, at the gate of the highroad, he came upon the women and children of the families of the crew he was in search of, and there, at the moment when the Bishop arrived for the funeral, he heard that the men had been at sea since the middle of the previous day. Confirmed in his suspicions, but concealing them, he returned to the village with the terrified women, and on the way he made his own sinister efforts to comfort them when they mourned as if their husbands had been lost. "Aw, no, no, no, never fear; we'll see them again soon enough, I'll go bail," he said, and in their guileless blindness the women were nothing loth to take cheer from the fellow's dubious smile.

His confidence was not misplaced, for hardly had he got back to the village, and stepped into the houses one after one, making his own covert investigations while he sandwiched his shrewd questions with solace, when the fishermen themselves, old Quilleash, Crennell, Teare, and Corkell, and the lad Davy Fayle, came tramping up the street. Then there was wild joy among the children, who clung to the men's legs, and some sharp nagging among the women, who were by wifely duty bound to conceal their satisfaction under a proper appearance of wrath. "And what for had they been away all night?" and "Didn't they take shame at treating a woman like dirt?" and "Just like a man, just, not caring a ha'p'orth, and a woman up all night, and taking notions about drowning, and more fool for it."

And when at length there came a cessation of such questions, and the fishermen sat down with an awkward silence, or grunted something in an evasive way about "Women preaching mortal," and "Never no reason in them," then the coroner began his more searching inquiries. When did they run in with the cod and ling that was found lying in the tent? Was there a real good "strike" on, that they went out again at half-flood last night? Doing much outside? No? He wouldn't trust but they were lying off the

Mooragh, eh? Yes, you say? Coorse, coorse. And good ground, too. And where was the capt'n? Out with them? He thought so.

Everything the coroner asked save the one thing on which his mind was set, but at mention of the Mooragh the women forgot their own trouble in the greater trouble that was over the parish, and blurted out, with many an expletive, the story of the coming to shore of the body of Ewan. And hadn't they heard the jeel? Aw, shocking, shocking! And the young pazon had sailed in their boat; so he had! Aw, ter'ble, ter'ble!

The coroner kept his eyes fixed on the men's faces, and marked their confusion with content. They on their part tried all their powers of dissembling. First came a fine show of ferocity. Where were their priddhas and herrings? Bad cess to the women, the idle shoulderin' craythurs, did they think a man didn't want never a taste of nothin' comin' in off the say, afther workin' for them day and night same as haythen naygroes, and no thanks for it?

It would not do, and the men themselves were the first to be conscious that they could not strike fire. One after another slunk out of his house until they were all five on the street in a group, holding their heads together and muttering. And when at length the coroner came out of old Quilleash's house, and leaned against the trammon at the porch, and looked toward them in the darkness, but said not a word, their self-possession left them on the instant, and straightway they took to their heels.

"Let's away at a slant over the Head and give warning to Mastha Dan," they whispered; and this was the excuse they made to themselves for their flight, just to preserve a little ray of self-respect.

But the coroner understood them, and he set his face back toward the churchyard, knowing that the Deemster would be there by that time.

The Bishop had gone through the ceremony at the graveside with composure, though his voice when he spoke was full of tears, and the hair of his uncovered head seemed to have passed from iron-gray to white. His grand, calm face was steadfast, and his prayer was of faith and hope. Only beneath this white quiet as of a glacier the red riot of a great sorrow was rife within him.

It was then for the first time in its fulness that—undisturbed in that solemn hour by coarser fears—he realized the depth of his grief for the loss of Ewan. That saintly soul came back to his memory in its beauty and tenderness alone, and its heat and uncontrollable unreason were forgotten. When he touched on the mystery of Ewan's death his large wan face quivered slightly and he paused; but when he spoke of the hope of an everlasting reunion, and how all that was dark would be made plain and the Judge of all the earth would do right, his voice grew bold as with a surety of a brave resignation.

The Deemster listened to the short night-service with alternate restlessness—tramping to and fro by the side of the grave—and cold self-possession, and with a constant hardness and bitterness of mind, breaking out sometimes into a light trill of laughter, or again into a hoarse gurgle, as if in scorn of the Bishop's misplaced confidence. But the crowds that were gathered around held their breath in awe of the mystery, and when they sang it was with such an expression of emotion and fear that no man knew the sound of his own voice.

More than once the Deemster stopped in his uneasy perambulations, and cried "What's that?" as if arrested by sounds that did not break on the ears of others. But nothing occurred to disturb the ceremony until it had reached the point of its close, and while the Bishop was pronouncing a benediction the company was suddenly thrown into a great tumult.

It was then that the coroner arrived, panting, after a long run. He pushed his way through the crowd, and burst in at the graveside between the Bishop and the Deemster.

"They've come ashore," he said, eagerly; "the boat's in harbor and the men are here."

Twenty voices at once cried "Who?" but the Deemster asked no explanation. "Take them," he said, "arrest them;" and his voice was a bitter laugh, and his face in the light of the torches was full of malice and uncharity.

Jarvis Kerruish stepped out. "Where are they?" he asked.

"They've run across the Head in the line of the Cross Vein," the coroner answered; "but six of us will follow them."

And without more ado he twisted about and impressed the five men nearest to him into service as constables.

"How many of them are there?" said Jarvis Kerruish.

"Five, sir," said the coroner, "Quilleash, Teare, Corkell, Crennell, and the lad Davy."

"Then is he not with them?" cried the Deemster, in a tone that went to the Bishop's heart like iron.

The coroner glanced uneasily at the Bishop, and said, "He was with them, and he is still somewhere about."

"Then away with you; arrest them, quick," the Deemster cried in another tone.

"But what of the warrant, sir?" said the coroner.

"Simpleton, are you waiting for that?" the Deemster shouted, with a contemptuous sweep of the hand. "Where have you been, that you don't know that your own warrant is enough? Arrest the scoundrels, and you shall have warrant enough when you come back."

But as the six men were pushing their way through the people, and leaping the cobble wall of the churchyard, the Deemster picked from the ground a piece of slate-stone that had come up from the vault, and scraped his initials upon it with a pebble.

"Take this token, and go after them," he said to Jarvis Kerruish, and instantly Jarvis was following the coroner and his constables, with the Deemster's legal warranty for their proceedings.

It was the work of a moment, and the crowd that had stood with drooping heads about the Bishop had now broken up in confusion. The Bishop himself had not spoken; a shade of bodily pain had passed over his pale face, and a cold damp had started from his forehead. But hardly had the coroner gone, or the people recovered from their bewilderment, when the Bishop lifted one hand to bespeak silence, and then said, in a tone impossible to describe: "Can any man say of his own knowledge that my son was on the 'Ben-my-Chree' last night?"

The Deemster snorted contemptuously, but none made answer to the Bishop's question.

At that moment there came the sound of a horse's hoofs on the road, and immediately the old archdeacon drew up. He had been preaching the Christmas sermons at Peeltown that day, and there he had heard of the death of his grandson, and of the suspicions that were in the air concerning it. The dour spirit of the disappointed man had never gone out with too much warmth to the Bishop, but had always been ready enough to cast contempt on the "moonstruck ways" of the man who had "usurped" his own place of preferment; and now, without contrition or pity, he was ready to strike his blow at the stricken man.

"I hear that the 'Ben-my-Chree' has put into Peel harbor," he said, and as he spoke he leaned across his saddle-bow, with his russet face toward where the Bishop stood.

"Well, well, well?" cried the Deemster, rapping out at the same time his oath of impatience as fast as a hen might have pecked.

"And that the crew are not likely to show their faces soon," the archdeacon continued.

"Then you're wrong," said the Deemster imperiously, "for they've done as much already. But what about their owner? Was he with them? Have you seen him? Quick, let us hear what you have to say."

The archdeacon did not shift his gaze from the Bishop's face, but he answered the Deemster nevertheless.

"Their owner was with them," he said, "and woe be to him. I had as lief that a millstone were hung about my neck as that I stood before God as the father of that man."

And with such charity of comfort the old archdeacon alighted and walked away with the Deemster, at the horse's head. The good man had preached with unwonted fervor that day from the Scripture which says, "With what measure ye mete, it shall be measured to you again."

In another instant the Bishop was no longer the same man. Conviction of Dan's guilt had taken hold of him. Thus far he had borne up against all evil shown by the strength of his great faith in his Maker to bring out all things well. But at length that faith was shattered. When the Deemster and the archdeacon went away together, leaving him in the midst of the people, he stood there, while all eyes were upon him, with the stupid bewildered look of one who has been dealt an unexpected and dreadful blow. The world itself was crumbling under him. At that first instant there was something like a ghastly smile playing over his pale face. Then the truth came rolling over him. The sight was terrible to look upon. He tottered backward with a low moan. When his faith went down his manhood went down with it.

"Oh, my son, my son!" he cried again, "how have you shortened my days! How have you clothed me with shame! Oh, my son, my son!"

But love was uppermost even in that bitter hour, and the good God sent the stricken man the gift of tears. "He is dead, he is dead!" he cried; "now is my heart smitten and withered like grass. Ewan is dead. My son is dead. Can it be true? Yes, dead, and worse than dead. Lord, Lord, now let me eat ashes for bread and mingle my drink with weeping."

And so he poured out his broken spirit in a torrent of wild laments. The disgrace that had bent his head heretofore was but a dream to this deadly reality. "Oh, my son, my son! Would God I had died before I saw this day!"

The people stood by while the unassuageable grief shook the Bishop to the soul. Then one of them—it was Thormod Mylechreest, the bastard son of the rich man who had left his offspring to public charity—took the old man by the hand, and the crowd parted for them. Together they passed out of the churchyard, and out of the hard glare of the torchlight, and set off for Bishop's Court. It was a pitiful thing to see. How the old father, stricken into age by sorrow rather than years, tottered feebly on the way. How low his white head was bent, as if the darkness itself had eyes to peer into his darkened soul.

And yet more pitiful was it to see how the old man's broken spirit, reft of its great bulwark, which lay beneath it like an idol that was broken, did yet struggle with a vain effort to glean comfort from its fallen faith. But every stray text that rose to his heart seemed to wound it afresh. "As arrows in the hand of a mighty man, so are children of the youth.... They shall not be ashamed.... Oh, Absalom, my son, my son!... For thy sake I have borne reproach; shame hath covered my face.... I am poor and needy; make haste unto me, O God.... Hide not thy face from thy servant, for I am in trouble.... O God, thou knowest my foolishness.... And Eli said, It is the Lord, let him do as seemeth him good.... The waters have overwhelmed me, the streams have gone over my soul; the proud waters have gone over my soul."

Thus tottering feebly at the side of Mylechreest and leaning on his arm, the Bishop went his way, and thus the poor dead soul of the man, whose faith was gone, poured forth its barren grief. The way was long, but they reached Bishop's Court at last, and at sight of it a sudden change seemed to come over the Bishop. He stopped and turned to Mylechreest, and said, with a strange resignation:

"I will be quiet. Ewan is dead, and Dan is dead. Surely I shall quiet myself as a child that is weaned of its mother. Yes, my soul is even as a weaned child."

And with the simple calmness of a little child he held out his hand to Mylechreest to bid him farewell, and when Mylechreest, with swimming eyes and a throat too full for speech, bent over the old man's hand and put his lips to it, the Bishop placed the other hand on his head, as if he had asked for a blessing, and blessed him.

"Good-night, my son," he said simply, but Mylechreest could answer nothing.

The Bishop was turning into his house when the memory that had gone from him for one instant of blessed respite returned, and his sorrow bled afresh, and he cried piteously. The inanimate old place was in a moment full of spectres. For that night Bishop's Court had gone back ten full years, and if it was not now musical with children's voices, the spirit of one happy boy still lived in it.

Passing his people in the hall and on the stairs, where, tortured by suspense, bewildered, distracted, they put their doubts and rumors together, the Bishop went up to the little room above the library that had once been little Danny's room. The door was locked, but the key was where it had been for many a day—though Dan in his headstrong waywardness had known nothing of that—it was in the Bishop's pocket. Inside the muggy odor was of a chamber long shut up. The little bed was still in the corner, and its quilted counterpane lay thick in dust. Dust covered the walls, and the floor also, and the table under the window was heavy with it. Shutting himself in this dusty crib, the Bishop drew from under the bed a glass-covered case, and opened it, and lifted out one by one the things it contained. They were a child's playthings—a whip, a glass marble, a whistle, an old Manx penny, a tomtit's mossy nest with three speckled blue eggs in it, some pearly shells, and a bit of shriveled seaweed. And each poor relic as it came up awoke a new memory and a new grief, and the fingers trembled that held them. The sense of a boy's sport and a boy's high spirits, long dumb and dead, touched the old man to the quick within these heavy walls.

The Bishop replaced the glass-covered case, locked the room, and went down to his library. But the child ghost that lived in that gaunt old house did not keep to the crib upstairs. Into this book-clad room it followed the Bishop, with blue eyes and laughter on the red lips; with a hop, skip, and a jump, and a pair of spectacles perched insecurely on the diminutive nose.

Ten years had rolled back for the broken-hearted father that night, and Dan, who was lost to him in life, lived in his remembrance only as a beautiful, bright, happy, spirited, innocent child that could never grow older, but must be a child forever.

The Bishop could endure the old house no longer. It was too full of spectres. He would go out and tramp the roads the long night through. Up and down, up and down, through snow or rain, under the moonlight or the stars until the day dawned, and the pitiless sun should rise again over the heedless sleeping world.

CHAPTER XXIX
BY BISHOP'S LAW OR DEEMSTER'S

The Bishop had gone into the hall for his cloak and hat when he came face to face with the Deemster, who was entering the house. At sight of his brother his bewildered mind made some feeble efforts to brace itself up.

"Ah, is it you, Thorkell? Then you have come at last! I had given you up. But I am going out to-night. Will you not come into the library with me? But perhaps you are going somewhere?"

It was a painful spectacle, the strong brain of the strong man tottering visibly. The Deemster set down his hat and cane, and looked up with a cold, mute stare in answer to his brother's inconsequent questions. Then, without speaking, he went into the library, and the Bishop followed him with a feeble, irregular step, humming a lively tune—it was "Salley in our Alley"—and smiling a melancholy, jaunty, bankrupt smile.

"Gilcrist," said the Deemster, imperiously, and he closed the door behind them as he spoke, "let us put away all pretense, and talk like men. We have serious work before us, I promise you."

By a perceptible spasm of will, the Bishop seemed to regain command of his faculties, and his countenance that had been mellowed down to most pitiful weakness, grew on the instant firm and pale.

"What is it, Thorkell?" he said, in a more resolute tone.

Then the Deemster asked deliberately, "What do you intend to do with the murderer of my son?"

"What do I mean to do! I? Do you ask me what I intend to do?" said the Bishop, in a husky whisper.

"I ask you what you intend to do," said the Deemster, firmly. "Gilcrist, let us make no faces. You do not need that I should tell you what powers of jurisdiction over felonies are held by the Bishop of this island as its spiritual baron. More than once you have reminded me, and none too courteously, of those same powers when they have served your turn. They are to-day what they were yesterday, and so I ask you again, What do you intend to do with the murderer of my son?"

The Bishop's breath seemed suspended for a moment, and then, in broken accents he said, softly, "You ask me what I intend to do with the murderer of our Ewan—his murderer, you say?"

In a cold and resolute tone the Deemster said again, "His murderer," and bowed stiffly.

The Bishop's confusion seemed to overwhelm him. "Is it not assuming too much, Thorkell?" he said, and while his fingers trembled as he unlaced them before him, the same sad smile as before passed across his face.

"Listen, and say whether it is not so or not," said the Deemster, with a manner of rigid impassibility. "At three o'clock yesterday my son left me at my own house with the declared purpose of going in search of your son. With what object? Wait. At half-past three he asked for your son at the house they shared together. He was then told that your son would be found at the village. Before four o'clock he inquired for him at the village pot-house, your son's daily and nightly haunt. There he was told that the man he wanted had been seen going down toward the creek, the frequent anchorage of the fishing-smack the "Ben-my-Chree," with which he has frittered away his time and your money. As the parish clock was striking four he was seen in the lane leading to the creek, walking briskly down to it. He was never seen again."

"My brother, my brother, what proof is there in that?" said the Bishop, with a gesture of protestation.

"Listen. That creek under the Head of Orrisdale is known to the fisher-folk as the Lockjaw. Do you need to be told why? Because there is only one road out of it. My son went into the creek, but he never left it alive."

"How is this known, Thorkell?"

"How? In this way. Almost immediately my son had gone from my house Jarvis Kerruish went after him, to overtake him and bring him back. Not knowing the course, Jarvis had to feel his way and inquire, but he came upon his trace at last, and followed Ewan on the road he had taken, and reached the creek soon after the parish clock struck five. Now, if my son had returned as he went, Jarvis Kerruish must have met him."

"Patience, Thorkell, have patience," said the Bishop. "If Ewan found Dan at the Lockjaw Creek, why did not the young man Jarvis find both of them there?"

"Why?" the Deemster echoed, "because the one was dead, and the other in hiding."

The Bishop was standing at that moment by the table, and one hand was touching something that lay upon it. A cry that was half a sigh and half a suppressed scream of terror burst from him. The Deemster understood it not, but set it down to the searching power of his own words. Shuddering from head to foot the Bishop looked down at the thing his hand had touched. It was the militia belt. He had left it where it had fallen from his fingers when the men brought it to him. Beside it, half hidden by many books and papers, the two small daggers lay.

Then a little low cunning crept over the heart of that saintly man, and he glanced up into his brother's face with a dissembled look, not of inquiry, but of supplication. The Deemster's face was imperious, and his eyes betrayed no discovery. He had seen nothing.

"You make me shudder, Thorkell," the Bishop murmured, and while he spoke he lifted the belt and dagger furtively amid a chaos of loose papers, and whipped them into the door of a cabinet that stood open.

His duplicity had succeeded; nor even the hollow ring of his voice had awakened suspicion, but he sat down with a crushed and abject mien. His manhood had gone, shame overwhelmed him, and he ceased to contend.

"I said there was only one way out of the creek," said the Deemster, "but there are two."

"Ah!"

"The other way is by the sea. My son took that way, but he took it as a dead man, and when he came ashore he was wrapped for sea-burial—by ignorant bunglers who had never buried a body at sea before—in a sailcloth of the 'Ben-my-Chree.'"

The Bishop groaned, and wiped his forehead.

"Do you ask for further evidence?" said the Deemster, in a relentless voice. "If so, it is at hand. Where was the 'Ben-my-Chree' last night? It was on the sea. Last night was Christmas Eve, a night of twenty old Manx customs. Where were the boat's crew and owner? They were away from their homes. To-day was Christmas Day. Where were the men? Their wives and children were waiting for some of them to eat with them their Christmas dinner and drink their Christmas ale. But they were not in their houses, and no one knew where they were. Can circumstances be more damning? Speak, and say. Don't wring your hands; be a man, and look me in the face."

"Have mercy, Thorkell," the Bishop murmured, utterly prostrate. But the Deemster went on to lash him as a brutal master whips a broken-winded horse.

"When the 'Ben-my-Chree' came into harbor to-night what was the behavior of crew and owner? Did they go about their business as they are wont to do when wind and tide has kept them too long at sea? Did they show their faces before suspicion as men should who have no fear? No. They skulked away. They fled from question. At this moment they are being pursued."

The Bishop covered his face with his hands.

"And so I ask you again," resumed the Deemster, "what do you intend to do with the murderer of my son?"

"Oh, Dan, Dan, my boy, my boy!" the Bishop sobbed, and for a moment his grief mastered all other emotions.

"Ah, see how it is! You name your son, and you know that he is guilty."

The Bishop lifted up his head, and his eyes flashed. "I do not know that my son is guilty," he said in a tone that made the Deemster pause. But, speedily recovering his self-command, the Deemster continued, in a tone of confidence, "Your conscience tells you that it is so."

The Bishop's spirit was broken in a moment.

"What would you have me do, Thorkell?"

"To present your son for murder in the court of your barony."

"Man, man, do you wish to abase me?" said the Bishop. "Do you come to drive me to despair? Is it not enough that I am bent to the very earth with grief, but that you of all men should crush me to the dust itself with shame? Think of it—my son is my only tie to earth, I have none left but him; and, because I am a judge in the island as well as its poor priest, I am to take him and put him to death."

Then his voice, which had been faint, grew formidable.

"What is it you mean by this cruel torture? If my son is guilty, must his crime go unpunished though his father's hand is not lifted against him? For what business are you yourself on this little plot of earth? You are here to punish the evil-doer. It is for you to punish him if he is guilty. But no, for you to do that would be for you to be merciful. Mercy you will not show to him or me. And, to make a crime that is terrible at the best thrice shameful as well, you would put a father as judge over his son. Man, man, have you no pity? No bowels of compassion? Think of it. My son is myself, life of my life. Can I lop away my right hand and still keep all my members? Only think of it. Thorkell, Thorkell, my brother, think of it. I am a father, and so are you. Could you condemn to death your own son?"

The sonorous voice had broken again to a sob of supplication.

"Yes, you are a father," said the Deemster, unmoved, "but you are also a priest and a judge. Your son is guilty of a crime—"

"Who says he is guilty?"

"Yourself said as much a moment since."

"Have I said so? What did I say? They had no cause of quarrel—Dan and Ewan. They loved each other. But I can not think. My head aches. I fear my mind is weakened by these terrible events."

The Bishop pressed his forehead hard, like a man in bodily pain, but the Deemster showed no ruth.

"It is now for you to put the father aside and let the priest-judge come forward. It is your duty to God and your Church. Cast your selfish interests behind you and quit yourself like one to whom all eyes look up. The Bishop has a sacred mission. Fulfil it. You have punished offenders against God's law and the Church's rule beforetime. Don't let it be said that the laws of God and Church are to pass by the house of their Bishop."

"Pity, pity! have pity," the Bishop murmured.

"Set your own house in order, or with what courage will you ever again dare to intrude upon the houses of your people? Now is your time to show that you can practise the hard doctrine that you have preached. Send him to the scaffold—yes, to the scaffold—"

The Bishop held up his two hands and cried: "Listen, listen. What would it avail you though my son's life were given in forfeit for the life of your son? You never loved Ewan. Ah! it is true, as Heaven is my witness, you never loved him. While I shall have lost two sons at a blow. Are you a Christian, to thirst like this for blood? It is not justice you want; it is vengeance. But vengeance belongs to God."

"Is he not guilty?" the Deemster answered. "And is it not your duty and mine to punish the guilty?"

But the Bishop went on impetuously, panting as he spoke, and in a faint, broken tone:

"Then if you should be mistaken—if all this that you tell me should be a fatal coincidence that my son can not explain away? What if I took him and presented him, and sent him to the gallows, as you say, and some day, when all that is now dark became light, and the truth stood revealed, what if then I had to say to myself before God, 'I have taken the life of my son?' Brother, is your heart brazed out that you can think of it without pity?"

The Bishop had dropped to his knees.

"I see that you are a coward," said the Deemster, contemptuously. "And so this is what your religion comes to! I tell you that the eyes of the people of this island are on you. If you take the right course now their reverence is yours; if the wrong one, it will be the worst evil that has ever befallen you from your youth upward."

The Bishop cried, "Mercy, mercy—for Christ's sake, mercy!" and he looked about the room with terrified eyes, as if he would fly from it if he could.

But the Deemster's lash had one still heavier blow.

"More, more," he said—"your Church is on its trial also, and if you fail of your duty now, the people will rise and sweep it away."

Then a great spasm of strength came to the Bishop, and he rose to his feet.

"Silence, sir!" he said, and the Deemster quailed visibly before the heat and flame of his voice and manner.

But the spasm was gone in an instant, for his faith was dead as his soul was dead, and only the galvanic impulse of the outraged thing remained. And truly his faith had taken his manhood with it, for he sat down and sobbed. In a few moments more the Deemster left him without another word. Theirs had been a terrible interview, and its mark remained to the end like a brand of iron on the hearts of both the brothers.

The night was dark but not cold, and the roads were soft and draggy. Over the long mile that divided Bishop's Court from Ballamona the old Deemster walked home with a mind more at ease than he had known for a score of years. "It was true enough, as he said, that I never loved Ewan," the Deemster thought. "But then whose was the fault but Ewan's own? At every step he was against me, and if he took the side of the Bishop and his waistrel son he did it to his own confusion. And he had his good parts, too. Patient and long-suffering like his mother, poor woman, dead and gone. A little like my old father also, the simple soul. With fire, too, and rather headstrong at times. I wonder how it all happened."

Then, as he trudged along through the dark roads, his mind turned full on Dan. "He must die," he thought, with content and a secret satisfaction. "By Bishop's law or Deemster's he can not fail but be punished with death. And so this is the end! He was to have his foot on my neck some day. So much for the brave vaunt and prophecy. And when he is dead my fate is broken. Tut, who talks of fate in these days? Idle chatter and balderdash!"

When the Deemster got to Ballamona he found the coroner, Quayle the Gyke, in the hall awaiting him. Jarvis Kerruish was on the settle pushing off his slush-covered boots with a bootjack.

"Why, what? How's this?" said the Deemster.

"They've escaped us so far," said the coroner, meekly.

"Escaped you? What? In this little rat-hole of an island, and they've escaped you?"

"We gave them chase for six miles, sir. They've taken the mountains for it. Up past the Sherragh Vane at Sulby, and under Snaefell and Beinn-y-Phott—that's their way, sir. And it was black dark up yonder, and we had to leave it till the morrow. We'll take them, sir, make yourself easy."

"Had any one seen them? Is he with them?"

"Old Moore, the miller at Sulby, saw them as they went by the mill running mortal hard. But he told us no, the captain wasn't among them."

"What! then you've been wasting your wind over the fishermen while he has been clearing away?"

Jarvis Kerruish raised his head from where he was pulling on his slippers.

"Set your mind at rest, sir," he said, calmly. "We will find him, though he lies like a toad under a stone."

"Mettle, mettle," the Deemster chuckled into his breast, and proceeded to throw off his cloak. Then he turned to the coroner again.

"Have you summoned the jury of inquiry?"

"I have, sir—six men of the parish—court-house at Ramsey—eight in the morning."

"We must indict the whole six of them. You have their names? Jarvis will write them down for you. We can not have five of them giving evidence for the sixth."

The Deemster left the hall with his quick and restless step, and turned into the dining-room, where Mona was helping to lay the supper. Her face was very pale, her eyes were red with long weeping, she moved to and fro with a slow step, and misery itself seemed to sit on her. But the Deemster saw nothing of this. "Mona," he said, "you must be stirring before daybreak to-morrow."

She lifted her face with a look of inquiry.

"We breakfast at half-past six, and leave in the coach at seven."

With a puzzled expression she asked in a low tone where they were to go.

"To Ramsey, for the court of inquiry," he answered with complacency.

Mona's left hand went up to her breast, and her breath came quick.

"But why am I to go?" she asked, timidly.

"Because in cases of this kind, when the main evidence is circumstantial, it is necessary to prove a motive before it is possible to frame an indictment."

"Well, father?" Mona's red eyes opened wide with a startled look, and their long lashes trembled.

"Well, girl, you shall prove the motive."

The Deemster opened the snuff-horn on the mantel-shelf.

"*I* am to do so?"

The Deemster glanced up sharply under his spectacles. "Yes, you child—you," he said, with quiet emphasis, and lifted his pinch of snuff to his nose.

Mona's breast began to heave, and all her slight frame to quiver.

"Father," she said, faintly, "do you mean that I am to be the chief witness against the man who took my brother's life?"

"Well, perhaps, but we shall see. And now for supper, and then to bed, for we must be stirring before the lark."

Mona was going out of the room with a heavy step, when the Deemster, who had seated himself at the table, raised his eyes. "Wait," he said; "when were you last out of the house?"

"Yesterday morning, sir. I was at the plowing match."

"Have you had any visitors since five last night?"

"Visitors—five—I do not understand—"

"That will do, child."

Jarvis Kerruish came into the room at this moment. He was the Deemster's sole companion at supper that night. And so ended that terrible Christmas Day.

CHAPTER XXX
THE DEEMSTER'S INQUEST

It was at the late dawn of the following morning that Dan Mylrea escaped from his night-long burial in the shaft of the disused lead mine. On his way to Ballamona he went by the little shed where Mrs. Kerruish lived with her daughter Mally. The sound of his footstep on the path brought the old woman to the doorway.

"Asking pardon, sir," the old body said, "and which way may you be going?"

Dan answered that he was going to Ballamona.

"Not to the Deemster's? Yes? Och! no. Why, d'ye say? Well, my daughter was away at the Street last night—where she allis is o' nights, more's the pity, leaving me, a lone woman, to fret and fidget—and there in the house where they tell all newses, the guzzling craythurs, they were sayin' as maybe it was yourself as shouldn't trouble the Deemster for a bit of a spell longer."

Dan took no further heed of the old woman's warning than to thank her as he passed on. When he got to Ballamona the familiar place looked strange and empty. He knocked, but there was no answer. He called, but there was no reply. Presently a foot on the gravel woke the vacant stillness. It was Hommy-beg, and at sight of Dan he lifted both his hands.

Then, amid many solemn exclamations, slowly, disjointedly, explaining, excusing, Hommy told what had occurred. And no sooner had Dan realized the business that was afoot, and that the Deemster, with Jarvis Kerruish and Mona, were gone to Ramsey on a court of inquiry touching Ewan's death, than he straightway set his face in the same direction.

"The court begins its business at eight, you say? Well, good-by, Hommy, and God bless you!" he said, and turned sharply away. But he stopped suddenly, and came back the pace or two. "Wait, let us shake hands, old friend; we may not have another chance. Good-by."

In a moment Dan was going at a quick pace down the road.

It was a heavy morning. The mists were gliding slowly up the mountains in grim, hooded shapes, their long white skirts sweeping the meadows as they passed. Overhead the sky was dim and empty. Underfoot the roads were wet and thick. But Dan felt nothing of this wintry gloom. It did not touch his emancipated spirit. His face seemed to open as he walked, and his very stature to increase. He reflected that the lumbering coach which carried the Deemster and his daughter and bastard son must now be far on its way through the ruts of this rough turnpike that lay between Michael and Ramsey. And he pushed on with new vigor.

He passed few persons on the roads. The houses seemed to be deserted. Here or there a little brood of children played about a cottage door. He hailed them cheerily as he went by, and could not help observing that when the little ones recognized him they dropped their play and huddled together at the threshold like sheep affrighted.

As he passed into Ballaugh under the foot of Glen Dhoo he came upon Corlett Ballafayle. The great man opened his eyes wide at sight of Dan and made no answer to his salutation; but when Dan had gone on some distance he turned, as if by a sudden impulse, and hailed him with scant ceremony.

"Ay, why do you take that road?"

Dan twisted his head, but he did not stop, and Corlett Ballafayle laughed in his throat at a second and more satisfying reflection, and then, without waiting for an answer to his question, he waved the back of one hand, and said, "All right. Follow on. It's nothing to me."

Dan had seen the flicker of good-will, followed by the flame of uncharity, that flashed over the man's face, but he had no taste or time for parley. Pushing on past the muggy inn by the bridge, past the smithy that stood there and the brewery that stood opposite, he came into the village. There the women, standing at their doors, put their heads together, looked after him and whispered, and, like Corlett Ballafayle, forgot to answer his greeting. It was then that over his new-found elevation of soul Dan felt a creeping sense of shame. The horror and terror that had gone before had left no room for the lower emotion. Overwhelmed by a crushing idea of his guilt before God, he had not realized his position in the eyes of his fellow-men. But now he realized it, and knew that his crime was known. He saw himself as a hunted man, a homeless, friendless wanderer on the earth, a murderer from whom all must shrink. His head fell into his breast as he walked, his eyes dropped to the ground, he lifted his face no more to the faces of the people whom he passed, and gave none his salutation.

The mists lifted off the mountains as the morning wore on, and the bald crowns were seen against the empty sky. Dan quickened his pace. When he came to Sulby it had almost quickened to a run, and as he went by the mill in the village he noticed that old Moore, the miller, who was a square-set, middle-aged man with a heavy jowl, stood at the open door and watched him. He did not lift his eyes, but he was conscious that Moore turned hurriedly into the mill, and that at the next instant one of his men came as hurriedly out of it.

In a few minutes more he was at the bridge that crosses the Sulby River, and there he was suddenly confronted by a gang of men, with Moore at their head. They had crossed the river by the ford at the mill-side, and running along the southern bank of it, had come up to the bridge at the moment that Dan was about to cross it from the road. Armed with heavy sticks, which they carried threateningly, they called on Dan to surrender himself. Dan stopped, looked into their hot faces, and said, "Men, I know what you think, but you are wrong. I am not running away; I am going to Ramsey court-house."

At that the men laughed derisively, and the miller said with a grin that if Dan was on his road to Ramsey they would take the pleasure of his company, just to see him safely landed there.

Dan's manner was quiet. He looked about him with calm but searching looks. At the opposite bank of the river, close to the foot of the bridge, there was a smithy. At that moment the smith was hooping a cart-wheel, and his striker set down his sledge and tied up his leather apron to look on and listen.

"Men," said Dan again, in a voice that was low but strong and resolute, "it is the truth that I am on my way to Ramsey court-house, but I mean to go alone, and don't intend to allow any man to take me there as a prisoner."

"A likely tale," said the miller, and with that he stepped up to Dan and laid a hand upon his arm. At the next moment the man of flour had loosed his grip with a shout, and his white coat was rolling in the thick mud of the wet road. Then the other men closed around with sticks uplifted, but before they quite realized what they were to do, Dan had twisted some steps aside, darted through them, laid hold of the smith's sledge, swung it on his shoulder, and faced about.

"Now, men," he said, as calmly as before, "none of you shall take me to Ramsey, and none of you shall follow me there. I must go alone."

The men had fallen quickly back. Dan's strength of muscle was known, and his stature was a thing to respect. They were silent for a moment and dropped their sticks. Then they began to mutter among themselves, and ask what it was to them after all, and what for should they meddle, and what was a few shillin' anyway?

Dan and his sledge passed through. The encounter had cost him some minutes of precious time, but the ardor of his purpose had suffered no abatement from the untoward event, though his heart was the heavier for it and the dreary day looked the darker.

Near the angle of the road that turns to the left to Ramsey and to the right to the Sherragh Vane, there was a little thatched cottage of one story, with its window level with the road. It was the house of a cobbler named Callister, a lean, hungry, elderly man, who lived there alone under the ban of an old rumor of evil doings of some sort in his youth. Dan knew the poor soul. Such human ruins had never been quarry to him, the big-hearted scapegrace, and now, drawing near, he heard the beat of the old man's hammer as he worked. The hammering ceased, and Callister appeared at his door.

"Capt'n," he stammered, "do you know—do you know—?" He tried to frame his words and could not, and at last he blurted out, "Quayle the Gyke drove by an hour ago."

Dan knew what was in the heart of the poor battered creature, and it touched him deeply. He was moving off without speaking, merely waving his hand for answer and adieu, when the cobbler's dog, as lean and hungry as its master to look upon, came from the house and looked up at Dan out of its rheumy eyes and licked his hand.

The cobbler still stood at his door, fumbling in his fingers his cutting-knife, worn obliquely to the point, and struggling to speak more plainly.

"The Whitehaven packet leaves Ramsey to-night, capt'n," he said.

Dan waved his hand once more. His heart sank yet lower. Only by the very dregs of humanity, the very quarry of mankind, and by the dumb creatures that licked his hand, was his fellowship rewarded. Thus had he wasted his fidelity, and thrown his loyalty away. In a day he had become a hunted man. So much for the world's gratitude and even the world's pity. And yet, shunned or hunted, a mark for the finger of shame or an aim for the hand of fate, he felt, as he had felt before, bound by strong ties to his fellow-creatures. He was about to part from them; he was meeting them for the last time. Not even their coldest glance of fear or suspicion made a call on his resolution.

At every step his impatience became more lively. Through Lezayre, and past Milntown, he walked at a quick pace. He dared not run, lest his eagerness should seem to betray him and he should meet with another such obstacle as kept him back at Sulby Bridge. At length he was walking through the streets of Ramsey. He noticed that most of the people who passed him gave him a hurried and startled look, and went quickly on. He reached the court-house at last. Groups stood about the Saddle Inn, and the south side of the enclosure within the rails was crowded. The clock in the church tower in the market-place beyond was striking nine. It was while building that square tower, twenty years before, that the mason Looney had dropped to his knees on the scaffold and asked the blessing of the Bishop as he passed. To the Bishop's son the clock of the tower seemed now to be striking the hour of doom.

The people within the rails of the courtyard fell aside as Dan pushed his way through, and the dull buzz of their gossip fell straightway to a great silence. But those who stood nearest the porch were straining their necks toward the inside of the court-house in an effort to see and hear. Standing behind them for an instant Dan heard what was said in whispers by those within to those without, and thus he learned what had been done.

The Deemster's inquest had been going on for an hour. First, the landlady of the "Three Legs of Man" had sworn that, at about three o'clock on Christmas Eve, Parson Ewan had inquired at her house for Mr. Dan Mylrea, and had been directed to the creek known sometimes as the Lockjaw. Then the butcher from the shambles in the lane had sworn that Parson Ewan had passed him walking toward the creek; and the longshore fishermen who brought the body to Bishop's Court gave evidence as to when (ten o'clock on Christmas morning) and where (the coral ground for herrings, called the Mooragh) it came ashore. After these, Jarvis Kerruish had sworn to following Parson Ewan within half an hour of the deceased leaving Ballamona, to hearing a loud scream as he approached the lane leading to Orris Head, and to finding at the creek the fisher-lad, Davy Fayle, whose manner awakened strong suspicion when he was questioned as to whether he had seen Parson Ewan and his master, Mr. Daniel Mylrea. The wife of one of the crew of the "Ben-my-Chree" had next been called to say that the fishing-boat had been at sea from high-water on Christmas Eve. The woman had given her evidence with obvious diffidence and some confusion, repeating and contradicting herself, being sharply reprimanded by the Deemster, and finally breaking down into a torrent of tears. When she had been removed the housekeeper at the old Ballamona, an uncomfortable, bewildered old body, stated that Mr. Dan Mylrea had not been home since the early morning on the day before Christmas Day. Finally, the harbor-master at Peel had identified the sailcloth in which the body had been wrapped as a drift yawlsail of the "Ben-my-Chree," and he had also sworn that the lugger of that name had come into the harbor at low-water the previous night, with the men Quilleash, Teare, Corkell, Crennell, and Davy Fayle, as well as the owner, Mr. Dan Mylrea, aboard of her.

Without waiting to hear more, Dan made one great call on his resolution, and pushed his way through the porch into the court-house. Then he realized that there was still some virtue left in humanity. No sooner had the people in the court become aware of his presence among them than one stepped before him as if to conceal him from those in front, while another tapped him on the shoulder, and elbowed a way out, beckoning him to follow as if some pressing errand called him away.

But Dan's purpose was fixed, and no cover for cowardice availed to shake it. Steadfast and silent he stood at the back of the court, half hidden by the throng about him, trying to look on with a cool countenance, and to fix his attention on the proceedings of his own trial. At first he was conscious of no more than the obscurity of the dusky place and a sort of confused murmur that rose from a table at the farther end. For a while he looked stupidly on, and even trembled slightly. But all at once he found himself listening and seeing all that was going on before him.

The court-house was densely crowded. On the bench sat the Deemster, his thin, quick face as sharp as a pen within his heavy wig. Jarvis Kerruish and Quayle, the coroner, stood at a table beneath. Stretched on the top of this table was a canvas sail. Six men from Michael sat to the right as a jury. But Dan's eyes passed over all these as if scarcely conscious of their presence, and turned by an instinct of which he knew nothing toward the witness-box. And there Mona herself was now standing. Her face was very pale and drawn hard about the lips, which were set firm, though the nostrils quivered visibly. She wore a dark cloak of half-conventual pattern, with a hood that fell back from the close hat that sat like a nun's cap about her smooth forehead. Erect she stood, with the fire of two hundred eager eyes upon her, but her bosom heaved and the fingers of her ungloved hand gripped nervously the rail in front of her.

In an instant the thin shrill voice of the Deemster broke on Dan's consciousness, and he knew that he was listening to his own trial, with Mona put up to give evidence against him.

"When did you see your brother last?"

"On the afternoon of the day before yesterday."

"At what hour?"

"At about two o'clock."

"What passed between you at that interview?"

There was no answer to this question.

"Tell the jury if there was any unpleasantness between you and your brother at two o'clock the day before yesterday."

There was a pause, and then the silence was broken by the reply, meekly spoken:

"It is true that he was angry."

"What was the cause of his anger?"

Another pause and no answer. The Deemster repeated his question, and still there was no reply.

"Listen; on your answer to this question the burden of the indictment must rest. Circumstance points but too plainly to a crime. It points to one man as perpetrator of that crime, and to five other men as accessories to it. But it is necessary that the jury should gather an idea of the motive that inspired it. And so I ask again, what was the difference between you and your brother at your interview on the afternoon of the day before yesterday?"

There was a deep hush in the court. A gloomy, echoless silence, like that which goes before a storm, seemed to brood over the place.

All eyes were turned to the witness-box.

"Answer," said the Deemster, with head aslant. "I ask for an answer—I demand it."

Then the witness lifted up her great, soft, liquid eyes to the Deemster's face, and spoke: "Is it the judge or the father that demands an answer?" she said.

"The judge, the judge," the Deemster replied with emphasis, "we know of no father here."

At that the burden that had rested on Mona's quivering face seemed to lift away. "Then, if it is the judge that asks the question, I will not answer it."

The Deemster leaned back in his seat, and there was a low rumble among the people in the court. Dan found his breath coming audibly from his throat, his finger-nails digging trenches in his palms, and his teeth set so hard on his lips that both teeth and lips were bleeding.

After a moment's silence the Deemster spoke again, but more softly than before, and in a tone of suavity.

"If the judge has no power with you, make answer to the father," and he repeated his question.

Amid silence that was painful Mona said, in a tremulous voice, "It is not in a court of justice that a father should expect an answer to a question like that."

Then the Deemster lost all self-control, and shouted in his shrill treble that, whether as father or judge, the witness's answer he should have; that on that answer the guilty man should yet be indicted, and that even as it would be damning to that man so it should hang him.

The spectators held their breath at the Deemster's words and looked aghast at the livid face on the bench. They were accustomed to the Deemster's fits of rage, but such an outbreak of wrath had never before been witnessed. The gloomy silence was unbroken for a moment, and then there came the sound of the suppressed weeping of the witness.

"Stop that noise!" said the Deemster. "We know for whom you shed your tears. But you shall yet do more than cry for the man. If a word of yours can send him to the gallows, that word shall yet be spoken."

Dan saw and heard all. The dark place, the judge, the jury, the silent throng, seemed to swim about him. For a moment he struggled with himself, scarcely able to control the impulse to push through and tear the Deemster from his seat. At the next instant, with complete self-possession and strong hold of his passions, he had parted the people in front of him, and was making his way to the table beneath the bench. Dense as the crowd was it seemed to open of itself before him, and only the low rumble of many subdued voices floated faintly in his ear. He was conscious that all eyes were upon him, but most of all that Mona was watching him with looks of pain and fear.

He never felt stronger than at that moment. Long enough he had hesitated, and too often he had been held back, but now his time was come. He stopped in front of the table, and said in a full clear voice, "I am here to surrender—I am guilty."

The Deemster looked down in bewilderment; but the coroner, recovering quickly from his first amazement, bustled up with the air of a constable making a capture, and put the fetters on Dan's wrists.

What happened next was never afterward rightly known to any of the astonished spectators. The Deemster asked the jury for their verdict, and immediately afterward he called on the clerk to prepare the indictment.

"Is it to be for this man only, or for all six?" the clerk asked.

"All six," the Deemster answered.

Then the prisoner spoke again. "Deemster," he said, "the other men are innocent."

"Where are they?"

"I do not know."

"If innocent, why are they in hiding?"

"I tell you, sir, they are innocent. Their only fault is that they have tried to be loyal to me."

"Were they with you when the body was buried?"

Dan made no answer.

"Did *they* bury it?"

Still no answer. The Deemster turned to the clerk, "The six."

"Deemster," Dan said, with stubborn resolution, "why should I tell you what is not true? I have come here when, like the men themselves, I might have kept away."

"You have come here, prisoner, when the hand of the law was upon you, when its vengeance was encircling you, entrapping you, when it was useless to hold out longer; you have come here thinking to lessen your punishment by your surrender. But you have been mistaken. A surrender extorted when capture is certain, like a confession made when crime can not be denied, has never yet been allowed to lessen the punishment of the guilty. Nor shall it lessen it now."

Then as the Deemster rose a cry rang through the court. It was such a cry out of a great heart as tells a whole story to a multitude. In a moment the people saw and knew all. They looked at the two who stood before them, Dan and Mona, the prisoner and the witness, with eyes that filled, and from their dry throats there rose a deep groan from their midst.

"I tell you, Deemster, it is false, and the men are innocent," said Dan.

The clerk was seen to hand a document to the Deemster, who took a pen and signed it.

"The accused stands committed for trial at the Court of General Jail Delivery."

At the next moment the Deemster was gone.

CHAPTER XXXI
FATHER AND SON

The prison for felons awaiting trial in the civil courts was in Castle Rushen, at Castletown, but Dan Mylrea was not taken to it. There had been a general rising in the south of the island on the introduction of a coinage of copper money, and so many of the rioters had been arrested and committed for trial, without bail, at the Court of General Jail Delivery, that the prison at Castle Rushen was full to overflowing. Twenty men had guarded the place day and night, being relieved every twenty-four hours by as many more from each parish in rotation, some of them the kith and kin of the men imprisoned, and all summoned to Castletown in the morning by the ancient mode of fixing a wooden cross over their doors at night.

Owing to this circumstance the Deemster made the extraordinary blunder of ordering his coroner to remove Dan to the prison beneath the ruined castle at Peeltown. Now, the prison on St. Patrick's islet had for centuries been under the control of the Spiritual Courts, and was still available for use in the execution of the ecclesiastical censures. The jailer was the parish sumner, and the sole governor and director was the Bishop himself. All this the Deemster knew full well, and partly in defiance of his brother's authority, partly in contempt of it, but mainly in bitter disdain of his utter helplessness, where his son's guilt was manifest and confessed, he arrogated the right, without sanction from the spiritual powers, of committing Dan to the Church prison, the civil prison being full.

It was a foul and loathsome dungeon, and never but once had Bishop Mylrea been known to use it. Dark, small, damp, entered by a score of narrow steps, down under the vaults on the floor of the chapel, over the long runnels made in the rock by the sea, it was as vile a hole as the tyranny of the Church ever turned into a jail for the punishment of those who resisted its authority.

The sumner in charge was old Paton Gorry, of Kirk Patrick, a feeble soul with a vast respect for authority, and no powers of nice distinction between those who were placed above him. When he received the Deemster's warrant for Dan's committal, he did not doubt its validity; and when Quayle, the coroner, for his own share ordered that the prisoner should be kept in the close confinement of the dungeon, he acquiesced without question.

If Dan's humiliation down to this moment had not been gall and wormwood to his proud and stubborn spirit the fault did not lie at the door of Quayle the Gyke. Every indignity that an unwilling prisoner could have been subjected to Dan underwent. From the moment of leaving the court-house at Ramsey, Dan was pushed and huddled and imperiously commanded with such an abundant lack of need and reason that at length the people who crowded the streets or looked from their windows—the same people, many of them, who had shrunk from Dan as he entered the town—shouted at the coroner and groaned at him. But Dan himself, who had never before accepted a blow from any man without returning it, was seen to walk tamely by the coroner's side, towering above him in great stature, but taking his rough handling like a child at his knees.

At the door of the prison where Quayle's function ended that of the sumner began, and old Gorry was a man of another mold. Twenty times he had taken charge of persons imprisoned six days for incontinence, and once he had held the governor's wife twelve hours for slander, and once again a fighting clergyman seven days for heresies in looking toward Rome, but never before had he put man, woman, or child into the pestilential hole under the floor of the old chapel. Dan he remembered since the Bishop's son was a boy in corduroys, and when the rusty key of the dungeon turned on him with a growl in its wards, and old Gorry went shivering to the guard-room above and kindled himself a fire there and sat and smoked, the good man under his rough surtout got the better of the bad jailer. Then down he went again, and with a certain shame-facedness, some half-comic, half-pathetic efforts of professional reserve, he said he wouldn't object, not he, if Dan had a mind to come up and warm himself. But Dan declined with words of cold thanks.

"No, Gorry," he said, "I don't know that I feel the cold."

"Oh, all right, all right, sit ye there, sit ye there," said Gorry. He whipped about with as much of largeness as he could simulate, rattled his keys as he went back, and even hummed a tune as he climbed the narrow stairs. But, warming itself at the fire, the poor human nature in the old man's breast began to tear him pitilessly. He could get no peace for memories that would arise of the days when Dan plagued him sorely, the sad little, happy dog. Then up he rose again, and down he went to the dungeon once more.

"I respects the ould Bishop," he said, just by way of preliminary apology and to help him to carry off his intention, "and if it be so that a man *has* done wrong I don't see—I don't see," he stammered, "it isn't natheral that he should be starved alive anyway, and a cold winter's night too."

"It's no more than I deserve," Dan mumbled; and at that word old Gorry whipped about as before, repeating loftily, "Sit ye there, sit ye there."

It was not for him to cringe and sue to a prisoner to come out of that foul hole, och! no; and the Bishop's sumner inflated his choking chest and went back for another pipe. But half an hour later the night had closed in, and old Gorry, with a lantern in his hand, was at the door of Dan's prison again.

"To tell the truth, sir," he muttered, "I can't get lave for a wink of sleep up yonder, and if you don't come up to the fire I wouldn't trust but I'll be forced to stay down here in the cold myself."

Before Dan could make answer there came a loud knocking from overhead. In another moment the key of the door had turned in its lock from without, and Gorry's uncertain footfall was retreating on the steps.

When Dan had first been left alone in his dark cell he had cast himself down on the broad slab cut from the rock, which was his only seat and bed. His suspense was over; the weight of uncertainty was lifted from his brain; and he tried to tell himself that he had done well. He thought of Ewan now with other feelings than before—of his uprightness, his tenderness, his brotherly affection, his frequent intercession, and no less frequent self-sacrifice. Then he thought of his own headlong folly, his blank insensitiveness, his cold ingratitude, and, last of all, of his blundering passion and mad wrath. All else on both sides was blotted from his memory in that hour of dark searching. Alone with his crime—tortured no more by blind hopes of escaping its penalty, or dread misgivings as to the measure of his guilt—his heart went out to the true friend whose life he had taken with a great dumb yearning and a bitter remorse. No cruel voice whispered now in palliation of his offense that it had not been murder, but the accident of self-defense. He had proposed the fight that ended with Ewan's death, and, when Ewan would have abandoned it, he, on his part, would hear of no truce. Murder it was; and, bad as murder is at the best, this murder had been, of all murders, most base and foul. Yes, he had done well. Here alone could he know one hour of respite from terrible thoughts. This dark vault was his only resting-place until he came to lie in the last resting-place of all. There could be no going back. Life was forever closed against him. He had spilled the blood of the man who had loved him with more than a brother's love, and to whom his own soul had been grappled with hooks of steel. It was enough, and the sick certainty of the doom before him was easiest to bear.

It was with thoughts like these that Dan had spent his first hours in prison, and when old Gorry had interrupted them time after time with poor little troubles about the freezing cold of the pestilential place he hardly saw through the old man's simulation into the tender bit of human nature that lay behind it.

A few minutes after Gorry had left the cell, in answer to the loud knocking that had echoed through the empty chambers overhead, Dan could hear that he was returning to it, halting slowly down the steps with many a pause, and mumbling remarks meantime, as if lighting some one who came after him.

"Yes, my lord, it's dark, very dark. I'll set the lantern here, my lord, and turn the key."

In another moment old Gorry was at Dan's side, saying, in a fearful undertone, "Lord 'a' massy! It's the Bishop hisself. I lied to him mortal, so I did—but no use—I said you were sleeping, but no good at all, at all. He wouldn't take rest without putting a sight on you. Here he is—Come in, my lord."

Almost before Dan's mind, distraught by other troubles, had time to grasp what Gorry said, the old jailer had clapped his lantern on the floor of the cell, and had gone from it, and Dan was alone with his father.

"Dan, are you awake?" the Bishop asked, in a low, eager tone. His eyes were not yet familiar with the half-light of the dark place, and he could not see his son. But Dan saw his father only too plainly, and one glance at him in that first instant of recovered consciousness went far to banish as an empty sophism the soothing assurance he had lately nursed at his heart that in what he had done he had done well.

The Bishop was a changed and shattered man. His very stature seemed to have shrunk, and his Jovian white head was dipped into his breast. His great calm front was gone, and in the feeble light of the lantern on the floor his eyes were altered and his face seemed to be cut deep with lines of fear and even of cunning. His irresolute mouth was half-open, as if it had only just emitted a startled cry. In one of his hands he held a small parcel bound tightly with a broad strap, and the other hand wandered nervously in the air before him.

Dan saw everything in an instant. This, then, was the first-fruits of that day's work. He rose from his seat.

"Father!" he cried, in a faint, tremulous voice.

"My son!" the Bishop answered, and for some swift moments thereafter the past that had been very bitter to both was remembered no more by either.

But the sweet oblivion was cruelly brief. "Wait," the Bishop whispered, "are we alone?" And with that the once stately man of God crept on tiptoe like a cat to the door of the cell, and put his head to it and listened.

"Art thou there, Paton Gorry?" he asked, feebly simulating his accustomed tone of quiet authority.

Old Gorry answered from the other side of the door that he was there, that he was sitting on the steps, that he was not sleeping, but waiting my lord's return.

The Bishop crept back to Dan's side, with the same cat-like step as before. "You are safe, my son," he whispered in his low eager tone. "You shall leave this place. It is my prison, and you shall go free."

Dan had watched his father's movements with a sickening sense.

"Then you do not know that I surrendered?" he said, faintly.

"Yes, yes, oh, yes, I know it. But that was when your arrest was certain. But now—listen."

Dan felt as if his father had struck him across the face. "That was what the Deemster said," he began; "but it is wrong."

"Listen—they have nothing against you. I know all. They can not convict you save on your own confession. And why should you confess?"

"Why?"

"Don't speak—don't explain—I must not hear you—listen!" and the old man put one arm on his son's shoulder and his mouth to his ear. "There is only one bit of tangible evidence against you, and it is here; look!" and he lifted before Dan's face the parcel he carried in his other trembling hand. Then down he went on one knee, put the parcel on the floor, and unclasped the strap. The parcel fell open. It contained a coat, a hat, two militia daggers, and a large heavy stone.

"Look!" the Bishop whispered again, in a note of triumph, and as he spoke a grin of delight was struck out of his saintly old face.

Dan shuddered at the sight.

"Where did you get them?" he asked.

The Bishop gave a little grating laugh.

"They were brought me by some of my good people," he answered. "Oh, yes, good people, all of them; and they will not tell. Oh, no, they have promised me to be silent."

"Promised you?"

"Yes—listen again. Last night—it was dark, I think it must have been past midnight—I went to all their houses. They were in bed, but I knocked, and they came down to me. Yes, they gave me their word—on the Book they gave it. Good people, all—Jabez the tailor, Stean the cobbler, Juan of Ballacry, and Thormod in the Street. I remember every man of them."

"Father, do you say you went to these people—these, the very riff-raff of the island—you went to them—you, and at midnight—and begged them—"

"Hush, it is nothing. Why not? But this is important." The Bishop, who was still on his knees, was buckling up the parcel again. "You can sink it in the sea. Did you mark the stone? That will carry it to the bottom. And when you are in the boat it will be easy to drop everything overboard."

"The boat?"

"Ah! have I not told you? Thormod Mylechreest—you remember him? A good man, Thormod—a tender heart, too, and wronged by his father, poor misguided man. Well, Mylechreest has promised—I have just left him—to come down to the harbor at nine to-night, and take the fishing-smack, the 'Ben-my-Chree,' and bring her round to the west coast of St. Patrick's Islet, and cast anchor there, and then come ashore in the boat, and wait for you."

"Wait for me, father?"

"Yes; for this prison is mine, and I shall open its doors to whomsoever it pleases me to liberate. Look!"

The Bishop rose to his full height, threw back his head, and with a feeble show of his wonted dignity strode to the door of the cell and cried, in a poor, stifled echo of his accustomed strong tone, "Paton Gorry, open thou this door."

Old Gorry answered from without, and presently the door was opened.

"Wider."

The door was thrown wide.

"Now, give me the keys, Paton Gorry," said the Bishop, with the same assumption of authority.

Old Gorry handed his keys to the Bishop.

"And get thee home, and stay there."

Old Gorry touched his cap and went up the steps.

Then, with a bankrupt smile of sorry triumph, the Bishop turned to his son. "You see," he said, "you are free. Let me look—what is the hour?" He fumbled for his watch. "Ah, I had forgotten. I paid my watch away to poor Patrick Looney. No matter. At nine by the clock Mylechreest will come for you, and you will go to your boat and set sail for Scotland, or England, or Ireland, or—or—"

Dan could bear up no longer. His heart was choking. "Father, father, my father, what are you saying?" he cried.

"I am saying that you are free to leave this place."

"I will not go—I can not go."

The Bishop fetched a long breath and paused for a moment. He put one trembling hand to his forehead, as if to steady his reeling and heated brain.

"You can not stay," he said. "Hark! do you hear the wind how it moans? Or is it the sea that beats on the rock outside? And over our heads are the dead of ten generations."

But Dan was suffocating with shame; the desolation around, the death that was lying silent above, and the mother of sorrows that was wailing beneath had no terrors left for him.

"Father, my father," he cried again, "think what you ask me to do. Only think of it. You ask me to allow you to buy the silence of the meanest hinds alive. And at what a price? At the price of the influence, the esteem, the love, and the reverence that you have won by the labor of twenty years. And to what end? To the end that I—I—"

"To the end that you may live, my son. Remember what your father's love has been to you. No, not that—but think what it must have been to him. Your father would know you were alive. It is true he would never, never see you. Yes, we should always be apart—you there, and I here—and I should take your hand and see your face no more. But you would be alive—"

"Father, do you call it living? Think if I could bear it. Suppose I escaped—suppose I were safe in some place far away—Australia, America, anywhere out of the reach of shame and death—suppose I were well, ay, and prosperous as the world goes—what then?"

"Then I should be content, my son. Yes, content, and thanking God."

"And I should be the most wretched of men. Only think of it, and picture me there. I should know, though there were none to tell me, I should remember it as often as the sun rose above me, that at home, thousands of miles away, my poor father, the righteous Bishop that once was, the leader of his people and their good father, was the slave of the lowest offal of them all, powerless to raise his hand for the hands that were held over him, dumb to reprove for the evil tongues that threatened to speak ill. And, as often as night came and I tried to sleep, I should see him there growing old, very old, and, maybe, very feeble, and wanting an arm to lean on, and good people to honor him and to make him forget—yes, forget the mad shipwreck of his son's life, but with eyes that could not lift themselves from the earth for secret shame, tortured by fears of dishonor, self-tormented and degraded before the face of his God. No, no, no, I can not take such sacrifice."

The Bishop had drawn nearer to Dan and tried to take his hand. When Dan was silent he did not speak at once, and when Dan sat on his stone seat he sat beside him, gentle as a child, and very meek and quiet, and felt for his hand again, and held it, though Dan would have drawn it away. Then, as they sat together, nearer the old Bishop crept, nearer and yet nearer, until one of his trembling arms encircled Dan's neck and the dear head was drawn down to his swelling, throbbing breast, as if it were a child's head still, and it was a father's part to comfort it and to soothe away its sorrows.

"Then we will go together," he said, after a time, in a faint forlornness of voice, "to the utmost reaches of the earth, leaving all behind us, and thinking no more of the past. Yes, we will go together," he said, very quietly, and he rose to his feet, still holding Dan's hand.

Dan was suffocating with shame. "Father," he said, "I see all now; you think me innocent, and so you would leave everything for my sake. But I am a guilty man."

"Hush! you shall not say that. Don't tell me that. No one shall tell me that. I will not hear it."

The hot eagerness of the Bishop's refusal to hear with his ears the story of his son's guilt told Dan but too surely that he had already heard it with his heart.

"Father, no one would need to tell you. You would find it out for yourself. And think of that awful undeceiving! You would take your son's part against the world, believing in him, but you would read his secret bit by bit, day by day. His crime would steal in between you like a spectre, it would separate you hour by hour, until at length you would be forever apart. And that end would be the worst end of all. No, it can not be. Justice is against it; love is against it. And God, I think God must be against it, too."

"God!"

Dan did not hear. "Yes, I am guilty," he went on. "I have killed the man who loved me as his own soul. He would have given his life for my life, even as he gave his honor for my honor. And I slew him. Ewan! Ewan! my brother, my brother!" he cried, and where he sat he buried his face in his hands.

The Bishop stood over his son with the same gentle calm that had come upon him in the cell, and with not one breath of the restless fever with which he entered it. Once again he tried to take Dan's hand and to hold it, and to meet with his own full orbs Dan's swimming eyes.

"Yes, father, it is right that I should die, and it is necessary. Perhaps God will take my death as an atonement—"

"Atonement!"

"Or, if there is no atonement, there is only hell for my crime, and before God I am guilty."

"Before God!"

The Bishop echoed Dan's words in a dull, mechanical underbreath, and stood a long time silent while Dan poured forth his bitter remorse. Then he said, speaking with something of his own courageous calm of voice, from something like his own pure face, and with some of the upright wrinkles of his high forehead smoothed away: "Dan, I will go home and think. I seem to be awakening from a dreadful nightmare in a world where no God is, and no light reigns, but all is dark. To tell you the truth, Dan, I fear my faith is not what it was or should be. I thought I knew God's ways with his people, and then it seemed as if, after all these years, I had not known him. But I am only a poor priest, and a very weak old man. Good-night, my son, I will go home and think. I am like one who runs to save a child from a great peril and finds a man stronger than himself and braver—one who looks on death face to face and quails not. Good-night, Dan, I will go home and pray."

And so he went his way, the man of God in his weakness. He left his son on the stone seat, with covered face, the lantern, and the parcel on the floor, and the door of the cell wide open. The keys he carried half-consciously in his hand. He stumbled along in the darkness down the winding steps, hewn from the rock, to the boat at the little wooden jetty, where a boatman sat awaiting him. The night was very dark, and the sea's loud moan and its dank salt breath were in the air. He did not see, he did not hear, he did not feel. But there was one in that lonesome place who saw his dark figure as he passed. "Who is there?" said an eager voice, as he went through the deep portcullis and out at the old notched and barred door ajar. But the Bishop neither answered nor heard.

At the house in Castle Street, near to the quay, he stopped and knocked. The door was opened by the old sumner.

"I've brought you the keys, Paton Gorry. Go back to your charge."

"Did you lock the doors, my lord?"

"Yes—no, no—I must have forgotten. I fear my mind—but it is of no moment. Go back, Paton—it will be enough."

"I'll go, my lord," said the sumner.

He went back, but others had been there before him.

CHAPTER XXXII
DIVINATION

Well satisfied with this day's work the Deemster drove from the Ramsey court-house to midday dinner with his father-in-law, the old archdeacon, taking Jarvis Kerruish with him. Mona he sent home in the lumbering car driven by the coroner. It suited well with the girl's troubled mind to be alone, and when night fell in and the Deemster had not returned, the grim gloom of the lonely house on Slieu Dhoo brought her no terrors. But toward nine o'clock the gaunt silence of the place was broken, and from that time until long after midnight Ballamona was a scene of noise and confusion.

First came blind Kerry, talking loudly along the passages, wringing her hands, and crying, "Aw, dear! oh, mam! oh, goodness me!"

Mastha Dan was no longer in prison, he had been kidnapped; four men and a boy had taken him by main force; bound hand and foot he had been carried through the mountains to a lonely place; and there at daybreak to-morrow he was to be shot. All this and more, with many details of place and circumstance, Kerry had seen as in a flash of light, just as she was raking the ashes on the fire preparatory to going to bed.

Mona had gone through too much to be within touch of the blind woman's excitement.

"We must not give way to these fancies, Kerry," she said.

"Fancies, mam? Fancies you're saying? Scoffers may mock, but don't you, mam—brought up with my own hand, as the saying is."

"I did not mean to mock, Kerry; but we have so many real troubles that it seems wicked to imagine others—and perhaps a little foolish, too."

At that word the sightless face of Kerry grew to a great gravity.

"Foolish, mam? It is the gift—the gift of the good God. He made me blind, but he gave me the sights. It would have been hard, and maybe a taste cruel, to shut me up in the dark, and every living craythur in the light; but he is a just God and a merciful, as the saying is, and he gave me the gift for recompense."

"My good Kerry, I am so tired to-night, and must go to bed."

"Aw, yes, and well it has sarved me time upon time—"

"We were up before six this morning, Kerry."

"And now I say to you, send immadient, mam, or the Lord help—"

The blind woman's excitement and Mona's impassibility were broken in upon by the sound of a man's voice in the hall asking sharply for the Deemster. At the next moment Quayle, the coroner, was in the room. His face was flushed, his breath came quick, and his manner betrayed extreme agitation.

"When the Deemster comes home from Kirk Andreas tell him to go across to Bishop's Court at once, and say that I will be back before midnight."

So saying, the coroner wheeled about without ceremony, and was leaving the room.

"What has happened at Bishop's Court?" Mona asked.

"Nothing," he said, impatiently.

"Then why should I tell him to go there?"

The tone of the question awakened the curmudgeon's sense of common policy.

"Well, if you must know, that man has escaped, and I'm thinking the Bishop himself has had his foot in the mischief."

Then Kerry, with a confused desire to defend the Bishop, interrupted, and said, "The Bishop's not at the Coort—let me tell ye that."

Whereupon the coroner smiled with a large dignity, and answered, "I know it, woman."

"When did this happen?" said Mona.

"Not an hour ago; I am straight from Peeltown this minute."

And without more words the coroner turned his back on her, and was gone in an instant.

When Quayle had left the room Kerry lifted both hands; her blind face wore a curious expression of mingled pride and fear. "It is the gift," she said, in an awesome whisper.

Mona stood a while in silence and perplexity, and then she said, in tremulous voice, "Kerry, don't think me among those that scoff, but tell me over again, my good Kerry, and forgive me."

And Kerry told the story of her vision afresh, and Mona now listened with eager attention, and interrupted with frequent questions.

"Who where the four men and the boy? Never saw their faces before? Never? Not in the street? No? Never heard their voices? Ah, surely you remember their voices? Yes, yes, try to recall them; try, try, my good Kerry. Ah! the fishermen—they were the voices of the fishermen! How were you so long in remembering? Quilleash? Yes, old Billy. And Crennell? Yes, and Teare and Corkell, and the boy Davy Fayle? Poor young Davy, he was one of them? Yes? Oh, you dear, good Kerry!"

Mona's impassibility was gone, and her questions, like her breath, came hot and fast.

"And now tell me what place they took him to. The mountains? Yes, but where? Never saw the place before in all your life? Why, no, of course not; how could you, Kerry? Ah, don't mind what I say and don't be angry. But what kind of place? Quick, Kerry, quick."

Kerry's blind face grew solemn, and one hand, with outstretched finger, she raised before her, as though to trace the scene in the air, as she described the spot in the mountains where the four men and the boy had taken Dan.

"It was a great lone place, mam, with the sea a-both sides of you, and a great large mountain aback of you, and a small low one in front, and a deep strame running under you through the gorse, and another shallow one coming into it at a slant, and all whins and tussocks of the lush grass about, and maybe a willow by the water's side, with the sally-birds hanging dead from the boughs, and never a stick, nor a sign of a house, nor a barn, but the ould tumbled cabin where they took him, and only the sea's roar afar away, and the sheep's bleating, and maybe the mountain geese cackling, and all to that."

Mona had listened at first with vivid eagerness and a face alive with animation, but as Kerry went on the girl's countenance saddened. She fell back a pace or two, and said, in a tone of pain and impatience:

"Oh, Kerry, you have told me nothing. What you say describes nearly every mountain-top in the island. Was there nothing else? Nothing? Think. What about the tumble-down house? Had it a roof? Yes? No one living in it? No buildings about it? A shaft-head and gear? Oh, Kerry, how slow you are! Quick, dear Kerry! An old mine? A worked-out mine? Oh, think, and be sure!"

Then the solemnity of the blind woman's face deepened to a look of inspiration. "Think? No need to think," she said in an altered tone. "Lord bless me, I see it again. There, there it is—there this very minute."

She sunk back into a chair, and suddenly became motionless and stiff. Her sightless eyes were opened, and for the first few moments that followed thereafter all her senses seemed to be lost to the things about her. In this dream-state she continued to talk in a slow, broken, fearsome voice, exclaiming, protesting, and half-sobbing. At first Mona looked on in an agony of suspense, and then she dropped to her knees at Kerry's feet, and flung her arms about the blind woman with the cry of a frightened bird.

"Kerry, Kerry!" she called, as if prompted by an unconscious impulse to recall her from the trance that was awful to look upon. And in that moment of contact with the seer she suffered a shock that penetrated every fibre; she shuddered, the cry of pain died off in her throat, her parted lips whitened and stiffened, her eyes were frozen in their look of terror, her breath ceased to come, her heart to beat, and body and soul together seemed transfixed. In that swift instant of insensibility the vision passed like a throb of blood to her from the blind woman, and she saw and knew all.

Half an hour later, Mona, with every nerve vibrating, with eyes of frenzy and a voice of fear, was at Bishop's Court inquiring for the Bishop.

"He is this minute home from Peel," said the housekeeper.

Mona was taken to the library, and there the Bishop sat before the fire, staring stupidly into the flame. His hat and cloak had not yet been removed, and a riding-whip hung from one of his listless hands.

He rose as Mona entered. She flew to his arms, and while he held her to his breast his sad face softened, and the pent-up anguish of her heart overflowed in tears. Then she told him the tangled, inconsequent tale, the coroner's announcement, Kerry's vision, her own strange dream-state, and all she had seen in it.

As she spoke, the Bishop looked dazed; he pressed one hand on his forehead; he repeated her words after her; he echoed the questions she put to him. Then he lifted his head to betoken silence. "Let me think," he said. But the brief silence brought no clearness to his bewildered brain. He could not think; he could not grasp what had occurred. And the baffled struggle to comprehend made the veins of his forehead stand out large and blue. A most pitiful look of weariness came over his mellow face, and he said in a low tone that was very touching to hear, "To tell you the truth, my dear child, I do not follow you—my mind seems thick and clouded—things run together in it—I am only a feeble old man now, and—But wait" (a flash of light crossed his troubled face)—"you say you recognize the place in the mountains?"

"Yes, as I saw it in the vision. I have been there before. When I was a child I was there with Dan and Ewan. It is far up the Sulby River, under

Snaefell, and over Glen Crammag. Don't say it is foolish and womanish, and only hysteria, dear uncle. I saw it all as plainly as I see you now."

"Ah, no, my child. If the Patriarch Joseph practised such divination, is it for me to call it foolishness? But wait, wait—let me think." And then, in a low murmur, as if communing with himself, he went on: "The door was left open ... yes, the door ... the door was...."

It was useless. His brain was broken, and would not link its ideas. He was struggling to piece together the fact that Dan was no longer in prison with the incidents of his own abandoned preparations for his son's escape. Mumbling and stammering, he looked vacantly into Mona's face, until the truth of his impotence forced itself upon her, and she saw that from him no help for Dan could come.

Then with many tears she left him and hastened back to Ballamona. The house was in confusion; the Deemster and Jarvis Kerruish had returned, and the coroner was with them in the study.

"And what of the Peeltown watch?" the Deemster was asking sharply. "Where was he?"

"Away on some cock-and-bull errand, sir."

"By whose orders?"

"The Bishop's."

"And what of the harbor-master when the 'Ben-my-Chree' was taken away from her moorings?"

"He also was spirited away."

"By whom?"

"The same messenger—Will-as-Thorn, the parish clerk."

"Old Gorry, the sumner, gave up the prison keys to the Bishop, you say?"

"To the Bishop, sir."

"And left him in the cell, and found the door open and the prisoner gone upon his return?"

"Just so, sir."

"What have you been doing in the matter?"

"Been to Ramsey, sir, and stationed three men on the quay to see that nobody leaves the island by the Cumberland packet that sails at midnight."

"Tut, man, who will need the packet?—the man has the fishing-boat."

Mona's impatience could contain itself no longer. She hurried into the study and told her tale. The Deemster listened with a keen, quick sense; he questioned, cross-questioned, and learned all. This done, he laughed a little, coldly and bitterly, and dismissed the whole story with contempt.

"Kidnapped? No such matter. Escaped, woman—escaped! And visions, forsooth! What pedler's French! Get away to bed, girl."

Mona had no choice but to go. Her agitation was painful; her sole thought was of Dan's peril. She was a woman, and that Dan was a doomed man, whether in prison or out of it, whether he had escaped or been kidnapped, was a consideration that had faded from her view. His life was in imminent danger, and that was everything to her. She had tried to save him by help of the Bishop, and failing in that direction, she had attempted the same end by help of the Deemster, his enemy.

The hours passed with feet of lead until three o'clock struck, and then there was a knock at her door. The Deemster's voice summoned her to rise, dress quickly and warmly, and come out immediately. She had not gone to bed, and in two minutes more was standing hooded and cloaked in the hall. The Deemster, Jarvis, the coroner, and seven men were there. At the porch a horse, saddled and bridled, was pawing the gravel.

Mona understood everything at a glance. Clearly enough the Deemster intended to act on the guidance of the vision which he had affected to despise. Evidently it was meant that she should go with the men to identify the place she had described.

"An old lead mine under Snaefell and over Glen Crammag, d'you say?"

"Yes, father."

"Daybreak?"

"It was daybreak."

"You would know the place if you saw it again?"

"Yes."

The Deemster turned to the coroner.

"Which course do you take?"

"Across Glen Dhoo, sir, past Ravensdale, and along the mountain-path to the Sherragh Vane."

"Come, girl, mount; be quick."

Mona was lifted to the saddle, the coroner took the bridle, and they started away, the seven men walking behind.

CHAPTER XXXIII
KIDNAPPED

What had happened was a strange series of coincidences. Early that day the crew of the "Ben-my-Chree," in the mountain solitude where they found freezing and starving safety, had sent one of their number back to Sulby village to buy a quarter of meal. Teare was the man chosen for the errand, and having compassed it, he was stealing his way back to the mountains, when he noticed that great companies of people were coming from the direction of Ramsey. Lagging behind the larger groups on the road was a woman whom he recognized as his wife. He attracted her attention without revealing himself to the people in front. She was returning from the Deemster's inquest, and told what had occurred there: that Dan, the Bishop's son, had surrendered, and that the indictment to the Court of General Jail Delivery had been made out not only in his name, but in the names of the four men and the boy of the "Ben-my-Chree."

Teare carried back to the mountains a heavier burden than the quarter of meal. His mates had watched for him as he plodded up the bank of the Sulby River with the bag on his back. When he came up his face was ominous.

"Send the lad away for a spell," he muttered to old Billy Quilleash, and Davy Fayle was sent to cut gorse for a fire.

Then the men gathered around Teare and heard what had happened. The disaster had fallen which they foresaw. What was to be done? Crennell, with a line from a psalm, was for trusting in the Lord; and old Quilleash, with an oath, was for trusting in his heels. After a pause Teare propounded his scheme. It centred in Dan. Dan with his confession was their sole danger. Once rid of Dan they were as free men. Before his confession of guilt their innocence was beyond his power to prove or their power to establish. On his way up from the valley Teare had hit on a daring adventure. They were to break into the castle at Peel, take Dan by force, bring him up to the mountains, and there give him the choice of life or death: life if he promised to plead Not Guilty to the indictment, death if he adhered to the resolution by which he had surrendered.

The men gathered closer about Teare, and with yet whiter faces. Teare gave his plan; his scheme was complete; that night they were to carry it out. Paton Gorry was the jailer at Peel Castle. The lad Davy was the old sumner's godchild. Davy was to go forth and smuggle Gorry's keys out of the guard-room. If that were found impossible—well, Paton was an old man; he might be put quietly out of harm's way—no violence—och! no, not a ha'p'orth. Then Corkell was son-in-law of the watch at Peeltown, and hence the watch must take the harbor-master to the "Jolly Herrings," in Castle Street, while they themselves, Teare, Quilleash, Crennell, and Corkell, took the "Ben-my-Chree" from her moorings at the mouth of the harbor. On the west coast of St. Patrick's Isle they must bear down and run the dingey ashore. Then Dan must be seized in his cell, bound hand and foot, and brought aboard. With a fair wind—it was blowing east-sou'east—they must set sail for Ramsey Bay, put about at Lague, anchor there, and go ashore.

"That'll lave it," said Teare, "to raisonable inf'rence that Mastha Dan had whipped off to England by the Whitehaven packet that sails at midnight from the quay."

This done, they were to find a horse, strap the fettered man to its back, fetch him into the mountains in the dark hours of the night, and at daybreak try him solemnly and justly on the issue they had hit upon of life or death. No violence! Aw, no, all just and straight! If so be that the man was hanging them, they'd do him justice man to man, as fair as the backbone lies down the middle of a herring. Deemster's justice couldn't be cleaner; no, nor as clean. Aw, yes, no violence!

It was an intricate plan, involving many risks, presupposing many favorable chances. Perhaps it was not a logical computation of probabilities. But, good or bad, logical or illogical, probable or improbable, easy of accomplishment or full of risk and peril, it was the only alternative to trusting in the Lord, as Crennell had suggested, or in their heels, as Quilleash had preferred. In the end they took it, and made ready to act on it.

As the men arrived at their conclusion Davy Fayle was returning with an armful of withered gorse for a fire. The first move in that night's adventure was to be made by him. "Lave the lad to me," whispered Quilleash, and straightway he tackled Davy. Veracity was not conspicuous in the explanation that the old salt made. Poor Mastha Dan had been nabbed, bad cess to it, and jiggered up in Peel Castle. He would be hanged sarten sure. Aw, safe for it, if some chaps didn't make an effort immadient. They meant to do it, too. Ay, that very evenin'! Wouldn't they let him help? Well, pozzible, pozzible. They wasn't no objection to that. Thus, Davy fell an eager victim to a plan that was not propounded to him. If saving Mastha

Dan from the dirts that had nabbed him was the skame that was goin', why, nothin' would hould him but he would be in it. "Be aisy with the loblolly-boy and you have him," whispered old Billy behind the back of his hand, as he spat a long jet from his quid.

Relieved of doubt as to their course of action, they built a fire and warmed themselves, and with water from the river below they made cold porridge of the meal, and ate and drank, and waited for the night. The darkness came early—it was closing in at four o'clock. Then the men smothered their fire with turf and earth and set out for Peeltown. Their course was over Colden, and between Greeba and Beary, to the breast of Slieu Whallin, and then down to St. Patrick's Isle by the foot of Corrin's Hill. It was twelve miles over hill and dale, through the darkness and the muggy air of the winter's night. They had to avoid the few houses and to break their pace when footsteps came their way. But they covered the distance in less than four hours. At eight o'clock they were standing together on the south of the bridge that crosses the Neb River at the top of Peel Harbor. There they separated. Corkell went off to the market-place by a crooked alley from the quay to find the watch and dispose of him. When the harbor-master had been removed, Corkell was to go to the "Ben-my-Chree," which was moored in deep water at the end of the wooden pier, open the scuttle on the south, and put the lamp to it as a signal of safety to Quilleash, Teare, and Crennell above the bridge on the headland opposite. They were then to come aboard. Davy Fayle took the south quay to St. Patrick's Isle. It was now the bottom of the ebb-tide, and Davy was to wade the narrow neck that divided the isle from the mainland. Perhaps he might light on a boat; perhaps cross dry-shod. In half an hour he was to be on the west of the castle, just under a spot known as the Giant's Grave, and there the four men were to come ashore to him in the dingey. Meantime he was to see old Paton Gorry and generally take the soundings. Thus they parted.

Davy found the water low and the ford dry. He crossed it as noiselessly as he could, and reached the rocks of the isle. It was not so dark but he could descry the dim outlines of the ruined castle. A flight of steps ascended from the water's edge to the portcullis. Davy crept up. He had prepared to knock at the old notched door under the arch, but he found it standing open. He stood and listened. At one moment he thought he heard a movement behind him. It was darkest of all under these thick walls. He went on; he passed the doorway that is terrible with the tradition of the Moddey Dhoo. As he went by the door he turned his head to it in the darkness, and once again he thought he heard something stir. This time the sound came from before him. He gasped, and had almost screamed. He stretched his arms toward the sound. There was nothing. All was still once more.

Davy stepped forward into the courtyard. His feet fell softly on the grass that grew there. At length he reached the guard-room. Once more he had lifted his hand to knock, and once more he found the door open. He looked into the room. It was empty; a fire burned on the hearth, a form was drawn up in front of it; a pipe lay on a bare deal table. "He has gone down to the cell," Davy told himself, and he made his way to the steps that led to the dungeon. But he stopped again, and his heart seemed to stand still. There could now be no doubt but some one was approaching. There was the faint jingle as of keys. "Paton! Paton!" Davy called, fearfully. There was no answer, but the footsteps came on. "Who is there?" he cried again, in a tremulous whisper. At the next instant a man passed in the darkness, and Davy saw and knew him. It was the Bishop.

Davy dropped to his knees. A moment afterward the Bishop was gone through the outer gate and down the steps. His footsteps ceased, and then there were voices, followed by the plash of an oar, and then all was silence once more, save for the thick boom of the sea that came up from the rocks.

Davy rose to his feet and turned toward the steps that led down to the door of the dungeon. A light came from below. The door was open also, and, stretching himself full-length on to the ground, Davy could see into the cell. On the floor there was a lantern, and beside it a bundle lay. Dan was there; he was lying on the stone couch; he was alone.

Breathless and trembling, Davy rose again and fled out of the old castle and along the rocky causeway to a gullet under the Giant's Grave. There the men were waiting for him.

"The place is bewitched," he said, with quick-coming breath; and he told how every door was open, and not a soul was in the castle except Dan. The men heard him with evident terror. Corkell had just told them a similar story. The watch and the harbor-master had both been removed before he had gone in search of them. Everything seemed to be done to their hands. Nothing was left to them to do but simply to walk into the castle and carry out their design. This terrified them. "It's a fate," Corkell whispered; and Crennell, in white awe of the unseen hand that was helping them, was still for trusting in the Lord. Thus they put their heads together. Quilleash was first to recover from superstitious fears. "Come, lay down, and no blather," he said, and stalked resolutely forward, carrying a sack and a coil of rope. The other men followed him in silence. Davy was ordered to stay behind with the small-boat.

They found everything as the lad had left it: the notched door of the portcullis was open, the door of the guard-room was open, and when they came to the steps of the dungeon the door there was also open. A moment they stood and listened, and heard no sound from below but a light, regular breathing, as of one man only. Then they went quietly down the steps and into the cell. Dan was asleep. At sight of him, lying alone and unconscious, their courage wavered a moment. The unseen hand seemed to be on them still. "I tell thee it's a fate," Corkell whispered again over Quilleash's shoulder. In half a minute the sleeping man was bound hand and foot, and the sack was thrown over his head. At the first touch he awoke and tried to rise, but four men were over his prostrate body, and they overpowered him. He cried lustily, but there was none to hear. In less time than it takes to tell it the men were carrying Dan out of the cell. The lantern they left on the floor, and in their excitement they did not heed the parcel that lay by it.

Over the courtyard, through the gate, along the ledge under the crumbling walls, they stumbled and plunged in the darkness. They reached the boat and pushed off. Ten minutes afterward they were aboard the "Ben-my-Chree" and were beating down the bay.

Dan recognized the voices of the men, and realized his situation. He did not shout again. The sack over his head was of coarse fibre, admitting the air, and he could breathe through it without difficulty. He had been put to lie on one of the bunks in the cabin, and he could see the tossing light of the horn lantern that hung from the deck-planks. When the boat rolled in the strong sea that was running he could sometimes see the lights on the land through the open scuttle.

With a fair wind for the Point of Ayr, full sail was stretched. Corkell stood to the tiller, and, when all went smoothly, the three men turned in below, and lighted a fire in the stove and smoked. Then Davy Fayle came down with eyes dull and sick. He had begun to doubt, and to ask questions that the men could not answer. What for was Mastha Dan tied up like a haythen? And what for the sack? But the men were in no humor for cross-examination. No criss-crossing! The imperent young idiot waistrel, let him keep his breath to cool his porridge. To quiet the lad the men plied him with liquor, and at the second draft he was reeling drunk. Then he laughed a wild laugh, and sang a mad song, and finally stood up to dance. It was a grim sight, but it was soon ended, and Davy was put to sleep in another of the bunks. Then two hours passed, and there was some growling and quarreling.

Crennell and Teare went up on deck. Quilleash remained below, sitting before the stove cleaning with oil and a rag a fowling-piece that Dan had brought aboard at the beginning of the herring season. Sometimes he crooned a Manx carval, and sometimes whistled it, as he worked, chewing his quid meantime, and glancing at intervals at Dan's motionless figure on the bunk:

With pain we record
The year of our Lord
Sixteen hundred and sixty and sayven,
When it so come to pass
A good fishing there was
Off Dooglas, and a wonderful sayson.

There was no other sound in the cabin, except Davy's heavy breathing and the monotonous beat of the water at the boat's bow. Dan lay as quiet as the dead. Never once had he spoken or been spoken to.

The boat was flying before the wind. The sky had cleared, and the stars were out, and the lights on the shore could be plainly seen. Orrisdale, Jurby, and the Rue went by, and when Bishop's Court was passed the light in the library window burned clear and strong over the sea. Toward ten o'clock the lighthouse on the Point of Ayr was rounded, and then the boat had to bear down the Ramsey Bay in tacks. Before eleven they were passing the town, and could see the lights of the Cumberland packet as she lay by the quay. It was then three-quarter tide. In half an hour more the lugger was put about at Port Lague, and there Dan was taken ashore by Teare and Crennell. Quilleash went with them, carrying the fowling-peace.

Corkell and Davy Fayle, who had recovered from his stupor, were to take the "Ben-my-Chree" back into Ramsey Bay, to drop anchor under Ballure, and then to rejoin their companions at Lague before twelve o'clock. This was to divert suspicion, and to provoke the inference, when the fishing-boat would be found next morning, that Dan had escaped to England by the Whitehaven packet.

The "Ben-my-Chree" sailed off with Corkell and Davy. Teare went in search of a horse, Quilleash and Crennell remained on the shore at Lague with Dan. It was a bleak and desolate place, with nothing to the south but the grim rocks of the Tableland Head, and with never a house to the north nearer than Folieu, which was half a mile away. The night was now bitterly cold. The stars were gone, the darkness was heavy, and a nipping frost was in the dense atmosphere. But the wind had dropped, and every sound sent a dull echo through the air. The two men waited and listened. Thus far all had gone well with them, but what remained to do was perilous enough. If Corkell and the lad happened to be seen when coming from the boat, if Teare were caught in the act of borrowing a horse without leave, then all would be over with them. Their suspense was keen.

Presently there came up to them from the bay, over the dull rumble of the waves on the shore, a quick creaking sound, followed by a splash and then a dead roll. They knew it was the anchor being slipped to its berth. Soon afterward there came from the land to the south the sharp yap of dogs, followed at a sharp interval by the heavy beat of a horse's hoofs on the road. Was it Teare with the horse? Was he pursued? The men listened, but could hear no other noise. Then there came through the dense air the muffled sound of a bell ringing at the quay. It was the first of three bells that were rung on the Cumberland packet immediately before it set sail.

The horse behind drew nearer, the bell in front rang again. Then Teare came up leading a big draft mare by the bridle. He had been forced to take it from the stable at Lague, and in getting it away he had aroused the dogs; but he had not been followed, and all was safe. The bell rang a third time, and immediately a red light crept out from the quay toward the sea, which lay black as a raven below. The Cumberland packet had gone.

At that moment Corkell and Davy Fayle returned, Corkell holding Davy by the neck of his guernsey. The lad had begun to give signs of a mutinous spirit, which the man had suppressed by force. Davy's eyes flashed, but he was otherwise quiet and calm.

"What for is all this, you young devil?" said Quilleash. "What d'ye mean? Out with it, quick! what tricks now? D—— his fool's face, what for does he look at me like that?"

"Dowse that, Billy, and bear a hand and be quiet," said Crennell.

"The young pauper's got the imperence of sin," said Quilleash.

Then the man lifted Dan on to the back of the big mare, and strapped him with his covered face to the sky. Never a word was spoken to him, and never a word did he speak.

"Let's make a slant for it," said Teare, and he took the bridle. Corkell and Crennell walked on either side of the horse. Quilleash walked behind, carrying the fowling-piece over his left shoulder. Davy was at his right hand.

The journey thereafter was long and heavy. They took the path that is to the north by Barrule and Clag Ouyre and runs above Glen Auldyn and winds round to the south of Snaefell. Ten miles they plodded on in the thick darkness and the cold, with only the rumbling rivers for company, and with the hidden mountains making unseen ghosts about them. On they went, with the horse between them, taking its steady stride that never varied and never failed, even when the rivers crossed the path and their own feet stumbled into ruts. On and on, hour after hour, until their weary limbs dragged after them, and their gossip ceased, and even their growling and quarreling was no more heard. Then on and still on in the gruesome silence.

Under the breast of Snaefell they came into the snow of two days ago, which had disappeared in the valleys but still lay on the mountains, and was now crisp under their feet. It seemed, as they looked down in the darkness, to pass beneath them like short, smoky vapor that dazed the eyes and made the head giddy. Still higher, the sound of running waters suddenly stopped, for the rivers were frozen and their voices silenced. But the wind blew more strongly as they ascended the chill heights.

Sometimes at the top of a long rise they stopped to breathe the horse, and then, with no sound above or around except the shrill sough of the wind in the gorse, their courage began to fail. Ghostly imaginings would not be kept down.

"Did you ever hear the Lockman!" said Crennell beneath his breath.

"I never come agen him," said Quilleash. "When I see anything at night on the mountains I allis lave it alone."

The other men shuddered, and forthwith began to whistle right lustily.

Sometimes they passed a mountain sheep-pen, and the sheep being disturbed, would bleat. Sometimes a dog at a distant house would hear them and bark; and even that, though it was a signal of danger, was also a sort of human companionship on the grim mountain-side.

It was a dreary walk, and to Dan, bound hand and foot on the horse, it was a painful ride—a cold one it could not be, for the awkward motion brought warmth. The night wore on, and the air grew keener; the men's beards became crisp with the frost

At length the silent company rounded Snaefell to the north of Cronk-y-Vane and Beinn-y-Phott. Then Teare at the horse's head twisted about. "Do we take the ould mine-shed for it?" he asked.

"Ay," said Quilleash.

Their journey was almost ended. The sky over the sea behind them was then dabbled with gray, and a smell of dawn was coming down from the mountains.

CHAPTER XXXIV
A RUDE TRIBUNAL

The course taken by the coroner and his seven men, with Mona on the horse, came to a triangle of mountain-paths above a farm known as the Sherragh Vane. One path wound close under the west foot of Snaefell, another followed the bed of the river that ran through a glen called Crammag, and the third joined these two by crossing the breast of Beinn-y-Phott. At the acute angle of the Sherragh Vane the coroner drew up.

"Can any one see the lead shaft?" he asked. None could see it. The darkness had lifted away, and the crown of Snaefell was bare against the sky, like an islet of green floating over a cloud of vapor. But the mists still lay thick on the moorlands, and even the high glens were obscure.

"It must be yonder, about a mile and a half up the river," said the coroner.

The lead mine was in the southeast angle of the triangle of paths, under the southwest of Snaefell and the north of Beinn-y-Phott. For some minutes the company was at a stand while the coroner considered their movements.

Mona's impatience was manifest. "Let us push on," she said.

The coroner merely eyed her largely, and resumed his deliberations.

"Oh! how we waste our time," she said again. "If the lead mine is there, what have we to do but reach it?"

The coroner with an insolent smile inquired if the lady felt the cold.

"He is in danger for his life, and here we waste the precious minutes in idle talk," she answered.

"Danger for his life," the coroner echoed, and laughed coldly. Then in a tone of large meaning he added, "Possible, possible," and smiled at his own subtle thought.

Mona's anxiety mastered her indignation.

"Look, the mist is lifting. See, there is the shed—there in the gap between the hills, and it is the very place I saw. Come, make haste—look, it is daylight."

"Be aisy, be aisy. If they're in yonder shed, they are packed as safe as herrings in a barrel," said the coroner.

Then he divided his forces. Three men he sent down the path of the Glent Crammag. Two he left where they then stood to guard that outlet to the Curraghs of the north and west. Two others were to creep along the path under Snaefell, and shut out the course to the sea and the lowlands on the south and east. He himself would walk straight up to the shed, and his seven men as they saw him approach it were to close quickly in from the three corners of the triangle.

"Is it smoke that's rising above the shed? A fire? Possible. He thinks he's safe, I'll go bail. Och! yes, and maybe eating and drinking and making aisy. Now, men, away with you."

Within the shed itself at that moment there was as grim a scene as the eye of man has yet looked upon. The place was a large square building of two rooms, one on the ground-level and the other above it, the loft being entered by a trap in the floor with a wooden ladder down the wall. It had once served as gear-shed and office, stable, and store, but now it was bare and empty. In the wall looking east there was a broad opening without door, and in the wall looking north a narrow opening without window. To a hasp in the jamb of the doorway the big mare was tethered, and in the draught between the two openings the lad Davy with wandering mind was kindling a fire of gorse over two stones. The smoke filled the place, and through its dense volumes in the dusk of that vaporous dawn the faces of the men were bleared and green and haggard. The four fishermen stood in a group together, with old Quilleash a pace to the fore, the fowling piece in his hand, its butt on the ground. Before him and facing him, two paces in front, stood Dan, his arms still bound to his sides, his head uncovered, and his legs free. There was a gaunt earnestness in every face.

"Listen to me," said old Quilleash. "We're going to judge and jury you, but all fair and square, as God is above us, and doing nothing that we can't answer for when the big day comes and every man has to toe his mark. D'ye hear what we're saying, sir?"

Dan hoved his head slightly by way of assent.

"We've trapped you, it's true, and fetched you by force, that's sartin; but we mean to be just by you, and no violence; and it's spakin' the truth we're going to do, and never a word of a lie."

The other men muttered "Ay, ay;" and Quilleash went on: "We're chaps what believes in a friend, and buckin' up for them as bucks up for you, and being middlin' stanch, and all to that; but we're after doing it once too often."

"So we are," said Crennell, and the others muttered again, "Ay, ay."

Quilleash spat behind his hand and continued: "The long and short of it is that you're goin' middlin' straight for hanging us, and it isn't natheral as we're to stand by and see it done."

Dan lifted his face from the ground. "I meant to do you no harm, my good fellows," he said, quickly.

"Meaning's meaning, but doing's doing, and we've heard all that's going," said Quilleash. "You've surrendered and confessed, and the presentment is agen us all, and what's in for you is in for us."

"But you are innocent men. What need you fear?"

"Innocent we be, but where the Deemster comes there's not a ha'p'orth to choose between you and us."

Dan's face flushed, and he answered warmly, "Men, don't let your miserable fears make cowards of you. What have you done? Nothing. You are innocent. Yet how are you bearing yourselves? Like guilty men. If I were innocent do you think I would skulk away in the mountains?"

"Aisy, sir, take it aisy. Maybe you'd rather run like a rat into a trap. Cowards? Well, pozzible, pozzible. There's nothing like having a wife and a few childers for making a brave chap into a bit of a skunk. But we'll lave 'cowards' alone if you plaze."

Quilleash made a dignified sweep of the back of his hand, while the other men said, "Better, better."

"Why have you brought me here?" said Dan.

"There isn't a living sowl knows where you are, and when they find you're missing at the Castle they'll say you've thought better of it and escaped."

"Why have you brought me here?" Dan repeated.

"The Whitehaven boat left Ramsey after we dropped anchor in the bay last night, and they'll say you've gone off to England."

"Tell me why you have brought me to this place."

"We are alone and can do anything we like with you, and nobody a ha'p'orth the wiser."

"What do you mean to do?"

Then they told him of the alternative of life or death. There was nothing against him but his own confession. If he but held his tongue there was not enough evidence to hang a cat. Let him only promise to plead "Not guilty" when the trial came on, and they were ready to go back with him and stand beside him. If not—

"What then?" Dan asked.

"Then we'll be forced—" said Quilleash, and he stopped.

"Well?"

"I'm saying we'll be forced—" He stopped again.

"Out with it, man alive," Teare broke in—"forced to shoot him like a dog."

"Well, that's only spakin' the truth anyway," said Quilleash, quietly.

Davy Fayle leapt up from the fire with a cry of horror. But Dan was calm and resolute.

"Men, you don't know what you're asking. I can not do it."

"Aisy sir, aisy, and think agen. You see we're in if you're in, and who's to know who's deepest?"

"God knows it, and he will never allow you to suffer."

"We've childers and wives looking to us, and who can tell how they'd fend in the world if we were gone?"

"You're brave fellows, and I'm sorry for the name I gave you."

"Shoo! Lave that alone. Maybe we spoke back. Let's come to the fac's."

They stated their case again and with calm deliberation. He asked how it could mend their case if his life was taken. They answered him that they would go back and surrender, and stand their trial and be acquitted.

Those four men were as solemn a tribunal as ever a man stood before for life or death. Not a touch of passion, hardly a touch of warmth, disturbed their rude sense of justice.

"We're innocent, but we're in it, and if you stand to it we must stand to it, and what's the use of throwing your life away?"

Dan looked into their haggard faces without wavering. He had gone too far to go back now. But he was deeply moved.

"Men," he said, "I wish to God I could do what you ask, but I can not, and, besides, the Almighty will not let any harm come to you."

There was a pause, and then old Quilleash said with quiet gravity, "I'm for religion myself, and singing hymns at whiles, and maybe a bit of a spell at the ould Book, but when it comes to trusting for life, d— —d if I don't look for summat substantial."

As little was their stubborn purpose to be disturbed by spiritual faith as Dan's resolution was to be shaken by bodily terrors. They gave him as long to decide as it took a man to tell a hundred. The counting was done by Teare amid dead silence of the others.

Then it was that, thinking rapidly, Dan saw the whole terrible issue. His mind went back to the visit of the Bishop to the castle, and to the secret preparations that had been made for his own escape. He remembered that the sumner had delivered up his keys to the Bishop, and that the Bishop had left the door of the cell open. In a quick glance at the facts he saw but too plainly that if he never returned to take his trial it would be the same to his father as if he had accepted the means of escape that had been offered him. The Bishop, guilty in purpose, but innocent in fact, would then be the slave of any scoundrel who could learn of his design. Though his father had abandoned his purpose, he would seem to have pursued it, and the people whom he had bribed to help him would but think that he had used other instruments. There could be only one explanation of his absence—that he escaped; only one means of escape—the Bishop; only one way of saving the Bishop from unmerited and life-long obloquy—returning to his trial; and only one condition of going back alive—promising to plead "Not guilty" to the charge of causing the death of Ewan.

It was an awful conflict of good passions with passions that were not bad. At one moment the sophistry took hold of him that, as his promise was being extorted by bodily threats, it could not be binding on his honor; that he might give the men the word they wanted, go back to save his father, and finally act at the trial as he knew to be best. But at the next moment in his mind's eye he saw himself in the prisoner's dock by the side of these five brave fellows, all standing for their lives, all calmly trusting in his promise, and he heard himself giving the plea that might send them to their deaths. Better any consequences than such treachery. Truth it must be at all costs; truth to them and to himself. And as for the Bishop, when did the Almighty ask for such poor help as the lie of a blood-stained criminal to save the honor of a man of God?

It was a terrible crisis of emotion, but it was brief. The counting ended, and Quilleash called for the answer.

"No, I can not do it—God forgive me, I wish I could," said Dan, in a burst of impatience.

It was said. The men made no reply to it. There was awful quiet among them. They began to cast lots. Five copper coins of equal size, one of them marked with a cross scratched with the point of a nail, they put into the bag. One after one they dipped a hand and drew out a coin, and every man kept his fist clenched till all had drawn. The lad was not for joining, but the men threatened him, and he yielded. Then all hands were opened together.

The lot had fallen to Davy Fayle. When he saw this, his simple face whitened visibly and his lip lagged very low. Old Quilleash handed him the gun, and he took it in a listless way, scarcely conscious of what was intended.

"What's goin' doing?" he asked vacantly.

The men told him that it was for him to do it.

"Do what?" he asked, dazed and stupid.

Shamefully, and with a touch of braggadocio, they told what he had to do, and then his vacant face became suddenly charged with passion, and he made a shriek of terror and let the gun fall. Quilleash picked the gun from the ground and thrust it back into Davy's hand.

"You've got to do it," he said; "the lot's fallen to you, and it's bad work flying in the face of fate."

At first Davy cried that nothing on God's earth would make him do it; but suddenly he yielded, took the gun quickly, and was led to his place three of four paces in front of where Dan stood with his arms bound at his sides, his face of an ashy whiteness and his eyes fearful to look upon.

"I can't kill him while he's tied up like that," said Davy. "Loose him, and then I'll shoot."

The men had been startled by Davy's sudden acquiescence, but now they understood it. Not by so obvious a ruse were they to be deceived. They knew full well that Dan as a free man was a match for all four of them unarmed.

"You're meaning to fire over his head," they said to Davy; and carried away by his excitement, and without art to conceal his intention, the lad cried hysterically, "That's the truth, and so I am."

The men put their heads together, and there was some hurried whispering. At the next minute they had laid hold of Davy, bound him as Dan was bound, and put him to stand at Dan's side. This they did with the thought that Davy was now Dan's accomplice.

Then again they cast lots as before. This time the lot fell to Quilleash. He took his stand where the lad had stood, and put the trigger of the gun at cock.

"Men," he said, "if we don't take this man's life nothing will hould him but he'll take ours; and it's our right to protect ourselves, and the ould Book will uphold us. It isn't murder we're at, but justice, and Lord A'mighty ha' massy on their sowls!"

"Give him another chance," said Teare, and Quilleash, nothing loath, put his question again. Dan, with a glance at Davy, answered as before, with as calm a voice, though his face was blanched, and his eyes stood out from their sockets, and his lips and nostrils quivered.

Then there was silence, and then down on their knees behind Quilleash fell the three men, Crennel, Corkell, and Teare. "Lord ha' massy on their sowls!" they echoed, and Quilleash raised the gun.

Never a word more did Dan say, and never a cry or a sign came from Davy Fayle. But Quilleash did not fire. He paused and listened, and turning about he said, in an altered tone, "Where's the horse?"

The men lifted their heads and pointed, without speaking, to where the horse was tethered by the doorway. Quilleash listened with head aslant. "Then whose foot is that?" he said.

The men leapt to their feet. Teare was at the doorway in an instant. "God A'mighty, they're on us!" he said in an affrighted whisper.

Then two of the others looked, and saw that from every side the coroner and his men were closing in upon them. They could recognize every man, though the nearest was still half a mile away. For a moment they stared blankly in to each other's faces, and asked themselves what was to be done. In that moment every good and bad quality seemed to leap to their faces. Corkell and Crennell, seeing themselves outnumbered, fell to a bout of hysterical weeping. Teare, a fellow of sterner stuff, without pity or ruth, seeing no danger for them if Dan were out of sight, was for finishing in a twinkling what they had begun—shooting Dan, flinging him into the loft above, down the shaft outside, or into a manure-hole at the doorway, that was full of slimy filth and was now half-frozen over.

Quilleash alone kept his head, and when Teare had spoken the old man said, "No," and set his lip firm and hard. Then Dan himself, no less excited than the men themselves, called and asked how many they were that were coming. Crennell told him nine—seven men and the coroner, and another—it might be a woman—on a horse.

"Eight men are not enough to take six of us," said Dan. "Here, cut my rope and Davy's—quick."

When the men heard that, and saw by the light of Dan's eyes that he meant it, and that he whose blood they had all but spilled was ready to stand side by side with them and throw in his lot with their lot, they looked stupidly into each other's eyes, and could say nothing. But in another breath the evil spirit of doubt had taken hold of them, and Teare was laughing bitterly in Dan's face.

Crennell looked out at the doorway again. "They're running, we're lost men," he said; and once more he set up his hysterical weeping.

"Dowse that," said Quilleash; "where's your trustin' now?"

"Here, Billy," said Dan eagerly, "cut the lad's rope and get into the loft, every man of you."

Without waiting to comprehend the meaning of this advice, realizing nothing but that the shed was surrounded and escape impossible, two of them, Crennell and Corkell, clambered up the ladder to the loft. Old Quilleash, who from the first moment of the scare had not budged an inch from his place on the floor, stood there still with the gun in his hand. Then Dan, thinking to free himself by burning one strand of the rope that bound him, threw himself down on his knees by the fire of gorse and wood, and held himself over it until one shoulder and arm and part of his breast were in the flame. For a moment it seemed as if, bound as he was, he must thrust half his body into the fire, and roll in it, before the rope that tied him would ignite. But at the next moment he had leaped to his feet with a mighty effort, and the rope was burning over his arm.

At that same moment the coroner and the seven men with Mona riding behind them, came up the doorway of the shed. There they drew up in consternation. No sight on earth was less like that they had looked to see than the sight they then beheld.

There, in a dense cloud of smoke, was Davy Fayle, still bound and helpless, pale and speechless with affright; and there was Dan, also bound, and burning over one shoulder as if the arm itself were afire, and straining his great muscles to break the rope that held him. Quilleash was in the middle of the floor as if rooted to the spot, and his gun was in his hands. Teare was on the first rung of the wall-ladder, and the two white faces of Corkell and Crennell were peering down from the trap-hole above.

"What's all this?" said the coroner.

Then Teare dropped back from the ladder and pointed at Dan and said, "We caught him and were taking him back to you, sir. Look, that's the way we strapped him. But he was trying to burn the rope and give us the slip."

Dan's face turned black at that word of treachery, and a hoarse cry came from his throat.

"Is it true?" said the coroner, and his lip curled as he turned to Dan. Davy Fayle shouted vehemently that it was a lie, but Dan, shaking visibly from head to foot, answered quietly and said, "I'll not say no, coroner."

At that Quilleash stepped out. "But I'll say no," he said, firmly. "He's a brave man, he is; and maybe I'm on'y an ould rip, but d— — me if I'm goin' to lie like that for nobody—no, not to save my own sowl."

Then in his gruff tones, sometimes faltering, sometimes breaking into deep sobs, and then rising to deeper oaths, the old fellow told all. And that night all six of them—Dan, the four fishermen, and the lad Davy—were lodged in the prison at Castle Rushen.

CHAPTER XXXV
THE COURT OF GENERAL JAIL DELIVERY

From Christmas-tide onward through the dark months, until a "dream of spring" came once again on the slumbering face of winter, the six men lay in Castle Rushen. Rumors from within the gray walls of the jail told that some of them were restive under their punishment, and that the spirits of others sank under it, but that Dan bore up with the fortitude of resignation, and, though prone to much sadness, with even the cheerfulness of content. It was the duty of each man to take his turn at cleaning the cell, and it was said that Dan's turn seemed by his own counting to come frequently. Reproaches he bore with humility, and on one occasion he took a blow from Crennell, who was small of stature and had a slight limp in one leg. Constant bickerings were rife among them, and Dan was often their subject of quarrel, and still oftener their victim; but they had cheerful hours, too, and sometimes a laugh together.

Such were some of the reports that made gossip outside, where public curiosity and excitement grew keener as the half-yearly sitting of the Court of General Jail Delivery drew nearer. Copper riots and felonies of all descriptions, disputes as to tithe, and arbitrations as to the modes of counting the herrings, sank out of sight in prospect of the trial of Dan and his crew. From Point of Ayr to the Calf of Man it was the engrossing topic, and none living could remember a time when public feeling ran so high. The son of the Bishop was to be tried for the murder of the son of the Deemster, and a bigger issue could no man conceive. Variable enough was the popular sympathy—sometimes with Dan, sometimes against him, always influenced by what way the wave of feeling flowed with regard to the Deemster and the Bishop. And closely were these two watched at every turn.

The Deemster showed uncommon animation, and even some sprightliness. He was more abroad than at any time for fifteen years before, and was usually accompanied by Jarvis Kerruish. His short laugh answered oftener to his own wise witticisms than at any time since the coming to the island of his brother, the Bishop; but people whispered that his good spirits did not keep him constant company within the walls of his own house. There his daughter, Mona, still soft as the morning dew and all but as silent, sat much alone. She had grown "wae," as folk said, rarely being seen outside the gates of Ballamona, never being heard to laugh, and showing little interest in life beyond the crib of her foster-child, Ewan's orphaned daughter. And people remembered her mother, how silent she had been, and how patient, and how like to what Mona was, and they said now, as they had said long ago, "She's going down the steep places."

The Bishop had kept close to Bishop's Court. Turning night into day, and day into night, or knowing no times and seasons, he had been seen to wander at all hours up and down the glen. If any passed him as he crossed the road from the glen back to the house he had seemed not to see. His gray hair had grown snowy white, his tall figure drooped heavily from his shoulders, and his gait had lost all its spring. Stricken suddenly into great age, he had wandered about mumbling to himself, or else quite silent. The chapel on his episcopal demesne he had closed from the time of the death of Ewan, his chaplain. Thus had he borne himself shut out from the world, until the primrose had come and gone, and the cuckoo had begun to call. Then as suddenly he underwent a change. Opening the chapel at Bishop's Court he conducted service there every Sunday afternoon. The good souls of the parish declared that never before had he preached with such strength and fervor, though the face over the pulpit looked ten long years older than on the Christmas morning when the 'longshoremen brought up their dreadful burden from the Mooragh. Convocation was kept on Whit-Tuesday as before, and the Bishop spoke with calm and grave power. His clergy said he had gathered strength from solitude, and fortitude from many days spent alone, as in the wilderness, with his Maker. Here and there a wise one among his people said it might look better of him to take the beam out of his own eye than to be so very zealous in pointing out the motes in the eyes of others. The world did not stand still, though public interest was in suspense, and now and again some girl was presented for incontinence or some man for drunkenness. Then it was noticed that the censures of the Church had begun to fall on the evil-doer with a great tenderness, and this set the wise ones whispering afresh that some one was busy at sweeping the path to his own door, and also that the black ox never trod on his own hoof.

The day of the trial came in May. It was to be a day of doom, but the sun shone with its own indifference to the big little affairs of men. The spring had been a dry one, and over the drought came heat. From every corner of the island the people trooped off under the broiling sun to Castletown. The Court of General Jail Delivery was held in Castle Rushen, in the open square that formed the gateway to the prison chapel, under the clear sky, without shelter from any weather. There the narrow space allotted to spectators was thronged with hot faces under beavers, mutches, and sun-bonnets. The passages from the castle gate on the quay were also thronged by crowds who could not see, but tried to hear. From the lancet windows of the castle that overlooked the gateway eager faces peered out, and on the lead flat above the iron staircase and over the great clock-tower were companies of people of both sexes, who looked down and even listened when they could. The windows of the houses around the castle gate were thrown up for spectators who sat on the sills. In the rigging of the brigs and luggers that lay in the harbor, close under the castle walls, sailors had perched themselves to look on, and crack jokes and smoke. Nearly the whole floor of the market-place was thronged, but under the cross, where none could see or hear, an old woman had set up ninepins, tipped with huge balls of toffee, and a score of tipsy fellows were busy with them amid much laughter and noise. A line of older men, with their hands in their pockets, were propped against the castle wall; and a young woman from Ballasalla, reputed to be a prophetess, was standing on the steps of the cross, and calling on the careless to take note that, while they cursed and swore and forgot their Maker, six men not twenty yards away were on the brink of their graves.

The judges were the Governor of the island (who was robed), the Clerk of the Rolls, the two Deemsters (who wore wigs and gowns), the Water Bailiff, the Bishop, the Archdeacon, the Vicars-General, and the twenty-four Keys. All these sat on a raised platform of planks. The senior and presiding Deemster (Thorkell Mylrea), who was the mouthpiece of the court, was elevated on a central dais.

Thorkell was warm, eager, and even agitated. When the Bishop took his seat, amid a low murmur of the spectators, his manner was calm, and his quiet eyes seemed not to look into the faces about him.

The prisoners were brought in from the cell that opened to the left of the gateway. They looked haggard and worn, but were not wanting in composure. Dan, towering above the rest in his great stature, held his head low; his cheeks were ashy, but his lips were firm. By his side, half clinging to his garments, was the lad Davy, and at the other end of the line was old Quilleash, with resolution on his weather-beaten face. Crennell and Corkell were less at ease, but Teare's firm-set figure and hard-drawn mouth showed the dogged determination of a man who meant that day to sell his life dear. Sixty-eight men were present, summoned from the seventeen parishes of the island to compose a jury of twelve to be selected by the prisoners. Over all was the burning sun of a hot day in May.

When the officer of the court had made the presentment, and was going on to ask the prisoners to plead, the proceedings were suddenly interrupted. The steward of the spiritual barony of the Bishop, now sole baron of the island, rose to a point of law. One of the six prisoners who were indicted for felony was a tenant of the Bishop's barony, and as such was entitled to trial not by the civil powers of the island, but by a jury of his barony, presided over by the proper president of his barony. The prisoner in question was Daniel Mylrea, and for him the steward claimed the privilege of a remand until he could be brought up for trial before the court of the lord of the barony under which he lived.

This claim created a profound sensation in the court. Dan himself raised his eyes, and his face had a look of pain. When asked by the Deemster if the claim was put forward by his wish or sanction he simply shook his head. The steward paid no attention to this repudiation. "This court," he said, "holds no jurisdiction over a tenant of the Bishop's barony;" and forthwith he put in a document showing that Daniel Mylrea was tenant of a farm on the episcopal demesne, situate partly in Kirk Ballaugh and partly in Kirk Michael.

The Deemster knew full well that he was powerless. Nevertheless he made a rigid examination of the prisoner's lease, and, finding the document flawless, he put the point of law to the twenty-four Keys with every hampering difficulty. But the court was satisfied as to the claim, and allowed it. "The prisoner, Daniel Mylrea, stands remanded for trial at the court of his barony," said the Deemster, in a tone of vexation; "and at that trial," he added, with evident relish, "the president of the barony shall be, as by law appointed, assisted by a Deemster."

Dan was removed, his name was struck out of the indictment, and the trial of the five fishermen was proceeded with. They pleaded "Not guilty." The Attorney-General prosecuted, stating the facts so far as they concerned the remaining prisoners, and reflecting at the evidence against the prisoner who was remanded. He touched on the evidence of the sailcloth, and then on the mystery attaching to a certain bundle of clothes, belts, and daggers that had been found in the prison at Peel Castle. At this reference the steward of the barony objected, as also against the depositions that inculpated Dan. The witnesses were fewer than at the Deemster's inquest, and they had nothing to say that directly criminated the fishermen. Brief and uninteresting the trial turned out to be with the chief prisoner withdrawn, and throughout the proceedings the Deemster's vexation was betrayed by his thin, sharp, testy voice. Some efforts were made to prove that Dan's disappearance from Peel Castle had been brought about by the Bishop; but the steward of the barony guarded so zealously the privileges of the ecclesiastical courts that nothing less than an open and unseemly rupture between the powers of Church and State seemed imminent when the Deemster, losing composure, was for pressing the irrelevant inquiry. Moreover, the Keys, who sat as arbiters of points of law and to "pass" the verdict of the jury, were clearly against the Deemster.

The trial did not last an hour. When the jury was ready to return a verdict, the Deemster asked in Manx, as by ancient usage, *"Vod y fer-carree soie?"* (May the Man of the Chancel [the Bishop] sit?). And the foreman answered *"Fod"* (He may); the ecclesiastics remained in their seats; a verdict of "Not guilty" was returned, and straightway the five fishermen were acquitted.

Later the same day the Deemster vacated his seat on the dais, and then the Bishop rose and took it with great solemnity. That the Bishop himself should sit to try his own son, as he must have tried any other felon who was a tenant of his barony, made a profound impression among the spectators. The Archdeacon, who had hoped to preside, looked appalled. The Deemster sat below, and on either side were the ecclesiastics, who had claimed their right to sit as judges in the civil court. Another jury, a jury of the barony, was impaneled. The sergeant of the barony brought Dan to the bar. The prisoner was still very calm, and his lips were as firm, though his face was as white and his head held as low as before. When a presentment was read over to him, charging him with causing the death of Ewan Mylrea, deacon in holy orders, and he was asked to plead, he lifted his eyes slowly, and answered in a clear, quiet, sonorous voice, that echoed from the high walls of the gateway, and was heard by the people on the clock tower, "Guilty."

As evidence had been taken at the Deemster's inquest, no witnesses were now heard. The steward of the barony presented. He dwelt on the prisoner's special and awful criminality, in so far as he was the son of the Bishop, taught from his youth up to think of human life as a holy thing, and bound by that honored alliance to a righteous way in life. Then he touched on the peculiar duty of right living in one who held the office of captain of his parish, sworn to preserve order and to protect life.

When the steward had appended to his statement certain commonplaces of extenuation based on the plea of Guilty, the Deemster, amid a dead hush among the spectators, put questions to the prisoner which were intended to elicit an explanation of his motive in the crime, and of the circumstances attending it. To these questions Dan made no answer.

"Answer me, sir," the Deemster demanded, but Dan was still silent. Then the Deemster's wrath mastered him.

"It ill becomes a man in your position to refuse the only amends that you can make to justice for the pains to which you have put this court and another."

It was an idle outburst. Dan's firm lip was immovable. He looked steadily into the Deemster's face, and said not a word.

The steward stepped in. "The prisoner," he said, "has elected to make the gravest of all amends to justice," and at that there was a deep murmur among the people. "Nevertheless, I could wish," said the steward, "that he would also make answer to the Deemster's question."

But the prisoner made no sign.

"There is some reason for thinking that, if all were known, where so much is now hidden, the crime to which the prisoner pleads guilty would wear a less grievous aspect."

Still the prisoner gave no answer.

"Come, let us have done," said the Deemster, twisting impatiently in his seat. "Pronounce the sentence, and let your sergeant carry it into effect."

The murmur among the people grew to a great commotion, but in the midst of it the Bishop was seen to rise, and then a deep hush fell on all.

The Bishop's white head was held erect, his seamed face was firm as it was pale, and his voice, when he spoke, was clear and full. "Daniel Mylrea," he said, "you have pleaded guilty to the great crime of murder. The sergeant of your barony will now remove you, and on the morning of this day next week he will take you in his safe custody to the Tynwald Hill, in the centre of the island, there in the eye of light, and before the faces of all men, to receive the dreadful sentence of this court, and to endure its punishment."

CHAPTER XXXVI
CUT OFF FROM THE PEOPLE

During the week that followed the trial of Daniel Mylrea at the court of his barony the excitement throughout the island passed all experience of public feeling. What was to be the sentence of the barony? This was the one question everywhere—at the inn, the mill, the smithy, the market-cross, the street, in the court-house; and if two shepherds hailed each other on the mountains they asked for the last news from Peel.

With a silent acceptance of the idea that death alone could be the penalty of the crime that had been committed, there passed through the people the burden, first of a great awe, and then of a great dread that any Christian man should die the death of hanging. Not for nearly twoscore years had the island seen that horror, and old men shuddered at the memory of it.

Then it came to be understood in a vague way that after all Daniel Mylrea was not to die. Whispers went from mouth to mouth that old Quilleash had sailed down to the Calf Sound with the "Ben-my-Chree," well stored with provisions. In a few days the old salt returned, walking overland, preserving an air of vast mystery, and shaking his head when his gossips questioned him. Then poor human nature, that could not bear to see Daniel Mylrea die, could not bear to see him saved either, and men who had sworn in their impotent white terror that never again should a gallows be built in the island, lusty fellows who had shown ruth for the first time, began to show gall for the hundreth, to nudge, to snigger, and to mutter that blood was thicker than water, and there was much between saying and doing, as the sayin' was.

The compassion that had been growing in secret began to struggle with the ungentle impulses that came of superstitious fear. It seemed to be true, as old folk were whispering, that Daniel Mylrea was the Jonah of the island. What had happened in the first year of his life? A prolonged drought and a terrible famine. What was happening now? Another drought that threatened another famine. And people tried to persuade themselves that the sword of the Lord was over them, and that it would only rest and be quiet when they had executed God's judgment on the guilty man.

The day of Tynwald came, and the week before it had passed like a year. There was no sun, but the heat was stifling, the clouds hung low and dark and hot as the roof of an open oven, the air was sluggish, and the earth looked blue. Far across the sea to the northwest there was a thin streak of fiery cloud, and at some moments there was the smell of a thunder-storm in the heavy atmosphere. From north and south, from east and west, the people trooped to Tynwald Hill. Never before within the memory of living man had so vast a concourse been witnessed on that ancient ground of assembly. Throughout the island the mill-wheel was stopped, the smithy fire was raked over with ashes, the plow lay in the furrow, the sheep were turned out on to the mountains, and men and women, old men, old women, and young children, ten thousand in all, with tanned faces and white, in sun-bonnets, mutches, and capes, and some with cloaks in preparation for the storm that was coming, drove in their little springless carts, or rode on their small Manx ponies, or trudged on foot through the dusty roads, and over the bleached hillsides and the parched Curraghs.

At ten o'clock the open green that surrounds the hill of Tynwald was densely thronged. Carts were tipped up in corners, and their stores of food and drink were guarded by a boy or a woman, who sat on the sternboard. Horses were tethered to the wheels, or turned loose to browse on a common near at hand. Men lounged on the green and talked, their hands in their pockets, their pipes in their mouths, or stood round the Tynwald Inn, lifting pannikins to their lips, and laughing—for there was merriment among them though the work for which they had come together was not a merry one.

The mount itself was still empty, and twelve constables were stationed about the low wall that surrounded it, keeping the crowd back. And though, as the people met and mingled, the men talked of the crops and of the prospect for the fishing, and women of the wool and yarn, and boys tossed somersaults, and young girls betook themselves to girlish games, and girls of older growth in bright ribbons to ogling and giggling, and though there was some coarse banter and coarser singing, the excitement of the crowd, beneath all, was deep and strong. At intervals there was a movement of the people toward a church—St. John's Church, that stood a little to the east of Tynwald—and sometimes a general rush toward the gate that looked westward toward Peeltown and the sea. Earlier in the day some one had climbed a mountain beyond the chapel and put a light to the dry gorse at the top, and now the fire smoldered in the dense air, and set up a long sinuous trail of blue smoke to the empty vault of the sky. The mountain was called Greeba, which is the native word for grief.

Toward half-past ten old Paton Gorry, the sumner, went down the narrow, tortuous steps that led to the dungeon of Peel Castle. He carried fetters for the hands and legs of his prisoner, and fixed them in their places with nervous and fumbling fingers. His prisoner helped him as far as might be, and spoke cheerily in answer to his mumbled adieu.

"I'm not going to St. John's, sir. I couldn't give myself lave for it," the sumner muttered in a breaking voice. With a choking sensation in his throat Daniel Mylrea said, "God bless you, Paton," and laid hold of the old man's hand. Twenty times during the week the sumner had tried in vain to prevail on the prisoner to explain the circumstances attending his crime, and so earn the mitigation of punishment which had been partly promised. The prisoner had only shaken his head in silence.

A few minutes afterward Daniel Mylrea was handed over in the guard-room to the sergeant of the barony, and Paton Gorry's duties—the hardest that the world had yet given him to do—were done.

The sergeant and the prisoner went out of the castle and crossed the narrow harbor in a boat. On the wooden jetty, near the steps by which they landed, a small open cart was drawn up, and there was a crowd of gaping faces about it. The two men got into the cart and were driven down the quay toward the path by the river that led to Tynwald under the foot of Slieu Whallin. As they passed through the town the prisoner was dimly conscious that white faces looked out of windows and that small knots of people were gathered at the corners of the alleys. But all this was soon blotted out, and when he came to himself he was driving under the trees, and by the side of the rumbling water.

All the day preceding the prisoner had told himself that when his time came, his great hour of suffering and expiation, he must bear himself with fortitude, abating nothing of the whole bitterness of the atonement he was to make, asking no quarter, enduring all contumely, though men jeered as he passed or spat in his face. He thought he had counted the cost of that trial. Seven sleepless nights and seven days of torment had he given to try his spirit for that furnace, and he thought he could go through it and not shrink. In his solitary hours he had arranged his plans. While he drove from Peel to St. John's he was to think of nothing that would sap his resolution, and his mind was to be a blank. Then, as he approached the place, he was to lift his eyes without fear, and not let them drop though their gaze fell on the dread thing that must have been built there. And so, very calmly, silently, and firmly, he was to meet the end of all.

But now that he was no longer in the dungeon of the prison, where despair might breed bravery in a timid soul, but under the open sky, where hope and memory grow strong together, he knew, though he tried to shut his heart to it, that his courage was oozing away. He recognized this house and that gate, he knew every turn of the river—where the trout lurked and where the eels sported—and when he looked up at the dun sky he knew how long it might take for the lightning to break through the luminous dulness of the thunder-cloud that hung over the head of Slieu Whallin. Do what he would to keep his mind a blank, or to busy it with trifles of the way, he could not help reflecting that he was seeing these things for the last time.

Then there came a long interval in which the cart wherein he sat seemed to go wearily on, on, on, and nothing awakened his slumbering senses. When he recovered consciousness with a start he knew that his mind had been busy with many thoughts such as sap a man's resolution and bring his brave schemes to foolishness. He had been asking himself where his father was that day, where Mona would be then, and how deep their shame must be at the thought of the death he was to die. To him his death was his expiation, and little had he thought of the manner of it; but to them it was disgrace and horror. And so he shrunk within himself. He knew now that his great purpose was drifting away like a foolish voice that is emptied in the air. Groaning audibly, praying in broken snatches for strength of spirit, looking up and around with fearful eyes, he rode on and on, until at length, before he was yet near the end of his awful ride, the deep sound came floating to him through the air of the voices of the people gathered at the foot of Tynwald. It was like the sound the sea makes as its white breakers fall on some sharp reef a mile away: a deep, multitudinous hum of many tongues. When he lifted his head and heard it, his pallid face became ashy, his whitening lips trembled, his head dropped back to his breast, his fettered arms fell between his fettered legs, river and sky were blotted out of his eyes, and he knew that before the face of his death he was no better than a poor broken coward.

At eleven o'clock the crowd at Tynwald had grown to a vast concourse that covered every foot of the green with a dense mass of moving heads. In an enclosed pathway that connected the chapel with the mount three carriages were drawn up. The Deemster sat in one of them, and his wizened face was full of uncharity. By his side was Jarvis Kerruish. On an outskirt of the crowd two men stood with a small knot of people around them; they were Quilleash and Teare. The Ballasalla prophetess, with glittering eyes and hair in ringlets, was preaching by the door of the inn, and near her were Corkell and Crennell, and they sang when she sang, and while she prayed they knelt. Suddenly the great clamorous human billow was moved by a ruffle of silence that spread from side to side, and in the midst of a deep hush the door of the chapel opened, and a line of ecclesiastics came out and walked toward the mount. At the end of the line was the Bishop, bareheaded, much bent, his face white and seamed, his step heavy and uncertain, his whole figure and carriage telling of the sword that is too keen for its scabbard. When the procession reached the mount the Bishop ascended to the topmost round of it, and on the four green ledges below him his clergy ranged themselves. Almost at the same moment there was a subdued murmur among the people, and at one side of the green, the gate to the west, the crowd opened and parted, and the space widened and the line lengthened until it reached the foot of the Tynwald. Then the cart that brought the sergeant and his prisoner from the castle entered it slowly, and drew up, and then, with head and eyes down, like a beast that is struck to its death, Daniel Mylrea dropped to his feet on the ground. He was clad in the blue cloth of a fisherman, with a brown knitted guernsey under his coat, and sea-boots over his stockings. He stood in his great stature above the shoulders of the tallest of the men around him; and women who were as far away as the door of the inn could see the seaman's cap he wore. The sergeant drew him up to the foot of the mount, but his bowed head was never raised to where the Bishop stood above him. An all-consuming shame sat upon him, and around him was the deep breathing of the people.

Presently a full, clear voice was heard over the low murmur of the crowd, and instantly the mass of moving heads was lifted to the mount, and the sea of faces flashed white under the heaviness of the sky.

"Daniel Mylrea," said the Bishop, "it is not for us to know if any hidden circumstance lessens the hideousness of your crime. Against all questions concerning your motive your lips have been sealed, and we who are your earthly judges are compelled to take you at the worst. But if, in the fulness of your remorse, your silence conceals what would soften your great offense, be sure that your Heavenly Judge, who reads your heart, sees all. You have taken a precious life; you have spilled the blood of one who bore himself so meekly and lovingly and with such charity before the world that the hearts of all men were drawn to him. And you, who slew him in heat or malice, you he ever loved with a great tenderness. Your guilt is confessed, your crime is black, and now your punishment is sure."

The crowd held its breath while the Bishop spoke, but the guilty man moaned feebly and his bowed head swayed to and fro.

"Daniel Mylrea, there is an everlasting sacredness in human life, and God who gave it guards it jealously. When man violates it, God calls for vengeance, and if we who are His law-givers on earth shut our ears to that cry of the voice of God, His fierce anger goes forth as a whirlwind and His word as a fire upon all men. Woe unto us if now we sin against the Lord by falling short of the punishment that He has ordered. Righteously, and without qualm of human mercy, even as God has commanded, we, His servants, must execute judgment on the evil-doer, lest His wrath be poured out upon this island itself, upon man and upon beast, and upon the fruit of the ground."

At that word the deep murmur broke out afresh over the people, and under the low sky their upturned faces were turned to a grim paleness. And now a strange light came into the eyes of the Bishop, and his deep voice quavered.

"Daniel Mylrea," he continued, "it is not the way of God's worse chastisement to take an eye for an eye, a tooth for a tooth, and to spill blood for blood that has been spilled. When the sword of the Lord goes forth it is sometimes to destroy the guilty man, and sometimes to cut him off from the land of the living, to banish him to the parched places of the wilderness, to end the days wherein his sleep shall be sweet to him, to blot out his name from the names of men, and to give him no burial at the last when the darkness of death shall cover him."

The Bishop paused. There was a dreadful silence, and the distant sea sent up into the still air, under the low clouds that reverberated like a vault, a hoarse, threatening murmur:

"Daniel Mylrea, you are not to die for your crime."

At that ill-omened word the prisoner staggered like a drunken man, and lifted his right hand mechanically above his head, as one who would avert a blow. And now it was easy to see in the wild light in the eyes of the Bishop, and to hear in his hollow, tense voice, that the heart of the father was wrestling with the soul of the priest, and that every word that condemned the guilty man made its sore wound on the spirit of him that uttered it.

"You have chosen death rather than life, but on this side of death's darkness you have yet, by God's awful will, to become a terror to yourself; you have water of gall to drink; toilfully you have to live in a waste land alone, where the sweet light of morning shall bring you pain, and the darkness of night have eyes to peer into your soul; and so on and on from year to weary year, until your step shall fail and there shall be never another to help you up; hopeless, accursed, finding death in life, looking only for life in death, and crying in the bitterness of your desolation, 'Cursed be the day wherein I was born; let not the day wherein my mother bare me be blessed! Cursed be the man that brought tidings to my father, saying, "A man-child is born unto thee," making his heart glad.'"

One hoarse cry as of physical pain burst from the prisoner before these awful words were yet fully uttered. The guilty man gripped his head between his hands, and like a beast that is smitten in the shambles he stood in a stupor, his body swaying slightly, a film upon his eyes, and his mind sullen and stunned. There was silence for a moment, and when the Bishop spoke again his tempest-beaten head, white with the flowers of the grave, trembled visibly. The terrified people were grasping each other's hands, and their hard-drawn breath went through the air like the hiss of the sea at its ebb. As they looked up at the Bishop they understood that an awful struggle of human love and spiritual duty was going on before them, and over all their terror they were moved to a deep compassion.

"Daniel Mylrea," said the Bishop again, and notwithstanding his efforts to uphold it, his voice softened and all but broke, "vengeance belongs to God, but we who are men and prone to fall are not to deny mercy. When your fetters are removed, and you leave this place, you will go to the Calf Sound that flows at the extreme south of the island. There you will find your fishing-boat, stored with such as may meet your immediate wants. With that offering we part from you while life shall last. Use it well, but henceforward look for no succor whence it has come. Though you loathe your life, be zealous to preserve it, and hasten not, I warn you, by one hour the great day of God's final reckoning. Most of all be mindful of the things of an eternal concernment, that we who part from you now may not part forever as from a soul given over to everlasting darkness."

The prisoner gave no further sign. Then the Bishop turned with a wild gesture to the right and to the left and lifted both his hands. "Men and women of Man," he said, in a voice that rose to the shrillness of a cry, "the sentence of the court of the barony of the island is that this man shall be cut off from his people. Henceforth let him have no name among us, nor family, nor kin. From now forever let no flesh touch his flesh. Let no tongue speak to him. Let no eye look on him. If he should be an-hungered, let none give him meat. When he shall be sick, let none minister to him. When his death shall come, let no man bury him. Alone let him live, alone let him die, and among the beasts of the field let him hide his unburied bones."

A great hoarse groan arose from the people, such as comes from the bosom of a sullen sea. The pathos of the awful struggle which they had looked upon was swallowed up in the horror of its tragedy. What they had come to see was as nothing to the awfulness of the thing they had witnessed. Death was terrible, but this was beyond death's terror. Somewhere in the dark chambers of the memory of their old men the like of it lived as a grim gorgon from old time. They looked up at the mount, and the gaunt figure standing there above the vast multitude of moving heads seemed to be something beyond nature. The trembling upraised hands, the eyes of fire, the white quivering lips, the fever in the face which consumed the grosser senses, appeared to transcend the natural man. And below was the prisoner, dazed, stunned, a beast smitten mortally and staggering to its fall.

The sergeant removed the fetters from the prisoner's hands and feet, and turned him about with his face toward the south. Not at first did the man seem to realize that he was no longer a prisoner, but an outcast, and free to go whither he would, save where other men might be. Then, recovering some partial consciousness, he moved a pace or two forward, and instantly the crowd opened for him and a long, wide way was made through the dense mass, and he walked through it, slow, yet strong of step, with head bent and eyes that looked into the eyes of no man. Thus he passed away from the Tynwald toward the foot of Slieu Whallin and the valley of Foxdale that runs southward. And the people looked after him, and the Bishop on the mount and the clergy below followed him with their eyes. A great wave of compassion swept over the crowd as the solitary figure crossed the river and began to ascend the mountain-path. The man was accursed, and none might look upon him with pity; but there were eyes that grew dim at that sight.

The smoke still rose in a long blue column from the side of Greeba, and the heavy cloud that had hung at poise over the head of Slieu Whallin had changed its shape to the outlines of a mighty bird, luminous as a sea-gull, but of a sickly saffron. Over the long line of sea and sky to the west the streak of red that had burned duskily had also changed to a dull phosphoric light that sent eastward over the sky's low roof a misty glow. And while the people watched the lonely man who moved away from them across the breast of the hill, a pale sheet of lightning, without noise of thunder, flashed twice or thrice before their faces. So still was the crowd, and so reverberant the air, that they could hear the man's footsteps on the stony hillside. When he reached the topmost point of the path, and was about to descend to the valley, he was seen to stop, and presently to turn his face, gazing backward for a moment. Against the dun sky his figure could be seen from head to foot. While he stood the people held their breath. When he was gone, and the mountain had hidden him, the crowd breathed audibly.

At the next moment all eyes were turned back to the mount. There the Bishop, a priest of God no longer, but only a poor human father now, had fallen to his knees, and lifted his two trembling arms. Then the pent-up anguish of the wretched heart that had steeled itself to a mighty sacrifice of duty burst forth in a prayer of great agony.

"O Father in Heaven, it is not for him who draws the sword of the Lord's vengeance among men to cry for mercy, but rather to smite and spare not, yea, though his own flesh be smitten; but, O Thou that fillest heaven and earth, from whom none can hide himself in any secret place that Thou shalt not see him, look with pity on the secret place of the heart of Thy servant and hear his cry. O Lord on High, whose anger goes forth as a whirlwind, and whose word is like as a fire, what am I but a feeble, broken, desolate old man? Thou knowest my weakness, and how my familiars watched for my halting, and how for a period my soul failed me, and how my earthly affections conquered my heavenly office, and how God's rule among this people was most in danger from the servant of God, who should be valiant for the Lord on the earth. And if through the trial of this day Thou hast been strength of my strength, woe is me now, aged and full of days, feeble of body and weak of faith, that Thou hast brought this heavy judgment upon me. God of Goodness and Righteous Judge of all the Earth, have mercy and forgive if we weep for him who goeth away and shall return no more, nor see his home and kindred. Follow him with Thy Spirit, touch him with Thy finger of fire, pour upon him the healing of Thy grace, so that after death's great asundering, when all shall stand for one judgment, it may not be said of Thy servant, 'Write ye this old man childless.'"

It was the cry of a great shattered soul, and the terrified people dropped to their knees while the voice pealed over their heads. When the Bishop was silent the clergy lifted him to his feet and helped him down the pathway to the chapel. There was then a dull murmur of distant thunder from across the sea. The people fell apart in confusion. Before the last of them had left the green the cloud of pale saffron over the head of Slieu Whallin had broken into lightning, and the rain was falling heavily.

THE BRIEF RELATION OF DANIEL MYLREA

WRITTEN BY HIMSELF

CHAPTER XXXVII
OF HIS OUTCAST STATE

I, Daniel Mylrea, the son (God forgive me!) of Gilcrist Mylrea, Bishop of Man—grace and peace be with that saintly soul!—do set me down in the year (as well as my reckoning serves me) 1712, the month September, the day somewhere between the twentieth and the thirtieth, to begin a brief relation of certain exceeding strange accidents of this life that have befallen me since, at the heavy judgment of God, I first turned my face from the company of men. Not, as the good Bunyan was, am I now impelled to such a narration—bear with me though I name myself with that holy man—by hope or thought that the goodness and bounty of God may thereby be the more advanced before the sons of men, though it is for me also to magnify the Heavenly Majesty, insomuch as that by this door of my outcast state He has brought me to partake of grace and life. Alone I sit to write what perchance no eye may read, but it is with hope, perhaps only vain, that she who is dear to me beyond words of appraisement may yet learn of the marvels which did oft occur, that I try in these my last days to put my memory under wardship. For it has fastened on me with conviction that God has chosen me for a vessel of mercy, and that very soon he will relieve me from the body of the death I live in. If I finish this writing before I go hence, and if when I am gone she reads it, methinks it will come to her as a deep solace that her prayer of long since was answered, and that, though so sorely separated, we twain have yet been one even in this world, and lived together by day and hour in the cheer of the spirit. But if the gracious end should come before I bring my task to a period, and she should know only of my forlorn condition and learn nothing of the grace wherein much of its desolation was lost, and never come to an understanding of such of those strange accidents as to her knowledge have befallen, then that were also well, for she must therein be spared many tears.

It was on May 29, 1705—seven years and four months, as I reckon it, back from this present time—that in punishment of my great crime the heavy sentence fell on me that cut me off forever from the number of the people. What happened on that day and on the days soon following it I do partly remember with the vividness of horror, and partly recall with difficulty and mistrust from certain dark places of memory that seem to be clouded over and numb. When I came to myself as I was plodding over the side of Slieu Whallin, the thunder was loud in my ears, the lightning was flashing before my eyes, and the rain was swirling around me. I minded them not, but went on, hardly seeing what was about or above me, on and on, over mountain road and path, until the long day was almost done and the dusk began to deepen. Then the strength of the tempest was spent, and only the hinder part of it beat out from the west a thin, misty rain, and I found myself in Rushen, on the south brow of the glen below Carny-Gree. There I threw myself down on the turf with a great numbness and a great stupor upon me, both in body and in mind. How long I lay there I know not, whether a few minutes only, or, as I then surmised, near four-and-twenty hours; but the light of day was not wholly gone from the sky when I lifted my head from where it had rested on my hands, and saw that about me in a deep half-circle stood a drift of sheep, all still, save for their heavy breathing, and all gazing in their questioning silence down on me. I think in my heart, remembering my desolation, I drew solace from this strange fellowship on the lone mountain-side, but I lifted my hand and drove the sheep away, and I thought as they went they bleated, but I could hear nothing of their cry, and so surmised that under the sufferings of that day I had become deaf.

I fell back to the same stupor as before, and when I came to myself again the moon was up, and a white light was around the place where I sat. With the smell of the sheep in my nostrils I thought they might be standing about me again, but I could see nothing clearly, and so stretched out my hands either way. Then, from their confusion in scurrying away, I knew that the sheep had indeed been there, and that under the sufferings of that day I had also failed in my sight.

The tempest was over by this time, the mountain turf had run dry, and I lay me down at length and fell into a deep sleep without dreams; and so ended the first day of my solitary state.

When I awoke the sun was high, and the wheat-ear was singing on a stone very close above me, whereunder her pale-blue egg she had newly laid. I know not what wayward humor then possessed me, but it is true that I reached my hand to the little egg and looked at it, and crushed it between my finger and thumb, and cast its refuse away. My surmise of the night before I now found to be verified, that hearing and sight were both partly gone from me. No man ever mourned less at first knowledge of such infirmities, but in truth I was almost beyond the touch of pain, and a sorer calamity would have wanted strength to torture me. I rose and set my face southward, for it was in the Calf Sound, as I remembered, that I was to find my boat, and if any hope lived in my heart, so numb of torpor, it was that perchance I might set sail and get myself away.

I walked between Barrule and Dalby, and came down on the eastward of Cronk-na-Irey-Lhaa. Then I, who had never before known my strength to fail, grew suddenly weary, and would fain have cast me down to rest. So to succumb I could not brook, but I halted in my walking and looked back, and across the plain to the east, and down to the Bay of Fleswick to the west. Many times since have I stood there and looked on sea and sky, and mountain and dale, and asked myself was ever so fair a spot, and if the plains of heaven were fairer? But that day my dim eyes scoured the sea for a sail and the mountains for a man, and nothing did they see of either, and all else was then as nothing.

Yet, though I was so eager to keep within sight of my fellow-man, I was anxious not to come his way, and in choosing my path I walked where he was least likely to be. Thus, holding well to the west of Fleswick, I took the cliff-head toward Brada, and then came down between Port Erin and Port-le-Mary to the moors that stretch to the margin of the sound. Some few I met, chiefly shepherds and fishermen, but I lifted my eyes to none, and none gave me salutation. This was well, for my heart was bitter, and if any had spoken, not knowing me, I doubt not I should have answered ill. In my great heart-torpor, half-blind, half-deaf, I was that day like a wounded beast of the field, ranging the moorland with a wild abandonment and dangerous to its kind.

When I came to Cregneesh and saw it for the first time, a little disjointed gipsy encampment of mud-built tents pitched on the bare moor, the sky was reddening across the sea, and from that I knew how far advanced the day must be, how slow my course had been, and how low my strength. In half an hour more I had sighted my boat, the "Ben-my-Chree," where she lay in the Doon Creek of the sound, at the length of some fifty fathoms inside the rocks of Kitterland. When I came up to her I found her anchored in some five fathoms of water, with the small-boat lying dry on the shingly beach. Her cabin contained provisions enough for present needs, and more than that I was in no mood to think about. Since the morning of the day before I had not broken fast, but now I ate hungrily of oaten and barley cake. Later in the evening, when the stars were out and the moon, which was in its last quarter, was hanging over the Calf, I mixed myself some porridge of rye-meal and cold water, and ate it on the deck, and then went below to my bunk and lay me down alone. Between sleeping and waking I tried to think of my position and to realize it, but an owl was hooting somewhere on the land, and somewhere over the waters of the sound a diver was making his unearthly laugh. I could not think save of the hooting owl and the screaming diver, and when I thought of them, though their note was doleful and seemed to tell of suffering, or perhaps of demoniac delight, I could not thank God that I had been made a man. Thus, feeling how sore a thing it is to be a creature living under the wrath of God, I tossed on my bunk until I fell to sleep; and so ended the second day of my unblessed condition.

To follow closely all that befell on the next day, or the many days thereafter whereof I kept no reckoning, were to weary my spirit. One thing I know, that a sudden numbness of the spiritual life within me left me a worse man than I had been before the day of my cutting off, and that I did soon lose the little I had of human love and tenderness. My gun had been put in the boat, and with that I ranged the cliffs and the moor from the Mull Hills that lie to the west of Cregneesh to the Chasms that are to the east of it. Many puffins I shot, that much frequent these shores, but their flesh was rank and salt, and they were scarcely worth the powder I spent on them. Thus, it sometimes happened that, being in no straits for food, I cast the birds away, or did not put myself to the pains of lifting them up after they fell to my gun, but went on, nevertheless, to destroy them in my wanton humor. Rabbits I snared by a trick I learned when a boy, and sometimes cooked them in the stove and ate them like a Christian man, and at other times I sat me down on the hillside and rived them asunder as a wild creature of the hills might do. But whether I ate in my boat or on the cliff I took no religion to my table, and thought only that I liked my food or misliked it.

Many times in these first days I had to tear myself away from thinking of my condition, for to do so was like the stab of a knife to my brain, and I plainly saw that in that way madness itself would lie. If I told myself that other men had been cast alone ere now in desolate places where no foot of man was and no sound of a human voice, a great stroke would come upon my spirit with the thought that only their bodies had been cast away, but that my soul was so. The marooned seaman on an uninhabited island, when at length he set eyes on his fellow-man, might lift up his heart to God, but to me the company of men was not blessed. Free I was to go where men were, even to the towns wherein they herded together, but go where I would I must yet be alone.

With this thought, and doubting not that for me the day of grace was past and gone, since God had turned His face from the atonement I had erewhile been minded to make, I grew day by day more bitter in my heart, and found it easiest to shut my mind by living actively from hour to hour.

Then, like a half-starved hound, I went abroad at daybreak and scoured the hills the day long, and returned to my bed at night. I knew I was a baser thing than I had been, and it brought some comfort then to know that I was alone and no eye saw me as I now was. Mine was a rank hold of life, and it gave me a savage delight unknown before to live by preying on other creatures. I shot and slew daily and hourly, and if for a moment I told myself that what I had killed held its life on the same tenure that I did, my humanity was not touched except to feel a strange wild thrill that it was not I that lay dead. Looking back over these seven years, it comes to me as an unnatural thing that this mood can ever have been mine; but mine it was, and from the like of it may God in His mercy keep all Christian men.

One day—I think it must have been somewhere toward the end of the first month of my outcast state—I was ranging the cliff-side above the gray rocks of the Black Head, when I chanced on a hare and shot it. On coming up with it I found it was lean and bony, and so turned aside and left it as it squeaked and bounced from my feet. This was in the morning, and toward nightfall I returned by the same way and saw the hare lying by a brookside, ragged and bleeding, but still alive. At sight of me the wee thing tried to move away, but its weakness and a clot of its blood kept it down, and, feeling its extremity, it lifted its two slender paws in the air, while its glistening eyes streamed visibly, and set up a piteous cry like the cry of a little child. I can not write what then I did, for it wounds me sore to think of it, but when it was done, and that piteous cry was no more in mine ears, suddenly I said with myself this awful word, "I am no longer a man, but a beast of the field; and the God of mercy and of tenderness has cast me forever out of the hollow of His hand."

CHAPTER XXXVIII
OF HIS WAY OF LIFE

This meeting with the poor hare, though now it looks so trivial a thing, did then make a great seizure upon my mind, so that it changed my course and habit of life. For ceasing not to believe that I was wholly given over to a reprobate soul, I yet laid my gun aside, and locked my shot and powder in a drawer beneath my bunk, and set my face toward new ways of living. First I put myself to counting all that I possessed. Thus I found that of rye and Indian meal I had a peck each, of barley a peck, with two quarters of fine barley flour, of oats a peck, with two quarters of oaten meal, of potatoes two kischen, besides onions and a little common salt. In the hold under the hatches there were stored sundry useful implements—a spade, a fork, a hedge-knife, some hempen rope and twine, and with the rest were the four herring-nets which belonged to the boat, a mackerel-net, and some deep-sea lines. Other things there were that I do not name—wanting memory of them at this time of writing—but enough in all for most uses that a lone man might have.

And this had ofttimes set me wondering why, if it had been meant that I should be cast utterly away, I had been provided with means of life, who could well have found them for myself. But after that meeting with the hare I perceived the end of God in this, namely, that I should not, without guilt, descend from the state of a Christian man when hunger had to be satisfied.

And herein also I found the way of the stern Judge with guilty man, that, having enough for present necessities, I had little for the future, beyond the year that then was, and that if I must eat, so I must work. Thus, upon a day somewhere, as I reckon, about a month after my cutting off, I rose early, and set myself to delve a piece of fallow ground—where all was fallow—two roods or more in extent, lying a little to the north of the Black Head, and to the south of the circle of stones that stand near by. All day I wrought fasting, and when darkness fell in the fallows were turned. Next morning I put down my seed—of potatoes a half-kischen, cut in quarters where the eyes were many and also of barley and oats half a peck each, keeping back my other half-peck lest the ground were barren, or the weather against it, or the year too far worn for such-like crops.

And that day of the delving, the first on which I wrought as a man, was also the first on which I felt a man's craving for the company of other men. The sun was strong all the fore part of the day, and its hot rays scorched the skin of my back—for I had stripped to my waist for my labor—and that set me thinking what month it was, and wondering what was doing in the world, and how long I had been where I then was. When I returned to my boat at nightfall, the air, as I remember it, was quiet over the sound as it might be in a cloister, and only the gulls were jabbering on Kitterland and the cormorants at the water's edge. And I sat on the deck while the sun went down in the sea, and the red sky darkened and the stars began to show and the moon to look out. Then I went below and ate my barley bread and thought of what it was to be alone.

It was that night that I bethought me of my watch, which I had not once looked for since the day of my immersion in the Cross Vein on Orrisdale, when I found it stopped from being full of water. In my fob it had lain with its seals and chain since then, but now I took it out and cleaned it with oil from the fat of the hare and wound it up. For months thereafter I set a great store by it, always carrying it in my fob when I went abroad, and when I came home to the boat always hanging it on a nail to the larboard of the stovepipe in the cabin. And in the long silence of the night, when I heard it, sure, I thought, it is the same to me as good company. Very careful I was to wind it when the sun set, but if perchance it ran down, and I awoke in my bunk, and, listening, heard it not, then it was as if the pulse had stopped of the little world I lived in, and there was nothing but a great emptiness.

But withal my loneliness increased rather than diminished, and though I had no longer any hankering after my old way of life in ranging the moorlands with my gun, yet I felt that the activity of that existence had led me off from thinking too much of my forlorn condition. Wherefore, when my potatoes had begun to show above the ground, and I had earthed them up, I began to bethink me touching my boat, that it must be now the time of the herring-fishing come again, and that I would go out of nights and see what I could take. So, never doubting that single-handed I could navigate the lugger, I hoisted the nets out of the hold athwart the bunk-board, and took them ashore to mend and to bask them on the beach. I had spread them out on the shingle, and was using my knife and twine on the holes of the dogfish, when suddenly from behind me there came the loud bark of a dog. Well I remember how I trembled at the sound of it, for it was the nearest to a man's voice that I had heard these many lonesome days, and how fearfully I turned my head over my shoulder as if some man had touched me and spoken. But what I saw was a poor mongrel dog, small as a cur, and with ragged ears, a peaky nose, and a scant tail, which for all its loud challenge it dangled wofully between its legs. Until then I had never smiled or wept since my cutting off, and I believed myself to have lost the sense of laughter and of tears, but I must have laughed at the sight of the dog, so much did it call to mind certain brave vaunters I had known, who would come up to a bout of wrestling with a right lusty brag, and straightway set to trembling before one had well put eyes on them. At the sound of my voice the dog wagged his tail, and crept up timidly with his muzzle down, and licked the hand I held out to him. All day he sat by me and watched me at my work, looking up in my face at whiles with a wistful gaze, and I gave him a morsel of oaten cake, which he ate greedily, seeming to be half-starved of hunger. And when at dusk my task was finished and I rose and got into the dingey, thinking now he would go his ways and be seen of me no more, he leaped into the boat after me, and when we reached the lugger he settled himself in the corner under the locker as if he had now fully considered it that with me he would make his habitation henceforth.

Having all things in readiness for the fishing, I slipped anchor upon an evening toward autumn, as I reckoned, for the leaves of the trammon were then closing like a withered hand and the berries of the hollin were reddening. When the stars were out, but no moon was yet showing, I put about head to the wind, and found myself in nowise hampered because short-handed, for when I had to take in my sails I lashed my tiller, and being a man of more than common strength of arm, it cost me nothing to step my mainmast.

That night, and many nights thereafter, I had good takings of fish, and in the labor of looking after my corks and making fast my seizings the void in my mind was in somewise filled with other matter than thoughts of my abject state. But one thing troubled me at first, namely, that I took more fish by many meshes than I could ever consume. To make an end of my fishing was a thing I could not bring myself to, for I counted it certain that so to do would be to sink back to my former way of living. Wherefore I thought it safest to seek for some mode of disposing of my fish, such as would keep me at my present employment and do no harm to my feelings as a man, for with this I had now to reckon watchfully, being in constant danger, as I thought, of losing the sense of manhood.

So I soused some hundreds of my herrings with rought salt, which I distilled from the salt water by boiling it in a pan with pebbles. The remainder I concluded to give to such as would consume them, and how to do this, being what I was, cost me many bitter thoughts, wherein I seemed to be the most unblessed of all men. At length I hit on a device, and straightway brought it to bear. Leaving my fishing-ground while the night was not yet far spent, I ran into the sound before dawn, for soon I learned those narrow waters until they grew familiar as the palm of my hand. Then, before the sun rose above the Stack of Scarlet, and while the eastern sky was only dabbled with pink, I, with a basket of herrings on my shoulder, crossed the moor to Cregneesh, where the people are poor and not proud, and creeping in between the cabins, laid my fish down in the open place that is before the little chapel, and then went my way quickly lest a door should suddenly open or a window be lifted, and a face look forth. Thrice I did this before I marked that there were those who were curious to know whence the fish came, and then I was put on my nettle to go into the village and yet to keep myself from being seen, for well I knew that if any eye beheld me that knew who I was, there would thenceforward be an end of the eating of my herrings, even among the poorest, and an end of my fishing also. But many times I went into Cregneesh without being seen of any man, and now I know not whether to laugh or to weep when I look back on the days I write of, and see myself like a human fox stealing in by the gray of dawn among the sleeping homes of men.

CHAPTER XXXIX
OF THE GHOSTLY HAND UPON HIM

All that autumn I followed the herrings, choosing my ground mainly by guess, but sometimes seeing the blue lights of the herring fleet rise close under my quarter, and at other times, when the air was still, hearing voices of men or the sound of laughter rumored over the quiet waters. But ever fanciful to me, as a dream of a friend dead when it is past, was that sound on the sea, and as often as I heard it I took in my nets and hauled my sails, and stood out for the sound. Putting no light on my mitch-board, I would ofttimes pass the fleet within a cable's-length and yet not be known, but once and again I knew by the hush of voices and the dying away of laughter on the boats about me that my dark craft was seen scudding like a black bird of evil omen through the night.

In my cabin I was used to burn a tallow dip made of the fat of the birds I had shot and rushes from the soft places of the moor, and while my boat drifted under the mizzen between take and take of herrings I would go below and sit with my dog. He grew sleek with the fare I found him, and I in these days recovered in a measure my sense of sight and hearing, for the sea's breath of brine is good to man. Millish veg-veen I called him, and, though a man of small cheer, I smiled to think what a sorry misname that name would seem in our harder English tongue. For my poor mongrel cur had his little sorry vices, such as did oft set me wondering what the chances of his life had been, and whether, like his new messmate, he had not somewhere been driven out. Nevertheless, he had his good parts, too, and was a creature of infinite spirits. I think we were company each to the other, and if he had found me a cheerier mate-fellow, I doubt not we should have had some cheerful hours together.

But in truth, though my fishing did much to tear me away from the burden of myself, it yet left me many lonesome hours wherein my anguish was sore and deep, and, looking to the years that might be before me, put me to the bitter question whether, being a man outside God's grace, I could hold out on so toilsome a course. Also, when I fell to sleep in the daytime, after my work of the night was done, I was much wrought upon by troublous dreams, which sometimes brought back the very breath-odor of my boyish days with the dear souls that filled them with joy, and sometimes plagued me with awful questions which in vain I tried to answer, knowing that my soul's welfare lay therein. And being much followed by the thought that the spirit of the beast of the field lay in wait to fall on the spirit of the man within me, I was also put to great terror in my watchfulness and the visions that came to me in hours of idleness and sleep. But suddenly this sentence fell on my mind: Thou art free to go whithersoever thou wilt, though it be the uttermost reaches of the earth. Go, then, where men are, and so hold thy soul as a man.

Long did this sentence trouble me, not being able to make a judgment upon it, but at length it fastened on me that I must follow it, and that all the dread I had felt hitherto of the face of man was no more than a think-so. Thereupon I concluded that I would go into Castletown at high fair on the next market-day, which I should know from other days by the carts I could descry from the top of the Mull going the way of Rushen Church and Kentraugh. This resolve I never brought to bear, for the same day whereon I made it a great stroke fell upon my spirit and robbed me of the little wherewith I had tried to comfort me.

Going out of the sound that night by the Spanish Head, for the season was far worn, and the herrings lay to the eastward of the island, I marked in the dusk that a smack that bore the Peel brand on its canvas was rounding the Chicken Rocks of the Calf. So I stood out well to sea, and did not turn my head to the wind, and cast my nets, until I was full two leagues from shore. Then it was black dark, for the night was heavy, and a mist lay between sea and sky. But soon thereafter I saw a blue light to my starboard bow, and guessed that the smack from Peel had borne down in my wake. How long I lay on that ground I know not, for the takings were good, and I noted not the passage of time. But at short whiles I looked toward the blue light, and marked that as my boat drifted so did the smack drift, and that we were yet within hail. The moon came out with white streamers from behind a rack of cloud, and knowing then that the fishing was over for that night—for the herring does not run his gills into mischief when he has light to see by—I straightway fell to hauling my nets. And then it was that I found the smell of smoke in the nostrils, and heard loud voices from the Peeltown smack. Lifting my eyes, I could at first see nothing, for though the moon's light was in the sky, the mist was still on the sea, and through it there seemed to roll slowly, for the wind was low, a tunnel of smoke-like fog. Well I knew that something was amiss, and soon the mist lifted like a dark veil into the air, and the smoke veered, and a flash of red flame rose from the smack of the Peel-men. Then I saw that the boat was afire, and in two minutes more the silence of the sea was lost in the fire's loud hiss and the men's yet louder shouts. It was as if a serpent in the bowels of the boat struggled to make its way out, and long tongues of fire shot out of the scuttle, the hold, the combings, and the flue of the stove. Little thought had I then of those things, though now by the eye of memory I see them, and also the sinuous trail of red water that seemed to crawl over the dark sea from the boat afire to the boat I sailed in. I had stepped my mast and hoisted sail before yet I knew what impulse possessed me, but with my hand on the tiller to go to the relief of the men in peril. On a sudden I was seized with a mighty fear, and it was as though a ghostly hand laid on me from behind, and a voice above the tumult of that moment seemed to cry in my ears: "Not for you, not for you." Then in great terror I turned my boat's head away from the burning smack, and as I did so the ghostly hand did relax, and the voice did cease to peal in mine ears.

"They will drop into their dingey," I said with myself. "Yes," I said, as the sweat started cold from my forehead, "they will drop into the dingey and be saved;" and turning my head I saw, by the flame of the fire, that over the bulwark at the stern two men were tumbling down into the small-boat that they hauled behind. And I sped away in agony, for now I knew how deep was the wrath upon me, that it was not for me so much as to stretch my accursed hand to perishing men to save them. Scarce had I gone a cable's-length when a great shout, mingled with oaths, made me turn my head, thinking the crew of the boat were crying curses down on me, not knowing me, for deserting them in their peril, but I was then in the tunnel of smoke wherein I might not be seen, and, lo, I saw that the dingey with the two men was sheering off, and that other two of their mates were left on the burning boat.

"Haul the wind and run the waistrels down, d—— them," shouted one of the two men on the smack, and amid the leaping flames the mainsail shot up and filled, and a man stood to the tiller, and with an oath he shouted to the two in the small-boat that for their treachery they should go down to hell straightway.

In the glare of that fierce light and the turmoil of that moment my eyes grew dim, as they had been on the day of my cutting off, and I squeezed their lids together to relieve them of water. Then I saw how fearful a thing was going on within my cable's-length. Two men of a crew of four in the burning smack had got themselves into the small-boat and cleared off without thought of their comrades who were struggling to save their craft, and now the two abandoned men, doomed to near death in fire or water, were with their last power of life, and in life's last moments—for aught they could tell—thirsting for deadly vengeance. On the smack went, with its canvas bellied, and the flames shooting through and hissing over it, but just as it came by the small-boat the men therein pulled to the windward and it shot past.

Ere this was done, and while the smack's bow was dead on for the dingey, I too had sheered round and was beating up after the burning boat, and when the men thereon saw me come out of the smoke they ceased to curse their false comrades and made a great cry of thanks to God. At a distance of six fathoms I laid to, thinking the men would plunge into the sea and come to me, but, apprehending my thoughts, one shouted me to come closer, for that he could not swim. Closer to the burning smack I would not go from fear of firing my own boat, and I dared not to risk that fate wherein we might all have been swallowed up together. For despair, that fortifies some men, did make of me a coward, and I stood in constant terror of the coming of death. So I stripped me of my jacket and leaped into the water and swam to the boat, and climbed its open combings as best I could through the flame and heat. On the deck the two men stood, enveloped in swirling clouds of smoke, but I saw them where they were, and pulling one into the water after me, the other followed us, and we reached my boat in safety.

Then, as I rubbed my face, for the fire had burned one cheek, the men fell to thanking me in a shamefaced way—as in the manner of their kind, fearing to show feeling—when on a sudden they stopped short, for they had lifted their eyes, and in the flame of their boat had seen me, and at the same moment I had looked upon them and known them. They were Illiam Quilleash and Edward Teare, and they fell back from me and made for the bow, and stood there in silence together.

Taking the tiller, I bore in by tacks for Port-le-Mary, and there I landed the men, who looked not my way nor ever spoke word or made sign to me, but went off with their heads down. And when I stood out again through the Poolvash to round the Spanish Head and make for my moorings in the sound, and saw the burning smack swallowed up by the sea with a groan that came over the still waters, its small-boat passed me going into harbor, and the men who rowed it were Crennell and Corkell, and when they saw me they knew me, and made a broad sweep out of my course. Now all this time the ghostly hand had been on my shoulder, and the strange voice had pealed in mine ears, and though I wanted not to speak with any man, nor that any man should speak with me, yet I will not say but that it went to my heart that I should be like as a leper from whose uncleanness all men should shrink away.

For many days hereafter this lay with a great trouble upon me, so that I let go my strong intent of walking into Castletown at high fair, and put this question with myself, whether it was written that I should carry me through this world down to death's right ending. Not as before did I now so deeply abhor myself; but felt for myself a secret compassion. In truth, I had no bitterness left in my heart for my fellow-men, but tossed with the fear that if I lived alone much longer I must surely lose my reason, and hence my manhood, sinking down to the brute, this consideration fell with weight upon me. What thou hast suffered is from men who know thy crime, and stand in terror of the curse upon thee, wherein thou art so blotted out of the book of the living that without sin none may look thy way. Go therefore where no man knows thee, and the so heavy burden thou bearest will straightway fall from thee. Now, at this thought my heart was full of comfort, and I went back to my former design of leaving this place forever. But before I had well begun what I was minded to do a strange accident befell me, and the relation thereof is as followeth.

By half-flood of an evening late in autumn—for though the watch showed short of six the sun was already down—I left my old moorings inside the rocks of Kitterland, thinking to slip anchor there no more. The breeze was fresh in the sound, and outside it was stiff from the nor'east, and so I ran out with a fair wind for Ireland, for I had considered with myself that to that country I would go, because the people there are tender of heart and not favored by God. For a short while I had enough to think of in managing my cordage, but when I was well away to sou'west of the Calf suddenly the wind slackened. Then for an hour full I stood by the tiller with little to do, and looked back over the green waters to the purple mountains vanishing in the dusk, and around to the western sky, where over the line of sea the crimson streamers were still trailing where the sun had been, like as the radiance of a goodly life remains a while after the man has gone. And with that eye that sees double—the thing that is without and that which is within—I saw myself then in my little craft on the lonely sea like an uncompanionable bird in the wide sky, and my heart began to fail me, and for the first time since my cutting off I must have wept. For I thought I was leaving forever the fair island of my home, with all that had made it dear in dearer days. Though it had turned its back on me since, and knew me no more, but had blotted out my name from its remembrance, yet it was mine, and the only spot of earth on all this planet, go whither I would, that I could call my own. How long this mood lasted I hardly can say, but over the boat two gulls hovered or circled and cried, and I looked up at their white transparent wings, for lack of better employment, until the light was gone and another day had swooned to another night. The wind came up with the darkness, and more in heart than before, I stood out for the south of Ireland, and reached my old fishing port of Kinsale by the dawn of the next day.

Then in the gentle sun of that autumn morning I walked up from the harbor to the market-place, and there found a strange company assembled about the inn, and in the midst were six or seven poor ship-broken men, shoeless, half-naked, and lean of cheek from the long peril and privation that eats the flesh and makes the eyes hollow. In the middle of the night they had come ashore on a raft, having lost their ship by foundering twelve days before. This I learned from the gossip of the people about them, and also that they had eaten supper at the inn and slept there. While I stood and looked on there came out in the midst of the group two other men, and one of them was their captain and the other the innkeeper. And I noted well that the master of the inn was suave to his tattered customers, and spoke of breakfast as being made ready.

"But first go to the Mayor," said he, addressing the captain, "and make your protest, and he will lend whatever moneys you want."

The captain, nothing loth, set out with a cheerful countenance for the Mayor of the town, a servant of the inn going with him to guide him. The ship-broken crew stayed behind, and I, who was curious to learn if their necessities would be relieved, remained standing in the crowd around them. And while we waited, and the men sat on the bench in front of the inn, there came down on them from every side the harpies that find sea-going men with clothes. There was one with coats and one with guernseys, and one with boots of leather and one of neat's-skin, and with these things they made every man to fit himself. And if one asked the price, and protested that he had got no money, the Samaritans laughed and bade them not to think of price or money until their captain should return from the treasury of the Mayor. The seamen took all with good cheer, and every man picked out what he wanted, and put it on, throwing his rags aside, laughing.

But presently the master of the crew returned, and his face was heavy; and when his men asked how he had fared, and if the Mayor had advanced him anything, he told them No, and that the Mayor had said he was no usurer to lend money. At that there were groans and oaths from the crew, and looks of bewilderment among those who had fetched the clothes; but the innkeeper said all would be well, and that they had but to send for a merchant in the next street who made it his trade to advance money to ship-broken men. This news brought back the light to the dark face of the captain, and he sent the servant of the inn to fetch the merchant.

When this man came my mind misgave, for I saw the stamp of uncharity in his face. But the captain told his story, whereof the sum was this: That they were the English crew of the brig "Betsy," and were seven days out from Bristol, bound for Buenos Ayres, when they foundered on a rock, and had made their way thither on a raft, suffering much from hunger and the cold of the nights, and that they wanted three pounds' advance on their owners to carry them to Dublin, whence they could sail for their own port. But the merchant curled his hard lip and said he had just before been deceived by strangers, and could not lend money except to men of whom he knew something; that they were strangers, and, moreover, by their own words, entitled to no more than six days' pay apiece. And so he went his way.

Hardly had he gone when the harpies of the coats and boots and guernseys called on the men to strip off these good garments, which straightway they rolled in their several bundles, and then elbowed themselves out of the crowd. The poor seamen, resuming their rags, were now in sad case, scarce knowing whether most to curse their misfortunes or to laugh at the grim turn that they were taking, when the captain, in a chafe, called on the innkeeper to give breakfast to his men, for that he meant to push on to the next town, where people might be found who had more humanity. But the innkeeper, losing his by-respects, shook his head, and asked where was his pay to come from for what he had already done.

Now, when I heard this, and saw the men rise up to go on their toilsome way with naked, bleeding feet, suddenly I bethought me that, though I had little money, I had what would bring money, and before I had taken time to consider I had whipped my watch from my fob to thrust it into the captain's hands. But when I would have parted the crowd to do so, on a sudden that same ghostly hand that I have before mentioned seemed to seize me from behind. Then on the instant I faced about to hasten away, for now the struggle within me was more than I could bear, and I stopped and went on, and stopped again and again went on, and all the time the watch was in my palm, and the ghostly hand on my shoulder. At last, thinking sure that the memory of the seven sea-going men, hungry and ill-clad, would follow me, and rise up to torment me on land and sea, I wheeled around and ran back hot-foot and did as I was minded. Then I walked rapidly away from the market-place, and passing down to the harbor, I saw a Peeltown fisherman, and knew that he saw me also.

Now, I should have been exceeding glad if this thing had never befallen, for though it made my feeling less ungentle toward the two men, my old shipmates, who had turned from me as from a leper when I took them from the burning boat, yet it brought me to a sense that was full of terror to my oppressed spirit, namely, that though I might fly to lands where men knew nothing of my great crime, yet that the curse thereof was mostly within mine own afflicted soul, from which I could never flee away.

All that day I stayed in my boat, and the sun shone and the sky was blue, but my heart was filled with darkness. And when night fell in I had found no comfort, for then I knew that from my outcast state there was no escape. This being so, whether to go back to mine own island was now my question. Oh, it is a goodly thing to lie down in the peace of a mind at ease and rise up from the refreshment of the gentle sleep. But not for me was that blessed condition. The quaking of my spirit was more than I could well stand under without losing my reason, and in the fear of that mischance lay half the pain of life to me. Long were the dark hours, and when the soft daylight came again I did resolve that go back to my own island I would. For what was it to me though the world was wide if the little place I lived in was but my own narrow soul?

That night in the boat for lack of the tick of my watch there seemed to be a void in the air of my cabin. But when the tide was about the bottom of the ebb I heard the plash of an oar alongside and presently the sound of something that fell overhead. Next morning I found my watch lying on the deck, by the side of the hatches.

At the top of the flood I lifted anchor, and dropped down the harbor, having spoken no word to any man since I sailed into it.

CHAPTER XL
OF HIS GREAT LONELINESS

Back at my old moorings inside the rocks of Kitterland I knew full well that the Almighty Majesty was on this side of me and on that, and I had nothing to look for now or hereafter. But I think the extremity of my condition gave me some false courage, and my good genius seemed to say, What have you to lament? You have health and food and freedom, and you live under no taskmaster's eye. Let the morning see you rise in content, and let the night look on you lying down in thankfulness. And turn not your face to the future to the unsettling of your spirit, so that when your time comes you may not die with a pale face. Then did I laugh at my old yearning for fellowship, and asked wherefore I should be lonely since I lived in the same planet with other men, and had the same moon and stars above my sleep as hung over the busy world of men. In such wise did I comfort my torn heart, and shut it up from troubling me, but well I knew that I was like to one who cries peace where there is no peace, and that in all my empty sophistry concerning the moon and the stars there was no blood of poor human neighborliness.

Nevertheless, I daily went about my businesses, in pursuance whereof I walked up to the place over the Black Head where I had planted my corn and potatoes. These in their course I reaped and delved, cutting the barley and rye with my clasp-knife for sickle, and digging a burrow in the earth for my potatoes. Little of either I had, but enough for my frugal needs until more might grow.

When my work was done, and I had no longer any employment to take me ashore, the autumn had sunk to winter, for in this island of Man the cold and the mist come at a stride. Then sitting alone in my boat, with no task save such as I could make for myself, and no companion but little Veg-veen, the strength of the sophistry wherewith I had appeased myself broke down pitifully. The nights were long and dark, and the sun shone but rarely for many days together. Few were the ships that passed the mouth of the sound, either to east or west of it, and since my coming to moorage there no boat had crossed its water. Cold and bleak and sullen it lay around my boat, reflecting no more the forehead of the Calf, and lying now under the sunless sky like a dead man's face that is moved neither to smiles nor tears. And an awful weariness of the sea came to me then, such as the loneliest land never brought to the spirit of a Christian man, for sitting on the deck of my little swaying craft, with the beat of the sea on its timbers, and the sea-fowl jabbering on Kitterland, and perhaps a wild colt racing the wind on the Calf, it came into my mind to think that as far as eye could see or ear could hear there was nothing around me but the hand of God. Then all was darkness within me, and I did oft put the question to myself if it was possible for man to be with God alone and live.

Now it chanced upon a day that I wanted potatoes out of my burrow over the Black Head, and that returning therefrom toward nightfall, I made a circuit of the stone circle above the Chasm, and the northernmost side of it, midway to Cregneesh, came on a sight that arrested my breath. This was a hut built against a steepness of rugged land from which stones had sometimes been quarried. The walls were of turf; the roof was of gorse and sticks, with a hole in it for chimney. Window there was none, and the doorway was half closed by a broken gate whereof the bars were intertwined with old straw.

Mean it was, and desolate it looked on the wild moorland, but, it was a mark of the hand of man, and I, who had dwelt so long with God's hand everywhere about me, was touched with a sense of human friendliness. Hearing no voice within, I crept up and looked into the little place. A bed of straw was in one corner, and facing it was a lump of freestone hollowed out for the bed of a fire. A broken pipe lay near this rude hearth, and the floor was of mountain turf worn bare and hard. Two sacks, a kettle, a saucepan, and some potato-parings were the only other things in the hut, and poor as it all was it touched me so that in looking upon it I think my eyes were wet, because it was a man's habitation. I remember that as I turned to go away the rain began to fall, and the pattering drops on the roof seemed to my eye and ear to make the place more human.

In going back to my boat that day I came nearer to Cregneesh than was my wont in the daytime, and though the darkness was coming down from the mountains, I could yet see into the streets from the knoll I passed over. And there in the unpaved way, before a group of houses I saw a witless man in coat and breeches, but no vest or shirt, and with a rope about his waist, dancing and singing to a little noisy crowd gathered about him.

After that I had come upon the hut my mind ran much on the thought of it, and in three days or thereabouts I went back to look at it again, and coming near to it from behind, saw sundry beehives of a rude fashioning, made of straw and sticks. Veg-veen was with me, for he was now my constant company, and in a moment he had bounced in at the doorway and out again at yet more speed, with three of his kind close at his tail. Before I could turn me about to go away a man followed the dogs out of the hut, and he was the same witless being that I had seen at his dancing in the streets of Cregnesh. His lip lagged low and his eyes were dull as a rabbit's; on his head was a crownless hat through which his hair was seen, and I saw that his breast, where his shirt would be, was blackened as with soot. I would have gone about my own employments, but he spoke, telling me not to fear him, for it was false that he was possessed, as hard-spoken people said, with the spirit of delusion. I answered nothing to this, but stood and listened with eyes turned aside, while the broken brain of the poor creature rambled on.

"They call me Billy the Bees," he said, "because I catch them and rear them—look," and he pointed to his hives. He talked of his three dogs and named them, saying that they slept in a sack together, and that in the same sack he slept with them. Something he said of the cold that had been coming latterly, and pointed to the soot on his breast, saying that it kept him warm. He told how he made a circuit of the farmhouses once a week, dancing and singing at all of them, and how the people gave him barley-meal and eggs. Much more he said, but because the method of it—where method there was any—has gone from my memory I pass it. That the world was night about its end he knew of a surety, because he saw that if a man had money and great store of gear it mattered not what else he wanted. These with other such words he spoke ramblingly, and I stood aside and answered him nothing, neither did I look up into his face. At last he said, timidly, "I know I have always been weak in my intellects," and hearing that, I could bear to hear no more, but went about my business with a great weight of trouble upon me. And "O God," I cried that night in my agony, "I am an ignorant sot, without the grace of human tenderness, or the gift of understanding. I am guilty before Thee, and no man careth for my soul, but from this affliction, O Almighty Master save me; save me from this degradation, for it threatens me, and when death comes that stands at the foot of life's awful account, I will pay its price with thankfulness."

Now, after this meeting with the witless man the weariness that I had felt of my home on the sea lay the heavier on my spirits, and I concluded with myself that I should forsake my boat and build me a home on the land within sight of man's habitation. So I walked the cliffs from the Mull Hills to the Noggin Head, and at last I lit on the place I looked for. Near to the land where I had lately broken the fallows and grown me a crop of corn and potatoes, there were four roofless walls. Some time a house had stood there, but being built on the brink of the great clefts in the earth that we call the Chasms, it had shrunken in some settlement of the ground. This had affrighted the poor souls who inhabited it, and they had left it to fall into ruins. Such was the tale I heard long afterward, but none came near it then, and none have come near to it since. Save the four bare walls, and a wall that crossed it midway, nothing was left. Where the floor had been the grass was growing; wormwood was in the settle nook, and whinberries had ripened and rotted on the hearth. The door lintel was gone, and the sill of the window was fallen off. There was a round patch of long grass where the well had been, and near to where the porch once stood the trammon-tree still grew; and thus, though the good people who had lived and died there, been born and buried, were gone from it forever, the sign of their faith, or their superstition, lived after them.

Better for me than this forsaken place it was hard for any place to be. On a dangerous spot it stood, and therefore none would come anigh it. Near to Cregneesh it was, and from the rising ground above it I could look down on the homes of men. Truly it looked out on the sea, and had a great steepness of shelving rocks going down to an awesome depth, where, on the narrow beach of shingle, the tide beat with a woful moan; but though the sea was so near, and the sea-fowl screamed of an evening from the great rock like a cone that lifted its gaunt finger a cable's length away, yet to me it was within the very pulse of human life.

So I set to work, and roofed it with driftwood and turf and gorse; and then, with lime from a cliff at the Tubdale Creek in the Calf, I whitened it within and without, walls and roof. A door I made in somewise, and for a window I had a piece of transparent skin, having no glass. And when all was made ready I moved my goods from the boat to my house, taking all that seemed necessary—flour, and meat, and salt, and my implements, as well as my bed and the spare clothes I had, which were not many.

I had been in no haste with this work, being well content with such employment, but it came to an end at last, and the day that I finished my task was a day late in the first year after my cutting off. This I knew because the nights were long, and I had been trying with my watch to cast on the shortest day, and thereby recover my lost count of time. On the night of my first sleeping in my new home there came a fierce storm of wind and rain from the east. Four hours the gale lasted, and often the gulls were dashed screaming at the walls wherein I sat by the first fire I had yet kindled on my hearth. Toward midnight the wind fell suddenly to a dead calm, and, looking out, I saw that the moon was coming very bright in its rising from behind a heavy cloud over the sea. So, wondering what chance had befallen my boat—for though I had left it I had a tenderness for it and meant perchance to use it again—I set out for the sound. When I got to the head of the cliff I could plainly see the rocks of Kitterland, and the whole length of the Doon Creek, but where my boat had been moored no boat could I see, nor any trace of one from Fistard Head on the east to Half-Walk Rock on the west. Next morning, under a bright winter's sun, I continued the search for my boat, and with the rising tide at noon I saw her thrown up on to the beach of the Doon, dismasted, without spar or boom, bilged below her water-line, and altogether a hopeless hulk. I made some scabbling shift to pull her above high-water mark, and then went my ways.

Now this loss, for so I considered it, did at first much to depress me, thinking, with a bitter envy of my late past, that my future showed me a far more unblessed condition, seeing that I was now forever imprisoned on this island and could never leave it again whatsoever evil might befall. But when I had thought twice upon it, my mind came to that point that I was filled with gratitude; first, because the wrecking of my boat on the very day of my leaving it seemed to give assurance that, in making my home on the land, I had done that which was written for me to do; and next, because I must inevitably have been swallowed up in the storm if I had stayed on the sea a single night longer. And my terror of death was such that to have escaped the peril of it seemed a greater blessing than releasement from this island could ever be.

Every day thereafter, and oftenest at daybreak, I walked up to the crest of the rising ground at the back of my house, and stood awhile looking down on Cregneesh, and watching for the white smoke that lay like a low cloud over the hollow place wherein Port Erin lay. After that I had done this I felt strangely refreshed, as by a sense of companionship, and went about my work, such as it was, with content. But on a bitter morning, some time in December, as I thought, I came upon a sight that wellnigh froze my heart within me; for, outstretched on the bare moorland, under the bleak sky and in the lee of a thick gorse bush tipped with yellow, I found the witless man, Billy the Bees, lying cold and dead. His bare chest was blue, as with starvation, under the soot wherewith in his simpleness he had blackened it, and his pinched face told of privation and of pain. And now that he lay stretched out dead, I saw that he had been a man of my own stature. In his hut, which was farther away than my own house from the place where he lay, there was neither bite nor sup, and his dogs seemed to have deserted him in his poverty, for they were gone. The air had softened perceptibly for some minutes while I went thither, and as I returned to the poor body wondering what to do with it, the snow began to fall in big flakes. "It will cover it," I said with myself. "The snow will bury it," I thought; and casting a look back over my shoulder, I went home with a great burden of trouble upon me.

All that day, and other two days, the snow continued to fall, until the walls of my house were blocked up to the level of my window, and I had to cut a deep trench to the gable where I piled my wood. And for more than a week following, shut in from my accustomed walk I sat alone in the great silence and tried to keep my mind away from the one fearful thought that now followed it. Remembering those long hours and the sorry employments I found for them—scrabbling on all-fours in play with Millish-veg-veen, laughing loud, and barking back at the dog's shrill bark, I could almost weep while here I write to think of the tragic business that was at the same time lying heavy on my spirit. Christmas Day fell while thus I was imprisoned, for near to midnight I heard the church bells ring for Oiel Verree.

When the snow began to melt I saw that the dog put his muzzle to the bottom of the door instantly, and as often as I drove him away he returned to the same place. I will not say what awful thing came to my mind, knowing a dog's nature, and how near to my door lay the body of the witless man; only that I shuddered with a fear that was new to me when I remembered that, by the curse I lived under, the time would come when my unburied bones would lie on the bare face of the moor.

As soon as the snow had melted down to within a foot's depth of the earth I went out of my house and turned toward where my poor neighbor lay; but before I had come close to him I saw that three men were coming over the hillside by way of Port-le-Mary, and, wishing not to be seen by them, I crept back and lay by the hinder wall of my house to watch what they did. Then I saw that they came up to the body of the witless man and saw it, and stood over it some minutes talking earnestly, and then passed along on their way. And as they walked they turned aside and came close up by the front of my house, and looked in at the window, pushing the skin away. Standing by the wall, holding Veg-veen by the throat lest he should betray me, I heard some words the men said each to the other before they went on again.

"Well, man, he's dead at last, poor craythur," said one, "and good-luck too."

And the other answered, "Aw, dear, to think, to think! No man alive could stand up agen it. Aw, ter'ble, ter'ble!"

"I was at the Tynwald myself yander day," said the first, "and I'll give it a year, I was saying, to finish him, and behould ye, he's lying dead in half the time."

Then both together said, "God bless me!" and passed on.

At that moment my eyes became dim, and a sound as of running water went through my ears. I staggered into my house, and sat down by the cold hearth, for in my eagerness to go forth on my errand at first awakening, no fire had I kindled. I recalled the words that the men had spoken, and repeated them aloud one by one, and very slowly, that I might be sure I took their meaning rightly. This done, I said with myself, "This error will go far, until the wide island will say that he who was cut off, he who is nameless among men, is dead." Dead? What then? I had heard that when death came and took away a bad man, its twin-angel, the angel of mercy, bent over those who were left behind on the earth, and drew out of their softened hearts all evil reports and all uncharity.

And a great awe slid over me at that thought, and the gracious dew of a strange peace fell upon me. But close behind it came the other thought, that this error would reach my father also—God preserve him!—and Mona—God's holy grace be with her!—and bring them pain. And then it came to me to think that when men said in their hearing, "He whom you wot of is newly dead," they would take heart and answer, "No, he died long ago; it was only his misery and God's wrath that died yesterday."

With this thought I rose up and went out, and put some shovels of earth over the body of my poor neighbor, that his face might be hidden from the sky.

CHAPTER XLI
OF HOW HE KEPT HIS MANHOOD

The great snow lay long on the mountains, and died off in its silence like one who passes away in sleep. And the spring came, the summer and the winter yet again, and to set down in this writing all that befell would be a weariness, for I feel as I write that the pulse of my life is low; and neither am I one who can paint his words with wit. My way of life has now grown straight and even, and at my simple employments I wrought early and late, that by much bodily toil I might keep in check the distempers of my mind.

With my fishing-boat, my gun, which I had left behind me of design, had been carried to the bottom of the sound, and when the hulk of the lugger drifted up with the tide the gun was no longer within her. This I took for a direction to me that I should hunt no more. Nevertheless, for some while I went on to fish with a line from my small-boat, which, being on the beach, the storm had spared. But soon it was gotten into my head that, if to shoot a hare was an ill deed, to take a cod was but a poor business. Well I knew that there was some touch of insanity in such fancies, and that for man to kill and eat was the law of life, and the rather because it was enjoined of God that so he should do. But being a man like as I was, cut off from the land of the living, never more to have footing there for the great crime committed of spilling blood, I think it was not an ungentle madness that made me fear to take life, whether wantonly or of hunger's need. This dread lay close to me, and got to extremities whereat one of healthy mind might smile. For, being awakened some nights in succession by the nibble of a mouse, I arose from my bed in the dawn, and saw the wee mite, and struck it with an iron rod and killed it, and then suffered many foolish twitches, not from pity for the mouse, for of humanity I had none left, but from the sudden thought that the spirit of its life, which I had driven from its harmless body, was now about me as an invisible thing. Though I had fallen into such a weakness, yet I think that where choice was none for one like me between the weakness of a man and the strength of a beast, I did least injury to my own nature and disposition by yielding with childish indulgence toward the gentler side.

And truly, it is a beautiful thing to mark how the creatures of earth and air will answer with confidence to man's tenderness, whether, as with my saintly father, it comes of the love of them, or, as with me, of the love of myself. The sea-fowl flew in at my door and pecked up the morsels that fell at my feet; the wild duck on the moor would not rise though I walked within a stride of it; a fat hare nested in a hole under my house and came out at dusk to nibble the parings of potatoes that I threw at the door, and, but for Millish-veg-veen and his sly treacheries, with the rabbits of the Black Head I might have sported as with a kitten.

I could fill this account with the shifts I was put to by want of many things that even a lone man may need for his comfort or his cheer. Thus, I was at pains to devise a substitute for tinder, having lost much of all I had in the wrecking of my boat; and to find leather for the soles of my shoes when they were worn to the welt was long a search.

Yet herein my case was but that of many another man who has told of his privation, and the less painful was my position for that I had much to begin my battle of life with. In this first year of my unblessed condition my senses not only recovered their wonted strength, but grew keener than before my cutting off. Oft did my body seem to act without help of my intelligence, and, with a mind on other matters, I would find my way over the trackless moor back to my home in the pitch of darkness, and never so much as stumble by a stone. When the wind was from the north, or when the air lay still, I could hear the church bells that rang in the market square at Castletown, and thereby I knew what the day of the week was. None came nigh to my dwelling, but if a man passed it by at the space of two furlongs, I seemed to feel his tread on the turf.

And now, as I hold the pen for these writings, my hand is loth and my spirit is not fain to tell of the strange humors of these times. So ridiculous and yet so tragic do they look as they come back to me in the grave clothes of memory, that my imagination, being no longer turned wayward, shrinks from them as sorry things that none shall see to be of nature save he who has lived in an outcast state. But if the eyes I look for should ever read these lines, the tender soul behind them will bring me no laughter for my pains, and I ask no tears. Only for my weakness let it be remembered that the terror of my life was, that the spirit of madness and of the beast of the field waited and watched to fall upon me and to destroy the spirit of the man within me.

It is not to be expressed with what eagerness I strove to live in my solitude as a man should live in the company of his fellows. Down to the pettiest detail of personal manners, I tried to do as other men must be doing. Whatsoever seemed to be the habit of a Christian man that I practised, and (though all alone and having no man's eye to see me) with a grim and awesome earnestness. Thus before food, I not only washed but dressed afresh, taking off the sea-boots or the curranes I worked in, and putting on my shoes with silver buckles. My seaman's jacket I removed for a long coat of blue, and I was careful that my shirt was spotless. In this wise I also never failed to attire myself in the evening of the day for the short hours of rest between my work and my bed. That my cheeks should be kept clean of hair, and that the hair of my head should never outgrow itself, was a constant care, for I stood in fear of the creeping consciousness which my face in the glass might bring me, that I was other than other men. But I am loth to set down my little foolish formalities on sitting to meat and rising from it, and the silly ceremonies wherewith I indulged myself at going abroad and coming home. Inexpressibly comic and ridiculous some of them would seem to me now, but for the tragic meaning that in my terror underlay them. And remembering how much a defaulter I had been in all such courtesies of life when most they were called for, I could almost laugh to think how scrupulous I was in their observance when I was quite alone, with never an eye to see me, what I did or how I was clad, or in what sorry fashion I in my solitude acquitted myself like a man.

But though I could be well disposed to laugh at my notions of how to keep my manhood while compelled to live the life of a beast, alone like a wolf and useless for any purposes of man or the world, it is not with laughter that I recall another form of the insanity that in these times possessed me. This was the conviction that I was visited by Ewan, Mona, and my father. Madness, I call it, but never did my pulse beat more temperately or my brain seem clearer than when conscious of these visitations. If I had spent the long day delving, or gathering limestone on the beach of the sound, and returned to my house at twilight, I would perhaps be suddenly aware as I lifted the latch—having thought only of my work until then—that within my kitchen these three sat together, and that they turned their eyes to me as I entered. Nothing would be more convincing to my intelligence than that I actually saw what I say, and yet I always seemed to know that it was not with my bodily eyes that I was seeing. These indeed were open, and I was broad awake, with plain power of common sight on common things—my stool, my table, the settle I had made myself, and perhaps the fire of turf that burned red on the hearth. But over this bodily vision there was a spiritual vision more stable than that of a dream, more soft and variable than that of material reality, in which I clearly beheld Ewan and Mona and my father, and saw their eyes turned toward me. Madness it may have been, but I could say it at the foot of the White Throne that what I speak of I have seen not once or twice, but many times.

And well I remember how these visitations affected me: first as a terror, for when on a sudden they came to me as I lifted the latch I would shrink back and go away again, and return to my house with trembling; and then as a strange comfort, for they were a sort of silent company in my desolation. More than once, in these days of great loneliness, did I verily believe that I had sat me down in the midst of the three to spend a long hour in thinking of the brave good things that might have been for all of us but for my headstrong passion, helped out by the cruel tangle of our fate.

One thing I noted that even yet seems strange in the hours when my imagination is least given to waywardness. Throughout the period wherein I lived in the boat, and for some time after I removed me to my house, the three I have named seemed to visit me together; but after that I had found my witless neighbor lying dead on the moor, and after that I had heard the converse of the men who mistook his poor body for my own, the visitations of Mona and my father ceased altogether, and Ewan alone did I afterward seem to see. This I pondered long, and at length it fastened on me with a solemn conviction that what I had looked for had come about, and that the error that I was a dead man had reached the ears of my father and of Mona. With Ewan I sat alone when he came to me, and oft did it appear that we were loving company, for in his eyes were looks of deep pity, and I on my part had ceased to rail at the blind passion that had parted us flesh from flesh.

These my writings are not for men who will look at such words as I have here set down with a cold indifference, or my hand would have kept me back from this revelation. But that I saw apparently what I have described is as sure before God as that I was a man cut off from the land of the living.

A more material sequel came of the finding of the body on the moor. I was so closely followed by dread of a time that was coming when I must die, and stretch out my body on the bare ground with no man to give it Christian burial in the earth, that I could take no rest until I had devised a means whereby this terror might not haunt me in my last hours. In front of my house there were, as I have said, the places we call the Chasms, wherein the rock of this hungry coast is honeycombed into a hundred deep gullies by the sea. One of these gullies I descended by means of a cradle of rope swung overthwart a strong log of driftwood, and there I found a long shelf of stone, a deep fissure in the earth, a tomb of shelving rock coated with fungus and mold, whereto no dog could come, and wherein no bird of prey could lift its wing. To this place I resolved that I would descend when the power of life was on the point of ebbing away. Having lowered myself by my cradle of rope, I meant to draw the cordage after me, and then, being already near my end, to lie down in this close gully under the earth, that was to serve me for grave and death-bed.

But I was still a strong man, and, ungracious as my condition was, I shrank from the thought of death, and did what I could to put by the fear of it. Never a day did I fail to walk to the crest of the rising ground behind me and look down to where in the valley lay the habitations of men. Life, life, life, was now the constant cry of the voice of my heart, and a right goodly thing it seemed to me to be alive, though I might be said not to live, but only to exist.

Whether, from the day whereon I heard the converse of the two men who went by my house, I was ever seen of any man for a twelvemonth or more, I scarce can tell. Great was my care to keep out of the ways wherein even the shepherds walked, and never a foot seemed to come within two furlongs of these abandoned parts from the bleak Black Head to the margin of the sound. But it happened, upon a day toward winter, beginning the second year since my cutting off, that I turned toward Port-le-Mary, and walking on with absent mind, came nearer than I had purposed to the village over the Kallow Point. There I was suddenly encountered by four or five men who, much in liquor, were playing at leap-frog among the gorse. English seamen they seemed to be, and perhaps from the brig that some time before I had noted where she lay anchored to the lee of the Carrick Rock, in the Poolvash below. At sight of them I was for turning quickly aside, but they raised such a cry and shot out such a volley of levities and blasphemies that, try how I would to go on, I could not but stop on the instant and turn my face to them.

Then I saw that of me the men took no note whatever, and that all their eyes were on my dog Millish-veg-veen, who was with me, and was now creeping between my feet with his stump of a tail under his belly, and his little cunning face full of terror. "Why, here's the dog that killed our monkey," said one, and another shouted, "It's my old cur, sure enough," and a third laughed and said he had kept a rod in pickle for more than a year, and the first cried again, "I'll teach the beast to kill no more Jackeys." Then, before I was yet fully conscious of what was being done, one of the brawny swaggerers made toward us, and kicked at the dog with the fierce lunge of a heavy seaman's boot. The dog yelped and would have made off, but another of the blusterers kicked him back, and then a third kicked him, and whatever way he tried to escape between them, one of them lifted his foot and kicked again.

While they were doing this I felt myself struggling to cry out to them to stop, but not a syllable could I utter, and, like a man paralyzed, I stood stock-still, and did nothing to save my housemate and only companion in life. At length one of the men, laughing a great roistering laugh, stooped and seized the dog by the nape of the neck and swung him round in the air. Then I saw the poor cur's piteous look toward me, and heard its bitter cry; but at the next instant it was flying ten feet above our heads, and when it fell to the ground it was killed on the instant.

At that sight I heard an awful groan burst from my mouth, and I saw a cloud of fire flash before my eyes. When next I knew what I was doing I was holding one of the men by a fierce grip about the waist, and was swinging him high above my shoulders.

Now, if the good God had not given me back my consciousness at that moment, I know full well that at the next he who was then in my power would have drawn no more the breath of a living man. But I felt on a sudden the same ghostly hand upon me that I have written of before, and heard the same ghostly voice in mine ear. So, dropping the man gently to his feet, as gently as a mother might slip her babe to its cot, I lifted up my poor mangled beast by its hinder legs and turned away with it. And as I went the other men fell apart from me with looks of terror, for they saw that God had willed it that, with an awful strength, should I, a man of great passions, go through life in peril.

When I had found coolness to think of this that had happened, I mourned for the loss of the only companion that had ever shared with me my desolate state; but more than my grief for the dog was my fear for myself, remembering with horror that when I would have called on the men to desist I could not utter one word. Truly, it may have been the swift access of anger that then tied my tongue, but I could not question that my sudden speechlessness told me I was losing the faculty of speech. This conclusion fastened upon me with great pain, and I saw that for a twelvemonth or more I had been zealously preserving the minor qualities of humanity, while this its greatest faculty, speech, that distinguishes man from the brute, had been silently slipping from me. Preserve my power of speech also I resolved I would, and though an evil spirit within me seemed to make a mock at me, and to say, "Wherefore this anxiety to keep your speech, seeing that you will never require it, being a man cut off forever from all intercourse with other men?" yet I held to my purpose.

Then I asked myself how I was to preserve my speech, save by much and frequent speaking, and how I was to speak, having none—not even my dog now—to speak to. For, to speak constantly with myself was a practise I shrank from as leading perchance to madness, since I had noted that men of broken wit were much given to mumbling vain words to themselves. At last

I concluded that there was but one way for me, and that was to pray. Having lighted on this thought I had still some misgivings, for the evil spirit within me again made a mock at me, asking why I should speak to God, being a man outside God's grace, and why I should waste myself in the misspent desire of prayer, seeing that the Heavenly Majesty had set His face from me in rejecting the atonement of my life, which I had offered for my crime. But after great inward strivings I came back to my old form of selfishness, and was convinced that, though when I prayed God would not hear me, yet that the yearning and uplooking of prayer might be a good thing for the spiritual part of my nature as a man—for when was the beast known to pray?

At this I tried to recall a few good words such as my father used, and at length, after much beating of the wings of my memory, I remembered some that were the words of Bishop Jeremy Taylor, and did betake myself to prayer in this manner: "O most gracious God, I tremble to come into Thy presence, so polluted and dishonored as I am by my foul stain of sin which I have contracted; but I must come or I perish. I am useless to any purposes of God and man, and, like one that is dead, unconcerned in the changes and necessities of the world, living only to spend my time, and, like a vermin, eat of the fruits of the earth. O my God, I can not help it now; miserable man that I am, to reduce myself to so sad a state that I neither am worthy to come to Thee nor dare I stay from Thee. The greatness of my crime brings me to my remedy; and now I humbly pray Thee to be merciful to my sin, for it is great."

And this prayer I spoke aloud twice daily thenceforward, at the rising and the setting of the sun, going out of my house and kneeling on the turf on the top of the Black Head. And when I had prayed I sang what I could remember of the psalm that runs, "It is good for me that I have been in trouble, that I may learn Thy statutes."

In my mind's eye I see myself, a solitary man in that lone place, with the sea stretching wide below me, and only the sound of its heavy beat on the rocks rising over me in the quiet air.

CHAPTER XLII
OF THE BREAKING OF THE CURSE

Thus far have I written these four days past, amid pain and the quick lessening of the powers of life. In sleepless hours of the night I have made this writing, sitting oftenest by the light of my feeble candles until the day has been blue over the sea. And now that I glance back and see my own heart in the mirror I have made for it, I am like to one who has been brought through a fearsome sickness, that has left its marks upon him, to look for the first time at his altered face in the glass. And can it be that I, who have penned these words, am the man of seven years ago? Ah, now I see how profound has been the change that my great punishment has made in me, and perceive the end of God in refusing my poor atonement of life for life, and cutting me off from among men.

I will not say that what I have already written has not cost me some pangs, and perhaps some tears. But now I am come to that place where I must tell of the great turning-point in my sad state, and though the strength fails me wherewith I hold the pen to write of it, my spirit rises before it like as the lark awakened by the dawn.

This year—surely the darkest within the memory of our poor people of Man—began with more than its share of a winter of heavy rains. The spring that followed was also rainy, and when I looked for the summer to begin, the rains were still incessant. Heavy and sodden was the ground even of the moor whereon I lived, so that my feet sank into it as into a morass, and much of the seed I sowed was washed from it and wasted. When at length the long rains ceased to fall the year was far worn into June, and then the sun came quick and hot. My house stood on a brow descending to the cliffs of the coast, and beneath me were less than two feet of mold above the rock; but when the great heat came after the great rain, out of the ground there arose a thick miasmic mist that filled the air, obscured the light, lay heavy in sweat upon my hair and flesh, and made the walls and floor, the furniture, and the bed of my home, damp and dripping with constant dew.

Quickly I set myself to the digging of deep trenches that went vertically down the brow to the cliff head, and soon the ground about me across many acres was drained dry. But though I lived in a clear air, and could now see the sun as well as feel it, yet I perceived that the mists stood in a wide half-circle around me like walls of rain seen afar, while the spot whereon you stand is fair and in the sunshine. In my daily walks to the top of the moor I could no longer see the houses of Cregneesh for the cloud of vapor that lay over it, and when I walked to the Kallow Head for the first time since the day I lost my dog, the basin below, where Port-le-Mary stands, was even as a vast vaporous sea, without one islet of house or hill.

My health suffered little from this unaccustomed humidity, for my bodily strength was ever wonderful; but my spirits sank to a deep depression, and oft did I wonder how the poor souls must fare who lived on the low, wet Curraghs near to where my own home once lay. From day to day, and week to week, the mist continued to rise from the dank ground under the hot sun, and still the earth came up in thick clods to the spade.

The nights alone were clear, and toward midsummer I was witness to strange sights in the heavens. Thus I saw a comet pass close across the island from coast to coast, with a visible motion as of quivering flame. What this visitation could foretell I pondered long and sadly, and much I hungered for knowledge of what was being done in the world of men. But therein it seemed to my wayward mind that I was like a man buried in the churchyard while he is yet alive, who hears the bell in the tower that peals and tolls, but has no window in his tomb from which to see who comes to rejoice, and who to mourn.

When the fleet of fishing-boats should have put out from Port Erin for the ground that lies south of the Calf, scarce a sail could I see, and not a boat had I noted coming from the Poolvash, where Port-le-Mary stands above the bay. From the top of the Mull Hills I could faintly descry the road to Castletown, but never a cart on market-day seemed to pass over it. Groups of people I vaguely saw standing together, and once, at midday, from the middle of a field of new-mown hay, there came to me the sounds of singing and prayer. Oftener than at any period during my solitary life, I saw men on the mountains or felt their presence near me, for my senses were grown very keen. Oftener, also, than ever before, the sound of church bells seemed to come through the air. And going to the beach where my shattered boat lay, I one day came upon another boat beating idly down the waters of the sound, her sails flapping in the wind, and no hand at her tiller. I stood to watch while the little craft came drifting on with the flow of the tide. She ran head on to the cliff at Fistard, and then I went down to her, and found never a living soul aboard of her.

From these and other startling occurrences that came to me vaguely, as if by the one sense of the buried man, I felt that with the poor people of this island all was not well. But nothing did I know of a certainty until a day toward the first week of September—as I have reckoned it—and then a strange thing befell.

The sun was not shining, and when there was no sun there was little mist. A strong wind, too, had got up from the northeast, and the atmosphere over land and sea grew clearer as the day wore on. The wind strengthened after the turn of the ebb, and at half-flood, which was toward three in the afternoon, it had risen to the pitch of a gale, with heavy swirling rain. The rain ceased in a few hours, and in the lift of the heavy clouds I could see from the rising ground above my house a brig with shortened sail toiling heavily to the southwest of the Calf. She was struggling in the strong currents that flow there to get into the lee of the island, but was beaten back and back, never catching the shelter of the cliffs for the rush of the wind that swept over them. The darkness was falling in while I watched her, and when she was swept back and hidden from me by the forehead of the Calf I turned my face homeward. Then I noticed that on the top of the Mull Hills a great company of people had gathered, and I thought I saw that they were watching the brig that was laboring heavily in the sea.

That night I had close employment at my fireside, for I was finishing a coat that I had someways fashioned with my undeft fingers from the best pieces of many garments that of themselves would no longer hold together. Rough as a monk's long sack it was, and all but as shapeless, but nevertheless a fit companion for the curranes on my feet, which I had made some time before from the coat of my hapless Millish-veg-veen.

While I wrought with my great sail-maker's needle and twine, the loud wind moaned about the walls of my house and whistled through its many crevices, and made the candle whereby I worked to flicker and gutter. Yet my mind was more cheerful than had lately been its wont, and I sang to myself with my face to the glow of the fire.

But when toward ten o'clock the sea below sent up a louder hiss than before, followed by a deeper undergroan, suddenly there was a clash at my window, and a poor, panting sea-mew, with open beak, came through it and fell helpless on the floor. I picked up the storm-beaten creature and calmed it, and patched with the needle the skin of the window which it had broken by its entrance.

Then all at once my mind went back to the brig laboring in the sea behind the Calf. Almost at the same moment, and for the first time these seven years, a quick knock came to my door. I was startled, and made no answer, but stood stock-still in the middle of the floor with the frightened bird in my hand. Before I was yet fully conscious of what was happening, the wooden latch of the door had been lifted, and a man had stepped across the threshold. In another moment he had closed the door behind him, and was speaking to me.

"You will never find heart to deny me shelter on such a night as this?" he said.

I answered him nothing. Surely with my mind I did not hear him, but only with mine ears. I was like the one who is awakened suddenly out of a long dream, and can scarce be sure which is the dream and which the reality, what is behind and what is before.

The man stumbled a step forward, and said, speaking falteringly, "I am faint from a blow."

He staggered another pace forward, and would have fallen, but I, recovering in some measure my self-command, caught him in my arms, and put him to sit on the settle before the hearth.

Scarce had he gained this rest when his eyelids trembled and closed, and he became insensible. He was a large, swart, and bony man, bearing in his face the marks of life's hard storms. His dress was plainly the dress of a priest, but of an order of priesthood quite unknown to me. A proud poverty sat upon the man, and before I yet knew wherefor, my heart went out to him in a strange, uncertain reverence.

Loosening the hard collar that bound his neck, I made bare his throat, and then moistened his lips with water. Some other offices I did for him, such as with difficulty removing his great boots, which were full of water, and stretching his feet toward the fire. I stirred the peats, too, and the glow was full and grateful. Then I looked for the mark of the blow he spoke of, and found it where most it was to be feared, on the hinder part of the head. Though there was no blood flowing, yet was the skull driven in upon the brain, leaving a hollow spot over a space that might have been covered by a copper token.

He did not soon return to consciousness, but toiled hard at intervals to regain it, and then lapsed back to a breathless quiet. And I, not knowing what else to do, took a basin of water, lukewarm, and bathed the wound with it, damping the forehead with water that was cold. All this time the sea-mew, which I had cast from my hand when the priest stumbled, lay in one corner panting, its head down, its tail up, and its powerless wings stretched useless on either side.

Then the man, taking a long breath, opened his eyes, and seeing me he made some tender of gratitude. He told me that in being put ashore out of the brig "Bridget," from Cork, in Ireland, he had been struck on the head by the boom as it shifted with the wind, but that heeding not his injury, and thinking he could make Port-le-Mary to lie there that night, he had set out over the moor, while his late comrades of the brig put off from our perilous coast for England, whither they were bound.

So much had he said, speaking painfully, when again he fell in unconsciousness, and this time a strong delirium took hold of him. I tried not to hear what then he said, for it seemed to me an awful thing that in such an hour of reason's vanquishment the eye of man might look into the heart, which only God's eye should see. But hear him I must, or leave him alone in his present need. And he talked loudly of some great outrage wherein helpless women were thrown on the roads without shelter, and even the dead in their graves were desecrated. When he came to himself again he knew that his mind had wandered, and he told me that four years before he had been confessor at the convent of Port Royal in France. He said that in that place they had been men and women of the Order of Jansenists, teaching simple goodness and piety. But their convent had been suppressed by commission of the Jesuits, and being banished from France, he had fled to his native country of Ireland, where now he held the place of parish priest. More in this manner he said, but my mind was sorely perplexed, and I cannot recall his words faithfully, or rightly tell of the commerce of conversation between us, save that he put to me some broken questions in his moments of ease from pain, and muttered many times to himself after I had answered him briefly, or when I had answered him not at all.

For the sense that I was a man awakening out of a dream, a long dream of seven lonesome years, grew stronger as he told of what traffic the world had lately seen, and he himself been witness to. And my old creeping terror of the judgment upon me that forbade that any man should speak with me, or that I should speak with any man, struggled hard with the necessity now before me to make a swift choice whether I should turn away and leave this man, who had sought the shelter of my house, or break through the curse that bound me.

Choice of any kind I did not make with a conscious mind, but before I was yet aware I was talking with the priest, and he with me.

The Priest: He said, I am the Catholic priest that your good Bishop sent for out of Ireland, as you have heard I doubt not?

Myself: I answered No, that I had not heard.

The Priest: He asked me, did I live alone in this house, and how long I had been here?

Myself: I said, Yes, and that I had been seven years in this place come Christmas.

The Priest: He asked, What, and do you never go up to the towns?

Myself: I answered, No.

The Priest: Then, said the priest, thinking long before he spoke, you have not heard of the great sickness that has broken out among your people.

Myself: I told him I had heard nothing.

The Priest: He said it was the sweating sickness, and that vast numbers had fallen to it and many had died. I think he said—I can not be sure—that after fruitless efforts of his own to combat the disease, the Bishop of the island had sent to Ireland a message for him, having heard that the Almighty had blessed his efforts in a like terrible scourge that broke out two years before over the bogs of Western Ireland.

I listened with fear, and began to comprehend much that had of late been a puzzle to me. But before the priest had gone far his sickness overcame him afresh, and he fell in another long unconsciousness. While he lay thus, very silent or rambling afresh through the ways of the past, I know not what feelings possessed me, for my heart was in a great turmoil. But when he opened his eyes again, very peaceful in their quiet light, but with less than before of the power of life in them, he said he perceived that his errand had been fruitless, and that he had but come to my house to die. At that word I started to my feet with a cry, but he—thinking that my thoughts were of our poor people, who would lose a deliverer by his death—told me to have patience, for that God who had smitten him down would surely raise up in his stead a far mightier savior of my afflicted countrymen.

Then in the lapses of his pain he talked of the sickness that had befallen his own people; how it was due to long rains that soaked the soil, and was followed by the hot sun that drew out of the earth its foul sweat; how the sickness fell chiefly on such as had their houses on bogs and low-lying ground; and how the cure for it was to keep the body of the sick person closely wrapped in blankets, and to dry the air about him with many fires. He told me, too, that all medicines he had yet seen given for this disease were useless, and being oftenest of a cooling nature were sometimes deadly. He said that those of his own people who had lived on the mountains had escaped the malady. Much he also said of how men had fled from their wives, and women from their children in terror of the infection, but that, save only in the worst cases, contagion from the sweating sickness there could be none. More of this sort he said than I can well set down in this writing. Often he spoke with sore labor, as though a strong impulse prompted him. And I who listened eagerly heard what he said with a mighty fear, for well

I knew that if death came to him as he foretold, I had now that knowledge which it must be sin to hide.

After he had said this the lapses into unconsciousness were more frequent than before, and the intervals of cool reason and sweet respite from pain were briefer. But a short while after midnight he came to himself with a smile on his meagre face and peace in his eyes. He asked me would I promise to do one thing for him, for that he was a dying man; and I told him yes, before I had heard what it was that he wished of me. Then he asked did I know where the Bishop lived, and at first I made no answer.

Bishop's Court they call his house, he said, and it lies to the northwest of this island by the land they have named the Curraghs. Do you know it?

I bent my head by way of assent.

The Priest: I would have you to go to him, he said, and say—The Catholic priest you sent for out of Ireland, Father Dalby, fulfilled his pledge to you and came to your island, but died by the visitation of God on the night of his landing on your shores. Will you deliver me this message?

I did not make him an answer, and he put the question again. Still my tongue clave to the roof of my mouth and I could not speak.

The Priest: You need not fear, he said, to go to the Bishop, for he is a holy man, as I have heard, without pride of worldly place, and the poor and outcast are his constant guests.

Even yet I answered nothing, but only held down my head while my heart surged within me.

The Priest: The fame of him as a righteous servant of God had gone far into other lands, and therefore it was I, who love Protestantism not at all, and hold no dalliance with it, came to your island at his call.

He took my hand in his hands and asked me again if I would go to the Bishop to say the words which he had given me, and I, with swimming eyes that saw nothing of the dying face before me, bowed my head, and answered, I will go.

Near three hours longer he lived, and much of that time he passed in a feeble delirium. But just before the end came he awoke, and motioned to a small bag that hung about his waist. I guessed his meaning, and drawing out a crucifix I placed it in his hands.

Then he passed silently away, and Death, the black camel that had knelt at the gate of my lone house these seven years of death-in-life, had entered it at last to take another man than me.

CHAPTER XLIII
OF HIS GREAT RESOLVE

When he had ceased to breathe, the air of my house became suddenly void and empty. With a great awe upon me I rose and stretched him out on the settle, and covered his white face with a cloth. Then in the silence I sat and tried to think of the strange accident that had that night befallen. One thing I saw with a fearful certainty, that a great burden of responsibility had fallen upon me. I thought of the people of this island perishing in their sickness, and I remembered that I alone of all men here knew how to succor and save them. I alone, and who was I? The one man accursed among men; the one man cut off forever from the company of the living; the man without family or kin or name among the people; whose flesh no man might touch with his flesh; whose eye no other eye might look upon.

And thus with the burden of responsibility came a yet more terrible burden of doubt. Was it for me to break through the dread judgment pronounced upon me, and go down among the people to heal them? And if I went would the people receive me, even in this their last extreme? Before the face of death would all other fears sink out of their sight? Or, fearing death itself less than the curse, would they rise up and drive me from them?

Long I sat in the anguish of black misgivings, and then rose and ranged my room from side to side, if perchance I might find some light in my darkness. And oft did the strangeness of that night's accidents so far bewilder me that for an instant it would seem that I must be in a dream. Once I lifted the face-cloth from the face on the settle that I might be sure that I was awake.

At length it fixed itself on my mind that whatsoever the judgment upon me, and whatsoever the people's terror of it, I had no choice but to bear the burden that was now mine own. Go down among my sick countrymen I should and must, let the end be what it would! Accursed man though I was, yet to fulfil the dead priest's mission was a mission wherewith God Himself seemed to charge me!

And now I scarce can say how it escaped me that my first duty was to take the body of the priest who had died in my house to one of the churchyards for Christian burial. There must have been some end of Providence in my strange forgetfulness, for if this thing had but come into my wild thoughts, and I had indeed done what it was fitting that I should do, then must certain wonderful consequences have fallen short of the blessing with which God has blessed them.

What I did, thinking no evil, was to pick up my spade and go out on the moor and delve for the dead man a shallow grave. As I turned to the door I stumbled over something that lay on the floor. Stooping to look at it, I found it to be the poor sea-mew. It was dead and stiff, and had still its wings outstretched as if in the act of flight.

I had not noted until now, when with a fearful glance backward I stepped out into the night, that the storm had gone. A thick dew-cloud lay deep over the land, and the round moon was shining through it. I chose a spot a little to the south of the stone circle on the Black Head, and there by the moon's light I howket a barrow of earth. The better part of an hour I wrought, and when my work was done I went back to my house, and then the dead man was cold. I took a piece of old canvas, and put it about the body, from head to feet, wrapping it over the clothes, and covering the face. This done, I lifted the dead in my arms and carried it out.

Very hollow and heavy was the thud of my feet on the turf in that uncertain light. As I toiled along I recalled the promise that I had given to the priest to see my father and speak with him. This memory brought me the sore pain of a wounded tenderness, but it strengthened my resolve. When I had reached the grave which I had made the night was near to morning, the dew-cloud had lifted away, and out of the unseen, murmuring sea that lay far and wide in front of me a gray streak, like an arrow's barb, was shooting up into the darkness of the sky.

One glance more I took at the dead man's face in that vague foredawn, and its swart meagreness seemed to have passed off under death's composing hand.

I covered the body with the earth, and then I said my prayer, for it was nigh to my accustomed hour. Also I sang my psalm, kneeling with my face toward the sea. And while I sang in that dank air the sky lightened and the sun rose out of the deep.

I know not what touched me then, if it was not the finger of God Himself; but suddenly a great burden seemed to fall from me, and my heart grew full of a blessed joy. And, O Father, I cried, I am delivered from the body of the death I lived in! I have lived, I have died, and I live again!

I saw apparently that the night of my long imprisonment was past, that the doors of my dungeon were broken open, and that its air was to be the breath of my nostrils no more.

Then the tears gushed from mine eyes and rained down my bony cheeks, for well I knew that God had seen that I, even I, had suffered enough.

And when I rose to my feet from beside the dead man's grave I felt of a certainty that the curse had fallen away.

His Last Words

Three days have gone since last I put my hand to this writing, and now I know that though the curse has fallen from me yet must its earthly penalties be mine to the end. Sorely weary, and more sorely ashamed, I have, within these three hours past, escaped from the tumult of the people. How their wild huzzas ring in my ears! "God bless the priest!" "Heaven save the priest!" Their loud cries of a blind gratitude, how they follow me! Oh, that I could fly from the memory of them, and wipe them out of my mind! There were those that appeared to know me among the many that knew me not. The tear-stained faces, the faces hard and stony, the faces abashed and confused—how they live before my eyes! And at the Tynwald, how the children were thrust under my hand for my blessing! My blessing—mine! and at the Tynwald! Thank God, it is all over! I am away from it forever. Home I am at last, and for the last time.

Better than three weeks have passed since the priest died in my house and I buried him on the moor. What strange events have since befallen, and in what a strange, new world! The Deemster's terrible end, and my own going with the priest's message to the Bishop, my father. But I shall not live to set it down. Nor is it needful so to do, for she whom I write for knows all that should be written henceforward. Everything she knows save one thing only, and if this writing should yet come to her hand that also she will then learn.

God's holy grace be with her! I have not seen her. The Deemster I have seen, the Bishop I have spoken with, and a living vision of our Ewan, his sweet child-daughter, have I held to my knee. But not once these many days has she who is dearest of all to me passed before my eyes. It is better so. I shunned her. Where she was, there I would not go. Yet, through all these heavy years I have borne her upon my heart. Day and night she has been with me. Oh, Mona, Mona, my Mona, apart forever are our paths in this dim world, and my tarnished name is your reproach. My love, my lost love, as a man I yearned for you to hold you to my breast. But I was dead to you, and I would not break in with an earthly love that must be brief and might not be blessed on a memory that death has purified of its stains. Adieu, adieu, my love, my own Mona; though we are never to clasp hands again, yet do I know that you will be with me as an unseen presence when the hour comes—ah! how soon—of death's asundering.

For the power of life is low in me. I have taken the sickness. It is from the Deemster that I have taken it. No longer do I fear death. Yet I hesitate to do with myself what I have long thought that I would do when the end should come. "To-morrow," and "to-morrow," and "to-morrow," I say in my heart, and still I am here.

CHAPTER XLIV
THE SWEATING SICKNESS

I

When the sweating sickness first appeared in the island it carried off the lone body known as Auntie Nan, who had lived on the Curragh. "Death never came without an excuse—the woman was old," the people said, and went their way. But presently a bright young girl who had taken herbs and broths and odd comforts to Auntie Nan while she lay helpless was stricken down. Then the people began to hold their heads together. Four days after the girl was laid to rest her mother died suddenly, and two or three days after the mother's death the father was smitten. Then three other children died in quick succession, and in less than three weeks not a soul of that household was left alive. This was on the southwest of the Curragh, and on the north of it, near to the church of Andreas, a similar outbreak occurred about the same time. Two old people named Creer were the first to be taken; and a child at Cregan's farm and a servant at the rectory of the Archdeacon followed quickly.

The truth had now dawned upon the people, and they went about with white faces. It was the time of the hay harvest, and during the two hours' rest for the midday meal the haymakers gathered together in the fields for prayer. At night, when work was done, they met again in the streets of the villages to call on God to avert his threatened judgment. On Sundays they thronged the churches at morning and afternoon services, and in the evening they congregated on the shore to hear the Quaker preachers, who went about, under the shadow of the terror, without hindrance or prosecution. One such preacher, a town-watch at Castletown, known as Billy-by-Nite, threw up his calling, and traveled the country in the cart of a carrier, prophesying a visitation of God's wrath, wherein the houses should be laid waste and the land be left utterly desolate.

The sickness spread rapidly, and passed from the Curraghs to the country south and east of them. Not by ones but tens were the dead now counted day after day, and the terror spread yet faster than the malady. The herring season had run a month only, and it was brought to a swift close. Men who came in from the boats after no more than a night's absence were afraid to go up to their homes lest the sickness had gone up before them. Then they went out to sea no longer, but rambled for herbs in the rank places where herbs grew, and, finding them, good and bad, fit and unfit, they boiled and ate them.

Still the sickness spread, and the dead were now counted in hundreds. Of doctors there were but two in the island, and these two were closely engaged sitting by the bedsides of the richer folk, feeling the pulse with one hand and holding the watch with the other. Better service they did not do, for rich and poor alike fell before the sickness.

The people turned to the clergy, and got "beautiful texes," but no cure. They went to the old Bishop, and prayed for the same help that he had given them in the old days of their great need. He tried to save them and failed. A preparation of laudanum, which had served him in good stead for the flux, produced no effect on the sweating sickness. With other and other medicines he tried and tried again. His old head was held very low. "My poor people," he said, with a look of shame, "I fear that by reason of the sins of me and mine the Spirit of the Lord is gone from me."

Then the people set up a cry as bitter as that which was wrung from them long before when they were in the grip of their hunger. "The Sweat is on us," they groaned; and the old Bishop, that he might not hear their voice of reproach, shut himself up from them like a servant whom the Lord had forsaken.

Then terror spread like a fire, but terror in some minds begets a kind of courage, and soon there were those who would no longer join the prayer-meetings in the hay-fields or listen to the preaching on the shore. One of these was a woman of middle life, an idle slattern, who had for six or seven years lived a wandering life. While others prayed she laughed mockingly and protested that for the Sweat as well as for every other scare of life there was no better preventive than to think nothing about it. She carried out her precept by spending her days in the inns, and her nights on the roads, being supported in her dissolute existence by secret means, whereof gossip spoke frequently. The terrified world about her, busy with its loud prayers, took small heed of her blasphemies until the numbers of the slain had risen from hundreds to thousands. Then in their frenzy the people were carried away by superstition, and heard in the woman's laughter the ring of the devil's own ridicule. Somebody chanced to see her early one morning drawing water to bathe her hot forehead, and before night of that day the evil word had passed from mouth to mouth that it was she who had brought the sweating sickness by poisoning the wells.

Thereupon half a hundred lusty fellows, with fear in their wild eyes, gathered in the street, and set out to search for the woman. In her accustomed haunt, the "Three Legs of Man," they found her, and she was heavy with drink. They hounded her out of the inn into the road, and there, amid oaths and curses, they tossed her from hand to hand until her dress was in rags, her face and arms were bleeding, and she was screaming in the great fright that had sobered her.

It was Tuesday night, and the Deemster, who had been holding court at Peeltown late that day, was riding home in the darkness, when he heard this tumult in the road in front of him. Putting spurs to his horse, he came upon the scene of it. Before he had gathered the meaning of what was proceeding in the dark road, the woman had broken from her tormentors and thrown herself before him, crawling on the ground and gripping his foot in the stirrup.

"Deemster, save me! save me, Deemster!" she cried in her frantic terror.

The men gathered round and told their story. The woman had poisoned the wells, and the bad water had brought the Sweat. She was a charmer by common report, and should be driven out of the island.

"What pedler's French is this?" said the Deemster, turning hotly on the crowd about him. "Men, men, what forgotten age have you stepped out of that you come to me with such driveling, doddering, blank idiocy?"

But the woman, carried away by her terror, and not grasping the Deemster's meaning, cried that if he would but save her she would confess. Yes, she had poisoned the wells. It was true she was a charmer. She acknowledged to the evil eye. But save her, save her, save her, and she would tell all.

The Deemster listened with a feverish impatience. "The woman lies," he said under his breath, and then lifting his voice he asked if any one had a torch. "Who is the woman?" he asked; "I seem to know her voice."

"D—— her, she's a witch," said one of the men, thrusting his hot face forward in the darkness over the woman's cowering body. "Ay, and so was her mother before her," he said again.

"Tell me, woman, what's your name?" said the Deemster, stoutly; but this question seemed to break down as he asked it.

There was a moment's pause.

"Mally Kerruish," the woman answered him, slobbering at his stirrup in the dark road before him.

"Let her go," said the Deemster in a thick underbreath. In another moment he had disengaged his foot from the woman's grasp and was riding away.

That night Mally Kerruish died miserably of her fright in the little tool-shed of a cottage by the Cross Vein, where six years before her mother had dropped to a lingering death alone.

News of her end was taken straightway to Ballamona by one of the many tongues of evil rumor. With Jarvis Kerruish, who was in lace collar and silver-buckled shoes, the Deemster had sat down to supper. He rose, left his meat untouched, and Jarvis supped alone. Late that night he said, uneasily:

"I intend to send in my resignation to Castletown—burden of my office as Deemster is too much for my strength."

"Good," said Jarvis; "and if, sir, you should ever think of resigning the management of your estate also, you know with how much willingness I would undertake it, solely in order that you might spend your days in rest and comfort.

"I have often thought of it latterly," said the Deemster. Half an hour thereafter he spent in an uneasy perambulation of the dining-room while Jarvis picked his teeth and cleaned his nails.

"I think I must surely be growing old," he said then, and, drawing a long breath, he took up his bedroom candle.

II

The sickness increased, the deaths were many in the houses about Ballamona, and in less than a week after the night of Mally Kerruish's death, Thorkell Mylrea, a Deemster no longer, had made over to Jarvis Kerruish all absolute interest in his estates. "I shall spend my last days in the cause of religion," he said. He had paid up his tithe in pound-notes—five years' tithe in arrears, with interest added at the rate of six per cent. Blankets he had ordered for the poor of his own parish, a double blanket for each family, with cloaks for some of the old women.

This done, he relinquished his worldly possessions, and shut himself from the sickness in a back room of Ballamona, admitting none, and never stirring abroad except to go to church.

The Bishop had newly opened the chapel at Bishop's Court for daily prayers, and of all constant worshipers there Thorkell was now the most constant. Every morning his little shriveled figure knelt at the form before the Communion, and from his blanched lips the prayers were mumbled audibly. Much he sought the Bishop's society, and in every foolish trifle he tried to imitate his brother. A new canon of the Church had lately ordered that every Bishop should wear an episcopal wig, and over his flowing white hair the Bishop of Man had perforce to put the grotesque head-covering. Seeing this, Thorkell sent to England for a periwig, and perched the powdered curls on his own bald crown.

The sickness was at its worst, the terror was at its height, and men were flying from their sick families to caves in the mountains, when one day the Bishop announced in church that across in Ireland, as he had heard, there was a good man who had been blessed under God with miraculous powers of curing this awful malady.

"Send for him! send for him!" the people shouted with one voice, little heeding the place they sat in.

"But," said the Bishop, with a failing voice, "the good man is a Roman Catholic—indeed, a Romish priest."

At that word a groan came from the people, for they were Protestants of Protestants.

"Let us not think that no good can come out of Nazareth," the Bishop continued. "And who shall say, though we love the Papacy not at all, but that holy men adhere to it?"

There was a murmur of disapproval.

"My good people," the Bishop went on, falteringly, "we are in God's hands, and his anger burns among us."

The people broke up abruptly, and talking of what the Bishop had said, they shook their heads. But their terror continued, and before its awful power their qualms of faith went down as before a flood. Then they cried, "Send for the priest!" and the Bishop sent for him.

Seven weary days passed, and at length with a brightening countenance the Bishop announced that the priest had answered that he would come. Other three days went by, and the news passed from north to south that in the brig "Bridget of Cork," bound for Whitehaven, with liberty to call at Peeltown, the Romish priest, Father Dalby, had sailed for the Isle of Man.

Then day after day the men went up to the hilltops to catch sight of the sail of an Irish brig. At last they sighted one from the Mull Hills, and she was five leagues south of the Calf. But the wind was high, and the brig labored hard in a heavy sea. Four hours the people watched her, and saw her bearing down into the most dangerous currents about their coast. Night closed in, and the wind rose to the strength of a gale. Next morning at early dawn the people climbed the headlands again, but no brig could they now see, and none had yet made their ports.

"She must be gone down," they told themselves, and so saying they went home with heavy hearts.

But two days afterward there went through the island a thrilling cry, "He is here!—he has come!—the priest!" And at that word a wave of rosy health swept over a thousand haggard faces.

III

In the dark sleeping-room of a little ivy-covered cottage that stood end-on to the highroad through Michael a blind woman lay dying of the sickness. It was old Kerry; and on a three-legged stool before her bed her husband Hommy sat. Pitiful enough was Hommy's poor ugly face. His thick lubber lips were drawn heavily downward, and under his besom brows his little eyes were red and his eyelids swollen. In his hands he held a shovel, and he was using it as a fan to puff air into Kerry's face.

"It's all as one, man," the sick woman moaned. "Ye're only keeping the breath in me. I'm bound to lave ye."

And thereupon Hommy groaned lustily and redoubled his efforts with the shovel. There was a knock at the door, and a lady entered. It was Mona, pale of face, but very beautiful in her pallor, and with an air of restful sadness.

"And how are you now, dear Kerry?" she asked, leaning over the bed.

"Middling badly, mam," Kerry answered feebly. "I'll be took, sarten sure, as the saying is."

"Don't lose heart, Kerry. Have you not heard that the priest is coming?"

"Chut, mam! I'll be gone, plaze God, where none of the like will follow me."

"Hush, Kerry! He was in Patrick yesterday; he will be in German to-morrow, and the next day he will be here in Michael. He is a good man, and is doing wonders with the sick."

Kerry turned face to the wall, and Hommy talked with Mona. What was to become of him when Kerry was gone? Who would be left to give him a bit of a tidy funeral? The Dempster? Bad cess to the like of him. What could be expected from a master who had turned his own daughter out of doors?

"I am better where I am," Mona whispered, and that was her sole answer to the deaf man's too audible questions. And Hommy, after a pause, assented to the statement with his familiar comment, "The Bishop's a rael ould archangel, so he is."

Thereupon Kerry turned her gaze from the wall and said, "Didn't I tell ye, mam, that he wasn't dead?"

"Who?"

"Why—him—him that we mayn't name—*him*."

"Hush, dear Kerry, he died long ago."

"I tell ye, mam, he's a living man, and coming back—I know it—he's coming back immadient—I saw him."

"Drop it, woman, it's drames," said Hommy.

"I saw him last night as plain as plain—wearing a long gray sack and curranes on his feet, and a queer sort of hat."

"It must have been the priest that you saw in your dream, dear Kerry."

The sick woman raised herself on one elbow, and answered eagerly, "I tell you no, mam, but him—*him*."

"Lie still, Kerry; you will be worse if you uncover yourself to the cool air."

There was a moment's quiet, and then the blind woman said finally, "I'm going where I'll have my eyes same as another body."

At that Hommy's rugged face broadened to a look of gruesome sorrow, and he renewed his exertions with the shovel.

IV

At seven o'clock that day the darkness had closed in. A bright turf fire burned in a room in Bishop's Court, and the Bishop sat before it with his slippered feet on a sheepskin rug. His face was mellower than of old, and showed less of strength and more of sadness. Mona stood at a tea-table by his side, cutting slices of bread and butter.

A white face, with eyes of fear, looked in at the dark window. It was Davy Fayle. He was but little older to look upon for the seven years that had gone heavily over his troubled head. His simple look was as vacant and his lagging lip hung as low; but his sluggish intellect had that night become suddenly charged with a ready man's swiftness.

Mona went to the door. "Come in," she said; but Davy would not come. He must speak with her outside, and she went out to him.

He was trembling visibly.

"What is it?" she said.

"Mistress Mona," said Davy, in a voice of great emotion, "it's as true as the living God."

"What?" she said.

"He's alive—ould Kerry said true—he's alive, and coming back."

Mona glanced into his face by the dull light that came through the window. His eyes, usually dull and vacant, were aflame with a strange fire. She laid one hand on the door-jamb, and said, catching her breath, "Davy, remember what the men said long ago—that they saw him lying in the snow."

"He's alive, I'm telling you—I've seen him with my own eyes."

"Where?"

"I went down to Patrick this morning to meet the priest coming up—but it's no priest at all—it's—it's—it's *him*."

Again Mona drew her breath audibly.

"Think what you are saying, Davy. If it should not be true! Oh, if you should be mistaken!"

"It's Bible truth, Mistress Mona—I'll go bail on it afore God A'mighty."

"The priest, you say?"

"Aw, lave it to me to know Mastha—I mean—*him*"

"I must go in, Davy. Good-night to you, and thank you—Good-night, and—" the plaintive tenderness of her voice broke down to a sob. "Oh, what can it all mean?" she exclaimed more vehemently.

Davy turned away. The low moan of the sea came up through the dark night.

V

It happened that after service the next morning the Bishop and Thorkell walked out of the chapel side by side.

"We are old men now, Gilcrist," said Thorkell, "and should be good friends together."

"That is so," the Bishop answered.

"We've both lost a son, and can feel for each other."

The Bishop made no reply.

"We're childless men, in fact."

"There's Mona, God bless her!" the Bishop said, very softly.

"True, true," said Thorkell, and there was silence for a moment.

"It was partly her fault when she left me—partly, I say;—don't you think so, Gilcrist?" said Thorkell, nervously.

"She's a dear, sweet soul," the Bishop said.

"It's true."

They stepped on a few paces, and passed by the spot whereon the two fishermen laid down their dread burden from the Mooragh seven years before. Then Thorkell spoke again and in a feverish voice.

"D'ye know, Gilcrist, I sometimes awake in the night crying 'Ewan! Ewan!'"

The Bishop did not answer, and Thorkell, in another tone, asked when the Irish priest was to reach Michael.

"He may be here to-morrow," the Bishop said.

Thorkell shuddered.

"It must be that God is revenging himself upon us with this fearful scourge."

"It dishonors God to say so," the Bishop replied. "He is calling upon us to repent."

There was another pause, and then Thorkell asked what a man should do to set things right in this world if perchance he had taken a little more in usury than was fair and honest.

"Give back whatever was more than justice," said the Bishop promptly.

"But that is often impossible, Gilcrist."

"If he has robbed the widow, and she is dead, let him repay the fatherless."

"It is impossible—I tell you, Gilcrist, it is impossible—impossible."

As they were entering the house Thorkell asked if there was truth in the rumor that the wells had been charmed.

"To believe such stories is to be drawn off from a trust in God and a dependence on his good providence," said the Bishop.

"But I must say, brother, that strange things are known to happen. Now I myself have witnessed extraordinary fulfilments."

"Superstition is a forsaking of God, whom we have most need to fly to in trouble and distress," the Bishop answered.

"True—very true—I loathe it; but still it's a sort of religion, isn't it, Gilcrist?"

"So the wise man says—as the ape is a sort of a man."

VI

Three days later the word went round that he who had been looked for was come to Michael, and many went out to meet him. He was a stalwart man, straight and tall, bony and muscular. His dress was poverty's own livery: a gray shapeless sack-coat, reaching below his knees, curranes on his feet of untanned skin with open clocks, and a cap of cloth, half helmet and half hood, drawn closely down over his head. His cheeks were shaven and deeply bronzed. The expression of his face was of a strange commingling of strength and tenderness. His gestures were few, slow, and gentle. His measured step was a rhythmic stride—the stride of a man who has learned in the long endurance of solitude to walk alone in the ways of the world. He spoke little, and scarcely answered the questions which were put to him. "Aw, but I seem to have seen the good man in my drames," said one; and some said "Ay" to that, and some laughed at it.

Within six hours of his coming he had set the whole parish to work. Half of the men he sent up into the mountains to cut gorse and drag it down to the Curraghs in piles of ten feet high, tied about with long sheep lankets of twisted straw. The other half he set to dig trenches in the marshy places. He made the women to kindle a turf fire in every room with a chimney-flue, and when night came he had great fires of gorse, peat, withered vegetation, and dried sea-wrack built on the open spaces about the houses in which the sickness had broken out. He seemed neither to rest nor eat. From sick house to sick house, from trench to trench, and fire to fire, he moved on with his strong step. And behind him, at all times, having never a word from him and never a look, but trudging along at his heels like a dog, was the man-lad, Davy Fayle.

Many of the affrighted people who had taken refuge in the mountains returned to their homes at his coming, but others, husbands and fathers chiefly, remained on the hills, leaving their wives and families to fend for themselves. Seeing this, he went up and found some of them in their hiding-places, and shaming them out of their cowardice, brought them back behind him, more docile than sheep behind a shepherd. When the ex-town-watch, Billy-by-Nite, next appeared on the Curraghs in the round of his prophetic itineration, the strange man said not a word, but he cut short the vehement jeremiad by taking the Quaker prophet by legs and neck, and throwing him headlong into one of the drain-troughs newly dug in the dampest places.

But the strength of this silent man was no more conspicuous than his tenderness. When in the frenzy of their fever the sufferers would cast off their clothes, and try to rise from their beds and rush into the cooler air from the heat by which he had surrounded them, his big horny hands would restrain them with a great gentleness.

Before he had been five days in Michael and on the Curraghs the sickness began to abate. The deaths were fewer, and some of the sick rose from their beds. Then the people plied him with many questions, and would have overwhelmed him with their rude gratitude. To their questions he gave few answers, and when they thanked him he turned and left them.

They said that their Bishop, who was grown feeble, the good ould angel, thought it strange that he had not yet visited him. To this he answered briefly that before leaving the parish he would go to Bishop's Court.

They told him that Mistress Mona, daughter of the Deemster that was, bad cess to him, had been seeking him high and low. At this his lip trembled, and he bent his head.

"The good man's face plagues me mortal," said old Billy-the-Gawk. "Whiles I know it, and other whiles I don't."

VII

Only another day did the stranger remain in Michael, but the brief times was full of strange events. The night closed in before seven o'clock. It was then very dark across the mountains, and the sea lay black beyond the cliffs, but the Curraghs were dotted over with the many fires which had been kindled about the infected houses.

Within one of these houses, the home of Jabez Gawne, the stranger stood beside the bed of a sick woman, the tailor's wife. Behind him there were anxious faces. Davy Fayle, always near him, leaned against the door-jamb by the porch.

And while the stranger wrapped the sweltering sufferer in hot blankets, other sufferers sent to him to pray of him to come to them. First there came an old man to tell of his grandchild, who had been smitten down that day, and she was the last of his kin whom the Sweat had left alive. Then a woman, to say that her husband, who had started again with the boats but yesterday, had been brought home to her that night with the sickness. He listened to all who came, and answered quietly, "I will go."

At length a young man ran in and said, "The Dempster's down. He's shouting for you, sir. He sent me hot-foot to fetch you."

The stranger listened as before, and seemed to think rapidly for a moment, for his under lip trembled, and was drawn painfully inward. Then he answered as briefly as ever, and with as calm a voice, "I will go."

The man ran back with his answer, but presently returned, saying, with panting breath, "He's rambling, sir; raving mad, sir; and shouting that he must be coming after you if you're not for coming to him."

"We will go together," the stranger said, and they went out immediately. Davy Fayle followed them at a few paces.

VIII

Through the darkness of that night a woman, young and beautiful, in cloak and hood like a nun's, walked from house to house of the Curraghs, where the fires showed that the sickness was still raging. It was Mona. These three days past she had gone hither and thither, partly to tend the sick people, partly in hope of meeting the strange man who had come to cure them. Again and again she had missed him, being sometimes only a few minutes before or after him.

Still she passed on from house to house, looking for him as she went in at every fresh door, yet half dreading the chance that might bring them face to face.

She entered the house where he had received her father's message almost on the instant when he left it. The three men had gone by her in the darkness.

Jabez, the tailor, who sat whimpering in the ingle, told her that the priest had that moment gone off to Ballamona, where the Dempster that was—hadn't she heard the newses?—was new down with the Sweat.

Her delicate face whitened at that, and after a pause she turned to follow. But going back to the hearth, she asked if the stranger had been told that the Bishop wanted to see him. Jabez told her yes, and that he had said he would go up to Bishop's Court before leaving the parish.

Then another question trembled on her tongue, but she could not utter it. At last she asked what manner of man the stranger was to look upon.

"Aw, big and sthraight and tall," said Jabez.

And Billy-the-Gawk, who sat at the opposite side of the ingle, being kin to Jabez's sick wife, said, "Ay, and quiet like, and solemn extraordinary."

"A wonderful man, wonderful, wonderful," said Jabez, still whimpering. "And wherever he comes the Sweat goes down before him with a flood."

"As I say," said Billy-the-Gawk, "the good man's face plagues me mortal. I can't bethink me where I've seen the like of it afore."

Mona's lips quivered at that word, and she seemed to be about to speak; but she said nothing.

"And the strong he is!" said Jabez: "I never knew but one man in the island with half the strength of arm as him."

Mona's pale face twitched visibly, and she listened as with every faculty.

"Who d'ye mane?" asked Billy-the-Gawk.

At that question there was a moment's silence between the men. Then each drew a long breath, dislodged a heavy burden from his throat, glanced significantly up at Mona, and looked into the other's face.

"*Him,*" said Jabez, in a faint underbreath, speaking behind his hand.

"*Him?*"

Billy-the-Gawk straightened his crooked back, opened wide his rheumy eyes, pursed up his wizened cheeks, and emitted a low, long whistle.

"Lord A'mighty!"

For an instant Jabez looked steadily into the old mendicant's face, and then drew himself up in his seat—

"Lord a-massy!"

Mona's heart leaped to her mouth. She was almost beside herself with suspense, and felt an impulse to scream.

IX

Within a week after old Thorkell had conversed with the Bishop about the rumor that the wells had been charmed, his terror of the sickness had grown nigh to madness. He went to church no longer, but shut himself up in his house. Night and day his restless footstep could be heard to pass from room to room, and floor to floor. He ate little, and such was his dread of the water from his well that for three days together he drank nothing. At length, burning from thirst, he went up the Dhoon Glen and drank at a pool, going down on hands and knees to lap the water like a dog. Always he seemed to be mumbling prayers, and when the bell of the church rang, no matter for what occasion, he dropped to his knees and prayed audibly. He forbade the servants of the house to bring him news of deaths, but waited and watched and listened at open doors for their conversation among themselves. At night he went to the front windows to look at the fires that were kindled about the infected houses on the Curraghs. He never failed to turn from that sight with bitter words. Such work was but the devil's play; it was making a mock of God, who had sent the sickness to revenge Himself on the island's guilty people. Thorkell told Jarvis Kerruish as much time after time. Jarvis answered contemptuously, and Thorkell retorted angrily. At length they got to high words, and Jarvis flung away.

One morning Thorkell called for Hommy-beg. They told him that Hommy had been nursing his wife. The blind woman was now dead, and Hommy was burying her. At this Thorkell's terror was appalling to look upon. All night long he had been telling himself that he despised the belief in second sight, but that he would see if Kerry pretended to know whether he himself was to outlive the scourge. No matter, the woman was dead. So much the better!

Later the same day, Thorkell remembered that somewhere on the mountains there lived an old farmer who was a seer and bard. He would go to see the old charlatan. Yes, he would amuse himself with the superstition that aped religion. Thorkell set out, and found the bard's lonely house far up above the Sherragh Vane. In a corner of the big fireplace the old man sat, with a black shawl bound about his head and tied under his chin. He was past eighty years of age, and his face was as old a face as Thorkell had ever looked upon. On his knee a young child was sitting, and two or three small boys were playing about his feet. A brisk middle-aged woman was stirring the peats and settling the kettle on the chimney-hook. She was the old man's wife, and the young brood were the old man's children.

Thorkell began to talk of carvals, and said he had come to hear some of them. The old bard's eyes brightened. He had written a carol about the sickness. From the "lath" he took a parchment pan, full of papers that were worn, thumb-marked, and greasy. From one of these papers he began to read, and Thorkell tried to listen. The poem was an account of a dream. The dreamer had dreamt that he had gone into a church. There was a congregation gathered, and a preacher was in the pulpit. But when the preacher prayed the dreamer heard nothing of God. At length he discovered that it was a congregation of the dead in the region of the damned. They had all died of the Sweat. Every man of them had been warned by wise men and women in this world. The congregation sang a joyless psalm, and when their service was done they began to break up. Then the dreamer recognized some whom he had known in the flesh. Among them was one who had killed his own son, and he was afflicted with a burning thirst. To this unhappy man the dreamer offered a basin of milk-and-water, but the damned soul could not get the basin to his parched lips, struggle as he might to lift it in his stiff arms.

At first Thorkell listened with the restless mind of a man who had come on better business, and then with a feverish interest. The sky had darkened since he entered the house, and while the old bard chanted in his sing-song voice, and the children made their clatter around his feet, a storm of heavy rain pelted against the window-pane.

The ballad ended in the grim doggerel of a harrowing appeal to the sinner to shun his evil courses:

> "O sinner, see your dangerous state,
> And think of hell ere 'tis too late;
> When worldly cares would drown each thought,
> Pray call to mind that hell is hot.
> Still to increase your godly fears
> Let this be sounding in your ears,
> Still bear in mind that hell is hot,
> Remember, and forget it not."

Thus, with a swinging motion of the body, the old bard of the mountains chanted this rude song on the dangers of damnation. Thorkell leaped up from the settle and sputtered out an expression of contempt. What madness was this? If he had his way he would clap all superstitious people into the Castle.

The next morning, when sitting down to breakfast, Thorkell told Jarvis Kerruish that he had three nights running dreamt the same dream, and it was a terrible one. Jarvis laughed in his face, and said he was a foolish old man. Thorkell answered with heat, and they parted on the instant, neither touching food. Toward noon Thorkell imagined he felt feverish, and asked for Jarvis Kerruish; but Jarvis was at his toilet and would not be disturbed. At five o'clock the same day Thorkell was sweating from every pore, and crying lustily that he had taken the sickness. Toward seven he ordered the servant—a young man named Juan Caine, who had come to fill Hommy's place—to go in search of the Romish priest, Father Dalby.

When the stranger came, the young man opened the door to him, and whispered that the old master's wits were gone. "He's not been wise these two hours," the young man said, and then led the way to Thorkell's bedroom. He missed the corridor, and the stranger pointed to the proper door.

Thorkell was sitting up in his bed. His clothes had not been taken off, but his coat—a blue coat, laced—and also his long yellow vest were unbuttoned. His wig was perched on the top of a high-backed chair, and over his bald head hung a torn piece of red flannel. His long hairy hands, with the prominent blue veins, crawled over the counterpane. His eyes were open very wide. When he saw the stranger he was for getting out of bed.

"I am not ill," he said; "it's folly to think that I've taken the sickness. I sent for you to tell you something that you should know."

Then he called to the young man to bring him water. "Juan, water!" he cried; "Juan, I say, more water."

He turned to the stranger. "It's true I'm always athirst, but is that any proof that I have taken the sickness? Juan, be quick—water!"

The young man brought a pewter pot of cold water, and Thorkell clutched at it, but as he was stretching his neck to drink, his hot lips working visibly, and his white tongue protruding, he drew suddenly back. "Is it from the well?" he asked.

The stranger took the pewter out of his hands, unlocking his stiff fingers with his own great bony ones. "Make the water hot," he said to the servant.

Thorkell fell back to his pillow, and the rag of red blanket dropped from his bald crown. Then he lifted himself on one elbow and began again to talk of the sickness. "You have made a mistake," he said. "It is not to be cured. It is God's revenge on the people of this sinful island. Shall I tell you for what offense? For superstition. Superstition is the ape of religion. It is the reproach of God. Juan! Juan, I say, help me off with this coat. And these bedclothes also. Why are there so many? It's true, sir—Father, is it?—it's true, Father, I'm hot, but what of that? Water! Juan, more water—Glen water, Juan!"

The stranger pushed Thorkell gently back, and covered him closely from the air.

"As I say, it is superstition, sir," said Thorkell again. "I would have it put down by law. It is the curse of this island. What are those twenty-four Keys doing that they don't stamp it out? And the clergy—what are they wrangling about now, that they don't see to it? I'll tell you how it is, sir. It is this way. A man does something, and some old woman sneezes. Straightway he thinks himself accursed, and that what is predicted must certainly come about. And it does come about. Why? Because the man himself, with his blundering, doddering fears, *brings* it about. He brings it about himself—that's how it is! And then every old woman in the island sneezes again."

Saying this, Thorkell began to laugh, loudly, frantically, atrociously. Jarvis Kerruish had entered while he was running on with his tirade. The stranger did not lift his eyes to Jarvis, but Jarvis looked at him attentively.

When Thorkell had finished his hideous laugh, he turned to Jarvis and asked if superstition was not the plague of the island, and if it ought not to be put down by law. Jarvis curled his lips for answer, but his form of contempt was lost on old Thorkell's dim eyes.

"Have we not often agreed that it is so?" said Thorkell.

"And that you," said Jarvis, speaking slowly and bitterly, "are the most superstitious man alive."

"What? what?" Thorkell cried.

The stranger lifted his face, and looked steadily into Jarvis's eyes. "*You*," he said, calmly, "have some reason to say so."

Jarvis reddened, turned about, stepped to the door, glanced back at the stranger, and went out of the room.

Thorkell was now moaning on the pillow. "I am all alone," he said; and he fell to a bout of weeping.

The stranger waited until the hysterical fit was over, and then said, "Where is your daughter?"

"Ah!" said Thorkell, dropping his red eyes.

"Send for her."

"I will. Juan, go to Bishop's Court. Juan, I say, run fast and fetch Mistress Mona. Tell her that her father is ill."

As Thorkell gave this order Jarvis Kerruish returned to the room.

"No!" said Jarvis, lifting his hand against the young man.

"No?" cried Thorkell.

"If this is my house, I will be master in it," said Jarvis.

"Master! your house! yours!" Thorkell cried; and then he fell to a fiercer bout of hysterical curses. "Bastard, I gave you all! But for me you would be on the roads—ay, the dunghill!"

"This violence will avail you nothing," said Jarvis, with hard constraint. "Mistress Mona shall not enter this house."

Jarvis placed himself with his back to the door. The stranger stepped up to him, laid one powerful hand on his arm, and drew him aside. "Go for Mistress Mona," he said to the young man. "Knock at the door on your return. I will open it."

The young man obeyed the stranger. Jarvis stood a moment looking blankly into the stranger's face. Then he went out of the room.

Thorkell was whimpering on the pillow. "It is true," he said, with laboring breath, "though I hate superstition and loathe it, I was once its victim—once only. My son Ewan was killed by my brother's son, Dan. They loved each other like David and Jonathan, but I told Ewan a lie, and they fought, and Ewan was brought home dead. Yes, I told a lie, but I believed it then. I made myself believe it. I listened to some old wife's balderdash, and thought it true. And Dan was cut off—that is to say, banished, excommunicated; worse, worse. But he's dead now. He was found dead in the snow." Again Thorkell tried to laugh, a poor despairing laugh that was half a cry. "Dead! They threatened me that he would push me from my place. And he is dead before me! So much for divination! But tell me—you are a priest—tell me if that sin will drag me down to—to—But then, remember, I believed it was true—yes, I—"

The stranger's face twitched, and his breathing became quick.

"And it was you who led the way to all that followed" he said, in a subdued voice.

"It was; it was—"

The stranger had suddenly reached over the bed and taken Thorkell by the shoulders. At the next instant he had relinquished his hard grasp, and was standing upright as before, and with as calm a face. And Thorkell went jabbering on:

"These three nights I have dreamt a fearful dream. Shall I tell you what it was? Shall I? I thought Dan, my brother's son, arose out of his grave, and came to my bedside, and peered into my face. Then I thought I shrieked and died; and the first thing I saw in the other world was my son Ewan, and he peered into my face also, and told me that I was damned eternally. But, tell me, don't you think it was only a dream? Father! Father! I say, tell me—"

Thorkell was clambering up by hold of the stranger's coat.

The stranger pushed him gently back.

"Lie still; lie still—you, too, have suffered much," he said. "Lie quiet—God is merciful."

Just then Jarvis Kerruish entered, in wild excitement. "Now I know who this man is," he said, pointing to the stranger.

"Father Dalby," said Thorkell.

"Pshaw!—it is Dan Mylrea."

Thorkell lifted himself stiffly on his elbow, and rigidly drew his face closely up to the stranger's face, and peered into the stranger's eyes. Then he took a convulsive hold of the stranger's coat, shrieked, and fell back on to the pillow.

At that moment there was a loud knocking at the door below. The stranger left the room. In the hall a candle was burning. He put it out. Then he opened the door. A woman entered. She was alone. She passed him in the darkness without speaking. He went out of the house and pulled the door after him.

X

An hour later than this terrible interview, wherein his identity (never hidden by any sorry masquerade) was suddenly revealed, Daniel Mylrea, followed closely at his heels by Davy Fayle, walked amid the fires of the valley to Bishop's Court. He approached the old house by the sea-front, and went into its grounds by a gate that opened on a footpath to the library through a clump of elms. Sluggish as was Davy's intellect, he reflected that this was a path that no stranger could know.

The sky of the night had lightened, and here and there a star gleamed through the thinning branches overhead. In a faint breeze the withering leaves of the dying summer rustled slightly. On the meadow before the house a silvery haze of night-dew lay in its silence. Sometimes the croak of a frog came from the glen; and from the sea beyond (though seemingly from the mountains opposite) there rose into the air the rumble of the waves on the shore.

Daniel Mylrea passed on with a slow, strong step, but a secret pain oppressed him. He was walking on the ground that was dear with a thousand memories of happy childhood. He was going back for some brief moments that must be painful and joyful, awful and delicious, to the house which he had looked to see no more. Already he was very near to those who were very dear to him, and to whom he, too—yes, it must be so—to whom he, too, in spite of all, must still be dear. "Father, father," he whispered to himself. "And Mona, my Mona, my love, my love." Only the idle chatter of the sapless leaves answered to the yearning cry of his broken spirit.

He had passed out of the shade of the elms into the open green of the meadow with the stars above it, when another voice came to him. It was the voice of a child singing. Clear and sweet, and with a burden of tenderness such as a child's voice rarely carries, it floated through the quiet air.

Daniel Mylrea passed on until he came by the library window, which was alight with a rosy glow. There he stood for a moment and looked into the room. His father, the Bishop, was seated in the oak chair that was clamped with iron clamps. Older he seemed to be, and with the lines a thought deeper on his massive brow. On a stool at his feet, with one elbow resting on the apron in front of him, a little maiden sat, and she was singing. A fire burned red on the hearth before them. Presently the Bishop rose from his chair, and went out of the room, walking feebly, and with drooping head.

Then Daniel Mylrea walked round to the front of the house and knocked. The door was opened by a servant whose face was strange to him. Everything that he saw was strange, and yet everything was familiar. The hall was the same but smaller, and when it echoed to his foot a thrill passed through him.

He asked for the Bishop, and was led like a stranger through his father's house to the door of the library. The little maiden was now alone in the room. She rose from her stool as he entered, and, without the least reserve, stepped up to him and held out her hand. He took her tender little palm in his great fingers, and held it for a moment while he looked into her face. It was a beautiful child-face, soft and fair and oval, with a faint tinge of olive in the pale cheeks, and with yellow hair—almost white in the glow of the red fire—falling in thin tresses over a full, smooth forehead.

He sat and drew her closer to him, still looking steadily into her face. Then, in a tremulous voice he asked her what her name was, and the little maiden, who had shown no fear at all, nor any bashfulness, answered that her name was Aileen.

"But they call me Ailee," she added, promptly; "everybody calls me Ailee."

"Everybody? Who?"

"Oh, everybody," she answered, with a true child's emphasis.

"Your mother?"

She shook her head.

"Your—your—perhaps—your—"

She shook her head more vigorously.

"I know what you're going to say, but I've got none," she said.

"Got none?" he repeated.

The little maiden's face took suddenly a wondrous solemnity, and she said, "My father died a long, long, long time ago—when I was only a little baby."

His lips quivered, and his eyes fell from her face.

"*Such* a long, long while ago—you wouldn't think. And auntie says I can't even remember him."

"Auntie?"

"But shall I tell you what Kerry said it was that made him die?—shall I?—only I must whisper—and you won't tell auntie, will you?—because auntie doesn't know—shall I tell you?"

His quivering lips whitened, and with trembling hands he drew aside the little maiden's head that her innocent eyes might not gaze into his face.

"How old are you, Ailee ven?" he asked, in a brave voice.

"Oh, I'm seven—and auntie, she's seven too; auntie and I are twins."

"And you can sing, can you not? Will you sing for me?"

"What shall I sing?"

"Anything, sweetheart—what you sang a little while since."

"For grandpa?"

"Grandpa?"

"Kerry says no, it's uncle, not grandpa. But that's wrong," with a look of outraged honor; "and besides, how should Kerry know? It's not *her* grandpa, is it? Do *you* know Kerry?" Then the little face saddened all at once. "Oh, I forgot—*poor* Kerry."

"Poor Kerry?"

"I used to go and see her. You go up the road, and then on and on and on until you come to some children, and then on and on and on until you get to a little boy—and then you're there."

"Won't you sing, sweetheart?"

"I'll sing grandpa's song."

"Grandpa's?"

"Yes, the one he likes."

Then the little maiden's dimpled face smoothened out, and her simple eyes turned gravely upward as she began to sing:

> "O, Myle Charaine, where got you your gold?
> Lone, lone, you have left me here.
> O, not in the curragh, deep under the mold,
> Lone, lone, and void of cheer."

It was the favorite song of his own boyish days; and while the little maiden sang it seemed to the crime-stained man who gazed through a dim haze into her cherub face, that the voice of her dead father had gone into her voice. He listened while he could, and when the tears welled up to his eyes, with his horny hands he drew her fair head down to his heaving breast, and sobbed beneath his breath, "Ailee ven, Ailee ven."

The little maiden stopped in her song to look up in bewilderment at the bony, wet face that was stooping over her.

At that moment the door of the room opened, and the Bishop entered noiselessly. A moment he stood on the threshold, with a look of perplexity. Then he made a few halting steps, and said:

"My eyes are not what they were, sir, and I see there is no light but the firelight; but I presume you are the good Father Dalby?" Daniel Mylrea fell to his knees at the Bishop's feet.

"I come from him," he answered.

"Is he not coming himself?"

"He can not come. He charged me with a message to you."

"You are very welcome. My niece will be home presently. Be seated, sir."

Daniel Mylrea did not sit, but continued to stand before his father, with head held down. After a moment he spoke again.

"Father Dalby," he said, "is dead."

The Bishop sunk to his chair. "When—when—"

"He died the better part of a month ago."

The Bishop rose to his feet.

"He was in this island but yesterday."

"He bade me tell you that he had fulfilled his pledge to you and come to the island, but died by the visitation of God the same night whereon he landed here."

The Bishop put one hand to his forehead.

"Sir," he said, "my hearing is also failing me, for, as you see, I am an old man now, and besides, I have had trouble in my time. Perhaps, sir, I did not hear you aright?"

Then Daniel Mylrea told in few words the story of the priest's accident and death, and how the man at whose house he died had made bold to take the good priest's mission upon himself.

The Bishop listened with visible pain, and for a while said nothing. Then, speaking in a faltering voice, with breath that came quickly, he asked who the other man had been. "For the good man has been a blessing to us," he added, nervously.

To this question there was no reply, and he asked again:

"Who?"

"Myself."

The Bishop lifted with trembling fingers his horn-bridged spectacles to his eyes.

"Your voice is strangely familiar," he said. "What is your name?"

Again there was no answer.

"Give me your name, sir—that I may pray of God to bless you."

Still there was no answer.

"Let me remember it in my prayers."

Then in a breaking voice Daniel Mylrea replied:

"In your prayers my poor name has never been forgotten."

At that the Bishop tottered a pace backward.

"Light," he said, faintly. "More light."

He touched a bell on the table, and sank quietly into his chair. Daniel Mylrea fell to his knees at the Bishop's feet.

"Father," he said in a fervent whisper, and put his lips to the Bishop's hand.

The door was opened, and a servant entered with candles. At the same moment Daniel Mylrea stepped quickly out of the room.

Then the little maiden leaped from the floor to the Bishop's side.

"Grandpa, grandpa! Oh, what has happened to grandpa?" she cried.

The Bishop's head had dropped into his breast and he had fainted. When he opened his eyes in consciousness Mona was bathing his forehead and damping his lips.

"My child," he said, nervously, "one has come back to us from the dead."

And Mona answered him with the thought that was now uppermost in her mind:

"Dear uncle," she said, "my poor father died half an hour ago."

CHAPTER XLV
"OUR FATHER, WHICH ART IN HEAVEN"

Not many days after the events recorded in the foregoing chapter the people of Man awoke to the joyful certainty that the sweating sickness had disappeared. The solid wave of heat had gone; the ground had become dry and the soil light; and no fetid vapors floated over the Curraghs at midday. Also the air had grown keener, the nights had sharpened, and in the morning the fronds of hoar-frost hung on the withering leaves of the trammon.

Then the poor folk began to arrange their thoughts concerning the strange things that had happened; to count up their losses by death; to talk of children that were fatherless, and of old men left alone in the world, like naked trunks, without bough or branch, flung on the bare earth by yesterday's storm.

And in that first roll-call after the battle of life and death the people suddenly became aware that, with the sweating sickness, the man who had brought the cure for it had also disappeared. He was not on the Curraghs, he was no longer in Michael, and further east he had not traveled. None could tell what had become of him. When seen last he was walking south through German toward Patrick. He was then alone, save for the half-daft lad, Davy Fayle, who slouched at his heels like a dog. As he passed up Creg Willey's Hill the people of St. John's followed him in ones and twos and threes to offer him their simple thanks. But he pushed along as one who hardly heard them. When he came by the Tynwald he paused and turned partly toward Greeba, as though half minded to alter his course. But, hesitating no longer, he followed the straight path toward the village at the foot of Slieu Whallin. As he crossed the green the people of St. John's, who followed him up the hill road, had grown to a great number, being joined there by the people of Tynwald. And when he passed under the ancient mount, walking with long, rapid steps, his chin on his breast and his eyes kept steadfastly down, the gray-headed men uncovered their heads, the young women thrust their young children under his hands for his blessing, and all by one impulse shouted in one voice, "God bless the priest!" "Heaven save the priest!"

There were spectators of that scene who were wont to say, when this sequel had freshened their memories, that amid the wild tumult of the gratitude of the island's poor people he who was the subject of it made one quick glance of pain upward to the mount, now standing empty above the green, and then, parting the crowds that encircled him, pushed through them without word or glance or sign. Seeing at last that he shrunk from their thanks, the people followed him no further, but remained on the green, watching him as he passed on toward Slieu Whallin, and then up by the mountain track. When he had reached the top of the path, where it begins its descent to the valley beyond, he paused again and turned about, glancing back. The people below saw his full figure clearly outlined against the sky, and once more they sent up their shout by one great impulse in one great voice that drowned the distant rumble of the sea: "God bless the priest!" "Heaven save the priest!" And he heard it, for instantly he faced about and disappeared.

When he was gone it seemed as if a spell had broken. The people looked into one another's faces in bewilderment, as if vaguely conscious that somewhere and some time, under conditions the same yet different, all that they had then seen their eyes had seen before. And bit by bit the memory came back to them, linked with a name that might not be spoken. Then many things that had seemed strange became plain.

In a few days the whisper passed over Man, from north to south, from east to west, from the sod cabins on the Curragh to the Castle at Castletown, that he who had cured the people of the sickness, he who had been mistaken for the priest out of Ireland, was none other than the unblessed man long thought to be dead; and that he had lived to be the savior of his people.

The great news was brought to Bishop's Court, and it was found to be there already. Rumor said that from Castletown an inquiry had come asking if the news were true, but none could tell what answer Bishop's Court had made. The Bishop had shut himself up from all visits, even those of his clergy. With Mona and the child, Ewan's little daughter, he had passed the days since Thorkell's death, and not until the day of Thorkell's funeral did he break in upon his solitude. Then he went down to the little churchyard that stands over by the sea.

They buried the ex-Deemster near to his son Ewan, and with scarcely a foot's space between them. Except Jarvis Kerruish, the Bishop was Thorkell's sole mourner, and hardly had the service ended, or the second shovel of earth fallen from old Will-as-Thorn's spade, when Jarvis whipped about and walked away. Then the Bishop stood alone by his brother's unhonored grave, trying to forget his malice and uncharity, and his senseless superstitions that had led to many disasters, thinking only with the pity that is nigh to love of the great ruin whereunto his poor beliefs had tottered down. And when the Bishop had returned home the roll-call of near kindred showed him pitiful gaps. "The island grows very lonesome, Mona," he said.

That night Davy Fayle came to Bishop's Court with a book in his hand. He told Mona how he had found the "Ben-my-Chree" a complete wreck on the shingle of the Dhoon Creek in the Calf Sound, and the book in its locker. Not a syllable could Davy read, but he knew that the book was the fishing-log of the lugger, and that since he saw it last it had been filled with writings.

Mona took the book into the library, and with the Bishop she examined it. It was a small quarto, bound in sheepskin, with corners and back of untanned leather. Longways on the back the words "Ben-my-Chree Fishing-Log" were lettered, as with a soft quill in a bold hand. On the front page there was this inscription:

Ben-my-Chree.
Owner, Daniel Mylrea, Bishop's Court,
Isle of Man.
Master, Illiam Quilleash.

Over page was the word "Accounts," and then followed the various items of the earnings and expenditure of the boat. The handwriting was strong and free, but the bookkeeping was not lucid.

Eight pages of faintly-tinted paper, much frayed, and with lines ruled by hand one way of the sheet only, were filled with the accounts of the herring season of 1705. At the bottom there was an attempt at picking out the items of profit and loss, and at reckoning the shares of owner, master, and man. The balance stood but too sadly on the wrong side. There was a deficit of forty pounds four shillings and sixpence.

The Bishop glanced at the entries, and passed them over with a sigh. But turning the leaves, he came upon other matter of more pathetic interest. This was a long personal narrative from the owner's pen, covering some two hundred of the pages. The Bishop looked it through, hurriedly, nervously, and with eager eyes. Then he gave up the book to Mona.

"Read it aloud, child," he said, in a voice unlike his own, and with a brave show of composure he settled himself to listen.

For two hours thereafter Mona read from the narrative that was written in the book. What that narrative was does not need to be told.

Often the voice of the reader failed her, sometimes it could not support itself. And in the lapses of her voice the silence was broken by her low sobs.

The Bishop listened long with a great outer calmness, for the affections of the father were struggling with a sense of the duty of the servant of God. At some points of the narrative these seemed so to conflict as to tear his old heart wofully. But he bore up very bravely, and tried to think that in what he had done seven years before he had done well. At an early stage of Mona's reading he stopped her to say:

"Men have been cast on desert islands beforetime, and too often they have been adrift on unknown seas."

Again he stopped her to add, with a slow shake of the head:

"Men have been outlawed, and dragged out weary years in exile—men have been oftentimes under the ban and chain of the law."

And once again he interrupted and said, in a trembling undertone, "It is true—it has been what I looked for—it has been a death in life."

But as Mona went on to read of how the outcast man, kept back from speech with every living soul, struggled to preserve the spiritual part of him, the Bishop interrupted once more, and said, in a faltering voice:

"This existence has been quite alone in its desolation."

As Mona went on again to read of how the unblessed creature said his prayer in his solitude, not hoping that God would hear, but thinking himself a man outside God's grace, though God's hand was upon him—thinking himself a man doomed to everlasting death, though the blessing of Heaven had already fallen over him like morning dew—then all that remained of spiritual pride in the heart of the Bishop was borne down by the love of the father, and his old head fell into his breast, and the hot tears rained down his wrinkled cheeks.

Later the same night Mona sent for Davy Fayle. The lad was easily found; he had been waiting in the darkness outside the house, struggling hard with a desire to go in and tell Mistress Mona where Daniel Mylrea was to be found.

"Davy," she said, "do you know where he is?"

"Sure," said Davy.

"And you could lead me to him?"

"I could."

"Then come here very early in the morning, and we will go together."

Next day when Mona, attired for her journey, went down for a hasty breakfast, she found the Bishop fumbling a letter in his trembling fingers.

"Read this, child," he said in a thick voice, and he handed the letter to her.

She turned it over nervously. The superscription ran, "These to the Lord Bishop of Man, at his Palace of Bishop's Court," and the seal on the other face was that of the insular Government.

While the Bishop made pretense of wiping with his handkerchief the horn-bridged spectacles on his nose Mona opened and read the letter.

It was from the Governor at Castletown, and said that the Lord of Man and the Isles, in recognition of the great services done by Daniel Mylrea to the people of the island during their recent affliction, would be anxious to appoint him Deemster of Man, in succession to his late uncle, Thorkell Mylrea (being satisfied that he was otherwise qualified for the post), if the Steward of the Ecclesiastical Courts were willing to remove the censure of the Church under which he now labored.

When she had finished reading, Mona cast one glance of nervous supplication upward to the Bishop's face, and then with a quick cry of joy, which was partly pain, she flung her arms about his neck.

The old Bishop was quite broken down.

"Man's judgments on man," he said, "are but as the anger of little children—here to-day, gone to-morrow, and the Father's face is over all."

What need to tell of one of the incidents of Mona's journey, or of the brave hopes that buoyed her up on the long and toilsome way? Many a time during these seven years past she had remembered that it was she who had persuaded Dan to offer his life as an atonement for his sin. And often the thought came back to her with the swiftness of remorse that it was she who, in her blindness, had sent him to a doom that was worse than death. But Heaven's ways had not been her ways, and all was well. The atonement had been made, and the sin had been wiped out of the book of life. Dan, her love, her beloved, had worked out his redemption. He had proved himself the great man she had always known he must be. He was to come back loaded with honor and gratitude, and surrounded by multitudes of friends.

More than once, when the journey was heaviest, she put her hand to her bosom and touched the paper that nestled so warmly there. Then in her mind's eye she saw Dan in the seat of the Deemster, the righteous judge of his own people. Oh, yes, he would be the Deemster, but he would be Dan still, her Dan, the lively, cheerful, joyous, perhaps even frolicsome Dan, once more. He would sport with her like Ailee; he would play with her as he used to play long ago with another little girl that she herself could remember—tickling her under her armpits, and under her chin, and in twenty different cozy nests of her pretty body, where whole broods of birdies sent up a chorus of squealing song-laughter.

The burden of Mona's long years of weary sorrow had been so suddenly lifted away that she could not restrain her thoughts from childish sportiveness. But sometimes she remembered Ewan, and then her heart saddened, and sometimes she thought of herself, and then it flushed full of quick, hot blood. And, oh, how delicious was the secret thing that sometimes stole up between her visions of Dan and the high destiny that was before him. It was a vision of herself, transfigured by his noble love, resting upon and looking up to him, and thus passing on and on and on to the end.

Once she remembered, with a chill passing through her, that in the writing which she had read Dan had said he was ill? But what of that? She was going to him, and would nurse him back to health.

And Davy Fayle, walking at her side, was full of his own big notions, too. Mastha Dan would be Dempster, true; but he'd have a boat for his pleasure, sarten sure. Davy Fayle would sail man in her, perhaps mate, and maybe skipper some day—who knows? And then—lying aft and drifting at the herrings, and smokin', and the stars out, and the moon makin' a peep—aw, well, well, well!

They reached the end of their journey at last. It was in a small gorse-covered house far over the wild moor, on the edge of the Chasms, looking straight out on the hungry sea. In its one bare room (which was without fire, and was cheerless with little light) there was a table, a settle, a chair, a stool, and a sort of truckle-bed. Dan was there, the same, yet, oh, how different! He lay on the bed unconscious, near to death of the sickness—the last that the scourge was to slay.

Of this story of great love and great suffering what is left to tell?

There are moments when life seems like the blind swirl of a bat in the dusk—blundering, irresponsible, not to be counted with, the swift creature of evil chance. We see a little child's white face at a hospital window, a strong man toiling hopelessly against wrong, the innocent suffering with the guilty, good instincts thwarted and base purposes promoted, and we ask ourselves, with a thrill of the heart, What, after all, is God doing in this His world? And from such blind laboring of chance the tired and beaten generations of men seem to find it reward enough to drop one after one to the hushed realms of rest.

Shall we marvel very much if such a moment came to this pure and noble woman as she stood in the death-chamber of her beloved, with whom, after years of longing, she was at last brought face to face?

But again, there are other moments, higher and better, when there is such a thing in this so bewildering world as the victory of vanquishment, when the true man crushed by evil chance is yet the true man undestroyed by it and destroying it, when Job on his dunghill is more to be envied than Pharaoh on his throne, and death is as good as life.

And such a higher moment came to Mona in that death-chamber. She sat many hours by Dan's side, waiting for the breaking of his delirium and the brief space of consciousness and of peace which would be the beginning of the end. It came at long, long length, and, ah, how soon it came!

The night had come and gone while she sat and watched. When the sunrise shot red through the skin-covered window it fell on Dan and awakened him. Opening his eyes, he saw Mona, and his soul smiled over his wasted face. He could not speak, nor could he lift his worn hands. She knew that the time was near, and holding back her grief, like wild creatures held by the leash, she dropped to her knees, and clasped her hands together to pray. And while she prayed the dying man repeated some of the words after her. "Our Father—"

"Our—Father—"

"Which art in heaven, hallowed be Thy name—"

"Hallowed—be—Thy—name—"

"Thy kingdom come, Thy will be done in earth, as it is in heaven; give us this day our daily bread; and forgive us our trespasses, as we forgive them that trespass against us; and lead us not into temptation, but deliver us from evil—"

"But deliver us from evil—"

"Amen."

"Amen."